HUNTER AND HUNTED

Motive didn't come into it now, and hadn't for a long time. Did agents *have* any motives? Agents were normal, ordinary human beings. They undoubtedly acted from a wide variety of motives, but did that matter? The longer you pursued a profession, the less your motives counted.

He only knew that he had ceased to need a motive. His trade—the spy trade—was motive enough in itself for him to do a conscientious job.

Borchers left his post at the window and stowed the tapes in his briefcase. He had a long day behind him, but he didn't feel tired. He wasn't nervous any longer. He would continue to do what his "friends" expected of him.

The irony of it was he couldn't be shadowed inside the Center. He suddenly thought of the man in the car. He, too, was trying to do a conscientious job, nothing more. Prompted by a strange sense of kinship, Borchers switched on all the lights and walked back to the window to give the hunter a good-night view of his quarry.

Books by Hans Herlin

COMMEMORATIONS
WHICH WAY THE WIND
SOLO RUN

SOLO RUN

HANS HERLIN

TRANSLATED BY
J. MAXWELL BROWNJOHN

PINNACLE BOOKS NEW YORK

SOLO RUN

*English Translation Copyright ©1983 by Doubleday & Company,
Inc. and William Collins Sons & Company, Ltd.*

Copyright © 1981 by Marion von Schröder Verlag

A Pinnacle Books edition, published by special arrangement with
Doubleday & Company, Inc. Doubleday English edition published
by arrangement with Marion von Schröder Verlag. Originally published as *Satan ist auf Gottes Seite*.

Doubleday edition published in 1983
Pinnacle edition/October 1985

ISBN: 0-523-42279-2
Can. ISBN: 0-523-43274-7

Printed in the United States of America

PINNACLE BOOKS, INC.
1430 Broadway
New York, New York 10018

9 8 7 6 5 4 3 2 1

SOLO RUN

PROLOGUE

1

HE PAUSED FOR A MOMENT, breathing fast after toiling through a stretch of dense undergrowth. It was still too dark to see clearly, but ahead of him, where the forest sloped away, something glimmered between the trees. It could only be the tortuous little river that marked the frontier. Perhaps because his goal was so near, the dawn light lent it an air of enchantment, as if it were a silver thread lying unraveled in the wake of some ethereal creature hurrying through the woods.

He had known this part of the frontier since his childhood. The old map case slung over his shoulder was only a form of protective coloring—a memento. His father, a customs officer, had never used it as anything but a tobacco pouch, and he himself was carrying his report in it. Like his father, he needed neither map nor compass. Many landmarks were permanently imprinted on his memory: winding paths, deserted shacks, the abandoned graphite mine—all the trails and hideouts on the Czech-German border where his father had hunted smugglers in the old days. He had even come across isolated trees that still bore blaze marks dating from that time, and once he lingered to examine an unusually small, fine-leafed variety of fern that had long escaped inclusion in his father's set of botanical specimens.

He pressed on. In an area where no one thinned the trees

anymore, downhill stretches were easier going. It had rained yesterday, so the forest scents were fresh and new. Although the mid-September morning was chilly, he felt warm after his long trek—warm, too, with excitement at the prospect of meeting his supervisor. He was proud of the report in his map case. A stoke of luck, the whole thing. An unexpected windfall, but there was no need—or was there?—to say so to the man he would meet at the rendezvous.

He had been listening intently to the sounds of the forest: the snap of twigs beneath his feet, the whirr of birds taking wing, the rasp of squirrels' claws on spruce bark. Now came another sound, alien in such surroundings: a distant mechanical hum—his supervisor's car, most likely. A narrow track ran parallel to the frontier on the West German side, and he could picture the supervisor—whose name he didn't know—tensely watching for any signs of abnormal activity.

He himself felt in no danger. That lay behind him. He would naturally have to rerun the gauntlet when going back—the strip of open ground, the watchtowers, the patrolling scout cars—but here in the woods he was safe. After the rendezvous he would lie up for the rest of the day and wait until nightfall before retracing his steps.

The alien sound ceased. Its source was still invisible, but a pair of headlights flashed three times. Peering at his watch, he saw he was dead on time.

2

THE OPEN SCOUT car on the Czech side of the border was traveling without lights. The driver turned off down the track that led into the woods—gingerly, for fear of running into unexpected obstacles. The man beside him might have been asleep. A rifle lay across his knees, the stock resting on his palm, the small of the glossy wooden butt nestling in his right hand. Both soldiers were young—little more than twenty—and both held the same rank, but something about the man with the rifle conveyed that he was in charge.

The track had once been used for hauling logs, stacks of which stood moldering and disintegrating beside it. Neither man had so far said a word. At last, the one with the rifle spoke.

"That's far enough."

The driver pulled up to let him get out, then turned the jeep around and switched off the motor, leaving the key in the ignition. The sniper left the track and struck off into the trees. The driver followed him. Moving stealthily and unhurriedly, they reached the spot where the woods sloped down to embrace the silver thread of water at their lowest point.

The men were moving even more slowly now. The sniper circled an area only yards across. He raised his rifle once or twice and leveled it at a point below, but no position met his requirements. He shook his head and continued to prowl until he found an uprooted beech tree with a forked branch jutting at a convenient angle. His sigh of relief seemed to indicate that the hardest part of the job was over.

The driver sat down beside him. His hand went to his breast pocket, but the sniper shook his head. Reluctantly, the driver left his cigarettes where they were.

"Are you sure he'll come this way?"

Again the sniper said nothing. He produced a single round from his pocket and weighed it in his hand. The cartridge case shone like gold in the half-light. He took the round and inserted it in the chamber. Gently closing the bolt, he raised the rifle once more and peered through the telescopic sight. With another sigh, he lowered the weapon and felt in his pocket for a second round. "Just in case," he whispered. The words were barely audible. The driver tried again.

"Why let them rendezvous at all?"

He got no answer, and the expression on the sniper's face told him to expect nothing but silence from now on.

The sniper sat there like a statue, deaf to everything but

the sounds of the forest. Every falling leaf seemed to heighten the concentration on his face. The light grew stronger, intensifying the blue of his eyes and the yellow of his hair. Later, when he raised the butt from his lap and slowly—infinitely slowly—put it to his shoulder, the driver didn't even notice. The whiplash report made him jump to his feet as if he himself had been hit.

3

IT WAS INCOMPREHENSIBLE. The pain transfixed his chest as if he had blundered into a tree—the projecting branch of a fallen tree. Except that no one died of such a thing, and he, he knew, was going to die.

He fell with his arms outflung—subsided onto a bed of rotting twigs and vegetation. For one brief instant he experienced a surge of hope. No, not hope; that was too strong a word for the simple animal temptation to believe that escape and relief from the pain in his chest might lie in sheer movement, in running for as far and as long as possible, in keeping on the move till his lungs gave out, in following a route prescribed by instinct alone.

Another thought occurred to him, or part of one. What had gone wrong? How had they learned of the rendezvous? He clutched at the idea but it eluded his grasp, merely grazing his consciousness as it became just one more enigma in the great bewilderment of dying.

His body sank deeper into its bed of leaves and twigs. He felt he would never stop falling, never complete his slow, interminable descent. Though not the movement that had given him hope, it was at least a crumb of consolation. His hands had closed on something as he fell, and the touch of it became transmuted into a mental image: a small, fine-leafed fern. It held some significance, but he couldn't think what. His fingers relaxed their hold on the rough, serrated fronds.

The pain in his chest expanded and proliferated. He

thought he heard footsteps approaching, coming downhill, wading through leaves.

Perhaps they'll never find me, he thought. He felt as if the forest floor had swallowed him up.

1

CHAPTER I

1

CAROW STOOD AT HIS BEDROOM WINDOW, looking down at the swimming pool. Cradled in his hands was the mug of hot milk prescribed by the Organization's senior medical officer. He had lately been staving off his kidney pains with too many Darvon tablets, and in Carow's peculiar trade suspicion was aroused by any form of excess: too much hard liquor, too many women, too much financial expenditure, too many pills.

Carow detested hot milk—the very smell of it turned his stomach—so this dogged compliance with doctor's orders said much for his strength of character, not to mention his absolute loyalty to the Organization.

He was still in pajamas and dressing gown, debating whether or not to go for a swim. The pool heater was already off, and although September had been exceptionally fine and mild, the nights were growing chilly. The water temperature couldn't be more than sixty—unpleasantly cold for a slightly underweight fifty-seven-year-old with inflamed kidneys.

Unpleasant or not, Carow had swum his quota of lengths in the past few days. It was part of his routine, and routine mattered to a man who planned his schedule with scrupulous care. If he didn't take a dip, half an hour of his day would remain unfilled.

He knew, of course, that it was Saturday. Like every senior member of the Organization, Heiner Carow had assumed a second name. At weekends he was Heiner Grapentin, well-heeled vice-president of a reputable insurance company. Only the duty officer was authorized to contact the weekday persona of the man at the bedroom window—head of Section I, Procurement (Recruitment and Supervision of Agents in Foreign Countries)—but his weekends were seldom disturbed. Once it had been a different story; nowadays, even spies kept the Sabbath.

Carow laid the mug aside untouched and cleaned his teeth. He didn't use the Waterpik his wife had given him for his birthday a month ago. Where presents were concerned, Isabelle had rather lost her touch in the last ten years.

He shaved with ordinary soap and a cutthroat razor, a hangover from his own days as an agent in the field. Then he got dressed for golf—gray flannel slacks, polo-necked shirt, yellow cashmere sweater. He at once felt better in this outfit. Herr Grapentin favored worsted suits, white shirts, dark ties and socks, whereas Carow preferred flannels and tweeds and sweaters. This quick-change act, which he'd practiced for so many years, was far more than an outward transformation. The metamorphosis extended to his face. Grapentin's was smooth and bland, the face of a man with a capacity for inspiring trust and confidence. It wasn't until he changed into Carow that one noticed the broken nose sustained in a clumsy parachute landing. Quite suddenly, the face became harder, betraying a hint of the steel in Carow's rather frail-looking physique and the inner conflicts he carried around with him.

The two personae had one thing in common: both had aged early. They were gray by forty-five, almost as if they yearned to grow old in the hope that age might be a phase of life that suited them better than youth.

Carow finished dressing and went downstairs. He glanced into the drawing room. Like the entire house, it was furnished in Isabelle's taste: white carpet, white sofa and armchairs, pseudo-Japanese black lacquer coffee table plus matching bureau. There were ikebana flower arrangements everywhere.

The dog was lying on his old pigskin bed in front of the open fireplace. A few of last night's embers were still glowing on the hearth. The dog rose when Carow entered the room, slowly and laboriously, but his legs buckled twice before he made it. He was sixteen years old, a black-and-white-ticked pointer. Skin cancer had encrusted the joints of his forelegs and hind legs with sores, and he was steadily going blind.

The dog was the object of a long and largely silent battle of wills between Carow and his wife. Although they both agreed in principle that it would be better to put him to sleep, each left the decision to the other. If ever Carow got as far as calling the vet, Isabelle would abruptly put her foot down and complain that only he would have the cold-hearted cruelty to exterminate a helpless beast that had come to them as a month-old pup. Carow always lost such arguments, so the dog lived on.

He opened one of the french windows. The pointer followed him outside. The house stood at the end of a cul-de-sac in one of the most opulent and fashionable residential districts in the south of Munich, and the gently sloping site was bounded by a lake. All this luxury and seclusion had been purchased with Isabelle's money; on his salary, Carow would have found it hard to account for his ownership of such a property. Its view of the lake's broad expanse and the far shore, though almost obscured by greenery in summer, came to perfection when the leaves fell.

Rain had fallen during the night, and the sky was overcast. There was every chance of more rain to come. The possibility filled Carow with dismay. If golf was out, his daily routine would suffer a further upset.

2

ISABELLE WAS ALREADY having breakfast when he returned from walking the dog. She, too, was dressed for the course: slacks and twinset, pale blond hair held in place by a terrycloth bandeau. Isabelle's beauty was ageless. Even at fortynine, she seemed an unlikely mother of two—a daughter of twenty-one; a son who would have been twenty-six last month—and showed no signs of surrendering to the years.

He kissed her dutifully on both cheeks before sitting down across the table from her. This was part of their *modus vivendi*—a clause in the unwritten treaty concluded when he returned to her after a twelve-month separation: at weekends they played the polite, attentive married couple.

"You were late last night."

"There's a flap on," he said. The higher a man got, the less he told his wife—that was one of the Organization's golden rules, though they'd never observed it. "Trouble in the Eastern Bloc, but not the usual kind. They seem to be having some genuine problems over there."

Isabelle had always taken an interest in his career. Without her, Carow would never have risen to become C's deputy and potential successor. Such was the entire focus of her ambitions, the one thing that justified her marriage.

When he'd left her last year and asked for a divorce, Isabelle had confided in C. Carow was presented with a choice: either he went back to his wife, or he submitted his resignation. At first he'd felt relieved and ready to quit the Service, but the other two—C and Isabelle—knew better. They realized that his greatest weakness was his loyalty to the Organization; more simply, they knew how much he dreaded premature retirement.

Still answering her questions, he recalled the hours he'd spent with Anne the night before. Isabelle had never understood his streak of reckless, almost primitive masculinity. Why—why a woman like Anne? Isabelle had been speechless when he told her—reduced to unprecedented silence. Anne was twenty-five years his junior, dark-haired and beautiful but overweight. She had a skin that showed she drank and smoked too much, a body that had known too many lovers. Hers was a wild but already wilting beauty. Why, Heiner?

Because I can *feel* her, he thought as he looked across the table into Isabelle's flawless face—because I can feel her beneath me at this moment, feel her body arch itself, feel the thrust of her thighs and buttocks, hear the soft, gurgling laughter as she strains to reach her climax, hear her cry of unbridled delight when she comes. That's why: because of your silence and immobility. The sole indication that Isabelle had experienced an orgasm was her habit of falling fast asleep immediately afterward.

"Telephone, Heiner."

He pushed his chair back, alerted by a sense of the unusual. The direct line to the Center was in his study, which Isabelle had installed next door to the drawing room and furnished from floor to ceiling. He had never read any of the books on its well-stocked shelves, and the desk, which might have been made for Herr Grapentin, the insurance company vice-president, had seldom seen him at work. Bringing home files was taboo.

"Carow."

"Ritter here. A report from Outstation B3—urgent. Timed at nine zero five."

Carow glanced at his watch. Only three minutes had elapsed.

"Geissler wants to see you in person." The duty officer held his breath as though fearful of Carow's response. If there was one thing Carow couldn't stand, it was irregular procedure, and unheralded contact between outstation heads and senior Center executives was irregular in the extreme.

"He'd better have a damned good reason." Carow detected the duty officer's hesitation, and again he was assailed by a sense of foreboding.

"What's his problem?"

"He's lost a runner."

The Organization's term for an agent in the field. "Lost" was jargon too, and Carow was momentarily grateful for the euphemism. His principal emotion was surprise. In Cold War days—even in the early sixties—agents captured in the Eastern Bloc had been guillotined. But those days were gone. Since then, both sides had adopted a policy of sale or exchange.

"When did it happen?"

"Six fifty-eight this morning. I advised Geissler to go through channels, but—"

"Where is he now?"

"Somewhere on the Nuremberg-Munich Autobahn. I couldn't stop him."

Carow stared out at the garden, picturing Geissler alone at the wheel. He well knew what it was like to lose an agent, so he could imagine how Geissler must be feeling.

"I'll be at the golf club from ten o'clock on. Redirect him there when he turns up. This runner—do you have his code number?"

"CS 77."

"Dig out his personal file, curriculum vitae—all we've got on him. Keep it under lock and key, but have it ready for me. And Ritter, better inform C. Tell him I'll come to the Center as soon as I've had a word with Geissler." Carow felt a sudden stab of pain in his back. He turned to see Isabelle standing in the doorway between the study and the drawing room. She closed the sliding door behind her.

"Anything wrong?"

He remembered the day he'd come home with the news that their son, an Air Force lieutenant, had been killed in a Starfighter crash. She must have read it in his face, yet she'd stood there with the same composed expression and asked the selfsame question. It was her weakness—and, of course, her strength—that she could never break out of her shell or crack the carapace of discipline that had grown up around her over the years.

"We've lost an agent."

"You mean you won't be coming to the club?"

"No, we can still go, but you'd better take your own car. I'll have to drop in at the office later."

The pain became fiercer, and his body ached for relief.

"Ines is coming to lunch. You promised to talk to her about that apartment."

"I'm afraid I'll have to postpone it."

The bedroom he'd occupied since his return had belonged to his daughter. He went upstairs and took two Darvons in quick succession. He heard Isabelle get the cars out; first his elderly Porsche, then her BMW. The rain had held off, but the sky remained gray and overcast.

The pointer was back in front of the fireplace when he came downstairs again. He rubbed the animal's sores with an ointment prescribed by the vet. The whitish paste did little good because it must have contained some ingredient which pointers found palatable. It was licked off as soon as he applied it.

Later, during the drive to the golf club, when ingrained habit made him slip the gun he always carried into the Porsche's glove compartment, he realized what had been wrong with the idea of putting the dog to sleep. He pictured a consulting-room table draped in white oilcloth—pictured, more especially, a long-needled hypodermic poised above a quivering flank—and thought: No, that would be a shameful, almost obscene way for any pointer to die, however old and feeble.

CHAPTER II

THEY CONTINUED TO PLAY IN SPITE OF the light drizzle that set in after the first nine holes. One of the caddies was shielding Isabelle with an outsize umbrella. She was "Isabelle" to everyone at the club. She belonged to the committee and was the local women's champion. Isabelle never had trouble in finding caddies or partners to accompany her.

Her handicap for the course was better than Carow's. Although he had a good long drive, it often landed him in trouble. Once on the green his play improved, because that was where his quiet, methodical approach came into its own.

This morning he was playing particularly badly—four strokes behind after the first round. The second round promised to be even worse. He couldn't cope with the wet grass, tended to select the wrong club, sliced and hooked his ball all over the place.

They were on the seventh green when he spotted Geissler on the clubhouse terrace. Isabelle had holed out and was waiting. Carow putted rather carelessly but was surprised to see his ball head straight for the pin and drop. They filled in their score cards. He was relieved when Isabelle walked on with the caddie.

Geissler was wearing a long loden overcoat almost the color of the grass. The array of badges on his felt hat reminded Carow of the days when he and Geissler used to go mountain climbing as students. Neither of them had gradua-

ted. Carow, a stonemason's son, was drafted into the Army.
Geissler, a year or so younger, took over his father's farm.
There was something of the country boy about his broad
face even now, despite its pallor and fatigue.

"I know, Heiner, I shouldn't have—"

"Let me play this hole."

Carow's interruption was deliberately brusque. Nothing
could alter what had happened. Geissler must be blaming
himself for the loss of an agent. Though altogether natural,
reactions of this kind were unproductive. Feelings of guilt,
pangs of conscience—in their trade, all such emotions were
futile; they merely prevented a man from doing his duty.
Carow drove off.

"You've put on weight."

They followed the ball, Carow striding out briskly, Geissler puffing a little.

"I know. We haven't seen each other for ages."

"I've been chained to my desk."

"Is that Isabelle?" Geissler pointed ahead. They were approaching the next green. The rain had stopped and the umbrella had disappeared. The turf beneath their feet was wet
and slippery. "I heard you'd gone back to her."

Scuttlebutt had always flourished in the Organization. In
an environment where so much had to be kept secret, discussion of personal matters was incessant. Most of the gossip
was harmless, but one ill-considered word had been known
to blight a man's career.

"You heard right."

Carow's approach shot had landed in a bunker full of
coarse wet sand. He took a sand wedge and lofted the ball
with unsuspected strength.

"All right, Karl, fire away."

Geissler produced a slip of gray paper from his inside
pocket.

"Here's the report from CS 77."

Carow shook his head. "Background first. Tell me all I
need to know for now. I'll bone up on him properly later."

"You won't find much in Records. You've got him on file, but there's no C.V. or source book. He wasn't important enough for that."

"Not till today, you mean? All right, go on."

Carow had once held down an interrogator's job, and even the most tight-lipped subjects were reputed to have crumbled under his powers of gentle attrition.

"Name Cichosz, age forty-one—a Czech national. Came from a frontier family—customs officers one day, smugglers the next. That was probably my big mistake, Heiner. He had the frontier in his blood. It was his idea of romance."

Geissler's accent suddenly slipped. His Saxon origins were barely perceptible most of the time. He had moved west in 1950, after his farm was expropriated under the Communist land reforms. Like so many uprooted people, he was forever engaged in perfecting his new identity.

"Romantic impulses needn't be a bad thing," said Carow. "They only become dangerous when you can't keep them stabilized. How was he paid?"

"I couldn't persuade him to accept any money."

"I don't like the sound of that." Carow's voice had acquired a slight edge.

"Beggars can't be choosers, Heiner. I take what I can get. The days when I could pick and choose my agents are gone. I'm happy to have a runner in the field at all, whatever his idiosyncrasies."

Carow knew what he meant. Outstation heads like Geissler were important pieces on the espionage chessboard. They enjoyed the status of petty princes and ran the agents in their bailiwick as they thought fit. Their golden age had been the heyday of the Cold War, prior to the building of the Berlin Wall and the sealing of the eastern border, but much had changed since then. The princelings had forfeited most of their power, just as the Organization as a whole had lost ground inside the Eastern Bloc. Carow steered the conversation back to its starting point.

"What sort of goods had he delivered in the past?"

"Nothing earthshaking, but always sound. Pre-sixty-nine was his best period. He actually ran two subagents in those days—Russian servicemen of junior rank. Nothing exceptional even then, but all the items we managed to check were rated 'reliable' or at least 'possible'—I've looked through his worksheet. I dropped him a year ago. No special reason, except that I couldn't stabilize his romantic impulses, as you would put it."

They had reached the eighth green, where Isabelle and the caddie were waiting. Isabelle played the scene to perfection: Her husband was conferring with a valued client on the golf course. Only a fleeting shadow of annoyance crossed her face—and was reflected somewhat less subtly in that of the caddie—when she noticed Geissler's ankle boots. Visitors who trod the club's well-tended greens in ordinary footwear were anathema.

Geissler watched her head for the next tee. He said, "Shall I go on, or will it put you off your game?"

"Why did you reactivate CS 77?" Carow used the agent's coded designation as though the anonymous letters and figures could dispel his growing mental image of the man.

"Because of your 'Bear-Hug' project. Mind telling me which one of you dreams up all these names?"

Carow didn't reply. All knowledge had its limits, and in the Organization these were strictly circumscribed. Not even a man like Geissler needed to know everything. Recent weeks had brought growing signs of popular unrest among the Soviet satellites, hence Operation Bear-Hug: a directive to all outstations to focus their agents' efforts on the subject.

"As soon as I got your request, I activated everyone on my books."

The little gadget in the breast pocket of Carow's golfing jacket began to bleep, softly but insistently. For a moment, it dominated all other sounds: the smack of a ball being struck on the next fairway, the murmur of distant voices, the hum of traffic building up on the road beyond the course because the sun had finally emerged.

"Excuse me." Carow killed the signal that requested his presence at headquarters. He put his driver back in the bag and picked up his ball.

"I heard from CS 77 two days ago. We had a standing arrangement that guaranteed to get him out if it came to the pinch. You'll be getting the details in my written report. That's what was meant to happen this morning."

Carow was towing his golf cart behind him. Now that the rain had stopped and the sun was shining, the grass looked almost fluorescently green.

"That was my second mistake—my second blunder, if you like." Geissler mopped his brow. "He'd sent the escape signal, but he didn't want out at all, he wanted to go back for more. He'd stumbled on something big—a windfall was the word he used."

"You mean you actually saw him face to face?" Carow couldn't conceal his surprise.

"But don't you see? That's just what he wanted—a chance to throw off his anonymity. Cichosz was a little runner who'd always trailed along behind the field, and now he'd come home first and expected some kudos. A pat on the back, that's all: Well done, you ran a good race, et cetera. I know it was a mistake, Heiner, but I tried to put it right. I did my best to stop him going back—not that I had the faintest idea what would happen. He'd turned up on time and he knew those woods like the back of his hand. No misgivings, no ominous signs on my side of the fence. The same went for him, I'd swear to it. He was as proud and happy as any runner could be."

"How did it happen?"

"A single shot. No one else in sight. Sounded like a high-velocity rifle. He was back inside their territory—not a chance of getting to him."

"You're sure he's dead?" Carow didn't stress the words.

"Positive. I could see him through my binoculars."

"Did they remove the body?"

"I left a man behind and got his report *en route*. They waited for over an hour. Two of them—soldiers. They toted him off between them. Probably had a vehicle hidden somewhere nearby."

"Anything to connect him with us?"

"I checked before I let him go back. He was clean."

"May I see the report now? Your decoded text, not the original."

Geissler hesitated. "Agents always think they've struck oil, I know, but the poor devil really came up with something big this time."

His accent had slipped again. Carow realized that he wasn't talking about the agent any longer. It was Geissler who needed a pat on the back and a word of encouragement. Being familiar with the condition himself, Carow felt momentarily tempted to give him what he wanted. Grapentin might have made the gesture, but not Carow.

"The report, please."

Even a preliminary glance told Carow that CS 77 had indeed struck oil. The bare bones of the message were exceptional enough in themselves: A meeting to be attended by the heads of the Warsaw Pact secret services, venue Prague.

Carow tried to recall the last such occasion. Conferences of this caliber were reserved for extreme emergencies: 1953, after Stalin's death; 1956, Hungarian uprising; 1962, Cuban missile crisis; 1968, prior to the invasion of Czechoslovakia. But the main value of the report lay elsewhere. It was the piece missing from a puzzle which the Organization had so far failed to complete. At the same time, Carow's predominant emotion was almost trivial—or, if not trivial, ultraprivate and personal: he felt profoundly relieved. Instead of a weekend that would have dragged on forever, he could look forward to two days of unremitting activity.

"What's your own assessment of this report?"

"Reliable. So you really think it's important?"

Again Carow ignored the almost pleading note in Geissler's voice. "One thing puzzles me. A single shot, you said?"

"That's right."

"Why, Karl? Who else knew about your rendezvous?"

Carow could sense that Geissler was recovering his poise. Something inside the man was hardening. Even before the reply came, Carow knew it would be an attempt to turn the tables—to steer responsibility away from Geissler and divert it to himself.

"Well, I naturally informed your people in advance."

"Subsection Czechoslovakia?"

"It was their baby."

"Borchers is one of the old guard." Carow regretted his remark at once. It implied a commitment in favor of Borchers, and that was premature. Pocketing the original and the decoded text, he added, "Security will check it out."

They had reached the club's parking lot. The Porsche and Isabelle's BMW were standing side by side. Carow stowed his golf bag.

"Where's yours?"

Geissler pointed to a gray Mercedes Diesel. "I've been up since God knows when. I could use something warm inside."

"Like a slug of brandy?"

"Has Security been checking my liquor bills?"

"Let me phone in first. C doesn't like being kept waiting."

Geissler watched Carow until he disappeared into the clubhouse. Then he walked to his car. There was a bottle of brandy in a plain brown-paper bag on the rear seat, but he didn't feel like drinking alone.

Carow was the only person inside the Organization whom he could call a friend. Carow trusted him. What more could he expect? The case was still pending. Operatives from the Security Section would soon be on his doorstep—he could picture them turning the place upside down. Carow would stand by him, though. He might be an unfeeling man, but his friendship was proof against sudden squalls.

"I'm wanted at the Center," was all Carow said when he came back.

"Family gathering?"

"Yes, it looks that way."

"How's the old man?"

"Neither old nor human. He's a unique species, a relic of the past—some kind of dinosaur, maybe."

They looked at each other, both sensing that it had come at last, the token of intimacy and affection demanded by Geissler and denied him by Carow. Geissler held out his hand.

"Come and pay us a visit some time."

But Carow wasn't prepared to give more than he had already.

"You'll send me a written report?"

"Tomorrow."

"Make it as full as you can. Put in everything likely to confirm this story."

"Filing copy to Borchers?"

Carow's reply was unhesitating. "Normal procedure till further notice. We must naturally disguise the identity of our source."

"Naturally."

Carow sat in the Porsche until he was sure Geissler's Mercedes had a big enough start. His route to the Center took in a stretch of autobahn. Carow enjoyed letting the Porsche rip, but he somehow wouldn't have liked Geissler to catch him doing so.

CHAPTER III

IT WAS RAINING AGAIN BY THE TIME Carow drove up to the main gate of the Organization's headquarters. The security man emerged from his guardhouse. He recognized the head of Section I and was about to wave him on when he thought better of it. Carow always insisted on being asked for his identification and could turn nasty if someone neglected to do so.

A continuous stream of traffic passed in and out of the main gate on normal workdays, especially at shift-changing times. Now, Carow met no one on his way to the building that housed the offices of C and his two deputies. The only car in the reserved parking lot was the senior secretary's battered blue Renault Dauphine.

To many people, particularly those who only glimpsed it through the tall electrified fence that enclosed the whole complex, there was something sinister about the Center. One could readily understand the sentiments of such rare visitors as it received. After driving through a peaceful suburb on the banks of the Isar, with detached houses, well-kept gardens and quiet tree-lined streets, they were greeted inside by a hodgepodge of buildings ranging from old Quonset huts to a modern glass office block. Observers who confessed that the place made a bleak and cheerless impression on them—one more usually associated with East European architecture—were not so wide of the mark. It was almost as though the men who worked there hoped to get inside their enemies' skins by working in similar surroundings.

To Carow, who was now at his desk being briefed by the duty officer, a procedure that barely impinged on his train of thought, the atmosphere had a monastic flavor. A special feeling pervaded him whenever he entered the Organization's precincts. Not of sanctity—Carow wasn't a religious man, or didn't regard himself as such—but of something else. In allowing himself to be recruited by the Organization, he had undoubtedly been attracted by the aura of a secret fraternity, its strict code of conduct and articles of faith.

Not, of course, that his office bore the least resemblance to a cell. Carow would gladly have made do with less space—a desk, a safe and a filing cabinet would have sufficed—but space, and number of office windows in particular, were the Organization's caste marks.

He sat with his back to the three windows that were his due. His office being on the ground floor, he would hear the others' cars when they came. No fellow member of the "family" had yet turned up. This gave him time to scan the nightly influx of reports relating to his section. He had already conferred with Ritter and Kurella, the head of Security.

Kurella had been down with flu for days. Carow summoned him from his sickbed, puffy-eyed and running a slight temperature. His condition had not been improved by the prospect of investigating a possible leak in the Czech subsection. For the moment, however, neither of them needed to make a decision. That would rest with C. They had gone to Borchers' office and opened the safe together. Sure enough, Geissler's reports on CS 77 were there, all neatly filed away.

Carow was drafting his own report on the frontier incident for submission to the meeting. Geissler had been right: there was no curriculum vitae or source book for CS 77, merely a computer-printed index card. In default of anyone else who could have been entrusted with the job, Carow had asked the senior secretary to produce some fair copies. Five of them now lay in front of him. Pauly had stamped them SECRET and CLASSIFIED on her own initiative.

He leafed through the finished report, which had the original in CS 77's handwriting appended, without really reading it. The pain in his back was a mute cry for help, but he knew he was in for a long, tiring day and would be even more in need of pain-killers later on. His Darvon consumption was beginning to worry him, like anything beyond his control.

He opened his safe and took out the studies on Operation Bear-Hug. They had spent nearly a week working on them in the big upstairs conference room. All Eastern Bloc subsections had taken part, Borchers' Czech subsection included.

While the first cars were pulling up outside, Carow immersed himself in the material so as to be armed for any questions that might be raised at the forthcoming meeting. What was really going on inside the Eastern Bloc? How sound were recent reports of public disorder there? Poland and Czechoslovakia were involved; more importantly, so was the "Zone." The terms "German Democratic Republic" and "East Germany" were taboo in C's presence.

Some reports referred to troop movements in conspicuous strength round East Berlin and in the Magdeburg area, though these were exceptionally hard to interpret because the Warsaw Pact states were about to hold their regular end-of-summer maneuvers. News items of this type were processed, evaluated, circulated and filed. They poured in day after day, but their incidence had noticeably increased in the foregoing week. Many came from agents, but most were so-called "overt material" ranging from press reports and monitored radio broadcasts to a file that simply contained a selection of readers' letters printed by East German newspapers during the past two weeks. Efficient evaluation—"reading" the enemy's intentions by putting two and two together—had always been one of the Organization's greatest strengths, and evaluation was the domain of Ziegler, head of Section II, Carow's fellow Deputy Director.

Despite Ziegler's straightforward view of the matter, Carow had expressed misgivings at the absence of any hard facts. Why? Normal competition—the friction that was bound to arise between their two departments? A measure of personal rivalry—even jealousy?

Carow still felt satisfied that his suggestion hadn't been prompted by any form of personal grudge and was tailored to given circumstances. He'd proposed that their existing information be checked *in extenso* by agents in all districts.

"Oh, sure, *in extenso*!" Ziegler had scoffed at their last meeting. "Some day you'll admit that the tortoise got there before the hare, Heiner. I hope I'm around when you do."

Carow kept his temper and C, for reasons still obscure to him, endorsed the proposal. Being a file and dossier man by nature, C must have been predisposed in Ziegler's favor, but this time his decision went the other way. Orders were duly issued to all outstations, which was how the word had reached Geissler—and CS 77.

Meantime, more cars had rolled up. Two of them belonged to secretaries in C's outer office. Ziegler's Corvette was there, as was his baby-sitter's nondescript Taunus. Blumenschein and his own shadow would be coming by suburban train. C and Puck would use C's private entrance, which was well away from the main gate, escorted by another two cars. The rules that governed this game of code names and baby-sitters—personal bodyguards—were laid down by C himself. Carow alone had steadfastly declined to be shadowed wherever he went, preferring to rely on the gun he always carried.

One of the phones on his desk came to life. It was Isabelle, reminding him to call Ines. He put off doing so in the hope that the buzzer summoning him to C's office would forestall him.

His daughter lived in a commune. Whenever he phoned

her, a male voice defiantly demanded to know who he was. It embarrassed him to say "Ines' father," but calling himself "Heiner," as he did on one occasion, had made him feel even more of an old fool.

He'd been there once. A multipurpose living room with mattresses on the floor—three for the girls, two for the boys—and so littered with guitars and audio equipment that it looked like a recording studio. The kitchen was just as overcrowded with the organic foods they held sacred—a veritable warehouseful, as though the fivesome were counting on a prolonged state of siege. Oddly enough, he'd felt quite at ease there; naturally enough, he'd wondered who slept with whom.

Ines eventually came to the phone. He told her that their lunch date would have to be postponed. Conversation was difficult because "the others"—she'd warned him of this—had no need to know the score: Ines was moving out!

Carow had seen it coming—"formed a prognosis," as Ziegler would have put it. So much for her ardent political convictions, for the vehemence with which she had rebelled against her family, her teachers, the world at large and "your whole damned class-ridden system." So much, too, for the aggressive behavior that had alarmed her parents and caused such ructions at home. The fire had gone out at last. "Tear-gas days," she'd christened her student-demonstrator period, and laughed. "Know something? You wake up one morning and it's all over."

Carow hadn't rejoiced at her laughter. It was as though he himself could feel the deep disenchantment that should really have smitten her. He was distressed by her resignation—or, worse still, by her failure to show any. It seemed a betrayal: the Ines that had emerged from the chrysalis was merely a budding Isabelle.

He had liked the other Ines better. Above all, he had admired her rugged recalcitrance and inward refusal to compromise, perhaps because he saw them as attributes inherited from himself. But that thought surfaced only in his better moments. At times like this, he doubted if he'd ever possessed such qualities.

Even while trying to fix another time and place to meet, he regretted having telephoned at all. Private preoccupations didn't belong in this room, these surroundings. It wouldn't have happened if his secretary had been there because she had strict instructions to short-circuit any personal calls.

What were they talking about, anyway? The point of their conversation suddenly escaped him. Isabelle often reproached him for his startling ignorance and indifference where normal, everyday matters were concerned. Had he any idea what it cost to maintain their standard of living? Carow evinced surprise and indignation when he chanced to learn what his wife paid the housekeeper or when he came across the gardener's monthly account. He jibbed at buying a new pair of golf shoes as soon as he heard that they would cost him twice what he'd bargained for—and that in a man of his omniscience, a man who was privy to so many things concealed from the rest of the world. But maybe that was the trouble—maybe the Carow-Grapentin equation simply didn't add up.

They finally settled on another lunch date. Carow looked around for an appointment diary, but his secretary's desk was bare. Even her memo pad had been dutifully locked away. He was still looking when Pauly's voice came over the intercom.

CHAPTER IV

1

THE SECRETARIES SUFFERED MORE THAN MOST from the Organization's universal craze for sobriquets. They were simply known as "dragons," and no one disputed Pauly's claim to the title of head dragon. Pauly had been C's secretary from time immemorial. She would never leave while he was still around, and there were some who speculated that C, a widower of three years' standing, would end by marrying her when he retired.

His outer office was staffed by three secretaries, all of whom had turned up. One of the younger two was dressed for skiing, and Carow recalled that the early morning news roundup had spoken of snowfalls in the Bavarian Alps. She was typing a report. The other hovered over the photocopier while Pauly herself made entries in one of the diaries she kept on C's behalf.

No nails were painted in the anteroom, no eyebrows plucked or cigarettes left to smolder in ashtrays. No private conversation flourished either. Grim and humorless, with a masklike air of vigilant mistrust, Pauly made no concessions to human nature save one: an endless supply of fresh coffee. This she drank herself—despite chronic heart trouble—in copious quantities, black and unsweetened.

Ziegler and Blumenschein were already there. They stood

waiting, each with a cup of coffee poised. The red light glowed above the door to C's suite.

Blummenschein was a fat man whose predilection for flashy clothes made him look even fatter. He had once been something of a Communist whizz-kid—a lawyer and rising star in the Comintern. After renouncing his erstwhile gods, he had also transformed his outward appearance as though it wasn't enough to change his faith. Slim and youthful looking until well into his forties, with a mane of blond hair that had earned him the nickname "Fairy" among his former comrades, he had since become what he was today.

Ziegler eyed the folders under Carow's arm. "I gather we owe this meeting to you."

" 'Fraid so."

Everything about Ziegler was ramrod stiff and erect. Blumenschein bent over his coffee in the normal way; Ziegler raised the cup to his lips without modifying his pose in the least. The way he drank coffee cast doubt on the laws of physics.

"Have I spoiled your weekend?"

"I was just off to Brussels."

"Reconnaissance techniques?"

"NATO. Satellite surveillance."

"Sky spies," Blumenschein interjected. "They're stealing a march on your agents, Heiner."

Carow had more time for Ziegler than he did for "Stargazer," as Blumenschein was now known. Blumenschein's head was permanently in the clouds. Carow distrusted his flights of fancy when it came to determining Organization policy. Ziegler kept his feet on the ground and saw things as they were; with him, Carow knew where he was. They worked well together as a rule—in fact, after so many years in harness, they should really have been friends. Perhaps the gossips were right—perhaps it was only their wives that prevented them from becoming so; each anxious to see her spouse installed as C's successor.

They had now been waiting fifteen minutes or more.

Though customary, these delays in the outer office defied rational explanation because Pauly's main responsibility was to coordinate C's appointments. Junior members of the Organization called them "kowtow time"—not that many of them were privileged to enter the anteroom, still less the Director's office or "throne room" itself.

They all failed to notice the green light come on and did so only when Puck opened the door and ushered them inside. Puck's manner always reminded Carow that he had once been a steward in the first-class section of a big ocean liner. He preceded them, limping in his habitual way.

"He'll be with you in a minute, gentlemen. Something to drink? A Coke? Some fruit juice—orange, grapefruit, tomato?"

Puck's smile verged on a grimace. He was their age, around fifty-five, but looked younger because of his eternal grin and strange, almost frisky gait. The latter seemed less amusing when one learned that his limp, which he studiously tried to disguise, was a souvenir of polio contracted in childhood.

Although he held no official post inside the Organization, other than that of C's baby-sitter, no one doubted that Puck stood high in the hierarchy and belonged to the "inner circle," "palace guard," "gang of four," or whatever name one chose to give the members of C's immediate entourage.

Again they waited. The door to the next room was ajar, and through it came the hum of an electric razor.

"He didn't have time," whispered Puck. He might have been dispensing crumbs from a king's table.

Carow felt ill at ease, whether because of his golfing attire, which looked out of place in this setting, or because of the room itself, with its sterile olive-green walls and artificial lighting. The windows were obscured by white plastic Venetian blinds. One wall bore a photographic blowup of the Berlin Wall. It dated from 1963 and showed John F. Kennedy looking east across the Wall from a viewing stand.

"Sure you won't have a drink?"

Puck filled a glass with ice. They all knew that the ice machine, a gleaming contraption which spewed out an avalanche of cubes at the touch of a lever, had been a gift from the CIA to C on his sixty-fifth birthday. During a long session, Puck journeyed to it many times. No room could be hot enough for C's taste, but his insides seemed to need glasses of ice-cold fruit juice as a car needs a radiator.

At last the door swung open and C came in. He looked pale and weary, not like a man who had just freshened up. His dark suit, an old-fashioned double-breasted two-piece in heavyweight cloth, did nothing to dispel this impression, nor did the dark tie adrift on his crumpled white shirt. Not for the first time, Carow was reminded of a priest with a slovenly housekeeper.

"Tedious business, shaving every twenty-four hours. I find it more and more so every day."

C greeted them all in turn. Carow found it almost distasteful to return his limp, languid handshake.

"Why hasn't anyone got a drink?"

"They all said no."

One corner of the room was occupied by a big round conference table. They had their well-established seating order: C and Puck on one side, the other three in a semicircle opposite. Puck placed a brimming glass of fruit juice in front of his master.

"Very well, Heiner, you kick off."

"No shorthand record?" Ziegler was ever practical.

C surveyed the table as though to remind himself of where he was. His eyes were peculiarly colorless. He shook his head.

"Later, perhaps."

Carow handed out the folders but retained his separate memo on the suspicions attaching to Borchers and the Czech subsection. Ziegler, Blumenschein and Puck started reading. C left his folder unopened. What was the matter with him—was he too tired even to peruse a seven-page report? It puzzled Carow to see him in this condition.

"All right, let's hear what you have to say."

Even his voice sounded listless and weary. It was Ziegler who, after finishing the report, helped Carow over the hurdle.

"This bears us out, wouldn't you say? I mean, it confirms what we already knew about disturbances inside the Bloc. How reliable was the agent?"

"I had my doubts at first. A meeting between all the secret service chiefs—Polish, East German, Czech, Hungarian—with the Soviet Director holding a watching brief? It sounded almost too dramatic."

"Not necessarily," Blumenschein broke in. "Not if they can see the floodgates bursting."

"It was the details that convinced me. Page three—that bit about anti-bugging devices in the conference room—that was how CS 77 came to hear of it in the first place. Then there's page five, bottom para—to my mind, the most convincing item of all. They've agreed on German as the principal language—at a conference in Prague! That sounds like Zentner—you know how weak he is at foreign languages."

C came to with a jerk. He put on his old horn-rimmed glasses—the lenses were none too clean—and began to read. The more he read, the paler his face seemed to become. They waited, expecting him to make some comment, but he merely propped the horn-rims on his forhead and sat there staring into space.

"Your final conclusion?" Ziegler insisted.

"It tallies with our other data, as you yourself said just now. They must be up against some very serious problems."

"They're sitting on a powder keg, if you ask me." Blumenschein underlined his words with an emphatic gesture. "They can stamp out isolated sparks, but once the whole thing goes up . . ."

Ziegler interrupted him. "I suggest we take another look at what we've got, in the light of this report." His words were directed at C, but C's lack of response was a tacit injunction to proceed without him.

They embarked on a reappraisal of the past week's developments. Ziegler, in his methodical, matter-of-fact way, led off.

"We can forget about our overt material on the disturbances, Heiner. Let's confine ourselves to what we have from the Monitoring Service and our agents . . ."

Carow was so familiar with the report that he could afford to let his thoughts stray without being thrown by Ziegler's occasional questions. He couldn't help looking across at C and wondering if it wasn't too much for him—if the reins weren't slipping from his grasp.

C would be sixty-seven this year. No one in the profession had headed any secret service for as long as he had—effectively since 1943. When he turned sixty-five, the normal retirement age, there were many who thought he should have rested on his laurels. Since then, criticism of him had been rife. The chief complaint from outside the Organization was that it was obsolete, overmanned and—worst of all—inefficient; that it had been worsted in its most important theater of operations, the battlefield on its doorstep: the "Zone."

"To sum up," Ziegler concluded, "there are strong indications that the Eastern Bloc, and the Zone in particular, is in for a rough ride during the next few weeks. It's a highly explosive situation—one that could easily become as grave as sixty-one. We have to assume that the purpose of this secret meeting will be to approve measures designed to defuse the situation."

"It's a time bomb! If they don't locate the detonator in time, there'll be a bang to end all bangs."

"Stargazer," who was euphoric, could always be relied on to produce his forecast long before the others, conjuring up a course of events in the visionary style that had earned him his nickname. Struck by his extravagant tone and manner, Carow suddenly wondered if he was gay. Blumenschein's personal file was locked up in C's safe and accessible to no one else, but it was unlikely that a homosexual would have climbed so high. To C, that guardian of moral purity, even extra-marital relationships were grounds for dismissal.

"Why don't we call in S Section?"

The section invoked by Blumenschein was not to be found on any Organization chart. The S stood for "stinkers"—operatives who applied themselves to the technical aspects of active resistance in enemy countries. Carow felt it was time to comment.

"Strong indications, yes, but we'll need a whole lot more before they're confirmed. Our conjecture rests on evaluation and a report from one lone agent."

Ziegler turned to Puck, who was busy replenishing C's glass with ice.

"Puck?"

Puck seldom commented during these sessions. The other three felt sure he always reserved judgment until he was alone with C, and that that was precisely why he carried such weight in their councils. Everyone at the table was duly surprised when he answered. His voice was low and expressionless—almost inaudible, as though what he had to say was for C's ears alone.

"It looks like Zentner's handwriting."

Was that all? They waited, but he left it at that and resumed his seat. They looked at C. They had pointed out the symptoms; he would make the diagnosis and prescribe the treatment—that was how it had always been. But he sat there drowsing, seemingly having taken nothing in. He reached for his glass but didn't drink. He looked across the table at Carow as if it were all he could do to raise his head. Nothing in his colorless eyes appeared to convey genuine interest, and his voice, when he spoke, sounded faintly diffident.

"There's a problem relating to this agent CS 77, isn't there, Heiner? Why keep your cards up your sleeve?"

2

IT WASN'T UNTIL later, when the project took a turn which none of them now foresaw, that Carow first suspected C of hoodwinking them all.

Had his ostentatious display of fatigue, his diffidence and vacillation, been merely an act? Had he been laying his plans even then—the chrysalis phase, as the beginnings of an operation were known? Did he already have Martin in mind that morning, when all was still wrapped in a secret service cocoon? Had he really been toying with the idea of sending Martin to Prague—Martin, who was far away in his island retreat and had doubtless dismissed the possibility of ever being recalled? And Zimra—were the contents of her file already flitting through C's head?

At the time, however, there had been no reason to indulge in such conjectures. Carow distributed the folders he'd so far withheld and presented his oral report.

A long silence followed—a sudden rise in tension. The ice machine made noises no one had noticed before. Carow sensed what the others were thinking, knew what their first reaction was bound to be: disbelief. Everyone at the table knew what a leak inside the Center implied and how disastrously it might cripple their future operations. It implied what every secret service feared most: an enemy agent—a traitor—in its own ranks. Carow chose his words with care.

"In view of CS 77's death, we can't exclude the possibility that a leak exists in the Czech subsection. At the top."

"Borchers? Never!"

They stared at each other. Who had said that?

Ziegler again. "When was he last checked out?"

Carow tapped a passage in his report. "Just under two years ago. The Security Section gave him a clean bill of health. No abnormal expenditure, no sex problems. A pedantic type. Not overambitious, but he does a good job."

"Trips abroad?" asked Puck.

"None. How could he, with that mother of his?" Carow had no need to elaborate. They all knew that Borchers lived with and looked after an invalid mother confined to a wheel-chair.

"What about doctor's bills?" asked Blumenschein. "Ones we don't know about?"

Carow shook his head. "His mother owns the house they live in. There's a family firm, too—she's a major share-holder. You won't find an explanation there."

"Improbable, the whole thing. Highly improbable." C had suddenly joined in. "I expect CS 77 opened his mouth too wide, that's all."

Carow felt another pang of surprise. As a rule, C was the one who kept impressing on them that security took priority over results—"secure your rear before advancing," to use his military turn of phrase. That was one of the reasons for his long survival in the profession. Why did he fail to see the problem here? Why should he want it shelved so quickly?

"Everything we've heard up to now is guesswork, Hein-er. Security's in the picture. You and Kurella opened the man's safe together. He hasn't disposed of any evidence, you tell us. Has he been exceeding his authority in any way—poking his nose into things that don't concern him?"

"Not that we've managed to discover so far."

"So where's your evidence?"

"We'll have to dig for it. The question is, how far do we go? Wiretapping, personal surveillance—that's for you to decide."

"I know what they'd do in the East," muttered Blumen-schein, but this found no favor with C either.

"Take it easy!" His tone was impatient. "You want to stir up a hornet's nest? Reports in the press, questions in the Bundestag—a public hearing, maybe? At the moment, that would hurt us more than any leak."

Ziegler squared his shoulders. "All the same, we can't just sit back and hope there's nothing to it."

"Who said anything about sitting back?" C threw his other deputy a disapproving glance. "Naturally we'll con-duct an investigation, but on tiptoe. Personal surveillance if you like. No wiretapping, though. That would involve too many people."

"We could test the man," Puck suggested. "Feed him something."

Carow squelched the idea. "If Borchers is really working for them, he must have class. He'd spot a marked card in two minutes flat."

"The fact remains, it poses a problem," said Ziegler. "They're meeting in Prague, and that's his department. His subsection would normally be involved. He'd be bound to notice if we cut off his flow of information overnight, but how can we pursue the project if we don't?"

The question had been put. They all knew it wouldn't be easy to find an answer. Once again, it didn't occur to Carow until much later that C had hit on the solution long ago—that the cards had still to be correctly arranged; above all, that no one could ever accuse him of having shuffled and dealt them himself.

But none of this was evident now. C turned to Puck and said, "Let's adjourn." He rose to make himself an iced drink while Puck asked the others what they wanted for lunch.

CHAPTER V

1

THE JUNIOR DRAGONS SERVED THE MEAL, cleared the table, brought tea for Carow and C and coffee for the rest. Conversation ceased to revolve around Organization business and became personal. The climate changed too. Where tension and irritation had reigned, the five men were now infused with a growing sense of solidarity. Casual remarks and laughter could be heard. Even C, who had visibly relaxed, became infected with the new mood.

It all sprang, of course, from their frequent experience of similar situations in the past. They'd been sitting in conclave—not in this building, which hadn't existed at the time—when they heard that Brigitta Stein had gone to the guillotine: "Briggi" Stein, their best-ever agent in the Zone and a woman near the top of the Apparat, the East German Security Service itself. They had also been together when the Organization lost seventy-eight runners in a single week, when its surviving agents in the field became embittered and demoralized, when the Wall went up and tighter restrictions on border traffic cut the two-way flow of agents to a trickle.

They were innumerable, the defeats they'd undergone, and their consequence was that the veil which C had drawn round the Organization grew steadily thicker and more impenetrable. The gossamer web encasing the cocoon was hardening, its occupants' room for maneuver decreasing.

Doubts? They existed too. Carow felt them even now. The same old question: why and what for? Were they making legitimate use of their power? The question of motive also cropped up—his own and the others'—but this was no time for self-doubt; this was a time to close ranks. One way or another, they had always surmounted their defeats.

"Let's start again." C had accepted one of Blumenschein's cigars—a rare phenomenon. "What are we going to do?"

Blumenschein took advantage of the changed atmosphere. "Why don't *we* have an agent inside the Apparat, right under Zentner's desk?"

"Yes, Heiner," said C, "why don't we?" He forced a smile, but no one followed suit. "I'd like to hear your views in turn—in a nutshell. You first." He pointed to Blumenschein.

"Stargazer" didn't hesitate. "The only way to hurt a

Communist régime is by force. In my opinion, we should foment existing unrest, call in S Section—blow the Zone sky-high. Boom-boom!''

Ziegler might have been reading his words into the record. ''According to our present information, the Bloc is facing a crisis. We should notify the Chancellery—friendly intelligence services as well, perhaps. We can continue to observe developments and step up our electronic surveillance.''

''Heiner?''

''We need more to go on. More facts—fresh meat, not canned. We should really try to sneak someone under Zentner's desk.''

''Assign an agent to the Prague conference, you mean?''

''Yes.'' Was he right, Carow asked himself—was he stating a belief or simply trying to demonstrate the importance of his section, and thus of himself, in relation to Ziegler?

''Puck?''

Puck was clearly disconcerted by the question. He grinned and ran his fingers through his reddish hair. ''Does Procurement have the necessary resources?''

This time, C did not keep them waiting. ''I'm afraid you'll have to forgo your weekend, gentlemen. Get down to work. Run through all our information again. Blumenschein, try Records. You should find some data on similar conferences in the past.'' He paused. ''Split up the donkeywork between you and consult me if necessary. I want to be absolutely sure of my ground, do you understand? This is our big chance.''

''And the final decision?'' insisted Ziegler.

''We'll make that tomorrow. Puck will provide you with all you need for the night, and the dragons will keep you fed and watered.''

They knew they'd been dismissed.

2

CAROW'S WEEKEND turned into a nightmare. His back ached, he slept badly, and he was jolted awake on Sunday morning by a dream he'd often had before but not in recent years: his first parachute jump behind the Russian lines. The dream was a rerun of past experience. He was standing in the open door of a low-flying aircraft with a swath of forest beneath him, the trees so close they seemed to be reaching for him. From behind him came the dispatcher's irate, imploring voice: "Jump! *Jump*, damn you!" Carow woke up, less startled than oppressed by the emotion associated with this dream: a sense of having failed at the crucial moment. It was so intense that he often felt sick and sometimes had to vomit.

He shaved in the washroom along the corridor from his office, joined the rest for breakfast in the conference room and then went back to work. His desk was strewn with files and folders. The very act of reading wearied him. He felt superfluous, duplicating the others' work—in fact, he felt the work itself was superfluous. Ziegler's had been the only sensible suggestion: Put in a report and let the politicians decide what conclusions to draw from it. Tuesday was C's day in Bonn, his weekly session with the head of government.

What had he said? *This is our big chance* . . . The sudden animation in his voice had been a giveaway. C loved backstage maneuvers. Personal policy making, that was his pet temptation. He loved shuffling the cards—alias items of intelligence gleaned by the Center—in such a way that the game followed a predetermined course. But what, Carow wondered, was the game this time?

Sunday went by. They met a few times in the main conference room to correlate their results. Twice summoned by C to answer questions, they found the innner sanctum littered with files and looking like a ransacked records office. On the only occasion when Carow asked to speak to C himself, he and Puck were off the premises.

They had just sat down to supper, again in the main conference room, when Pauly's voice came over the intercom.

"C wants you. I repeat, C wants you."

They walked down from the third floor. Red fire buckets
filled with sand lined the corridors. Together with the ubiq-
uitous fire escapes, they reminded Carow of the period immediately after the war, when the Organization had been
working for the Americans. That, too, was part of C's legend: his preservation, complete with secret files and personnel, of an intelligence service that had worked for Hitler and
then, thanks to him, survived the German defeat intact.

They had now reached the first floor. The passage leading
to C's anteroom was under surveillance by closed circuit TV
cameras. C himself could switch on a screen in his office.
Was he watching it at this moment? C had a weakness for
the technological toys that abounded in his profession. Outside headquarters, the only operatives whose sections he
ever visited were the lab men, the forgers and the radio experts.

This interest did not extend to Carow's section. At heart,
C had no high opinion of agents. Carow sometimes thought
he even detected a certain contempt for them. In C's scheme
of things, agents represented a *quantité négligeable*. The
fate of CS 77 had left him unmoved, Carow felt sure. C was
a desk warrior, a file and dossier man. Carow felt equally
certain that none of them had enjoyed the weekend more.
He'd sucked up information like a sponge, showing no sign
of fatigue.

The litter of files had disappeared by the time they
trooped into his office. C was seated behind his desk without
a jacket on, the overlong sleeves of his shirt held up by a pair
of old-fashioned expanders. He hadn't shaved since yesterday morning. The white stubble made his face look even
leaner, even more reminiscent of a down-at-heel priest, but
his expression was very different from yesterday. His eyes
were alight with cunning.

"Puck, drinks."

He led off even before his own glass arrived. "I had a
long talk with Kurella. Nasty bout of flu—which reminds
me, Personnel should see that everyone gets inoculated.
Anyway, Security came up with another question mark
against Borchers. The 'washerwomen' ''—he meant the
Monitoring Section—"have an old radio message on file:
birthday greetings from over there for someone referred to
as W.B. Five years old, no indication then that it might have
been meant for Borchers.''

C continued to discourse without notes. He had an inex-
haustible and unfailing memory, even where the most outwardly trivial matters were concerned. None of them could
rival him in that respect.

"On balance," he wound up, "everything points to
Borchers being the leak, but there's no conclusive proof. He
won't provide it himself—or can we hope for a confession,
Heiner?''

''Not a chance.''

"So Kurella's section will have to look for evidence, but
quietly. Nothing official, no public inquiry, no wiretaps.
The bailiffs will take him in hand. For the moment, that's
it.''

It was clear that he didn't expect any comment or concur-
rence. The bailiffs were the members of the Surveillance
Section.

Ziegler said, "That still doesn't solve our problem.''

"Hang on, I'm coming to that.'' C took a swig of chilled
fruit juice. "Blumenschein has unearthed an agent's report
from the week before the Wall went up. Highly informative.
The same sort of meeting between the Bloc Directors, the
same people present. Zentner took the chair and advocated a
hard line. Even the Russian representative had qualms, but
Zentner backed his own information and swore the Americans wouldn't take a gamble.''

It didn't escape Carow, as C reeled off more data, still
without notes, that he continually reverted to Zentner. The
very way he uttered the name betrayed some secret stirring

of emotion. C's delivery was as drawling and monotonous as it was because he scarcely moved his lips, but this one word, Zentner, emerged from between his bared teeth like gases given off by a process of fermentation deep inside him. Carow sensed that there was a personal factor involved here. Recently, when an updated photograph of Zentner appeared, he'd been surprised to note that advancing years had created a growing resemblance between them, if only in expression.

"Well?"

C had asked him a question—he must have missed it. Everyone was looking at him, and he could see annoyance written on C's face. Again it was Ziegler who came to his rescue.

"The question is, Heiner, how good are your resources?"

Had they solved the Borchers problem? He didn't know. Had they reached some kind of decision? He didn't know that either. He should have taken a Darvon before supper, but he'd forgotten to.

"Mind if I top up my glass?"

He wondered how to sneak the pill into his mouth.

"What's the matter with you, Heiner? It was your idea, after all." C sounded genuinely irritated. "We all agree we need some fresh meat. What and whom do you suggest?"

So that was the question. The decision had been taken. It had fallen on him, Carow—his section, his runners. The old, time-honored method: an agent on the ground. As simple as that. He'd advocated it from the first, when the scheme was launched. He should have felt gratified.

"Thanks, Puck." He drank some juice but left the Darvon in his pocket. "We can't use anyone local"—he was playing for time—"aside from the fact that we don't have anyone in Prague who'd be up to the job."

"We've already discussed that, Heiner. It's quite clear we need an outside man, someone out of the freezer, someone who doesn't have any present connection with us. What's the matter with you?"

"It's this kidney trouble—I must do something about it." Having supplied an explanation, he unashamedly took a Darvon. "There's the time factor to be considered. We'll need a man who knows his way around and speaks the language. He'll have to be carefully coached, too." Why hesitate, why balk at the idea? "The Prague conference opens in—a week from now, isn't it?"

"Yes, if CS 77 was right."

"That doesn't give the headhunters much time."

"No headhunters," C said quickly. "Handle it yourself, and when you've found the right man, supervise the whole operation. Recruit him and run him yourself—from an outstation."

The picture had suddenly changed. That one remark—"run him yourself"—meant that C had cast his line, and Carow knew he would willingly take the bait. That was another respect in which C surpassed them all: he knew and saw through them so much better than they did him.

"I want him found before I go to Bonn."

Carow was already conducting another mental withdrawal from the others. He thought of the problems ahead. Who was the right man? Names surfaced in his memory, faces paraded before his mind's eye. The fivesome in C's office had other decisions to make. He took part in them, but only halfheartedly.

How much was the Chancellor to be told at his weekly briefing? Ziegler pressed for a comprehensive report—everything they had—and Carow seconded him. Blumenschein and Puck opposed this on the grounds that it was premature. C gave his casting vote: They would wait and see. Bonn was a hotbed of gossip—too many leaks. Should they inform their CIA "cousins"? Again C had the last word: Not yet.

The meeting neared its end. It was past 9 P.M. After thirty-six hours together, they had found the solution. C wound up, as was his right.

"Once you walk out of that door, the shutters come

down. Business will go on as usual, but so will the Borchers investigation. If our young Turks start grumbling that their elders are blindly twiddling their thumbs again, let them. And Heiner, drop a hint that you'll be going into the hospital for surgery in the very near future. Set the scene for the days you'll have to spend at the outstation.''

Carow was happy to regain the open air after so many hours. Not that he'd noticed it inside the air-conditioned Center, the weather had changed. It was very much warmer, even at this hour.

The second half of September often produced a fine spell like this. Carow hoped the change would hold. For many reasons, an agent would find it easier to carry out such an assignment in good weather. Carow made a note to consult the experts.

Later that night, in an hour or two, he would return to the Center and begin his quest for the right agent. Runners' source books were the kind of reading matter he didn't shun. He actually liked the windowless subterranean chamber—part of Records—in which they were kept under lock and key. By morning he would have made his selection, and the potential candidates' source books would be lying in his office safe.

He walked to his car. He was still in golfing attire, but he didn't propose to drive home and slip back into the Grapentin role. Opening the car door, he replaced the gun in the glove compartment. He started the Porsche up and reversed out. The others had already gone. Ziegler had shaken his hand before leaving. ''Congratulations!'' He'd struck just the right note—a man who knew how to lose with good grace.

Once out of the main gate, Carow headed for central Munich. He stopped at the next public call box. He longed to unwind—to put some distance between himself and recent developments—but nobody answered. Although Anne had no reason to expect him tonight, he felt disappointed.

He dialed the number again and let it ring, and this time

he felt a sudden pang of jealousy, sharp and virulent. He needed her badly. Why wasn't she there? What was she doing? Was she with someone else? For a moment, all kinds of jealous fancies gnawed at him.

He walked back to the car. He could undress, take a bath, shave, wait for her in bed. He pictured himself lying there . . . He turned the car. He would do some work first and then try again. But as soon as he was seated in Records, poring over agents' source books, he forgot Anne entirely.

CHAPTER VI

1

ALTHOUGH BORCHERS HAD NO CLOSE FRIENDS inside the Organization, he had no enemies either. He was pleasant looking in an unexceptional way, and neither his outward appearance nor anything else about him suggested that he might be leading a double life. All that ever surprised his colleagues was that, when initialing a document or signing a receipt for one, he did so with his left hand—as though the mere fact of his left-handedness was an eccentricity that somehow conflicted with the rest of him. Nobody thought twice about his only real departure from the norm—his extended lunch breaks—nor begrudged him such a liberty because the whole world knew that he had to look after a mother whose dependence on him was total.

"Lamb," as Borchers was known among his colleagues, had availed himself of his privilege this Monday and left the Center at 11:30 A.M. The bailiff's report was lying on Kurella's desk within minutes of his return. Borchers had gone straight home. At 12:30 he drove his mother to Nymphen-burg Park. There they remained for an hour, he on a bench, she in her wheelchair (sketch map of relative positions appended). No contact or conversation with any third party observed. Borchers had checked in at the main gate at 2:30 P.M. Since then, he had been at his desk.

Subsection Czechoslovakia was housed in one of the Quonset huts that dated from the time when the Center was a U.S. Army base. Borchers was still at his desk at 7 P.M. Passed to him by Carow, Geissler's report on the border incident lay open in front of him. Under the circumstances, it was only natural for Borchers to be working late.

It had been a shock when the report came in. Not so much because of what his last signal had portended for CS 77—that he would have to come to terms with later—but because of the suspicions it aroused in himself. He had sensed that something was in the air for days now, but he'd urged himself to tread carefully. Suspicion was his life's most constant companion. When would they finally unmask him? When would they put the pieces together? How imminent, how remote, was the day of discovery?

Borchers was not a man given to needless speculation. He was patient and persevering, never rushed things or threw caution to the winds. Of course he'd have liked to know the full picture, but his scope for confirming or disproving what he suspected was limited.

He couldn't do much inside the Center, just remain on his guard, check whether information was being witheld from his office and keep his eyes skinned for marked cards. Curiosity and overeagerness were the surest aids to detection. For the moment, he couldn't even communicate his suspicions to his "friends." He had never supplied them with flights of fancy, only hard facts.

There was one point, however, that made his position unusually awkward: the stage at which his suspicions had been aroused. Something was brewing—something connected with Operation Bear-Hug. Borchers had been "one of them'' for too long not to sense the heightened tension at headquarters. C's daily presence there was itself an omen that some major operation was about to be launched. With his hands tied at such a juncture, Borchers was in a cleft stick: the need to preserve his cover warred with his fear of missing out on something important.

There was a better chance of confirming his suspicions elsewhere, hence the idea of an outing with his mother. The grounds of Nymphenburg Palace, with their wide open stretches of grass and dead straight gravel paths, were hard to keep under covert observation. The one thing he knew for sure was that, as long as *he* made no mistakes, *they* would sooner or later show their hand.

The outcome was inconclusive. Although there had been some indications that the bailiffs were on his tail, he couldn't be certain. He decided to try a second experiment on the way home; that was why he lingered so patiently at his desk. By 8 P.M. the city-bound traffic would have thinned, making it easier for him to spot a shadow.

2

THE HOUSE STOOD in a quiet street bordering a small canal. The term house was inaccurate to the extent that it was one of several flat-roofed apartments built on different levels. Frau Borchers, a woman with a practical turn of mind, had decreed the demolition of her late husband's family home and redeveloped the site to suit her own needs. She and her son occupied one of the ground-floor apartments, direct access to the basement garage being provided by an elevator that could accommodate her wheelchair.

By the time Borchers reached home, he felt sure that his suspicions were unfounded—that he'd simply allowed himself to become infected by the Center's epidemic sense of unease. He'd done everything possible—observed the cars following him, left his own to be washed at a service station, taken a tram, completed the rest of the journey on foot.

Three cars were parked outside. Borchers eyed them carefully too, but their presence meant nothing in itself. As soon as the weather turned fine, tenants couldn't be bothered to drive down into the communal garage.

He could hear, even in the hallway, that a tape was playing. His mother was suffering from progressive arteriosclerosis—or so, at least, the doctors said—and her symptoms of paralysis had lately been accompanied by deteriorating eyesight. No longer able to read, she could only listen to taped books, which she preferred to music.

She was sitting in her wheelchair in the living room, well-groomed as ever. She liked crêpe de chine dresses that matched the pastel shades she favored for her makeup. It was her face that never failed to move him. Thin, fine-boned and taut-skinned, it lent her the pallid beauty of a young girl—as if her face were trying to compensate for the ravages in progress elsewhere.

The tape came to an end.

"Enjoying it?"

"Not specially."

"The librarian recommended it."

"*Death in Venice?* I'm surprised. She knows the kind of thing I like."

"I'll change it tomorrow." He switched the machine off. "What would you like for supper?"

"Nothing much." She sounded momentarily tired and forlorn, but corrected the impression at once. "Just tea and toast. There's some smoked salmon left."

He went into the kitchen, where there was a second telephone, and dialed an acquaintance. They swapped trivialities for a couple of minutes. When the other party hung up, he kept the receiver glued to his ear and listened, although he knew, of course, that modern technological refinements made it impossible to tell whether a line was being tapped or not.

Borchers pushed the trolley into the living room and laid the table, then wheeled his mother to her place beside the window. He himself sat where he could keep an eye on the street. He had switched off the center light. All three cars were still parked outside.

For a moment he debated whether to ask his mother how long they'd been there. He sometimes felt an urge to confide in her—tell her everything—but he naturally suppressed it.

"In the old days," she was saying, "we always used to go to Venice in the autumn."

"I know. That's why I thought you might enjoy the Thomas Mann."

"Ah, so it was *your* idea." She stared at him. "What's the matter?"

Perseverance had paid off. He had seen what he'd given up hope of seeing: a brief flicker of light inside the middle car. Someone had lit a cigarette. Just carelessness, or couldn't they afford to give the bailiffs cars equipped with dashboard lighters?

"Something worrying you?"

"I worked too late." In a way, it relieved him to know where he stood. Now that his suspicions had been confirmed, he could notify his friends with a good conscience. "I'll go to the library tomorrow morning and change it."

"See if you can get me a Vicky Baum. *Grand Hotel* would do."

"Haven't you had it already?"

"That or something else of hers."

Borchers briefly permitted himself to think ahead. It might be better to broach the subject now.

"Perhaps I need a break."

"Nurse Karin could come and spend a couple of days with me."

"A proper break, I mean."

Alone? She had no need to say the word aloud; her look of silent reproach was enough. Silence was her strongest weapon, the one she always used when he tried to escape her magnetic field.

He cleared his throat. "Something may crop up."

"A woman?"

He almost laughed at the misconception. There had been a time when he brought women home and introduced them to her. One of them had even had the temerity to move in with him, but his mother's eloquent silences had driven her away.

"No, not a woman."

Borchers had always believed that life's greatest divide lay between the haves and the have-nots. He now knew that an even wider gulf separated the healthy from the sick, the able-bodied from the infirm.

He had to wait a long time before she went to bed. She spoke of Venice, of the trips they'd made together in the past. At her request, he set up the projector and showed her some slides. It amused him to guess what his secret observer would make of that in his report.

When she had finally gone to bed and was asleep, he returned to the living room and drew the curtains.

He gathered her selection of recorded books together. Rewinding the tape on the machine, he listened until he reached a particular passage. Then he switched to "Record" and dictated his message, simultaneously erasing the words beneath. He stacked the tapes ready for tomorrow's trip to the library, turned out the light and drew back the curtains.

There were still three cars outside, but the middle one was a different make—the relief, presumably. What an expenditure of effort, he thought. It signified that they had nothing on him, or not enough.

Borchers was in no hurry—he would make no mistakes. A surprising thought occurred to him: How had it all begun? What was his motive in working for "the others"? It was so long ago he could hardly remember. England, 1944. The P.O.W. camp. How old had he been? Little more than twenty. How had they induced him to betray the specifications of that submarine? What carrot had they dangled in front of him? He had a clearer recollection of the final phase: his sudden repatriation when the war ended, his night flight to the British Zone, the car journey, the safe house where they'd given him civilian clothes, discharge papers and a traitor's reward. No prior warning, no explanation. Was that where his motive sprang from? Was that why he'd become so willing a tool in the hands of "the others"?

Motive didn't come into it now, and hadn't for a long time. Did agents *have* any motives? Agents were normal, ordinary human beings. They undoubtedly acted from a wide variety of motives, but did that matter? The longer you pursued a profession, the less your motives counted. What about men like Ziegler and Carow? They did a job, but were they motivated?

He only knew that he, "Lamb" Borchers, had ceased to need a motive. His trade—the spy trade—was motive enough in itself for him to do a conscientious job.

Borchers left his post at the window and stowed the tapes in his briefcase. He had a long day behind him, but he didn't feel tired. All things considered, he felt satisfied with his day and himself. The morning's news had been a shock, but he'd ridden it well. He wasn't nervous any longer. He would continue to do what his "friends" expected of him.

The irony of it was, he couldn't be shadowed inside the Center. He suddenly thought of the man in the car. He, too, was trying to do a conscientious job, nothing more. Prompted by a strange sense of kinship, Borchers switched on all the lights and walked back to the window to give the hunter a good-night view of his quarry.

CHAPTER VII

C HAD SUGGESTED THE RENDEZVOUS, a beer garden not far
from the military airfield where a helicopter was waiting to
fly him to Bonn. C had already arrived. He was sitting at a
table in the far corner, under some chestnut trees. Puck was
also there, covering his approaches from a table some yards
away.

Despite the heat, C was wearing a dark serge overcoat
with a fur-trimmed collar. In front of him stood a glass and a
bottle of Coca-Cola. The Coke had remained untouched,
presumably because it wasn't cold enough. He looked pale
and short of sleep. Carow knew how much he hated flying.

Carow kept the briefcase on his lap.

"I've got three candidates lined up."

"Good, excellent." C seemed in no hurry. He treated his
deputy to a smile. "If this thing goes well, Heiner . . .
Once it's over, I can think about retiring."

The same old story. Carow, who had heard it on and off
for the past two years, took it no more seriously than C's repeated hints, sometimes to Ziegler, sometimes to himself,
that they fitted his picture of a successor to a tee.

"I mean it, Heiner. I've been in the job long enough, and
it hasn't always been easy. These damned politicos! The
more vital our information is, the more they tend to dismiss
it. If you take over, never forget one thing: but for us, the
Reds would probably be sitting here right now."

55

Carow began to feel uncomfortable, as he always did when C embarked on this line of talk. Perhaps it was just a hangover from the disappointment that lingered with him after seeing his daughter. Ines had taken him on a guided tour of the new apartment, soft-soaping him all the way. A peck on the cheek here, a daughterly hug there. Wouldn't it be far too expensive? Oh, no. Mother had already said yes—and besides, she'd naturally pay her back. How? She was already on the track of a job, a "madly well-paid" one. She spoke three languages, remember? Well, she'd just been offered this job as a traveling secretary . . .

The man across the table had never had any problems with his own children, who appeared to have known by instinct what befitted the offspring of a secret service chief. All were now safely settled, the son in a "secure position," as C phrased it, the daughters married to members of the Organization. Carow had met them all, C's late wife included—a colorless woman whose self-effacing devotion to her husband was his sole surviving impression of her. To Carow, the entire family had seemed no more than a disguise selected by C for wear in his extramural role as Dr. Achternbusch, Curator of the Bavarian Castles and Lakes Authority.

Carow removed three gray folders from his briefcase. "As I say, I've picked out three possibles."

"Fine, let's see them."

"The top one's my first choice."

C took the files, which were not very bulky. "Rosell . . . I thought you'd short-list him. Pinkert? I wouldn't know—never met him, to be frank." He turned to the third file and looked up. "Martin too?"

"He's only my number three."

"But you included him. Why? Because he's a veteran—one of the old guard? To make the other two look better?"

"Martin was one of our best men—in his day. Years of field experience. Three in East Berlin, six in Dresden, seventeen in the Zone as a whole. A calm, stable character, but ambitious as well. Always on the *qui vive*, always what a textbook runner should be. Outstandingly good at solo assignments—a loner *par excellence*."

Carow broke off, realizing that he had fallen into C's trap. He was singing the praises of a man he'd described as his third choice.

"Our first contact with him was in forty-five?"

A reply would have been superfluous. The answer was on record, albeit summarized in a single sentence. The remnants of the Organization—most of its personnel and all of its records—had been in transit for prearranged hideouts in the spring of 1945. C planned to lie low until the Americans came to their senses and developed a proper appreciation of his value as a source of intelligence about their Soviet enemy. There were two copies of the records, one set of which was to be submerged in a lake in the Bavarian Alps. That was when young Martin had joined them, an eighteen-year-old frogman on detachment from a special army diving team.

"You recruited him yourself, didn't you?"

"It's all down there."

"That's not the same as hearing it from you."

"Yes, in forty-seven. I came across him on a recruiting tour in Dresden. I'd heard he'd ended up in a paramilitary unit—men who'd volunteered to clear East German waters of mines left over from the war. That was the side of his character that worried me sometimes—his tendency to court danger."

"They all get a taste for it sooner or later."

Carow didn't comment. "I asked him to do something small and unimportant. That's how it started. After a trial period, we let him off the leash."

C was looking for something in the file. "Don't I recall a reference to his wife?"

"Foot of page two. She was killed in an accident. Terrible business—an explosion at a chemical works. They'd been married less than a year."

"Any motive there?"

Though equally superfluous, this question was only to be expected from C.

"I doubt it. Martin was a born agent. Natural ability."

"Never remarried?"

"No."

"Any woman trouble?"

"Not to our knowledge."

"No family ties?"

"Both his parents are dead. The father was an ethnic German, but anti-Nazi. His mother was Czech; hence his command of the language."

C dug deeper into Martin's file, muttering to himself from time to time. "Electronic equipment of the MiG-15 . . . Tilted the whole Korean War in America's favor . . . That training film on tank tactics . . . Till then, everyone in Bonn refused to believe us when we said the Zone was re-arming . . ." C looked up. "He was good, Heiner. Really good."

Carow felt it was time to be blunt. "Yes, but it doesn't mean he's in good shape now. I can't vouch for his present condition. Rosell and Pinkert are temporarily on ice but still on our books. Martin quit the Service six years ago. We don't have much time—maybe not enough to prepare him." He opened Rosell's file. "This man's in training. He's all set to go—*and* he's got all the qualifications the assignment calls for. You did say I'd be running the agent myself."

"Of course I did, so the ultimate decision rests with you. It's just that I want to be absolutely sure." C leafed through Martin's file. "I don't see anything here to indicate why he left us."

C's memory seldom failed, but it may have done so in this case because he couldn't accept the fact that any man with long years of devoted service behind him had left the Organization of his own accord. Carow himself had been deeply disappointed at the time. Something close to envy had possessed him when he came across Martin's source book in

Records. That was his strongest recollection of the man, his stubborn independence. Perhaps that was what had prompted his inclusion among the candidates.

"Why did he, Heiner?"

"He was a victim of the Zentner offensive in nineteen sixty-four, don't you remember?" C studied his fingernails and said nothing. "It was a lousy year—our sources in the Zone completely dried up. Martin held out till the autumn because he was operating solo. They sentenced him to twenty years. His name turned up on their list in sixty-eight, so we managed to exchange him."

"There was a six-month gap, wasn't there?"

"That's right, no witnesses to his last six months in jail. It made us curious."

"But he cleared himself, didn't he? He told us they'd invited him to work for the Apparat?"

"Yes."

"Did he have a clearance certificate when he left us? He went of his own accord, didn't he—not because we had any lingering doubts about him?"

"He was absolutely clean."

"You debriefed him yourself?"

"Yes. Kurella assisted, of course."

"Am I wrong, or wasn't there some criticism of your methods?"

"They were quite appropriate, given the special circumstances. I had a feeling he was holding something back. Martin himself never complained. We didn't use physical pressure, if that's what you mean."

"Was he invited to stay on?"

"Yes, we offered him a slot in the courier service, with an eye to reactivating him later on. It was pretty much of a dead-end job, though—not his style at all."

"There's nothing in the file about financial compensation."

"He refused it. At the time I suspected he'd had an offer

from the CIA, but as far as we know he quit the profession for good. I requested confirmation from friendly services."

Seated at his separate table, Puck signaled that it was time for C to leave.

Carow said, "Puck's getting fidgety."

C was unmoved. "What happened to him?"

"He became a scuba instructor, first Elba, then Kenya, then Eilat on the Red Sea. He now runs his own diving school in Ibiza . . . You don't honestly think he's our man, do you? All my reservations still stand."

"Those debriefing sessions—did you keep the transcripts on file?"

"No point. He was quitting the Service anyway."

"Pity. You say you felt he was holding something back?"

"It was only a hunch. An unfounded one, as it turned out."

"Try to cast your mind back—this could be important, Heiner. While you were questioning him, did the name Steffin crop up at any stage? Mean anything to you?"

"Steffin? No. Male or female?"

"Zimra."

"I don't follow."

"Zimra Steffin. A woman's name."

"No, definitely not."

"I'd like you to check it in Records—carefully."

"I don't know what you have in mind, but I still think we ought to take Rosell. Martin must be forty-nine by now. That's pretty old for a tough field assignment."

"Very well, Heiner. Whoever he is, the runner's yours while the operation lasts. You'll keep his books, you'll have to coach him, and you'll be running him, so pick him yourself." The bland, benevolent note crept back into C's voice. "You'll be the advance guard, the pair of you, with us here backing you up. It'll be just like old times."

"Where shall I run him from?"

"That's up to you. Get the candidates here—think of some excuse, but keep them guessing. Martin especially."

"I've already fixed that. Is it really essential to put them all in quarantine?"

"You can forget about Pinkert as far as I'm concerned, but I wouldn't mind seeing the other two. You surely wouldn't object to my *seeing* them?"

What could he say? Carow replaced the folders in his briefcase. Pinkert's elimination simplified matters, but he was still puzzled by C's interest in Martin. He couldn't think of any overriding reason for it.

C rose. With Puck in tow, they left the beer garden and walked to their waiting cars.

"You're making all the necessary arrangements? Operational cover, signals, codes, insertion points, escape routes?"

"I'm working on them now. I think I've had a bright idea."

"When can you have the men here?"

"Rosell by this evening, Martin tomorrow night—if he bites. I can't tell him what it's about, so it doesn't give me much scope. Anything new on Borchers?"

"No, he's lying low."

"Will you be back today?"

"I may stay on till tomorrow—anything to divert attention from this end. Don't forget to smoke-screen your absence, Heiner. Go to the doctor and book a hospital bed. Then you can take your runner and hole up with him. Somewhere nice and quiet." C smiled and patted him on the back.

Carow was surprised. C's spirits were seldom as high as this when he went to Bonn. It only struck him later that he should have been warned.

2

CHAPTER VIII

1

THE GIRL IN THE RUBBER DINGHY WAS WAITING for the diver to break surface. She didn't know how long he'd been down. There was a stopwatch on the thong around her neck, but she never thought to look at it.

He should have come up somewhere between the anchored boat and the rocky shores of Tagomago. In her fear for his safety, she forgot that too. Frenziedly and unmethodically, she scanned the sea. She even looked in places far out of range. She mistook ripples for a floating body. Her sense of time and direction deserted her entirely. All that remained was sheer panic.

Oh God, she thought, what should I do? Dive in after him, bring up his body—was that it? She could picture him in the depths at a place he'd once shown her, enmeshed in long strands of submarine grass. She couldn't just leave him down there . . .

At that moment, not a yard from the boat and her straining eyes, something cleft the surface. It was a dark head of hair slicked down, so it seemed, with the utmost care. Then she saw the mouth, the lips a startling color—almost violet— expelling a cloud of spray. One arm emerged and hooked itself over the gunwale, the other heaved a lead belt into the boat. As he removed the mask, she saw blood coming from his nose, first a blurred red smudge, than a trickle.

He seemed unaware of it. He spat out some more water, still panting, and asked, "How long?"

She reached for the stopwatch and pressed the button. He had a thing about time. There wasn't a single clock in his house—or, if there was, she'd never seen it—and he never wore a watch. But out on the water, and more especially under it, he fretted about tenths of a second. The same applied when they were out walking. He would suddenly hold his breath and time his endurance by measuring it against roadside landmarks that meant nothing to anyone but himself.

"You're bleeding! Damn you, I hate it when you scare me like that."

He put his free hand to his face. When he took it away and saw the blood on his fingers, he smiled. She suddenly felt sick enough to vomit. It wasn't just the blood. It was her abrupt realization that summer was coming to an end.

He duck-dived, surfaced again, and clambered aboard. The water had washed away the blood, and the trickle from his nostrils had stopped. He removed his flippers and laid them aside, then laid the mask beside them—carefully, so as not to scratch the toughened glass faceplate. That was another thing you noticed about him when you'd known him for a while: the care he bestowed on inanimate objects.

"I wish you'd worry about me half as much as you do about your damned equipment." She still felt frightened. And the other thing, but that she couldn't talk about. "You really had me scared." She tossed him a towel, but it wasn't, in the present context, a gesture of affection.

He dried himself very thoroughly. For a man who spent so much time outdoors, he had surprisingly pale skin. He was built like a swimmer—not too tall and powerfully muscled where it mattered—but few would have classed him as an athlete on sight. His face was far too meditative to accord with the conventional picture of a man of action.

"How deep did you go?"

"Just short of the grotto. Seventy-five feet, at a guess." His answers were always precise, seldom qualified or amplified. Another man of his age might have said, "That's the best I can do these days. Once upon a time . . ." But that would have been out of character.

"Sorry, I forgot to stop the watch."

He went aft to start the outboard. "You never got scared before."

"Today was different, I don't know why."

She stood facing him. Her long blond hair, which hung down on either side of her head like a parted curtain, was bleached by sun and salt. Her body was deeply tanned, and because she wore bikinis of the same shade, an observer on the distant beach might have thought her naked. It was almost as if she possessed two bodies, one slender and almost dainty, the other—from the waist down—heavily built, with sturdy hips and thighs. She gave surfing lessons during the summer months. Her school was attached to the beach hotel near Martin's scuba club.

"What could I have done, actually?"

He started the motor. It fired, faltered for a moment, then idled gently.

"Taken the boat back."

Her laugh was a failure. "Have I ever mattered as much to you as your precious boat?"

"Sit down." He waited until she was seated on the gunwale, holding the grab line, before he went on. "A boat's different."

"More important, you mean?"

The meditative look descended on his face, as though answering her question posed a physical effort. "A boat is only as good as the way you maintain it. The same goes for diving equipment. What I'm trying to say is, you can look after things like that."

"Not people?"

"Look after them more easily, I mean."

He was perched beside the outboard, one hand gripping the rope, the other the tiller. The sea was choppy now they'd rounded the offshore island. He opened the throttle. They didn't speak as the boat leaped forward. Before them lay the wide-open bay and a semicircle of rocky coastline, the upper part wooded and green and punctuated with white houses.

To the west lay the beach and its three multistoried hotels. Below, on the narrow strip of silver sand between the rocks and the water, men were busy setting up deckchairs and sun umbrellas. There were no boats or swimmers out; it was still too early for that, but there wouldn't be many even during the day. High season was over. The hotels and the scuba club would be closing down in ten days' time.

Martin skirted the bay and the beach in a wide arc. They negotiated a narrow inlet flanked by walls of pitted volcanic rock and entered a smaller bay. The water underwent a transformation, becoming blue and still as a pool of spilled ink.

He killed the outboard and let the boat drift. While he went forward, she took the tiller. It was a wordless maneuver; obviously, they had performed it many times before.

He moored the dinghy to a buoy and tilted the outboard clear of the surface. With a thoughtful glance at the sky, he slid over the side. The water was only chest-deep. She passed him his diving equipment and followed him ashore. The bay was so pellucid that every little ripple of sand on the bottom could be seen.

On the beach stood a car—his battered old Seat—and her yellow moped. Their clothes were on the back seat, a sun dress and sandals for her, jeans and a T-shirt for him. Again she noted the care with which he stowed his equipment. She felt almost jealous, knowing that his first act on getting home would be to dump it all in the bath and douse it in water to remove the salt. Only then would he take a shower himself.

He was a strange man, and no less strange to her now than he had been two months ago. He made no pretense of being in love with her. This he could safely do because it had always been understood that she would quit his life at the end of the summer. She never had affairs back in Strasbourg, only a man who'd promised to divorce his wife four years ago and was still married. Here in Ibiza, men were part of her summer—free, so to speak, like her board and lodging at the hotel.

She sat astride the moped with her feet in the sand. "Shall I see you at the beach later on?" She started up.

He glanced at the sky again. "I may bring the boat ashore."

"You think it'll rain?"

"Could be. Come as soon as you're through. Happy with fish for supper?"

She let go of the handlebars, took his head between her hands and kissed him. Turning away, she put the moped into gear. It reared on one wheel for a moment, then bounded forward. Sand and pebbles spurted as she rode off at break-neck speed.

Her long hair fluttered in the wind, streaming out almost horizontally behind her. She raised one hand and waved before concentrating on the narrow, rocky path. It took her back to the bathing beach, the multistoried hotels, and the earth-bound surfboards on which she taught beginners how to keep their balance.

If only I could control my emotions half as well, she thought.

2

MARTIN TOOK THE ROAD that led inland. It was only a nar-row, winding dirt road, gooey with reddish-brown mud after rain but now an almost bone-dry expanse of loose stones and potholes. Anyone looking at the Seat could see how often it must have made the round trip.

The sound of the sea had faded, to be replaced by the chirp-ing of cicadas. The higher he climbed into the hills, the hotter it became. He relished the heat after the chill of the sea. Last year, he thought—last year it wouldn't have worried him, div-ing in these temperatures.

He still couldn't understand it. He'd felt the genuine thing at last. Not a momentary pang of anxiety, but stark, paralyzing fear. He'd dived too deep without a cylinder and found himself in real trouble. It wasn't the first time, but he'd never before experienced any underwater emotion that bore the least resemblance to fear. Fear and water simply didn't go together.

Water was the one element Martin had always felt safe in. During his childhood, when his father came off duty and asked where he was, his mother's ritual response had been, "In the water." She meant swimming in the Vltava's network of streams and tributaries, and her tone of voice implied that he was safe and happy. Hence his decision to return to the water six years ago, when all he craved at the nadir of his life was security.

By now he was far along the upland valley. He had passed some isolated houses. Here there was nothing but heat, parched soil and a scattering of carob trees. The dark pods had dropped off, forming a round black patch at the base of every trunk. No one would trouble to harvest them.

Crumbling terraces and dried-up wells denoted that the land had once been cultivated. He had bought one of the derelict farm houses four years ago. It stood on a flat-topped hill, shaded by a clump of olive trees. Not whitewashed like the majority of local buildings, it had outer walls of natural stone. Seen from a distance as he saw it now, it looked like a miniature fortress.

There was a second track linking the house with the highway. A pall of dust hung over the approach road. When he drove into the yard he saw a car parked there. Méray was sitting on the shady veranda, fanning himself with a panama hat.

"Good God, what brings you here at this hour?"

Méray was one of the doctors who practiced in the island's little capital. Everything about him was white— baggy trousers, shirt, shoes, even his moonlike face and mane of hair—except for the jet-black moustache that drooped from his upper lip. A Hungarian expatriate, vintage 1956, Méray had settled in Ibiza two years after the revolt. He still spoke Spanish with an excruciating accent.

"It's quite a drive."

That was his way of asking for a drink. Martin went into the house. It had a big living room, a kitchen and a rectangular annex containing a bedroom and bathroom. Everything looked scrupulously neat and tidy. There were few personal touches—none of the objects that might normally have accumulated in the space of four years. The single shelf held a few textbooks on civil engineering. In another world and another age, Martin might have become a builder of bridges and dams. A game of patience lay unfinished on a heavy circular table.

He put his flippers, mask and snorkel in the bath and turned on the tap. The water emerged in a thin, brownish trickle. He picked up a bottle of Herbas and carried it out to the veranda.

Méray helped himself. "If there's one thing I hate, it's having to bring a friend bad news." He sniffed the herb liqueur and took a hesitant sip.

Martin had often felt that his past would catch up with him sooner or later. Now it had returned for the first time in ages, that feeling, though muted as yet by his surroundings and the utter stillness of the morning.

"Remember that blood test? I go to a lot of trouble, and what happens? Some fool in Barcelona muddles up the specimens and sends me the wrong report." Méray pulled out a white handkerchief and dabbed his moist forehead. "They now say they've found signs of incipient capillary thrombosis."

"The symptoms haven't been so noticeable lately."

"That happens—it doesn't mean a thing. You'll have to give it up. You're too old for this kind of diving."

"Look, Méray, what's the real trouble?"

"I used to have a colleague in Buda, a gargantuan eater. Food meant everything to him. He didn't eat, he guzzled. I warned him he'd choke himself one day, but he only laughed. Know what he said? 'I'd sooner die eating than starve to death.' You remind me of him, except that with you it's diving. What you need is a thorough checkup.''

The whole thing sounded illogical. Had Méray really driven all this way to tell him that? Martin looked him full in the face.

''You want me to go to Barcelona?''

The basket chair creaked as Méray sat back, unable to disguise his relief. ''Yes, you'll have to repeat the test. Just to be on the safe side. You need the sort of treatment I can't give you here. They've got specialists in Barcelona . . .''

It might have been that word—specialists—which suddenly banished any lingering doubt from Martin's mind. He stood up. His chair fell over with a crash, startling them both. Then silence returned to the valley: not a breath of wind; not a bird in the sky. From far away came the echoes of a single rifle shot; the rabbit-shooting season had opened last Sunday. The generator came to life, pumping water from the cistern to the tank on the farmhouse roof.

''Who sent you, Méray?''

The doctor's brow was beaded with sweat. ''I don't understand.''

''Who was it, Méray? What's the proposition?''

Like other agents before him, Martin had known that the most he could hope for in retirement was an uneventful, unobtrusive existence in the lee of an assumed name. He realized what it would mean when he turned down Carow's offer of a job in the courier service. He'd had a special reason—Zimra—but it hadn't been easy for all that. He'd been proud of his refusal and he still was, in a way. This place was better than any he'd known since his childhood. He'd felt secure and happy here. His nightmares had stopped, but his sense of relief had worn thin. Security and contentment were one thing, the fever of his old profession another.

He couldn't have said exactly when it began—in fact,

he'd never admitted to himself that the virus was still at work inside him. There were times when he missed what he'd done before, missed the years spent in fear, even the dreams that had awakened him at night, sweating and shaking. This, he knew, was the moment he'd been waiting for.

"They put pressure on me, Martin. It's an old, old story. I really hate to do this to you."

"What's the proposition?"

Méray looked up, suddenly hopeful. "What I said. You fly to Barcelona."

"How and when?"

"Iberia, nine-thirty tomorrow morning. Who are you, Martin?"

"You mean you don't know?" Martin couldn't help laughing.

"They threatened to withdraw my resident's permit. What else could I do? All they asked me to do was get you to Barcelona."

"Germans?"

"One German, one Spaniard. So you'll go?"

They drank some Herbas. It was the only thing Martin ever drank apart from a glass of red wine with his meals. Both were made by his nearest neighbor, the farmer whose gun they had probably heard just now. He must be out after rabbits with his dogs.

"Tell me, Méray. That test—what did it really show?"

"Roughly what I said. A clear case of the bends—caisson disease. Regressing, but the symptoms are bound to recur. Pins and needles, aching joints—at worst, spells of unconsciousness and paralysis. You'll have to give up diving. I was planning to tell you at the end of the season."

"Only then? Wasn't that professionally irresponsible?"

"It depends on your point of view." Méray rose. "I still have some calls to make in the district."

Martin stared after the car for a long time. There were things to be done, but he had plenty of time. The rubber dinghy was the biggest job: beaching it, letting the air out, carting it up here, sluicing the salt off, oiling it, reinflating it. The outboard he would take to be overhauled—his neighbor could collect it later. He would also have to visit the school and arrange a stand-in for the remainder of the season.

The house presented no problem. Although he liked living there, his ties with it were nil—or rather, he'd never accumulated all the things that create an emotional bond. It was a house, and a place, which could be abandoned at a moment's notice.

The doctor's car had disappeared. A serpentine plume of dust was winding along the valley.

To Martin, the desolate landscape had something of Eden before the Fall. In retrospect, however, his life in this paradise seemed an endless voyage through purgatory.

He didn't know what they planned to do with him. He even had an admonitory feeling that prompted him to see himself and his position for what they were. He, Martin, the retired, aging runner, was being given another chance. Why was he seizing it so recklessly? To prove what? That he was still good? That he hadn't forgotten the tricks of the trade?

He knew for one instant, as he stood there looking down into the valley, that he ought to resist the temptation. But he also knew that it was already too late. I can always come back, he told himself. A worthwhile line of retreat—something to fall back on. But that wasn't true either. He guessed that, if he went, he would never return.

CHAPTER IX

1

HE WAS AWAKENED BY ONE OF HIS OLD NIGHTMARES, the first for two or three years—he couldn't recall exactly how long. They were all about his years behind the Curtain. There was the courtroom again: arrayed on a table in front of him were the radio, the minicamera, the microfilms, the cash in assorted currencies. And there, quite suddenly, was Zentner's face, heavy-jowled, unshaven, taut with strain and fatigue after hours of interrogation. And he himself, secretly afraid that the dams he'd built might give way, that he was nearing the point where a man feels the urge to talk, talk, talk . . .

"Wake up, Martin! Martin! What's the matter?"

Another, vaguer part of the dream was already receding, disturbed by the voice. Another interrogation in a different place. He couldn't see the man because the light that stabbed his eyes was so bright, but he recognized the voice as Carow's. "Zimra Steffin—why not admit you knew her? Why not, Martin? Why? The truth, Martin!"

"Please Martin, you aren't making sense. Please . . . Oh, hell! *Must* you keep scaring me like this?"

"It's raining, isn't it?" The window to the terrace was open, and he thought he could hear raindrops pattering on the flagstones.

"What was it, a dream?"

Arms were holding him against a body radiant with warmth. He was sure of it now: the drought had broken. He sat up, intending to light the lamp beside the bed, then saw that she was peering into his face. The final wisps of his nightmare dispersed.

"It must have been a bad one."

"I don't remember." A half-truth. He was usually quick to shrug off the effect of such dreams—he even enjoyed them in some crazy, perverted way.

Once, when he'd awakened in Zimra's arms, bathed in sweat and trembling all over, she'd said, "I think your dreams are the price you pay for wanting to see the devil." He hadn't grasped her meaning till later. The lure of evil, of danger; the devil, not as a spirit but as something real and substantial—that was a temptation he'd never been able to resist.

Getting up, he went into the living room and opened the front door. The rain was teeming down. The valley road would be choked with mud and debris by morning.

He returned to the bedroom and looked at the watch she'd left on the bedside table. It was just after 1 A.M. He smiled despite himself. It was precisely the time he'd always been roused by his nightmares in the old days.

The bedroom was stuffy. The chill of the rain had yet to penetrate the walls. She had lit the lamp and was sitting up in bed. It struck him that he'd seldom known a woman who sat up in bed as uninhibitedly as she did, with no instinctive attempt to cover her nakedness.

"You're lucky," he said, "having breasts like yours."

"Don't most men like them bigger?"

When he didn't reply, she said, "Have you had a lot of women?"

"How many are a lot?"

"I don't know, it doesn't matter anyway. Come here."

He touched her body—the part that differed so much from the rest. She'd been sitting up in bed like a statue, but the other part was vibrant and alive.

"Were you ever married?" she asked.

"Yes."

"Any children?"

"No." In his profession—Martin had always regarded it as such—love represented the supreme danger. It was a risk he'd never been prepared to run save once, with Zimra. "I have to go away," he said. "I'm catching the nine-thirty flight to Barcelona." He hadn't mentioned it before.

She barely hesitated. "I could see you off at the airport and bring the car back."

"I was hoping you would."

"Will you be back before I leave?"

"Possibly, but I doubt it."

"Do you want me to move out?"

"If I'm not back in time, shut the house up. No problem, just defrost the refrigerator and switch off the generator."

"What about the key?"

"I can show you all that in the morning."

"Now would be a waste of time, wouldn't it?" She laughed. It was a strange, almost childish laugh that escaped her lips in little morsels of sound. "Kiss me." Her hands grasped his head and showed him what she meant.

He slid down the bed until his lips met the fleece between her thighs. It was darker than the hair on her head and surprisingly crisp. After a while he felt her draw him up to her.

"Come, come quickly!"

Her eyes were closed and her head lay back on the pillow. It was as though the inert part of her body had dissociated itself from the part that was surging beneath him. Even her arms, which had begun by holding him, lay folded beneath her head, remote and uninvolved. This lack of involvement persisted until she came. Afterward, she laughed and said, "No, stay there. Let's go to sleep like this."

It was broad daylight when he awoke. She was still fast asleep on her back, arms folded beneath her head, fair hair spread across the pillow.

They spoke very little on the way to the airport. Martin

tried to imagine what it would be like if he came back some day, but he couldn't. He could only recall his old home. His mother had wanted to see it again, years after the war. They flew to Prague and took a train next morning, then walked from the last stop before the Austrian border. It was a hot summer day, and they underestimated the distance. Neither of them stopped to think that it was a frontier district where much might have changed since the old days.

He still remembered the shock when they finally got there. No village, only a hint of where the main street had been, everything flattened by bulldozers, mounds of mortar-encrusted brick overgrown with grass and weeds. One largish heap of bricks had recorded the outlines of a house. His mother peered helplessly in all directions. "Is this it?" He remembered the disbelief in her voice. The river was a gray ribbon, the distant forest slashed with fields of fire for watch-towers.

They had walked the whole way back without a word, under a scorching July sun.

2

IT WAS HOT in Barcelona—hotter than the island. Martin was glad of his lightweight suit, a bleached old khaki two-piece bought the day he left Israel. His only baggage was an El Al airline bag.

Nothing happened when he emerged into the airport's huge, dreary concourse. He had watched the other passengers from the moment he was handed his ticket at the Iberia desk in Ibiza. Nobody looked like the baby-sitter who might have been assigned to him. For a moment, as he stood in the concourse and still nothing happened, he toyed with the notion that it had all been a figment of his own—and Méray's—imagination.

He picked up his bag and walked over to the Departures board. The only flights leaving in the next two hours were domestic ones. The first international departures—Paris,

London, Frankfurt, Munich—were not scheduled until mid-day. When he heard his name being called, he headed for the information desk.

"Señor Martin?"

He only had eyes for the envelope the man put in front of him. It was a plain buff envelope, too small and flat to convey any inkling of its contents.

"May I see your passport, please? You've come from Ibiza? It's raining there, one can tell from the passengers' umbrellas."

The remark sounded oddly stilted—a reminder to stay alert. Martin scrutinized the man closely, trying to memorize every detail: age, dress, tricks of speech—even the words themselves. He would be questioned about them later.

"Please sign here." The man handed him the envelope. "Exit A18. You've plenty of time."

Martin pocketed the envelope. It was bound to contain more than an airline ticket. He would probably find a ticket, a typed address, and the keys to a safe house. He deliberately refrained from opening the envelope right away. If someone were shadowing him, his every move would be reported, and Martin was determined to conceal one thing at all costs: they mustn't know how *hungry* he was for an assignment.

He bought a newspaper and coffee. It's still up to me, he thought; as long as I haven't gone through passport control and customs, it's still my decision. He opened the airline bag and took out his thirty-two-card deck, the cards dog-eared and worn, the pictures faded.

Two cards. One for me and the island, one for them and the assignment, higher card wins. Mine first. He shuffled, turned up a card, and placed it on the table. A jack. With eight-card suits, the odds were slightly in favor of Ibiza. He turned up the next card and smiled when he saw it was a king. He put the deck away, finished his cup of coffee and took out the envelope.

CHAPTER X

1

CAROW WAS GETTING READY FOR HIS STAY in the hospital. His things were laid out on the bed. The thought of having to make do with only one bag pleased him. He left the room and went to fetch one.

He had examined one of the candidates this afternoon and was satisfied with the result; Rosell fulfilled all his requirements. He had also received two reports on Martin, a lengthy wire from Barcelona and a telephone call from the man who'd been shadowing him since he landed in Munich. Contrary to custom, Martin hadn't moved into his quarters right away; he'd first gone shopping in town for an overcoat and a watch. He may have needed both, but it was a black mark. He had now been waiting in the rented apartment for four hours. Carow took his time; the longer he left him to sweat, the better.

Tomorrow morning—C had fixed an appointment with each—Carow would present both candidates for inspection. After that, the chosen agent would be entirely in his hands. Carow was feeling good. He'd done a lot of spadework in the past twenty-four hours, but he didn't feel tired in the least. It occurred to him that he hadn't taken a single pill since his last meeting with C.

He was looking for a particular bag when he heard footsteps in the hall downstairs. Isabelle was back from town—he saw her from the landing, still in her coat. The evenings were growing chilly, but the day had been dry and sunny. The experts had assured him that the fine weather would hold for the next ten days. All the omens were good.

"I can't find that checked bag of mine."

"Mind if I take my coat off first?"

Other women, he thought, needed a visit to the masseuse or hairdresser, a game of tennis or bridge, to set them up for the day; Isabelle needed a daily trial of strength. Once upon a time he'd shared the burden with his children; now he bore the brunt of her alone.

"I've looked everywhere."

Since when had their marriage been like this? Ten years; fifteen? With a touch of humor, which was not his strong point and could only be ascribed to his general elation, he decided on a specific date: ten years ago. The twilight of the gods of espionage had coincided with the end of his marriage.

She came upstairs polishing her wedding ring on the sleeve of her woolen dress. It was a habit she no longer noticed.

"Can't you ever find anything by yourself?"

"It was here last time I looked." He opened a built-in wardrobe in the passage. Carow had discovered over the years that Isabelle nursed a fundamental hatred of all men. It was probably because she couldn't live without their appreciation, their constant admiration, that she hated them with such singular intensity.

"So what's this?" She pulled the checked grip out from behind some hanging clothes.

"I'm sorry."

"You're going away? Where?"

"Wiesbaden. For a week or ten days. It's this kidney trouble. Dr. Reile insists—he says I can't put it off any longer."

She followed him as far as his bedroom and stood in the doorway, watching him pack. "Is it serious?"

"We'll have to wait and see."

"Does it mean an operation?"

"Not necessarily. I'll let you know." It was unusual for him to lie to her. "I'll leave you the address and phone number, and the doctor's name." The line would be manned day and night by an operative.

"Are you leaving today?"

"No, tomorrow."

She didn't inquire why he was packing so soon. Her mood seemed to change for the better. "I'd vaguely been planning a trip myself."

He turned. No, he hadn't imagined it; she was different. Or rather, he thought, she'd always been the same: a wealthy girl from a wealthy family, ex-pupil of schools for the wealthy, member of clubs for the wealthy.

"Where to?"

"Johannesburg. The Nine Nations' Cup. Of course, if you don't think I should . . ."

He was bound to be wrong whatever he said, so he said the first thing that came into his head. "No, no, for heaven's sake go."

"If you need me . . ."

"Really not."

"What about the dog?"

"How long will you be away?"

"Only for the tournament. Three days, but I might tack on an extra day or two."

"There's no problem, then. Can't the housekeeper look after him for that long?"

"I'll ask her."

He finished packing. Her mood remained amicable and relaxed until he left the house. He noticed when he kissed her that she was wearing a different perfume.

2

MARTIN'S QUARTERS WERE in an eighteen-story apartment block on the outskirts of Munich, immediately overlooking the start of the expressway to the airport. It was inhabited by an ever-changing population of tenants who took no interest in their neighbors. The Organization rented several apartments there in the name of one of its numerous bogus companies.

Carow had received another report before leaving home. The man on the spot reported nothing new. The subject—Martin's name was unknown to him—had stayed put and made no phone calls.

Model behavior, thought Carow. He ran another mental check on the debriefing sessions of six years ago, held in a lakeside safe house in Upper Bavaria. Cooperative but wary: that was his final verdict. He had never seriously credited the possibility that Martin had been turned by the East German Apparat. It wouldn't have been in character. Martin wasn't the sort of man to change sides. He would never betray his beliefs—probably, thought Carow, because he didn't have any. A man like Martin constituted the ideal agent—the professional, the specialist. With his kind, not that C would ever grasp the fact, you could forget about beliefs.

Carow drove along the outer ring road in his Porsche. The lights of the city were on his left, their reflection in the sky muted by smog. He liked the city best at night because its magnitude and extent were mirrored in a way that never became apparent by day.

He was glad to be getting out of town for a while. He'd decided on Geissler's outstation. The briefing period would give him an opportunity for some long country walks with the agent under preparation.

Carow loved endless plains and wide open spaces. He had often wondered, though not recently, what would have become of him if he'd stayed in America in 1946. He was only twenty-nine then. Perhaps he'd have managed to acquire the farm of his dreams. He visualized it: wheat fields stretching away for as far as the eye could see, the sun blazing down out of a sky embellished with puffs of cumulus. The same fields in winter: a broad white expanse, the snow almost bluish . . .

He had been on the point of communicating his decision to C, who was busy hammering out his contract with the Americans, when Isabelle's telegraphically worded letter arrived: "Return at once, wedding set for March 15." There had never been any talk of marriage between them. She was pregnant, it turned out. The news had only reinforced his decision to stay in America. He countered by asking her to join him there.

The reply had not come from Isabelle. It was C who summoned him back, appealed to his "sense of responsibility" and wound up with a stark allusion to the "consequences." It transpired that his prospective father-in-law had approached C direct. Perhaps that was why Carow hated the wealthy—for the way they used the power their wealth conferred on them.

The Porsche had left the ring road. Anne's apartment was near Martin's temporary quarters. As usual, Carow parked some distance away. He took out his briefcase and gun. The three-storied apartment blocks were built round an inner courtyard, most of which was lawn. Anne received an allowance from the married father of her child, an eleven-year-old girl at boarding school, but Carow paid her rent. He didn't wait for the elevator but climbed to the second floor. He put the key in the lock. It wouldn't turn; the inside catch was on.

His back started aching again. He glared at the door suspiciously. Behind him, the time switch on the landing clicked. He waited in the darkness, listening. Anne had had other men since he went back to Isabelle, but they had a tacit agreement: she would never bring them back here.

He rang the bell. He hated himself for doing it, but he wanted to make sure—wanted her to open up. Nothing else mattered to him at this moment, not even the man who was with her. He would let the interloper walk past him without saying a word. Far from having a row, they would end up—he knew it—in the bed she'd just been sharing with someone else.

"Open up! I know you're in there!"

In his fury, he could have kicked the door down. All that stopped him was a sudden pang of self-contempt, as though he could see himself standing there, an old man begging for love.

That was what eventually drove him away. Instead of waning, however, his jealousy only increased. He looked up at her windows from the courtyard. No sign of life. He was sure there'd been a light on when he arrived. Perhaps she was standing behind the curtain, naked except for a bathrobe round her shoulders. Perhaps they were both standing there, the man whispering something in her ear, both of them grinning, both amused by the sight of the figure below.

There was a call box near his parked car, but he resisted the temptation to dial her number.

═══════════ CHAPTER XI ═══════════

1

MARTIN WAS STANDING AT THE WINDOW of the sixteenth-floor apartment. The city lay spread out below him, not unlike some vast spaceship that had emerged from the cosmos and landed at his feet. The soft, sterile music oozing into the room strengthened this unearthly impression. Far below, a multilane expressway ran past. Dark metallic shapes moved silently along it, imbued with buglike animation by red and white lights. From time to time, one of them turned off and vanished beneath the tower block's projecting canopy.

The apartment comprised a living room, bedroom, bathroom and kitchenette. It was furnished in an impersonal style, hotel fashion. Concealed lighting, windows that couldn't be opened and an air-conditioning system that blew down his neck in a way that summoned up visions of a machine with lungs of preternatural size—Martin's immediate reaction had been one of unease.

He'd forced himself to sleep for two dreamless hours. Then he restored everything to its original state, made the bed and replaced his washing things in the airline bag. He was hungry when he woke but kept his resolution not to touch the contents of the icebox.

His impatience and uneasiness dwindled as time went by. All the advantages were on *their* side at the moment, he knew. They had probably been kept informed of every move he made. They could read his mind—the very fact that he'd taken their bait proved that. On the other hand, they must have an angle of their own. They must want something from *him*. Where did the center of gravity lie, on his side or theirs? Having no means of knowing, he banished the question from his mind.

He was still watching the bugs crawling in and out of the covered forecourt when the apartment door opened. Martin had some difficulty in concealing his surprise when he saw that it was Carow himself; in the normal course of events, Carow wouldn't have appeared on the scene until a later stage. The scales had tilted infinitesimally in his favor. He noticed something else: a hint of stiffness and uncertainty, as if Carow were momentarily doubtful whether he'd come to the right apartment—yes, as if their roles were reversed. It might have been Carow who was waiting to be put through the mill by *him*.

Perhaps because there was a barrier of years to surmount, or because they both knew that the room was bugged—that a nearby tape recorder would be activated by the sound of their voices—neither man spoke for the first few seconds.

"Did you have a good flight?"

Carow had still not fully recovered from his shock. The jealousy had gone, but not the feeling of self-contempt. He knew, only too well, that this was a handicap. Personal preoccupations impaired the efficiency of any interrogator.

"Yes, thanks. It's only a stone's throw."

"Got all you need?" Carow surveyed the room. He noted the airline bag, still zippered, and the deck of cards on the table. He strolled into the kitchenette and checked the icebox. He'd been given a list of the contents, notably the hard liquor, so he knew that Martin hadn't touched a thing. He himself felt tormented by the craving for something sweet that periodically overcame him now he no longer smoked. He longed for a candy bar. "We'll get some food sent up later."

"No hurry." Martin recalled his previous sessions with Carow. Hunger had often given him trouble, whereas Carow seemed immune to it.

Carow had taken off his jacket. He removed a folder from his briefcase and deposited it in front of him, unopened. "Where shall we start?"

Martin found the question puzzling—Carow wouldn't have asked it in the old days—so he said nothing. He took the deck and put it on the edge of the table. He itched to turn up two cards, one for Carow and one for himself.

"Very well, let's get one thing straight. Do you bear us a grudge of any kind?"

"No."

"We had to make sure." You're talking too much, Carow told himself. Don't let this interview run away from you. Is he any good still, that's the only point at issue. What's he worth?

"That job we offered you . . ."

Martin shook his head.

"It wouldn't have been for long, believe me."

"I couldn't see any future in it. I was . . ." Martin groped for the right words. "I was used to bigger things."

Carow indicated the folder. "I see you had an offer from the Israelis after you left us. The terms were excellent. Why didn't you take it up?"

Martin looked at the folder too. "You kept me alive?"

"Resurrected you, let's say. All right, why did you turn the offer down? You could have proved how dumb we were to shelve you. Or were you scared? Five years in an East German jail—that's enough to knock the stuffing out of any man, however good. Had you lost confidence in yourself?"

Martin didn't avoid Carow's eye. He pointed to the deck of cards. "First card or second?" They'd often done that at the end of a day's debriefing, before going off to eat nearby. The loser picked up the tab.

"Wait a minute." Carow reached for the cards. He looked through them suspiciously and shuffled them, then turned the top card up. It was a seven. Without a moment's hesitation, Martin exposed the next one.

"Ten beats seven," he said. He sat back in his chair.

"That doesn't answer my question," said Carow.

2

THEY HAD GONE through the whole procedure, been over Martin's last six years and brought the picture up to date, explored his state of health, his powers of observation and recall. Could he describe the man at the information desk in Barcelona? Could he repeat their conversation—word for word, if possible? Carow consulted his folder. Could he describe the man who'd been tailing him since his arrival in Munich?

They'd eaten a meal toward the end of these preliminaries. That, they both knew, was all they were, a mere preamble. Martin again had the feeling that their roles were reversed. Carow left the opening move to him.

"Why did you bring me here?"

Carow was playing with the cards, spilling them from one hand into the open palm of the other. "A trip to the Eastern Bloc."

Martin felt nothing. All at once, he became blind to everything but the sight of the cards sliding from one hand to the other, deaf to everything but the sound they made. "Do I know the area?"

"You're jumping the gun a little."

I shouldn't have asked, Martin thought. They never tell you everything at once; sometimes they tell you less than you ought to know. "Who'd be involved?"

"Just the agent and his case officer."

"A solo run, you mean?"

"That's right, solo."

"No trailblazers? No network?"

"No time to set one up. Anyway, it would only cramp the agent's style. No trailblazers, no tricks, no technology, just the agent's eyes and ears. We'll identify the target for him—"

"Which is?"

"—and he'll hit it, we hope."

"Who'd bring the goods out?"

"We're still working on that."

"Radio communication?"

"Probably not available. I told you, it's a solo run. The kind of job you always liked best and were best at."

Let's hope I still am, thought Martin. Another thought struck him—it's a job for a younger man—but he naturally didn't say that either. He recalled a similar situation. During the autumn prior to his arrest in the Zone, Carow had bombarded him with exhortations. We're dry, he'd said, we need new sources. Come on out of your hole, build up something new, recruit some subagents. Martin had resisted for a long time. When he finally yielded to Carow's urgings, it was the beginning of the end. Was he making the same mistake now—letting himself be talked into something too hot to handle?

''How would you insert me?''

''No problem there. Absolutely straightforward—a tailor-made cover. It would look quite natural.'' Carow refused to be drawn any further.

''When?'' asked Martin.

''That's a problem, I admit. Our man will be leaving in four days' time. More precisely, he'll be back on the eighth day after that.''

Four days' preparation wasn't enough for him; Martin didn't say so, but he thought it. Still, he'd gleaned something important. The timing of the run was the one hard fact Carow had given him. Four days . . . That meant leaving next Saturday and getting back the Sunday after that. He wondered if the information had slipped out, or was Carow being deliberately misleading?

''The time factor—will it count against me?''

''Codes, local knowledge, emergency procedures . . . I've no need to spell it out for you. Four days wouldn't give us much time. You'd have to work like a beaver.''

''Any other candidates in the running?''

''Of course, for fairness' sake. Only one, though.''

''Do I know him?''

''No, he's one of the younger generation.''

''How do you rate his chances?''

''High. He's very good.''

''The man you select—who'll be running him?''

Carow laid the cards aside at last. ''I will.''

This time Martin didn't even try to conceal his surprise. ''Pretty unusual, isn't it, a case officer of your seniority? May I ask you something? Why me? How did I get short-listed?''

''It has to be an outsider—someone who doesn't have any discernible links with us at present.''

''You must be really up against it.''

He's good, thought Carow, who had mastered his initial weakness. He had the situation in hand now. He studied Martin's reactions, trying to locate his Achilles' heel. Out-

wardly, the man seemed calm, but there was something almost palpable behind his air of serenity—an inner tension
born of self-control, a determination to conceal how much
he wanted this assignment. Oh, yes, Martin was hungry all
right.

Hungry agents were a rarity these days. They were the
best kind of all. There was a concomitant danger, of course:
they tended to overshoot the target and do more than was
asked of them. Nevertheless, Carow felt good in Martin's
company. They were well suited and had much in common.
Rereading Martin's curriculum vitae, Carow had been reminded of many aspects of his own life. Country-bred children of modest background, fathers dead at a relatively early
age, families held together by robust, strong-willed mothers
with a talent for survival. Later on, two young men who had
both sought, in their own ways, to escape from lives that had
grown too constricted for them. Above all, Carow had an
understanding of Martin's innermost nature. They were
both loners. Little things mattered to men like them, and an
agent's success—and survival—could all too often hinge on
a trifle.

I'd enjoy working with him, Carow thought. We could
depend on each other. All things considered, there was
much to be said in Martin's favor.

"That's all I can tell you for now. However, there is one
point we can clear up. The question of payment." It was always a good thing to talk about money when your emotions
gained the upper hand. "Don't expect too much. Accounts
are as tight-fisted as ever."

"It isn't a question of money."

"There are two options. You could do the job free
lance—payment on delivery, plus expenses. On the other
hand, you could rejoin the Service. If you did, I could guarantee we'd revive your original pension rights. Minus the
last six years, of course. That I couldn't swing."

"I'd sooner do it the first way."

"Suit yourself."

"When will I know?"

"Tomorrow. If the other man gets it, we'll keep you in quarantine for the duration of the assignment. Then you can go home. I'll need your decision first, though."

"I want the job, you know damned well I do."

"Fine." Carow rose. "Learned any new card tricks?"

"Four spies in the house—seen that one? No?" Martin fanned out the pack and looked for the jacks. He longed to know what had really made them pick on him. *The reason mattered.* They must have had a dozen to choose from. Of course he wanted the job. He couldn't imagine Carow coming to him tomorrow and saying no—it just wasn't conceivable. But the question remained: Why him?

He handed Carow the four jacks. "Four spies, okay?"

Carow recalled C's question about the name Steffin and his own feeling that C had a trump up his sleeve.

"Now give them back." Martin opened his palm and showed him the jacks once more. "Four spies." He put them on top of the deck. "They've been sent on a general reconnaissance . . ."

Carow had followed it up but found no trace of anyone by that name. Nothing in Records, nothing in Missing Persons, no card in the EDP section. Simply no trace at all.

"Number one heads south." Martin removed the top card and inserted it near the bottom of the deck. "Number two goes north." He took the second card and inserted it higher up. "Number three goes east." Another card vanished into the deck. "Number four stays in the west, in reserve." The next card he left on top. "Have you been watching?" He pushed the whole deck across to Carow. "They're working for you. Recall them for debriefing."

"What do I do?"

"Turn up the top four cards."

Carow turned up one after the other. One jack, two, three, four . . . They were all back on top.

"Tell me, do you know anyone by the name of Steffin?"

"Like me to show you how it's done? What was the name again?"

Steady hands, steady voice—nothing that might have led Carow to suspect that Martin was holding out on him, and yet . . . Carow thought he detected a sudden heightening of concentration.

"Steffin. No ideas?"

"Can't you give me a clue?"

He's digging in, thought Carow. He's on the defensive, so he knows something—something they *both* know, C and Martin, and don't want me to find out.

"The name cropped up recently."

"Nothing more to go on? When and where? Can't you tell me a bit more?"

"No." Carow decided to try the truth. "It was something C asked me in connection with your candidacy. He told me to search our files."

"Well?"

"No dice."

"He likes his little mysteries, so I've heard."

"You've never met him?"

"No. Here, I'll show you the secret. I already have three cards hidden in my left hand—any cards—when you give me back the jacks. That's all there is to it."

He's relieved, thought Carow—perceptibly relieved. *He's hiding something.* For the moment, however, Carow saw no way of extracting anything more.

CHAPTER XII

MARTIN HAD BEEN STARTLED WHEN the name came up. All that saved him from self-betrayal was the fact that he had buried Zimra as deep in his memory as any living soul could lie. He had numbered her among the dead, as it were—interred her with those who had once been loved but were now out of reach forever. His father, his mother, his wife: all lay in graves beyond the Iron Curtain, in another, alien land.

But Zimra was *his* secret, something that belonged to him alone, buried in the deepest recesses of his mind. Now they had dragged her back into the light of day. That changed everything. How could he trust them? Martin knew that he would have to do something, come to terms with the altered situation.

At the moment, he was glad not to have to concentrate on his shadow. He'd had little difficulty in identifying him. As soon as he left the elevator after riding down from the sixteenth floor, the man had risen a trifle too briskly from one of the armchairs in the lobby. He was oldish and looked tired. Although he smiled at Martin when he saw he'd been spotted, his resentment at being given the night shift was obvious. Martin smiled back and took him in tow. He went outside and stood beneath the canopy, stretching and inhaling deeply like a man in need of fresh air.

"I've been cooped up in here for seven hours." That was

his excuse to Carow, who'd given him an hour's leave of absence. After that, more work awaited. Carow had sent for two men to do a job on him—stage designers, as the Organization called those responsible for an agent's accessories: false papers, labels, clothing, luggage.

An hour wasn't much, but it ought to be long enough to evade surveillance, make his phone call and get back in time. He headed for the bus stop, covertly watching for a probable backup man. He spotted him when he leaped aboard at the last moment, an athletic-looking youngster with a round, boyish face.

Two of them—so much the better. It would make it easier to explain to Carow why he hadn't been able to resist the urge to shake them off—another demonstration that his agent's faculties were still intact.

His thoughts returned to Zimra and the dream he'd had last night, on the island, of Carow trying to browbeat him into an admission that he knew her. The strange thing about the dream was that the scene with Carow had never taken place. He'd never even mentioned her name before tonight.

It was after his release, when an operative named Kurella took charge of him at Wartha-Herleshausen and escorted him to Bavaria for debriefing, that Martin had made his resolution. Not a word about Zimra Steffin, he told himself. Even if they knew about her, which was unlikely, he wouldn't admit a thing. There was no need to lie outright; he would simply keep silent and resign.

As it turned out, the problem never arose. They naturally questioned him about his mysterious removal from Rummelsburg jail and the missing six months thereafter. He had no reason to keep silent about *that*. He told them everything, held nothing back, because *her* name never crossed their lips. That accounted for his genuine sense of shock at Carow's unexpected reference to it. More than that, he'd been scared—so scared that he seriously wondered if he had the nerve for another assignment. Above all, though, how could he carry it out if he suspected that they planned to involve Zimra?

He had now exchanged his bus for a subway train. Not knowing Munich well, he surfaced at a station near the heart of the city and led his shadows down a street thronged with window-shoppers and couples painting the town. They stayed with him, one to the side and rear, the other across the way and slightly ahead of him. Carow was bound to have briefed them. They had probably begun by treating their assignment as a harmless exercise, but Martin could sense them becoming more alert.

He went below ground again. Subway, streetcar, subway; steep, narrow escalators. The first man he shook off by the simple but effective expedient of wedging his foot in an automatic door and jumping off at the last moment. The second man, whom Martin had christened Babyface, was a tougher proposition. He stuck like glue, abandoning any attempt at concealment. Martin eventually lost him in an underground shopping arcade because he remembered a cafeteria—Kurella had bought him a snack there six years before—which had a rear entrance for goods deliveries. To make doubly sure, he took a subway to the central station and leaped aboard a suburban train just as it was pulling out, then alighted at the next stop. He used two cabs to get him back to the point where the game had begun. His hour was almost up.

Luckily, the public call box near the bus stop was vacant. He had some coins ready and the number in his head. He dialed with one eye on the passersby. A recorded voice answered.

"ATAP Airlines. This office is temporarily unoccupied. At the third pip, please leave your name and number."

Martin hung up. His new watch said just before ten. He would have to make a snap decision; there was no time to dwell on his disappointment. He looked up the number of the airport, but ATAP maintained no desk there and was unrepresented by a larger airline.

"I can give you another number to try," said the operator.

"No, wait!" He had change for only one more call. "Please put me through to the Tower."

Two more voices who couldn't be of help, then a third.

"Miroslav Sěnk . . . Gypsy, you mean?"

"That's right."

"Who wants him?"

"An old friend."

"Sorry, he isn't here. Today? I can tell you precisely. Took off fourteen zero five. Multiple pile-up on the Innatal Triangle—he flew two casualties to the hospital. When did he get back? Fifteen fifty-five. Refueled and took off again at seventeen-forty. Five passengers, destination St. Moritz . . . What's that? No, definitely not tonight."

"Was he piloting them himself?"

A laugh. "That's all ATAP Airlines consists of, just Sěnk and his Bell JetRanger."

"Thanks a lot."

So Gypsy Sěnk was still around—at least he knew that much. Still around and still flying. He even had a chopper of his own. He didn't have, six years ago in Elba.

What should he do? Not a hope of running Senk to earth in St. Moritz. On the other hand, he'd never get another chance to call if he landed the assignment. They wouldn't be as slipshod as they'd been tonight; they'd never let him out of their sight. Maybe the call wasn't necessary after all. Maybe he was being overcautious. Maybe Zimra's name wouldn't crop up again. That was a lot of maybes—too many for his liking.

He remembered what Carow had said about timing: off in four days, back eight days after that. Carow had confirmed this when speaking of the need to put him in quarantine if he wasn't selected. Martin deliberated: that would mean Sunday the thirtieth. His only recourse was to assume that Carow had been telling the truth.

He composed a message while dialing his second call to

ATAP—"Any Time, Any Place"—and waited till the voice had said its piece. Then he started dictating. "Carros Estate, Elba. Have three thousand acres of winter corn requiring fertilizer. Would like book helicopter for thirtieth instant. I repeat: Sunday, September thirtieth. Is it a deal? Acceptance definite on our side . . ." Martin was watching the second hand of his watch as he spoke. He spun out the message so the tape cut him short, making it look as if he'd had no time to sign off.

A secretary would audiotype the tape next morning and inform Sěnk when he called his office during the day. Martin felt sure he'd understand the message, know who'd left it and what was in the wind. He was gambling that Sěnk hadn't changed, of course, but men like him seldom did.

He left the call box feeling better. His shadows were nowhere to be seen. You've broken the rules, he thought, but he still felt he'd done the right thing.

He crossed the expressway by an underpass and walked back to the tower block. Seen from a distance and in darkness, it resembled a two-dimensional facade, an architectural flat on a film set, propped up from behind like a billboard and sprinkled with lights to simulate rooms. Yet one of the compartments in that big up-ended honeycomb was ready and waiting to receive him—a little cell whose walls would soon close around him . . .

He bumped into Carow in the lobby. Carow had just emerged from one of the phone booths, looking harrassed. Had the tails been in touch with him? If so, he didn't say. They walked to the elevators in silence.

They chose the wrong one. As they were moving across to the other, Babyface came dashing into the lobby. He caught sight of Carow and hurried over.

"Just a minute, sir! Our man—he gave us the slip."

"What do you mean?" Carow sounded preoccupied.

Babyface spotted Martin. As though he couldn't accept the sight of him standing there at Carow's side, he ignored him and went on. "The subject lost us half an hour ago. I tried to inform you at once, but there wasn't any reply from 1614.''

Carow looked at Martin.

Martin had had time to ponder his words. ''I couldn't pass up a chance to show you how good I am—still.''

Babyface turned puce but controlled himself in Carow's presence. All he said was, ''Do I enter this in my report?''

''Yes, of course.'' Carow turned to Martin. ''You've just made yourself a friend for life.''

''Sorry, I couldn't resist it.''

''Congratulations. They're pretty good as a rule. Losing three tails in half an hour—you can't have forgotten all you ever knew.''

Three, thought Martin with belated alarm. He'd never noticed the third tail, just been lucky. He needed preparation, he told himself. Four days, Carow had said. He would need every hour of every day.

Carow was pursuing a different line of thought as he watched the pinpoints of light that charted their ascent to the sixteenth floor. Martin was probably the better of the two candidates. On balance, though, his vote still went to Rosell. Rosell was younger and not so desperately hungry. Above all, when two men were roughly on a par, it was wiser to pick the one less close to you personally. Detachment made it easier to take the decisions that might, at a pinch, be forced on you.

But fundamentally, he thought, C's instinct had been right yet again.

CHAPTER XIII

HE HAD NEVER NEEDED MUCH SLEEP, and he always woke punctually at a predetermined time. It was still dark outside. The house was brilliantly illuminated by four floodlights throughout the night—so much so that a residual glow penetrated the curtains of his bedroom. The external lighting circuit and other security systems could be controlled from his bed.

Something important had occurred to C before he went to sleep, something he had to tell Puck, but it temporarily escaped him. He could recall past events far more clearly and vividly than things less remote from the present. They said it was a sign of age. Of course he was growing old; in fact, he was past growing old: he *was* old. "Dinosaur"—he knew there were some who called him that behind his back. Couldn't they see that age had the edge on youth?

He didn't get fully dressed, nor did he shave. Mirrors held no appeal for him at this hour. The morning agreed with some people—his wife had been one—but to him the opposite applied. Putting on his old blue dressing gown and a pair of leather slippers, he left the bedroom and went downstairs, still unable to recall what he'd meant to tell Puck. The house was far too big for him now—just him, Puck and the housekeeper—but he loved its quasi-monastic hush.

His study was a sort of alcove leading off the drawing

room. The window afforded a view of the garden and the erstwhile summerhouse, now converted for occupation by the security men who relieved each other at four-hour intervals. C saw his current watchdog emerge, submachine gun slung. The man stretched, yawned and looked across at the main house, waiting for the desk lamp in his alcove to come on at six o'clock sharp.

C thumbed the switch. The sentry retired into the summerhouse, reassured by this portent of a normal day's routine. A few minutes later, the floodlights went out.

Inside the alcove, C opened the combination safe. He removed a thin yellow folder and placed it in the pool of light shed by the desk lamp. On the cover, inscribed in his neat, microscopically fine hand, were the words "Zimra (?) Steffin."

The contents of the folder, a few sheets only, had dominated his thoughts since the start of the operation. He had read and reread them only the night before. Although it was unlikely that another look at the folder would increase his store of knowledge, this was precisely what he hoped. The typewritten sheets were a guide to buried treasure. They gave the name of the island, charted the route there and pinpointed the site of the cache. All that was missing was some clue to the size of the cache itself, some measure of its value. A few old coins or a genuine fortune? That was the question that haunted him: Did the treasure rate an expedition to distant shores?

His train of thought was interrupted. His daughter appeared, also in her dressing gown. Her hair, which she wore in a bun by day, hung loose. It looked stringy and badly in need of a wash. She's your daughter all right, thought C, without a trace of sentimentality. The mornings didn't suit her either.

"I'll bring your breakfast right away."

"I'd sooner wait till everyone's up."

"Nonsense, you can't work on an empty stomach."

He remembered what he'd meant to tell Puck and jotted it

down on his memo pad. "Just a glass of orange juice. And don't wake the children."

But that was just what she would do—take ages preparing breakfast in the kitchen, get the children dressed between times and fill the house with shouted injunctions not to disturb their grandfather.

"And kindly shut the door!"

Both his daughters had an inalienable belief that he needed cosseting. Although he never openly demurred, he loathed their visits and the turmoil they caused in the household.

C was content with his widower's state. He had always, even as a young man, nursed a distaste for his own carnal appetites—a phrase adopted from his clergyman father. Having yielded to them notwithstanding, he never did so without feeling disappointed in himself. Fortunately, his wife had not been an overly demanding bedmate.

He saw no contradiction in the fact that his thoughts had returned to her more often of late. Now that he was exempted from a husband's obligations, sexual and social, he could at last play the role he liked best: the ascetic, the pure soul, the man who lived out his ideals unfettered by the instincts that so often prevented his sex from accomplishing great things. *She* had always understood that—never obstructed his true mission in life.

Even her death had been the height of consideration—nothing that might have disrupted his routine to any undue extent. She had quit his life in a characteristically unobtrusive, unflamboyant way. He recalled her sitting at an open window in the room next door—an act of self-indulgence rare in someone so constantly, if undramatically, occupied with household tasks. When asked what the matter was, she merely replied, "Oh, nothing. I needed a spot of fresh air, that's all." And so it went on for three short weeks, not more. Her increasing breathlessness was a symptom of terminal lung cancer, but that he hadn't known till afterward. For her last four days in a hospital ward—four only—she chose a time that coincided with one of his absences on official business. Yes indeed, she'd been a damned good wife to him . . .

His daughter returned with a tray. Arrayed on it in addition to the orange juice he'd asked for were tea, toast, a boiled egg—she knew he wouldn't touch the toast or the egg—and a newspaper.

"Thanks. Now leave me alone, I'm busy."

He sipped a little tea. Outside, the light was growing stronger. Carow would report by 8 A.M. at the latest. At midday he would inspect both candidates, though his interest was confined to Martin alone. Hoping that Carow's assessment would turn out to be favorable, he plunged into the file again. The plan he had in mind contained an element of desperation, but was there a better alternative? The first sheet in the folder was devoted to the transcript of a Soviet defector's statement. The synopsis read as follows:

CIA/8044, Camp King, Oberursel, recorded February 7, 1970. Soviet defector (Admin. Center, Moscow) claims Org. agent currently detained at Bernau. Said to enjoy special privileges and relative freedom of movement. Name: Martin, Martini (?). Defector assumes agent in process of recruitment.

Head of Apparat alleged to have visited Bernau and conducted M's interrogation in person (!) Stenographic record kept by female aide named Zimra (?) Steffin. According to guards, M and Steffin on intimate terms.

Evaluation of statement: Defector 8044 has proved far less productive than originally hoped. Discovery of weakness for drink and women prompted Moscow Center to withhold high-grade information from him in recent months. Decision to seek political asylum possibly inspired by fear of recall to Moscow. Statement therefore suspect.

C had pursued the matter himself, as some notes in his own handwriting indicated. The first concerned Martin: *No reference by Martin to Zimra Steffin in debriefing records. According to Carow, M's attitude cooperative in every way. Deliberate suppression of a material fact? If so, why?!*

C compared dates. Martin had been exchanged in September 1969. The defector's statement was dated February 1970, by which time Martin had already left the Service.

C's second note related to the defector: *CIA's response to our request for personal reexamination of Defector 8044 negative. ("8044 already stateside and currently receiving new identity. Regret unable oblige.") They regret! Typical CIA cooperation!*

Judging by his personal comments, thought C, he had already decided, even at that stage, to keep the matter to himself. Why? Had he hoped that his information might bear fruit at some later date? He couldn't have seen this far ahead. No, he knew the reason perfectly well. The report hadn't ended up in his safe because of Martin and Steffin, but because of its allusion to "Head of Apparat." It was simply a part of the extensive Zentner dossier he'd built up over the years.

Zentner . . . The very name was enough to destroy his composure. Anger smote him, surged through his body like a hot flush. His wife had suffered from menopausal flushes into late middle age. Just as she had done on such occasions, C felt an urge to strip off his clothes. He reached for the glass of orange juice and drained it.

Zentner and himself! It had been *their* fight throughout the years, round after round of it won by each of them in turn. Not East versus West, not freedom versus oppression, but *their* fight alone—something he never admitted to others and seldom conceded to himself.

A light flashed on one of his telephones. Puck would take the call on his own extension. C had no wish to be disturbed at present. He reapplied himself to the yellow folder.

The second sheet was a curriculum vitae. Most of the details were unclassified material culled from outside sources. C hadn't wanted to draw anyone's attention to his interest in the subject by making inquiries at the Center, let alone filing his results there.

> *Steffin, Zimra (origin of name unknown), born Poznań, March 7, 1933. Father: noted Communist veteran of Spanish Civil War, pseudonym "General Moro." Interned France, deported Auschwitz. Member of SED Central Committee, Zone; fell into disfavor 1951; rehabilitated 1953; renewed "disappearance" 1969; died 1971 (suicide). Mother: Anna (née) Jensky, resident East Berlin. No known relatives or contacts in German Federal Republic.*
>
> *Education: junior high school graduate, East Berlin, interpreter's diploma. Memberships: Free German Youth Movement, Socialist Unity Party, Democratic Women's League. Employed Ministry of State Security since 1956. Last-known post: supervisor, central secretariat to Director of Apparat ("Zentner's right-hand woman"). No known sexual relationships. Details of foreign travel not ascertainable. Last-known address: 11 Gotlindenstrasse (Lichtenberg).* Here, too, C had made a handwritten addition: *October 4, 1972. $10,000 from Special Fund credited to G.M.'s Basle A/C against undertaking to contact Z.S. Secure exit guaranteed, also for mother. February 15, 1973. No result, but both parties still exercising previous functions.*

He laid the sheet aside. So he'd taken the first step all that time ago. A risky business, gambling blind. Not the contact with G.M.—the danger didn't lie there. G.M. was unimportant—a Communist lawyer, well known on both sides of the Curtain, who was busy amassing a numbered Swiss bank account. Communist or not, men like him had existed in every age and would continue to do so. Ten thousand dollars was a lot to ask, but you never got anything cheap from the G.M.s of this world. No result . . . Even that wasn't the whole story. G.M. had probably kept his word and made contact. He hadn't suffered in consequence, so the outcome was far from negative. Shouldn't the Steffin woman have done her patriotic duty and reported him at once for trying to suborn her? Didn't that signify something in itself?

Zentner's right-hand woman! The temptation had proved too much for him. Was he daydreaming—seeing chances that didn't exist at all? Caution was imperative. In his fight with Zentner he stood with his back perilously close to the ropes. And yet, the opening was there. A source near the top of the Apparat itself . . . They'd had one once. Why not again?

Martin and Zimra. That was it—that was where the solution lay. G.M. had simply been the wrong contact.

Again the light flashed on one of C's telephones, and again Puck took the call. This time, however, Puck buzzed him. He lifted the receiver.

"Morning, Chief. I'm holding a call from Bonn."

"No, not now."

"U. S. Embassy, Don Langtree . . ."

"On the line? At this hour?"

"No, someone in the Finance Section. He's got a personal message for you. Langtree will be in Bonn for a few days next week. He'd like you to keep an evening free."

"Tuesday's the only possibility. Our agent will be over there by then. Tell him Tuesday evening, after I've briefed the Chancellor. Only a meal, though—I want to be back the same night. Has Carow called yet?"

"Half an hour ago."

'Good. Come in here, would you?"

For a moment, C let his mind dwell on Langtree. The banker had played a major part in keeping the Organization alive after the war. Above all, he'd handled the financial aspects of its contract with the CIA. "Mr. Honeypot," they'd called him in the days when the dollar stood at over four marks and jeep loads of Luckies—by far the most popular brand with agents—represented a valuable form of currency. C and Langtree had continued to meet, even after Langtree's direct connection with the CIA lapsed. Insofar as the term existed in his vocabulary, C might have described Don Langtree as a friend.

He didn't bother to lock the folder away. Of the members of his inner circle, Puck was the one he trusted most. Some day, when he retired and the others weren't around anymore, Puck would still be at his side, still be his baby-sitter and factotum.

Puck limped in. C waved him into the chair facing his and switched off the desk lamp.

"Any idea what brings Don Langtree to Bonn?"

"None at all."

"Put someone on it."

"I thought I'd better get your say-so first."

Nobody understood their relationship, thought C, but it was all quite simple and straightforward. It had to do with Puck's deformity—his withered leg. C had found the explanation in Greek mythology, his favorite spare-time reading. In ancient times, children born deformed were killed— condemned to be thrown off a cliff into the sea. Although C approved of this practice in principle, he'd overridden it sufficiently in Puck's case to preserve him from the human scrap heap. His reward was absolute devotion.

"What did Carow say?"

"His candidates are all lined up."

"Has he made his choice?"

"He didn't say, but I get the feeling it's Rosell."

C indicated the folder. "You realize we'll never get anywhere without Martin, don't you? He's the only one with any chance of reaching Steffin."

"Do we know for sure she'll be going to Prague?"

"It's highly probable."

"You're taking quite a gamble. If it turns sour—"

"If it does, no one will be able to connect us with it."

"What about the agent? He might talk."

"That could be prevented."

"Any agent Carow runs is his own flesh and blood. You could have problems with *him*."

"Personal sentiments don't come into this."

"But isn't that just what you're banking on? A man like Martin—won't his personal feelings be involved?"

"I'll know that when I've seen him."

The conversation appeared to be over. Puck rose. Casually, as if the idea had only just struck him, he said, "Doesn't it ever occur to you that *he* may be trying to find out what *you* have in mind? He could be sitting there right now, thinking, 'What's he up to? What's going on in his head? Where will he make his next move?' "

C shrugged. "Of course it occurs to me, but I tell myself Zentner doesn't operate that way—it isn't his style. He's always going for a knockout, never thinking about the scorecard. Most people fight like that. We don't. We build up points, Puck, slowly and steadily, round by round, and that's how we'll win, on points—a slow and steady accumulation of points."

"It's *your* style, I know."

"And it's the only way I've ever won a round. Zentner thinks the fight's in his pocket, just because he's dumped me on the canvas a few times. But in the end, Puck, when all the points are totted up, I'll be ahead. When the Zone goes bang, he'll be finished."

"We still don't have the minutes of that conference."

"No, but we'll get them—Martin will get them for us. Don't you understand, Puck? I want to see Zentner floundering—I live for the day . . ."

Puck was inured to these one-sided conversations in which C cast him as a silent listener, but again he stepped out of character.

"And afterward? Are you seriously thinking of retiring?"

C looked so taken aback that Puck saw he'd gone too far. He sought refuge in one of his impish grins. That was *his* little secret—something he'd discovered early in life. Every-one had poked fun at his limp until he found he could escape his schoolmates' jeers and bullying by pulling faces and making them laugh. All of them, especially the bigger and stronger ones, had responded by taking him under their wing.

"Anyway," he said, grinning still more broadly, "I doubt if they'd let you go."

"Incidentally, Puck, I forgot to tell you something last night. Have a word with Personnel about my younger son-in-law. I want him transferred to another section."

Puck said nothing, relieved that C had gone off at a tangent.

"That courier job takes him away too often for my liking. My daughter descends on me every damned time. See he's given something else. Central Records, P.R.—anything that'll keep him at home."

He won't like it."

"Well, he'll have to lump it—on the same salary, of course. Handle it discreetly, so he doesn't know it's my doing." C smiled. "I'm an old man, and old men need their peace and quiet."

CHAPTER XIV

HIS SHADOWS HAD BEEN CHANGED. They sat in the car with him, one at the wheel, the other two flanking him in the back. They had tough, tight-lipped faces and an air of su-preme efficiency, especially one of them. He wore his hair in a fringe, the line across his forehead drawn with a preci-

sion that suggested it might be a toupee, and his nose stuck
out like a clothespin. Martin had privately christened him
"Pinocchio."

The car was parked outside Nymphenburg Palace. Sunlight glittered on the handsome building's multitudinous
windows, but Martin was too much on edge to appreciate
the view. All three men were smoking. When he asked if
they couldn't open a window, all he got was a blank stare.
He guessed they'd heard what he'd done to their colleagues.

Over half an hour went by. That morning, Carow had
paid him a brief visit. "Have a wash and brushup. You're
on parade at midday." Carow had been different, brusquer
and more aloof, as though at pains to put some distance between them.

A second car was parked nearby. Just then, the other
candidate—if that was who he was—returned. Martin put
him in his early thirties. His lean face and wiry physique
were reminiscent of a juggler he'd once seen perform in a
Barcelona circus.

The radio emitted a bleep. The driver acknowledged.
"Car Two here." A rasping voice filled the smoke-laden interior. "Next one!"

Pinocchio got out and held the door. "Now you. Past the
main building and down the central avenue. Count the statues on your left. After the fifth, turn left across the foot-
bridge. Then right, the sixth bench. And not too fast. Make
like you're taking a stroll—killing time."

"I'm in no hurry."

"Not like last night, eh?"

Pinocchio's hostility was written all over his face. He
climbed back inside and slammed the door behind him.

The juggler had climbed aboard too. When Martin passed
the other car he glimpsed him through the window, smiling
a self-absorbed, self-satisfied smile. What the hell, he
thought, I can always go back to the island. He felt like a
child whistling to keep his spirits up.

Now that he was free to move at last, his tension evaporated. He took in the beauty of his surroundings, the sun-kissed gravel of the broad central avenue. Roses were still blooming in front of the statues, though the trees in the background had already started to turn. Martin was only one of many strollers. A guide was lecturing a party of American tourists on local history—wearily, like a parent reciting a twice-told tale.

The old man on the sixth bench was wearing an overcoat with a rabbit's fur collar, a black homburg and black lace-up boots. He sat doubled over as though trying to catch his breath. Martin, who had never met C, experienced a moment's uncertainty. Glancing round to check his bearings, he saw a man with reddish hair on the next bench. The man grinned at him and nodded.

Martin sat down. He was determined to keep his guard up, remain coolly matter-of-fact, volunteer nothing, but the old man's silence and immobility drew him out.

"Beautiful grounds, these. Really lovely."

The old man looked up in surprise. He peered round, then stared at his neighbor on the bench. When he spoke, his voice was dry and expressionless.

"We didn't pick the spot for its scenic charm."

The voice and the appraising look in the cold blue eyes told Martin how misplaced his fleeting sense of pity had been.

"You have a sentimental streak?"

The question came as another surprise. In Martin's profession, sentimentality paid no dividends. No one had ever accused him of it, but C was probably right.

"I've never seen myself that way. Still, you may have a point."

"I like that. The harder-nosed the better, that's what most people think. Personally, I disagree. I prefer the sensitive type of agent—the kind who's got a heart and knows what it beats for. Or whom."

C looked down at his boots. They were old, wrinkled and rather dirty. Martin said nothing, if only because he didn't know what to say. The old man's words sounded half sincere, half sardonic. Whichever they were, they made him uneasy. C looked up again.

"Any doubts about this assignment?"

"None."

"You want it?"

"Yes."

"You'll get us what we need?"

"I still know very little."

"But the *will*—do you have the *will*?"

Martin nodded.

"Let's walk."

The red-haired man rose too. Martin noticed his limp. He followed them, never more than five paces behind. They strolled along the banks of a moat. The water was very low and soupy with algae.

"Tell me something. When they transferred you from the jail to Bernau, was it Zentner himself who invited you to work for the Apparat?"

"Not at first. He didn't turn up till later. I had no idea who he was, to begin with."

"What did he appeal to, your heart?"

Again Martin was forced to conceal his surprise. "It was a deal. They offered me something; I was to give them something in return."

"What did they offer you?"

"I still had fifteen years to serve."

"Of course, I understand. That was certainly a *quid pro quo*."

C spoke quietly, almost musingly, as if voicing a random series of ideas. Martin felt sure he had mapped everything out in advance—every move he meant to make.

"So that was it. Your freedom or a full term in jail. Nothing else?"

"Money, you mean?" Martin knew he didn't mean that, but he said it just the same.

"Zentner always looks for the weakest point in a line of

defense. He strikes where his victims are weak, not strong. Money and betrayal aren't your weak points. A man like Zentner can't have taken long to spot that. So . . ."

C sighed and left the sentence in midair, as though it wasn't his business to complete it. Here it comes, thought Martin. At least he wasn't unprepared.

"Sometimes women are the weak point . . ."

"I'm sure my file will tell you all there is to know." Martin hoped his smile was as self-assured as the juggler's.

"Perhaps I didn't express myself correctly. I meant *a* woman, of course." C's voice changed, lost its hesitancy. "Zimra Steffin. Is that any clearer?"

So they knew. It didn't matter how they'd found out. The fact itself was all that mattered—that and the question of why. What did they hope to gain?

"Let us assume that my information is accurate," C went on. "In other words, you knew her. You were in love with her. Let us further assume that Zentner knew this. If so, his offer might have included freedom for you both. Well, was that the bait?" C paused, seemingly tired. "Tell me about her. What sort of person was she?"

THEY HAD ALLOWED him to go for walks at Bernau too, though not in well-kept grounds like these, and there, too, his footsteps were dogged by someone never more than five yards behind. The Bernau equivalent of the red-haired man was a guard with a submachine gun.

He'd been allocated a log cabin containing a sizable living room, a kitchen and a cramped little bedroom. His transfer from the prison was so sudden and unexpected that he made no attempt to go outside for the first few days. He simply sat there like an animal whose cage has been unlocked, not knowing what to do with his new-found freedom.

They offered no reason for his transfer, though the reason was plain enough. He didn't avail himself of his exercise privileges until the fourth day, and then only because he was told that "talks" would begin on the morrow.

That morning he sat on a bench outside the cabin, waiting for the car to arrive. A farm track, waterlogged with rain when he'd been brought there but now dried out, led away from his quarters and disappeared into a swath of birches and beeches. Sentries were posted beyond the fence enclosing the cabin—two men in long greatcoats with submachine guns and binoculars slung round their necks. They sauntered idly to and fro with their hands behind their backs. It was their sudden quickening of attention—they came to a halt and leveled their binoculars at the track—which made him look up.

It wasn't a car—that would come later—but a lone figure on a bicycle. There was a thick hawthorn hedge between him and the track, so the first he saw of her was her head and shoulders as she pedaled along it. He could tell from her strenuous movements that the uneven surface was giving her a rough ride. She wore a gray forage cap secured at the side with a clasp. What with that, her plain gray uniform jacket, gray-blue shirt and black tie, she looked at a distance like a slim young soldier—not a real one, but one of the make-believe soldiers he'd seen as a boy in plays performed at Christmas in the local inn.

She reached the gate, showed the sentries her pass and wheeled her bicycle inside. He stood up—a prisoner's instinctive reaction. She walked past, apparently without noticing him, and propped her bicycle against the wall. Then, looking quite at home, she disappeared into the cabin.

He could see her setting the stage through the window—pulling chairs up to the table, pushing a smaller table to one side, laying out shorthand pads and pencils, wielding a pencil sharpener. Two minutes later she emerged and, as though it were the most natural thing in the world, sat down beside him on the bench. It was then that she said her name—nothing else, just her name—and relapsed into silence.

"Zimra Steffin."

He didn't introduce himself, partly because it seemed inappropriate and she knew his name anyway, and partly because he found her own so intriguing.

"What an unusual name."

She removed the barrette, took her cap off and shook her hair loose. He was surprised to see so much gray in it—a dense mesh of fine gray strands that made her age hard to determine. It meant little even when he learned, later on, that she was thirty-six. Just as her moods varied widely, so she seemed able to expand and contract her sum of years.

"What does it mean: Zimra?" He hadn't exchanged a word with his guards. It was the first time he'd spoken for a week, and he suddenly felt starved of conversation.

"I couldn't say. It comes from the Bible."

"You've never looked it up?"

She turned her head. She had brown eyes so dark they were almost black. The look on her face conveyed an inability to understand why anyone would consult the Bible.

"It was my father's idea. He detested the Poles, you see. He spent his whole life fighting dictatorships, but he had this utter hatred of all things Polish. When I was born at Poznań—not that he ever called it that, of course; the place was always Posen to him—he made a bet with some friends. He swore he'd give his daughter a name no one could translate into Polish. That was the law—every member of the German minority had to comply with it. Anyway, my father swore he'd find a name that would stump the Polish authorities."

Was his memory playing tricks? Had she really told him this at their very first encounter? Could he be certain of it, after all those interrogations, all those hours in the courtroom? He'd had to remember so much, remain on his guard for so long. What he'd said, where and when he'd said it, what he'd admitted, what he'd concealed, what he'd lied about.

"When the time came, he went to get me registered. His friends were waiting outside the office. The Poles tried to ban the name, but he had a Bible ready—he'd actually gone and bought one, Communist or no Communist. Here you are, he told them, it's in the Bible. What could they do, being good Catholics like all the Poles were? So my father won his bet and I was stuck with this funny name. I still am.''

''It sounds—well, very Old Testament.''

''Heroic, anyway. I suspect that's why my father chose it, not just to win a bet. He was a born fighter—something of a national hero—so he naturally expected his daughter to take after him. I've often thought my life might have been quite different with another name.''

It wasn't likely that she'd told him this on the very first day—or was it? At all events, he soon realized that Zimra hadn't been picked for the job because she was such an efficient stenographer, sitting quietly at her side table hour after hour, never asking for a word to be repeated, swiftly filling pad after pad in a kind of abstracted silence.

He guessed—he *knew*, thanks to the antennae which had equipped him to become a first-class agent—that the whole thing was a well-laid trap; that every step had been planned and pondered in advance, down to and including her first lone appearance on the scene.

They saw each other for nearly six months; at first only during the hours-long ''talks'' she recorded in shorthand, sometimes two, sometimes three times a week. Then, toward the end, when they were pressing for a decision, she was allowed to stay overnight.

Ever since his wife's death and his recruitment by the Organization, Martin had confined himself to affairs with women he didn't love. This time the position was different. He fell in love with Zimra long before he yielded to the emotion. The whole thing was too preposterous. What with the exceptional circumstances, the time limit imposed from the outset and the element of duress, their love stood no chance at all.

''I'll never pay the price.'' He must have told her that quite early on. ''They'll either send me back to jail or exchange me by myself. We'll never be able to stay together. There's no future in it.''

He could see it all too clearly, the way it would end, the price they would exact. But could love be thwarted like that—love, which existed in the mind and was fueled by wishful thinking? And so the cool-headed, circumspect, emotionally self-controlled agent had surrendered to his weaker alter ego, the fear- and nightmare-ridden prisoner. What a set of alternatives, though! A choice between fear and hatred inside prison walls and the fear and love of two human beings.

When the six months were up, he was just where they wanted him: ready to do as they asked, but only if both of them were guaranteed their freedom.

"I REALLY THINK you ought to clear the air.'' C's voice brought him back to the present. "Why so reticent? Is it because you concealed these facts from us at the time?''

C sensed that he was failing to penetrate Martin's guard. His only hope was that Carow had been right—that the man was hungry, that he wanted the assignment with all his heart and soul.

"You were trying to protect her, I imagine. Well, why not? Every agent does that some time or other. Anyway, it's water under the bridge.'' C paused for a moment. "At least tell me why you finally rejected their terms for you both.''

"Both? I don't follow you.''

Although Martin hadn't fallen into the trap, he knew his defenses were weak. Carow had said there wasn't a file on Zimra. Everything inside him rebelled against the idea of such a thing, of Organization men—of C himself—holding it and thumbing through it. He felt as if their hands were on her body, touching her, running the length of her.

"Is there a dossier on her?''

"Not a dossier, exactly.''

C's reply was almost inaudible. Did Martin realize that his question was an acknowledgment of her existence—of her importance to him? C was ecstatic but took care not to show it. He mustn't do anything to repair the breach in Martin's wall of silence.

"Have you contacted her since?"

"How could I?"

"Ever thought of telling us about her? We might have found some way of getting her out."

"Why should you have done that?"

"What about you?"

"Me?" Martin understood the question all too well, but he needed time.

"Did you ever try to get her out yourself—afterward, I mean?"

He can't know that, Martin thought, *not that*. Only one other person did, and Sěnk he was sure of. C had simply shaken the tree to see what fell out.

"There wasn't any way, not one with any prospect of success."

"There may be now. Did Carow tell you where the assignment would take you?"

"Into the Bloc."

"Prague, to be exact. A conference between the secret service chiefs of several Warsaw Pact countries. That's our agent's target."

Martin didn't trouble to conceal his surprise, not only because it would have been unnatural, but because Zimra was the heart of all his defenses, the focus of all his efforts.

"We want a record of what goes on at this meeting, preferably a verbatim transcript." C gave a thin smile. "The impossible, as usual."

He shouldn't be telling me this, Martin thought again—not yet. Another thought struck him. If they really wanted a verbatim record, their sole recourse would be to install some kind of electronic listening device.

"Carow said no technology."

"Correct. Bugging is out."

"Then . . ." Martin broke off. Suddenly, everything fell

into place. Neither of them spoke for a while. They both knew that the moment of truth had come at last. It was C who took the wraps off.

"That's our problem. We've only one chance of getting what we want. For all our electronic espionage, and for all our weird and wonderful hardware, we're sometimes dependent on the human factor." C gave Martin time to say something, but Martin didn't speak. He went on, swiftly and incisively now, as though to get it over fast. "That's where you come in. You and Zimra Steffin. We must activate her—or try to, at least. She still works for the Apparat; what's more, she's been promoted. Over here she'd be called the head dragon—supervisor of the central secretariat."

"There has to be another way."

C seemed not to have heard. "She'll be coming to Prague with the rest of them. It'll be her job to keep a verbatim record of every session, or so experience suggests. Those people don't trust each other. They like everything down in black and white—every last word they utter in conference—so no one can impute things to them later on. They're always on the lookout for scapegoats." C paused. "There are bound to be separate tapes or transcripts for each Service. Your target is Zentner's master copy. That's your assignment."

Martin felt momentarily overwhelmed, nothing more. Then his head became flooded with a swirling, tumultuous torrent of thoughts: that the assignment offered him a chance of seeing her again; that the scenario they'd concocted was far too hazardous; that he'd be risking his own life and endangering hers, possibly to no purpose.

"You might as well plant me under the table with a tape recorder."

"I don't object to your taking that attitude, Martin. It's a unique opportunity for an agent to show what he's made of."

Very clever, thought Martin. C had read his mind, but he

overlooked the fact that his plan was based on a false prem-
ise. How could C, with his meager knowledge of Zimra, his
slender file on her, cling to such a vague hope?

He knew her. He recalled her voice, dredged his memory
for the gist of their conversations during those last few days
at Bernau. The final day, his last chance: Zentner had threatened to have him taken straight back to jail unless he
changed his mind. He'd discussed it with Zimra, told her he
was ready to accept Zentner's offer.

"WHY NOT, IF it brings us our freedom?"

"What freedom, Martin? If you do it, you'll come to hate
me. Not them, but me."

"Once we're out of here . . ."

"You're dreaming."

"I can quit. Not work for either side."

"You know it won't work out like that."

"We'll find ourselves a place."

"You think it exists?"

"Yes, somewhere."

"You're incredibly romantic for an agent. Anyway,
that's not the only consideration. In spite of everything, this
is my country. You might be able to find another one—in
fact, I'm sure you could, somewhere. You can live with
your roots in the air, I can't. I need proper roots, deep ones.
Like a vine. Vines take years to mature, don't they? Well,
it's the same with me. This is where I grew up, don't forget.
Whatever its failings, I owe everything to this country.
There's my father, too. He's pinned so many hopes on
me . . ."

"YOU DON'T KNOW her," Martin said. "She won't play the
part you've cast her in."

"You haven't seen her for nearly six years, right? That's
a long time. A lot can happen in six years."

"The whole scheme sounds like Russian roulette."

"Odds of six to one?" C was unruffled. "To the man we

need for the job, I thought that would seem a reasonable proposition. Was I wrong? Anyway, we're only at the discussion stage. The deal's still open on either side—you can turn it down without prejudice to yourself." His voice hardened for the first time. "Could you do the same over there?"

They had come to a halt and were looking at each other. Martin knew he'd lost the game from the outset because C had detected how much he needed the assignment. Outsiders condemned the Organization's sinister tactics, but they were made possible only by men like himself—men who, when it came to the pinch, swallowed their misgivings because they couldn't live without one thing. His nightmares would return, and he yearned for the time when they did. He simply couldn't go back to the island. A quiet life generated no bad dreams; that was his problem.

The game was over. C had drawn the higher card. Wherever it had come from, the deck or his sleeve, it was better than his own. All that remained was to protect Zimra.

"I'll take the contract. I'll get you what you want. How I get it is my business."

"Agreed."

"If I did enlist her help, what could I offer her?"

"If she plays, we'll get her out."

"With me. The two of us together."

"It would probably mean a change of plan."

"If I'm the only one she trusts, as you assume . . ."

"Very well, we'll retrieve you together. Discuss it with Carow. He'll have to decide how it's done."

"Has Carow approved all this?"

C smiled. "Why shouldn't he? It's his scheme. Any points we haven't covered yet?" He looked round as if checking on their whereabouts in the park.

Martin couldn't disown the fear he felt at what lay ahead, now that it had become a reality, not a contingency to be toyed with in his head. He abruptly felt sick, the way he used to feel after too many cigarettes in the old days. It mortified him that his body was letting him down, showing signs of weakness, at this of all moments.

C put his hand out. The beginnings of a farewell handshake, Martin thought, until he saw that it was merely a gesture aimed at their surroundings.

"You're right. Lovely grounds, these—really lovely." C's voice was as desiccated and colorless as it had been when their conversation began. "Good luck."

It was his last chance to resist temptation and say no, but C had evidently discounted the possibility. He turned and shuffled off—back in his servile role once more—with the limping baby-sitter five yards behind.

Martin waited for his own shadows to pick him up. They didn't take long. Pinocchio materialized, still wearing the hostile expression that conveyed his unshakable dislike of agents in general.

═══════ CHAPTER XV ═══════

To OUTWARD APPEARANCES, CAROW WAS MAKING his official adieus before going on sick leave. He went through the whole performance, handed over his duties to a deputy— even threw a little party in his office suite. Festivities like these were popular in the Organization. Even Pauly, usually the soul of grim austerity, used to sneak away from C's anteroom to attend them. Carow could recall one such party in Records at which she'd unexpectedly mounted a table and danced—slipped off her shoes, lifted her skirt and kicked up her sturdy legs in their black lisle stockings.

She came to his party too, smiling and relaxed until the intercom crackled. "Carow to Director," it announced. She instantly resumed her mask, escorted him upstairs and sternly offered him some coffee while waiting for the green light to come on. It did so surprisingly soon.

C was seated at his desk on the mahogany and black-vinyl throne that always reminded Carow, when vacant, of the electric chair he'd once been shown in a U.S. penitentiary.

"You're all set to go, I gather."

They were alone. No sign of Puck, though one always felt he was there, omnipresent as a shadow and ever at hand when C had need of him. Carow deposited the yellow folder on the desk. He remained standing as though standing might help him to argue more effectively.

"We agreed that the final decision would be yours. Are we also agreed that Martin is our man?"

Carow's immediate reaction, when C had handed him the Steffin file that morning, was anger: at Martin for having deceived him under interrogation; at himself for failing to winkle out the truth; at C for keeping him so long in the dark. Since then his anger had evaporated. Carow was an admirer of courage, and courage was what Martin had undoubtedly shown. As for C . . .

"I might have known you had an ace up your sleeve."

"So it's Martin? Why not sit down while I tell you about my interview with him?"

Even as he listened, Carow's existing suspicion that something was wrong with the plan grew stronger still. It wasn't until much later that he wondered whether this hadn't been the moment when he could have squelched the whole thing—told C to drop the idea and rest content with what Ziegler's section had already unearthed. But wouldn't that have overtaxed his character? Wasn't he merely confused by their temporary exchange of roles: he, Carow, the cautious, diffident skeptic; C the reckless gambler?

"So we're agreed?" C sounded annoyed at having to belabor the question.

"You've never based your decisions on—well, instinct,

but that's what you're doing here. What makes you so sure this plan will deliver the goods? Why take the risk?''

''I don't see any risk. Did you find anything on Steffin in Records? No! There you are, then—it's absolutely water-tight. Besides, even if Martin does fail to produce what we want, he can always activate her for future use. That would be just as valuable, acquiring another high-grade source inside the Apparat.''

''I still think Rosell might be preferable. His approach would be more detached.''

''How would he contact the Steffin woman? Of course, we could tell him about the G.M. business and get him to put the squeeze on her, but you've always been opposed to any form of blackmail.''

''Yes, because the cons outweigh the pros.''

''In that case, what? You want to call the whole thing off at this stage? Everyone's breathing down our neck, don't forget. I don't just mean Zentner and the Apparat, I mean our friends as well. Nobody has ever handed us anything on a plate, Heiner. Look at the Zone—remember what it cost us to get that earmarked as our private preserve. Our friends let us operate in peace there, but only as long as we *produce*. All right, so let's start producing.''

''If Martin succeeds, they're bound to identify his source sooner or later.''

''I promised to get them out.''

''Both of them? Together?''

C's annoyance was quite undisguised now. ''I wonder if you'd mind . . .'' He rose instead and walked over to the drinks dispenser himself. ''Yes, together, damn it!''

''That complicates matters.''

''I know. Leaving her there would naturally be best. It's a crying shame to cut off such a fresh source so soon.''

''If you promised, it's in his contract.''

''Hell's bells!'' For C, it was an uncharacteristic explosion. ''What do you want to do, debate ethics with me? What attracts a man like Martin to an assignment like this?

Does he do it for love of us—for purely patriotic reasons—or because he's got a hankering, an *addiction*? Agents aren't saints, so don't pretend they are. If ever a situation arose in which Martin had to choose between his life and hers, he'd save his own skin." C drew a deep breath. "So let's drop the subject. Either get them both out or not, it's up to you, but tell me something first. Are you with me, yes or no? If you've any reservations at all, I can take the job off your hands—I can get Geissler to run him instead."

Carow found himself admiring C, even now. Or would it have been more accurate to say that he envied him? Envied his absolute and unquestioning belief that every consequence of a policy decision was fully justified? Carow had never detected any weakness in him.

He, Carow, knew his own Achilles' heel. His faith in C's leadership might falter—he might even oppose his decisions—but only up to a point. In the end he gave way. Open rebellion was the sole alternative, and he'd never summoned up the energy for that.

"Okay, I'll find some way of retrieving them together."

"Good. One more thing: I get the feeling Martin regards the Steffin woman as his own private problem. He may try to solve it in his own way, so watch him."

"We will, round the clock."

"Keep me posted. Has he left for the outstation yet?"

"He should be there by now."

"Make him sweat. I want him thoroughly prepared. When does he leave?"

"Saturday night, from Salzburg."

"Wait for my signal."

"Can we fix that now?"

"Any suggestions?"

"Not offhand."

"How about 'The wedding's on' if we send him in? If not, the opposite."

Carow raised his eyebrows. "You mean it might be scratched?"

"Something could always crop up."

"Anything new on Borchers?"

"You've read Kurella's reports. That's as much as I know myself. He seems to be lying low."

"Wouldn't it be safer to pull him in before the operation starts?"

"Without firm evidence? Don't worry, we'll keep that problem under control—I'll make it my personal business, right? Lots of luck with the operation. How's the kidney trouble?"

"Fine, thanks." In fact, the pain in his back was worse than ever. He would really have to do something about it when Bear-Hug was over. If it hadn't been for the pain, he might have put up a better fight.

Carow was far from happy with the way the interview had gone. Another thought kept nagging him, too: he and C made their decisions from behind a desk, encased in a cocoon of security. Nothing could happen to them. They weren't even required to justify the directives that affected those outside the cocoon—in this instance, Martin and Zimra Steffin among others. Martin and she would be out in the field by themselves, out in the cold and beyond his power to assist them.

As he boarded his car and headed for the outstation in Martin's wake, Carow presented himself with an ultimatum: either he would get them both out alive, or he himself would be the one to die. It was a notion whose melodramatic flavor seemed a product of the moment; of his awareness that the operation had now passed, wholly and irrevocably, into his hands. He must have been in earnest, though, because he felt himself break out in a cold sweat—a chill tide that trickled down his spine and seeped from his armpits.

CHAPTER XVI

1

By now, BORCHERS WAS WELL ACCUSTOMED to being shadowed and observed. To a certain extent, the process amused him. The irony of it was that he'd always longed to discard his outsider's role at the Center and gain recognition. So far, success had eluded him. Sacrificing himself to his mother's needs and running his office with exemplary efficiency had availed him nothing. For the first time ever, "Lamb" felt genuinely noticed and appreciated—felt personally important because of all the attention bestowed on him.

There were even times when he caught himself picturing the final act: his trial in front of innumerable TV cameras; the great day when he could at last speak out and parade his achievements before those who had always ignored him. But apart from the fact that he couldn't hurt his mother that way, everything was bound to follow a different course. His "friends" would first get him out and then assign him to some minor post in which he would merely become an outsider again. Either that, or he would be quietly arrested and tried in secret.

It might, in part, have been this melancholy prospect that inspired Borchers to reverse his decision—the one he'd so strictly adhered to till now—to lie low.

The whole change of plan was born of coincidence. He had just returned some files to Records when he saw Carow emerging from the so-called poison cupboard. They exchanged a few words and Carow invited him to his farewell party. That, of course, was the logical reason for Carow's presence: he'd been handing in some classified documents before going into the hospital. But Borchers had never contented himself with simple explanations. Following up "coincidences" had yielded some of his very best coups, so he decided to take the risk and terminate his dormant role.

The poison cupboard, also known as the dispensary, was the heart of the Records Office—a repository for everything to do with agents, active and on ice. It was an artificially lit subterranean chamber lined with shelves which, as in a pharmacy, could be swung back in layers. To Borchers, it always seemed to emit a medicinal smell.

"Yes?"

The guardian of the poison cupboard was nicknamed "Peppermint" because of his addiction to the little white peppermint drops he kept popping into his mouth. Grayhaired and close to retirement age, he had the bleached complexion of a cave dweller.

"I'd like all you've got on CS 77."

"Didn't we go through this before—a few days back?"

"I have to double-check something."

Borchers, kindred spirit that he was, had always treated Peppermint with extreme courtesy. His courtesy now paid off: Peppermint took the poison register—the massive ledger that every customer had to sign—and slid it across to him.

Borchers opened it at the most recent page. Carow's signature was down there, twice. As Borchers had surmised, he had returned two agents' source books. His momentary disappointment almost made him overlook a significant detail: both code numbers indicated that the agents were temporarily on ice. When had Carow withdrawn the files and why? Borchers ran his finger back up the page. Tuesday, Monday, nothing. Sunday . . . Carow's signature again, *three* times. Three source books, but he'd only returned two!

Peppermint shuffled round the desk and peered over his shoulder. "You won't find anything in there," he muttered. He turned away and headed for another part of the labyrinthine chamber. "Maybe under the name Cichosz," Borchers called after him. He knew Peppermint wouldn't find anything there either.

Though not easily rattled, Borchers was on tenterhooks. He had to keep an eye on Peppermint, watch the door, and—most important of all—memorize the coded designation of the third agent: A7Z115(NLA).

Why had Carow retained this particular file? Was it still in his safe? That would be a violation of standing orders, and Carow was a stickler for the rule book. So why?

Peppermint reappeared. "Nothing there, just his index card."

"We've got him in the computer as NLA."

"Then he's no longer active."

"On ice, you mean?"

"No, retired."

Borchers gestured at the shelves. "So his records wouldn't be here anymore?"

"Only if he was important enough."

"How long would you keep them?"

"Forever and a day. We're bursting at the seams in here. That damned computer—that's the only thing they've plenty of room for."

Was it worth the risk, Borchers wondered. Was it worth asking the question on the tip of his tongue? What if Kurella's men came asking what he'd wanted? It would then be Peppermint's well-drilled memory against the host of inquiries he handled every day.

"He had connections with another agent, A7Z115."

"That doesn't concern your subsection—I'd need Carow's approval in writing. Sorry."

"Z . . . Doesn't that mean the Zone?"

"Have you signed yet?"

Borchers signed with Peppermint looking over his shoulder. For whatever reason, the old man suddenly said, "That's right, the Zone. One of the really early birds, he was—joined in forty-seven. Don't forget the time, please."

Borchers entered the time. Now they could prove he'd been here whenever they liked. Was it worth it, for the sake of the little he'd gleaned? Carow was checking on three agents, presumably with an assignment in view. He'd retained one file: Agent A7Z115. No longer active, used to work in the Zone, recruited 1947 . . .

What could his "friends" make of that? Possibly nothing, but hadn't they always urged him to pass on every last little snippet of information, however seemingly unimportant, because it might be just what they needed?

2

BORCHERS WAS STANDING at the end of the queue. A second counter opened for business. The people ahead of him turned and stared, wondering why he didn't cross over, but he waited patiently in line as if he hadn't noticed. When his turn came, he removed the three cassettes from his briefcase and pushed them across the counter.

"Back so soon?"

The husky voice was almost certainly the result of an operation on her larynx, to judge by the scar on her neck. Her round face and old-fashioned bobbed hair made her look almost doll-like, or would have if it hadn't been for the shadows under her eyes.

"Weren't the books satisfactory?"

"Oh yes, especially *Frenchman's Creek*, but I'd like to stock up a little."

She took the cassettes and noted them down on a card. Her hands betrayed her real age, which must have been all of sixty. Borchers had no idea how she'd become involved or how she passed on the relevant cassettes. It wasn't his job to know.

"There's one tape missing. *Mrs. Miniver*."

He took it out of his briefcase and handed it over separately.

"You haven't had it long. Didn't your mother enjoy it?"

"Very much. I even listened to some of it myself."

"We don't get many requests for it these days." She made another entry. "You want to stock up, you said? Have you made a list, or will you leave the choice to me?"

"I'd be grateful—you know her taste. Hasn't *Grand Hotel* been returned yet?"

"I'm afraid not. Are you going on holiday?"

"It's still in the air, but I may not be able to come again for quite a while."

"I understand."

Was she worried? Borchers wondered. He knew nothing about her but her name, Sara Urbanic. He had no idea where she came from, what her motives were, whereabouts in Munich she lived, what sort of life she led or what the future held for her.

Because this was probably their last meeting, he felt tempted to say something, make some gesture that would convey his sense of common purpose—some sign that would, for the first and only time, bridge the gulf between them. But he knew, of course, that he couldn't afford to do anything of the kind. The most he could do was rely on his "friends" to ensure that, when the jaws of the trap closed on him, they failed to capture her too.

She fed some titles and code numbers into an electronic reservation machine.

"Next time you come, you must tell me if your mother approved of my selection."

"She's always been most satisfied. It's only my choices that usually turn out to be wrong."

"The tapes won't be long. Enjoy your holiday."

"Thank you."

There was no more to be said, no reason for him to linger. He knew this contact had to be abandoned. He could still use the telephone, but only in a real emergency. It was going to be hard, reverting to the dormant state.

He walked over to the "Out" desk and waited there, nerves jangling, until the cassettes were delivered by conveyor belt. Paradoxically, he didn't relax until he left the library and found his shadow waiting for him.

══════ CHAPTER XVII ══════

1

HARVESTED GRAIN FIELDS STRETCHED FOR MILES beneath a sky pregnant with cumulus. The clouds were forever changing shape without moving, or so it seemed. Martin had grown unused to such skies. Ibiza's clouds were never left in peace by the wind.

"Not a poppy or cornflower in sight," said Carow. "Is it something to do with these modern synthetic fertilizers?"

It was the fourth and last day of preparation. It had been Carow's idea to drive out here. They were sitting on the edge of a still uncut field of rye. Combine harvesters could be heard in the distance. Their car, with Pinocchio at the wheel, stood some way off at the mouth of a farm track.

"There were masses of them when I was a boy."

"Maybe you're right—maybe it's the fertilizers."

Other and more urgent considerations were running through Martin's head. He'd been looking for a chance to get in touch with Sĕnk ever since the die was cast, so far without success. If the go-ahead came through, he would have to board the Salzburg-Vienna express at 1:23 A.M.

"My daughter used to campaign against the stuff like a

maniac. 'We've got to stop polluting the soil, we're great at nuclear physics but we can't bake bread anymore, we send space probes to Uranus but we can't produce an exhaust-free car,' et cetera. You can't really blame the youngsters. It isn't a very pretty world we've brought them into.''

The days of waiting and preparation didn't seem to have done Carow's nerves much good. Martin found him far more on edge than he was himself. The other thing was that, since they'd been closeted together, Carow had tried to draw closer on a personal plane—more or less overtly thrust his friendship on him.

The professional side of their relationship was another matter. Martin had enjoyed their work on essentials such as codes, addresses, phone numbers, contact procedures, lines of withdrawal, ''emergency exits.'' He admired the care with which Carow had coached him, above all the brilliant simplicity of the cover background or ''legend'' he'd devised for the assignment. And now Carow was sitting here brooding aloud on the state of the world. An edgy, jittery, emotional case officer was the last thing Martin needed.

''I mean, how do you cope with that sort of argument?''

Martin glanced across at the mouth of the lane where the car was parked. The day was warm, almost sultry, and all four doors were open wide. Pinocchio was smoking a cigarette.

''You think they may call it off at the last minute?''

Carow's return to the terra firma of reality was an almost physical, visible process. He straightened up and stretched as though his body were made of some tensile material that could resume its original shape.

''That was my first impression of you, Martin: hungry as hell. It's a potentially dangerous condition. I hope you keep it under control.''

''I will, as soon as I'm on my own and over there.''

''We all want this thing to go off well.''

The combines had stopped to refuel. Carow cleared his throat and went on.

"I've never broached the subject, but there's something I'd dearly like to know. Didn't you ever try to get her out yourself? If not, I'm puzzled. It doesn't tally with my picture of you."

"C asked me the same question. I can only tell you what I told him: it couldn't be done."

"There are always ways and means. Are you telling me you never even tried?"

Involuntarily, Martin's thoughts returned to Sěnk and the plans and preparations they'd made: studying maps, reconnoitering the frontier, fixing dates and times, scouting around for ways of letting Zimra know.

"She didn't want to come—I couldn't persuade her. Later on, I sometimes thought I should have dragooned her into it, but how?"

"You think she'll want to now?"

"She won't have changed much—she's not the type. I honestly don't know. That's the shakiest feature of this whole exercise. You all seem to think she'll play."

"C does."

Martin looked at him quickly. "Meaning you don't?"

Carow was absolved from the need to reply. The receiver in his breast pocket started bleeping. He switched it off and hurried to the car without waiting for Martin.

Carow was leaning on the roof with one foot inside and the phone to his ear when Martin reached the mouth of the lane. He turned, still holding the receiver.

"It's the go-ahead."

The three men stood there for a moment, each digesting the news in his own way. Martin had thought that his tension would disappear as soon as the go-ahead was given, leaving him relaxed and clear-headed, but the opposite happened. All that had seemed so straightforward became confused and chaotic. His next moves had been clearly defined and carefully rehearsed, but what were they? From one moment to the next, he failed to perceive the logic in what had been devised and prepared for him by a whole team of human intellects.

He looked at the sky as if expecting to find the reason there; as if the cloud castles had descended and engulfed him in his present fog of bewilderment.

2

THE BACKGAMMON BOARD was still on the table, the game frozen at the stage it had reached when they left for their excursion into the country. The playing cards were there too. Before removing his jacket, Martin emptied the pockets. His small leather wallet was bulging with the money he'd won from Geissler, Pinocchio and the manager of the shop whose back room this was.

"They'll be glad to see the last of you." Carow took the wallet, counted the money, and called out the total to Geissler. "I don't know why you ever became an agent. You could make a living at cards."

Geissler took the jacket and deposited it in an open cardboard box. "Now your trousers." He had lost less than the other two. Stolzer had fared worst of all. He was a lean, elderly man—"H. Stolzer, Dealer in Ornamental Rocks and Minerals"—who spent his days among the bizarre-shaped stones that constituted his stock-in-trade. Stolzer had lost an ear; its gnarled remains looked like a peculiarly freakish mineral specimen. His deformity stemmed from an infection, but Pinocchio claimed that it had been progressively nibbled away by youthful lovers. Stolzer was a homosexual.

Martin, now stripped to the skin, cupped his hands over his genitals like a bashful young army recruit. His new outfit was lying on another table. Geissler picked up the first item and handed it to Carow for inspection.

Señor Martin—the name had been retained—was a schoolteacher from Albacete. He was traveling to Prague as a guest of the International Association of Teachers' Trade Unions to attend a week-long congress on "Educational

Freedom.'' Delegates from West European countries had to be in Vienna by next morning so as to catch a special train from there to Prague. The Albacete schoolteacher, who actually existed, had been taken into custody for the duration of the assignment by some helpful Spanish ''friends'' of the Organization.

Carow looked closely at each item, checked each label with the calm concentration of one who had ceased to be anything but a case officer responsible for his agent's welfare and security. After articles of clothing came the little things a teacher would normally carry: ball-points, for example, and a diary full of entries relating to teachers' conferences, textbooks, examinations, vacations.

With every piece of clothing he put on, and with every object he pocketed, Martin felt more and more at ease. It wasn't just the care with which Carow and Geissler proceeded or the perfection of the disguise itself, every component of which was old, well-worn and somehow ''alive.'' As he reequipped his body with all these things, Martin felt himself slipping into the other Martin's mind and taking on his personality.

Carow stepped back and surveyed him. ''Right,'' he said. ''The rest is up to you.'' That was the moment when Martin finally felt united with Carow in a perfect identity of interests and ideas. *That* he could give him—*that* kind of friendship he could feel. His life depended on it, after all. Despite his relief, what lay ahead had now acquired an inexorable quality. He knew that Carow's failure would entail his own, and that the converse would apply if he fell down on the job. From that angle, friendship was a key to joint survival.

''Official invitation, airline ticket from Madrid, rail tickets . . .''

Martin put them in his pocket. Should he drop the Šenk plan, he debated—was it necessary after all?

''Now the briefcase.''

Carow took it from Geissler and checked the contents;

passport last. It bore Martin's photograph, but the date of birth made him forty-six, three years less than his real age.

Next came the shoulder bag and suitcase. Carow showed him once more where the money was hidden: U.S. dollars, German marks, Czech korunas.

There was no passport for Zimra. It hadn't been possible to produce one here without a photo, so that would be handed over in Prague. They couldn't come out together, either. Although he accepted the logic of this, Martin still felt uneasy. Could Carow sense it?

"All clear on the Steffin front? Sunday, seven-thirty A.M., half an hour before your train leaves. The newspaper kiosk at the west exit, our man reading a copy of *Rudé Pravo*. Remember your code?"

" 'The Bohemians have played better.' His reply: 'What do you expect, with that new trainer of theirs?' "

"He'll drive her out to Ruzyně to catch the morning flight to Vienna. I'll meet her off the plane myself. She'll be home and dry before your train crosses the border. There wasn't any other way."

"Of course not."

"Well, I think that's it." Carow glanced at his watch. "We still have plenty of time. Anyone want to lose some more of his money to Martin?"

"Who's driving me to Salzburg?"

"Pinocchio." Carow had adopted the nickname.

"Can't we leave right away? I couldn't concentrate on a game, not now." Martin started to put the cards in his shoulder bag. Carow took the deck, examined it and handed it back. "All right." He turned to Geissler. "Tell Pinocchio to get the car out."

Geissler left the room. As he did so, Martin caught a fleeting glimpse of the showroom at the end of the passage. The light was fading, and Stolzer's shelves full of rock and mineral specimens glittered in the setting sun. Similar shops existed in a number of countries. They conducted a brisk correspondence and sent specimens back and forth, the valuable ones by courier—ideal camouflage for the kind of business they really transacted. All of them were owned by the Organization.

"Pinocchio will take you to the station. You can both eat there. Once you board that train you're on your own."

"Will you be staying on here?"

Carow's reply was almost a murmur. "Yes, and I won't rest easy till you're out again."

Martin recalled the question he'd asked before the go-ahead interrupted them. "You feel doubtful about the scenario because of Zimra?"

"It's your doubts that matter, not mine. I trust you don't have any."

"Not really. I think I stand a chance. I also think you'll get what you want however I play it." Martin did something with the cards, then peeled two off the deck and handed them to Carow. "Okay, take a good look. Ready? Now put them back in the deck—separately, anywhere you like."

He handed the deck to Carow, averting his head, and took it back. Again his hands did something. Then he tossed the deck onto the table. Only two cards landed face up, the seven of clubs and the eight of spades. Carow stared at them incredulously—touched them with his fingertips as though to satisfy himself that they were real.

"How on earth . . ."

"Sure they're the ones?" Martin seemed almost depressed by his success. "Tell me, if you had to choose between two colors—red and black—which would you say was the color of love and which of death?"

"That's easy. Red for love, black for death."

"Now watch I'll do the whole thing again, but with two red cards." He picked out the seven of diamonds and the eight of hearts. The procedure was repeated and two cards landed face up, but Carow promptly objected. "Those aren't the ones. Seven of hearts and eight of diamonds is the wrong way round . . ." He broke off and looked at Martin, then found the answer by himself. "You mean it was the same the first time?"

"Yes, that's the strange thing. The switch works with black cards, never with red ones—people spot it straight off. Nobody has ever managed to produce a satisfactory explanation. It happens, that's all. Red gives the game away at once." Martin gathered up the cards and put them in his pocket.

Carow watched him. "Feeling all right?"

Martin nodded. He regretted having voiced emotions he couldn't define himself. Besides, everything worth saying had already been said.

"Play it strictly by the book. If you pull it off, pass on the goods as arranged, then keep your head down. Preserve your cover—that way you'll be safe. And please don't try to do anything more. Don't be too hungry."

"Carow . . ."

"Yes?"

"I've a favor to ask. I know it isn't in my contract, but once the operation's over—whichever way it goes—I'd like her file destroyed." It seemed unnecessary to utter the name.

"You know we never—"

"Please, Carow. Destroy it!"

Martin himself was surprised by the urgency and entreaty in his voice. It was, after all, a matter of secondary importance.

CHAPTER XVIII

MARTIN STILL WASN'T SURE, WHEN the train pulled out and left Pinocchio standing on the platform, his expression no less hostile than it had been on the first day, whether he'd given Sěnk enough time.

He picked up his bags. Luckily, the train appeared to be quite empty. "The first non-smoker in front of the sleeping car"—he hadn't been able to tell Sěnk much more than that. In retrospect, he felt he'd pushed his luck a second time: to think that Gypsy had actually been hovering over the phone . . . He and Pinocchio had eaten and killed time in a restaurant opposite the station. His first stroke of luck had been that the phone booths were right beside the men's room. To the very last, Pinocchio showed none of the laxity that usually afflicted a shadow after several days of constant coexistence with his "subject."

Martin had never been able to sleep in trains—a minor flaw in any agent. He would have preferred to make the night trip to Vienna in a first-class compartment, but that would have strained the pocket of a humble Spanish schoolteacher, not to mention his Czech hosts' foreign exchange reserves.

The second compartment was empty. Martin chose a window seat as far away as possible from the corridor. He stowed his bags on the rack, hung up his coat and switched off the overhead light, leaving only his reading lamp on. If

140

Sěnk was on board, he would soon show up, It was over an hour to the next stop.

He was feeling better, relieved at being alone at last with his new persona, Señor Martin the schoolteacher. He had a natural talent for languages—the sort of mimicry that stood an agent in good stead. He had never forgotten his childhood Czech, either, and part of the last four days had been devoted to a refresher course.

An official program of events had been forwarded from Spain with the invitation and other documents. He studied it closely. Numerous last-minute changes would be made, he knew, but one thing was certain: his major problem in Prague would be freedom of movement.

Apart from general lectures and debates in the Congress Hall and a building entitled the Academy of Pedagogic Sciences, their hosts had arranged a full and intensive program of entertainment: a performance of *Turandot*, an ice hockey match, a steamer trip, a communal souvenir-buying excursion "for foreign currency." Between now and the gala "Friendship Evening" that concluded the seven-day schedule, every waking hour was filled with some kind of activity. Getting time to himself without attracting undue attention would be a headache—only one among many, but no less troublesome for that—from the moment he boarded the Vienna-Prague Special, Car 301, Compartment 15, Seat 89.

He didn't hear the door slide back. A voice said, in strongly accented German, "Any of these seats taken?"

Martin didn't speak—he couldn't. He simply shook his head and watched Sěnk take the corner seat farthest away from him. Sěnk had to stand on tiptoe to get his suitcase into the rack. He was short, even for a flyer, with the swarthy skin and dark hair that had earned him his nickname. People seeing Gypsy for the first time gained the impression that he was a shy, diffident little man, but that was only on the outside; inwardly, he was the toughest character Martin had ever met.

"Going far?" Šěnk's conversational gambit was suitably casual.

"Vienna."

"Vienna's nice at this time of year."

"I'm only changing there—going on to Prague."

"Prague, eh? Very nice too."

A man appeared in the corridor. He lit a cigarette. They fell silent like any two strangers on a train who retire into their shells after exchanging a few words.

Pinocchio had stayed behind in Salzburg. Despite Carow's assurance that he wouldn't be shadowed, it was always possible that they would continue to keep an eye on him, at least as far as the frontier. Martin was glad he didn't have to sound a note of warning, not with Gypsy.

Miroslav Šěnk had hit the headlines only once in his life, on the day he fled to the West—his "day of wine and roses," as he wryly called it. That was in March 1953, when a twenty-four-year-old lieutenant in the Czech Air Force flew his Russian MiG to Frankfurt. The CIA took charge of him, spirited him off to the States, squeezed him dry and then dropped him because his one real interest was flying, not spying.

Šěnk tried to get work with an airline company, but the CIA had neglected to honor its pledge of U.S. citizenship. He was obliged to make do with any odd jobs that came his way: dusting crops, spraying forest fires, even stunt flying—slave labor, to quote his own description. Miroslav Šěnk had joined the ranks of those aerial desperadoes who have so little in common with the dapper, godlike pilots of the major airlines.

When competition became still hotter—the end of the Korean War had dumped a mass of pilots on the market—Šěnk retreated to Europe and set up on his own. ATAP Airlines was based first in Elba, then in Munich. It was rumored, even in those days, that Gypsy accepted under-the-counter commissions to fly refugees out of Communist Czechoslovakia, which was how Martin got to know him.

The passenger in the corridor had disappeared. The train, which had been traveling quite slowly, speeded up. Martin could see no lights outside. Were they crossing an expanse of open countryside, or was it the lateness of the hour?

Sěnk grinned at him. "I didn't know you were back in business."

Martin had no need to explain his motives. As for Gypsy, he would go on flying for as long as he could climb into a cockpit. Martin recalled another of his sayings: "Some pilots reach for the stick the way others reach for the bottle."

"How are things at ATAP?"

"I've kept the date free. Sunday the thirtieth." His eyes were on the corridor, not Martin.

"Thanks."

"That scheme we never put into effect—any regrets?"

Martin came quickly to the point. "Could it still be done?"

"How many passengers?"

"Two."

"I've got a Bell JetRanger. It's the ideal chopper for the job."

"Would you handle it yourself?"

"I've given up flights behind the Curtain. Too many salary checks to meet—I'm almost a capitalist these days. Still, as long as it's you . . . Of course I'll do it."

"The Tower would want a flight plan."

"Couldn't be done, not without violating half a dozen laws and conventions. Leave it to me, though. I'll only charge you for fuel and flying time. My own services come free. I liked the plan then and I still do now—it appeals to me."

"What are the odds?"

"Fair. Better than in sixty-nine, I'd say. The Austrian border's pretty quiet, and I've got a better chopper this time."

"Same spot?"

"Sure, the same field. I still have the maps. What time?"

"Six-thirty?"

"Too early. I'll need daylight. If I'm going to sneak in under their radar, I'll have to fly at three-feet maximum in places. How about nine?"

Martin thought of the long wait between their dawn arrival and Sěnk's proposed collection time, but he said, "All right, make it nine A.M. And Gypsy, if we're there, pick us up. If not, don't wait."

"Okay, the same arrangement stands. No changes. If a plan's good, it stays good."

The man had reappeared, smoking again. He must be in a nonsmoker too; that was the logical explanation. Sěnk took a newspaper from his overcoat pocket. Martin stared out into the darkness. Still no lights. Where were they?

There was no need to speak again. They'd already said all there was to say. It was wiser to keep silent than attract attention. For all that, Martin yearned to go on talking. They were two men who spoke the same language, felt alike, shared a taste for danger, but it wasn't only that. More important to Martin just then was his sudden realization that this would be his last chance to converse with someone freely.

From the moment when the train slowed down—the moment when Sěnk rose and bade him a casual farewell before getting out at the next station—he would have to weigh every word he uttered, watch himself for signs of emotion and ruthlessly suppress them. And as soon as he crossed the frontier into an unfree country, sheer survival would require him to restrict his personal freedom and become an unfree man himself.

He glanced across the compartment, but Sěnk was engrossed in his newspaper.

C had talked of loyalty and duty. Martin had no time for such sentiments. He felt no part of what Zimra must have felt when she spoke of "her country." A country, a nation, a fatherland, a flag—Martin was motivated by none of these. He was no patriot. He had no country worth dying for. He carried his country around with him wherever he went. He was his own country, a land owned and ruled by him alone; he flew his own colors.

He wasn't there, sitting in this train, doing this job, preparing to cross the frontier and put his freedom in jeopardy, because he harbored any such sentiments. And yet, at this one moment, he came as close to them as he ever could, borne there by the thought that had just occurred to him—the knowledge of how much it meant to be a man who could speak out freely wherever he was.

"Gypsy . . . ."

Sěnk lowered the newspaper. "Yes?"

The words had no apparent bearing on what Martin meant to convey: "You never did come to the island."

"I know. Something always cropped up, but I will. After this."

Martin recalled his last dive, the morning before he left. He hadn't reached the grotto, partly because he'd spent too long savoring the beauty of a whole forest of spirographis. The outspread, flowerlike gills had resembled white palm fronds.

"You'd enjoy diving, I think. It's a different world down there."

"With me, it's up there. I'll come."

Was it possible for the train to put on still more speed? It seemed to be racing along like the only living thing in a dark, dead landscape. Martin felt as if they were already nearing the border; as if the train, past halting in its headlong career, would be bathed at any moment in the harsh beams of searchlights glaring down from a row of grim wooden watchtowers beside the track.

He peered out of the window, waiting, holding his breath. He felt afraid. His ears detected the change before he realized that the train was braking, at first by slow degrees, then in sharp bursts, then gently and smoothly again. As the first lights swam into view, he heard Sěnk getting ready behind him.

The feeling of dread still puzzled him. He couldn't quite make up his mind: was it the nervous excitement of a Castilian schoolteacher, or a secret agent's stage fright?

3

CHAPTER XIX

1

MARTIN LISTENED TO THE VOICE WITH mounting irritation. It wasn't so much what the man on the platform was saying; there were other reasons for his impatience. This was his second day in Prague—his third, counting the Sunday of his arrival—and all his efforts to date had proved abortive.

Two clocks, one on either side of the stage, supplied a clue to the Forum's original function. The Congress Hall hadn't been available after all, so the delegates were meeting in a former newsreel theater. The clocks were out of sync. One said five to three, the other five past. A half-hour break was scheduled for three o'clock, to be followed by another lecture which would take them up to five-thirty. The man on the platform was an Italian Communist. His theme: "The Scope for Revolution in a Capitalist Society."

"He talks a lot of sense. That bit about bourgeois society and the machinery of government . . ."

Martin squelched the simultaneous translation by removing his earphones. He turned to the woman beside him and smiled the uncomprehending smile of someone baffled by a foreign tongue, but his next-door neighbor refused to be discouraged. "I still can't take it in," she hissed. "I'm *here*, really and truly here!" Her upswept hairdo had begun to disintegrate, and isolated wisps were straggling down her face. "I mean, when the invitation came, I said to myself . . ."

A hand insinuated itself between them from behind, reducing her to silence. The speaker was still holding forth. It had to be after three by now. Martin knew that he must make a decision. He also knew that he was still trying to dodge it—still hoping to accomplish his mission without involving Zimra.

The lecture finally ended. The speaker gathered up his notes while the audience clapped. The applause was brisk but brief. Everyone rose swiftly, thankful for any respite from the Forum's abysmal seating accommodation. The wooden tip-ups were hard, shiny and installed at an angle that tended to eject their occupants.

"We'd better hurry or there'll be nothing left," said the woman at Martin's side.

They all streamed out, heading for the cold buffet in the foyer. It still surprised Martin to see how these delegates from Western countries swooped on anything their hosts had to offer in the way of food and drink, like famished new arrivals in a land of milk and honey. It had started in the train, the moment they crossed the border and were welcomed by officials bearing hot dogs and crates of Pilsener. The same behavior persisted in Prague itself, where even the most ample and formidable meals disappeared with miraculous speed from the Hotel Nltava's damask-covered tables. Perhaps it was just a sign of professional penury. Schoolteachers confronted by the sight of free food seemed prone to insatiable greed.

Martin waited for his next-door neighbor to fight her way back from the buffet, cheeks flushed and fair hair more disheveled still. Elsa Baum was a schoolmarm from the Rhineland. At thirty-two, she was already trying to paint the acid disenchantment out of her face with rouge and lipstick.

"You really don't want anything?"

Martin shook his head, watching the smokers drift outside. He wondered whether to seize the chance and play truant till the end of the second lecture.

"I always eat too much on these trips, I know I do. I just

can't bear to miss anything—it's my weakness.'' She laughed. ''Other people bring back snaps from abroad. With me, it's extra pounds.''

Elsa, who'd shared his compartment in the special train, had attached herself to him from the outset. That was another of Martin's discoveries. People had paired off, even in the train; tentatively at first, but now, after two days, on a firmly established basis. Couples sat together in buses, were inseparable at lectures, meals and evening functions, and doubtless slunk along the Nltava's corridors at night, bound for each other's bedrooms. The train had scarcely left Vienna when Elsa caused a momentary stir by addressing the compartment at large. ''Do you believe in free love?'' she asked, much as if she were inquiring whether her fellow passengers drank beer. Maybe she'd hit the nail on the head, Martin reflected. Maybe she'd merely voiced the thought that was flitting through every head—the feeling that no congress in Prague would be complete without a lightning affair.

''I'll dive into the fray and get you something—you only have to say the word.''

''Really not, thanks.'' He wondered whether to shake her off or use her to make his absence seem more natural.

''Whenever I look back on a trip abroad, it's never anything I've seen that comes to mind. I always think, that's where I ate such-and-such.''

Acting off the cuff was risky from an agent's point of view, but time was not on Martin's side. He simply didn't have enough to spare.

''I think I'll take a stroll.''

She smiled at him. ''Isn't it a bit early for that? You caused a fine old commotion that first evening.''

That, too, had been a risk, but a calculated risk designed to gain himself some elbowroom. He'd left the hotel at 6 P.M., visited a string of bars and deliberately turned up twenty minutes late for dinner. The officials, guides and interpreters assigned to their party were waiting for him in the lobby, filled with trepidation. Dismay yielded to evident relief when he reappeared, slightly the worse for wear and happily singing the praises of their city.

He had repeated the whole performance on Monday, invoking the fact that their daily schedule defined the period between 6 and 8 P.M. as "available for private recreation." Again he upset the organizers, but their disapproval was tempered with smiles which, though still uneasy, conveyed a hint of indulgence. Obviously, the teacher from Albacete was a man who liked a drink in the evening.

"Mind if I join you?" As though aghast at her own temerity, she quickly added, "I can catch up on the lecture later. There'll be transcripts in our rooms by dinner time."

Two empty seats were more noticeable than one. On the other hand, their simultaneous absence would seem more natural and understandable to the others. Elsa's interest in him was quite undisguised. Martin had qualms about taking advantage of it, but only for a moment. He shrugged and said, "Suit yourself."

Parked in the square outside the Forum were the Čedok buses that would take them back to their various hotels.

They were adorned with slogans such as "Education Means Freedom!" and "The Masses Are the True Intelligentsia!" Over on the right lay the National Museum and the Smetana Hall. To their left, the broad Václavské led straight into the old quarter of the city.

"Where shall we go?"

He shrugged again, knowing perfectly well. "Anywhere. Let's just walk."

A couple of drivers were standing beside their buses. They turned to stare. "We aren't doing anything illegal, are we?" Elsa hung back with a sudden look of anxiety. "It's just talk, isn't it—I mean, about not being able to take a step without being watched? And all that stuff about microphones hidden in our rooms—it's ridiculous, isn't it? I tell you, back where I come from, we . . ."

He tried not to listen to her.

2

THEY HEADED FOR the oldest part of town. The sunless sky was gray and overcast, and the traffic was surprisingly heavy—or perhaps it only seemed so as the streets grew steadily narrower.

Martin had sometimes visited Prague with his mother in the distant past. Having expected everything to look smaller and more cramped than he remembered, he was surprised to find how far it seemed from one intersection to the next.

Many of the old town houses had been converted into office blocks. Looking up, Martin saw a multitude of television aerials sprouting from the roofs like the sensors of some elaborate alarm system. He was assailed by a sudden and unaccountable presentiment of danger close at hand.

He made a beeline for a stand-up bar and knocked back two drinks for Elsa's benefit. He didn't feel like drinking in the middle of the afternoon—in fact, he had to grit his teeth to get them down. Aimlessly, or so it seemed, he strolled within a certain radius, returning full circle to streets and squares they'd already passed. His game of blindman's buff brought Elsa ever nearer the building he had in mind. The problem was how to unload her, if only for ten or fifteen minutes.

He paused, looking hesitant. Visible through a tall iron gate was a courtyard with a former convent in the background. The courtyard had been deserted the first time round. Now some children in gray button-up smocks were playing there under the supervision of three elderly women.

"Didn't we come this way already?" Martin peered about him uncertainly. "We'd better turn back."

"Yes, we mustn't miss the bus whatever we do!"

"You mean we'd get teased by the others?" He felt a swine for saying it. "Don't worry, I'll find us a cab." He took her arm and steered her across a little square to the window of a cafe. "I won't be long. Have a coffee while you're waiting. My treat."

Elsa gave him no trouble. She pointed to a *gâteau* smothered in pink-and-white whipped cream. "And maybe a slice of that too, just to remind me of our outing."

He reached the shop inside two minutes. It was one of the addresses salted away in his head. Carow had warned him not to expect too much of Dlubek. "He was the one who tipped our agent off about the conference. He may be so scared he'll refuse to speak to you at all."

There was a handwritten "Closed" sign hanging inside the glass door. The shop was filled with old television sets, hi-fi rigs and electronic equipment. Martin wasted no time on the deserted shop. He entered the building through a narrow door in the big wooden gate beside it. The flagstoned entrance was flanked by two flights of worn stairs. There were countless names on the rusty mailboxes at their foot.

The stairway was dark—lit only by windows caked with grime and exhaust fumes. Martin almost turned tail at the smell that hung in the air. Chloroform was yet another reminder of Prague. His mother had taken him to the capital to have some polyps removed. He remembered fighting the doctor's attempts to clamp the evil-smelling gauze mask over his nose and mouth, remembered the grip on his neck growing steadily tighter and more brutal as he screamed and bit and kicked with all his might. It was one of the most humiliating, and thus terrifying, experiences he had ever undergone, never to be equaled until he saw the inside of a prison cell.

The apartment was on the third floor. There was no doorbell, just a handle attached to a wire threaded through the door frame—surprisingly, in view of Dlubek's professional interest in electronic gadgets. The bell jangled faintly. Silence followed. Even when the door opened, all that could be heard was the gentle twittering of some birds.

As soon as Martin saw the woman, he knew he was too late. He found himself looking into a face rendered ageless by grief. In the room beyond, where two canaries were hopping around in a wire pagoda, he could see the table she'd been ironing on.

"I'd like a word with Stefan."

"He's gone." Her voice was expressionless.

"He promised to repair my set for me."

She looked at him with eyes as empty of emotion as her voice. "He's gone, don't you understand?"

Martin was gripped by the feeling he'd had in the street. This time the sense of danger was so immediate that he swung round. The scene unfolded in his mind's eye: two men mounting the stairs, the bell jangling, Dlubek opening the door and being led away. No need to use force, brandish guns, fend off a hysterical wife . . . He owed these mental images neither to the woman in front of him nor to his own imagination: they were transmitted by the *objects* around him—the gray, heavily waxed floorboards of the landing, the peeling brown paintwork on the door.

At last he understood the nature of his forebodings. They were a product of the city itself, the courtyards, the buildings, the aerials that seemed to keep a wary eye on strangers. The city and the things around him were as much to be feared as any member of a secret police force or counterespionage service.

"Any idea where he is?" Martin realized the futility of the question. He was merely groping for an exit line.

"They'll tell me sooner or later." She turned and closed the door behind her.

Long before he got back to the cafe—he told Elsa that he'd failed to find a cab but been directed to the hotel by a friendly policeman—Martin had overcome his fears. His recollection of the woman's face had been banished to the realm where it belonged, his storehouse of nightmares. The present consisted solely in his burning resolve to do the job he'd been given. Postponing a decision had cost him precious time. Now, there was only one course left.

CHAPTER XX

1

MARTIN STARED DOWN AT THE BRIDGE from the window of his hotel room. By day it was merely a drab gray means of conveyance across the murky waters of the Vltava, built on piers so often restored as to resemble the skin of a mangy beast. There was something equally drab and monotone about the traffic that crossed it during daylight hours. Now that it was dark, however, the old-fashioned candelabra lamps and the floodlit bridge tower on the far bank inbued the Karluv Most with a grandeur that went some way toward explaining its fame.

Almost no traffic was crossing at present. Even such few cars as there were had slowed and pulled into the curb as though making way for an ambulance. The ambulance proved to be a column of soldiers. Watching the men swing their arms, Martin had an involuntary notion that they must be singing at the tops of their voices.

He turned back into the room. Despite its size, it was so crammed with furniture that little scope for movement remained. The Hotel Nltava possessed a certain grandeur too—a seedy magnificence that extended to its bedrooms. This one boasted dark red-velvet curtains, gilt-framed pictures, plush armchairs, a huge black wardrobe and a pair of canopied beds. The bathroom—in which Martin could hear his roommate moving around—had the acoustics of a cathedral crypt, and the hot tap ran cold before the marble tub was even half full.

The telephone reposed on an occasional table in front of a large wall mirror. It was a ponderous, antiquated instrument that looked capable of compressing any voice into a whisper. The question was, did the whisper get monitored on its way from A to B? Carow had given Martin the names of two secretaries who would, according to his information, be accompanying Zentner's staff to Prague with Zimra Steffin. Martin debated whether to ask for them or not. There were only two or three hotels that qualified for consideration.

His roommate emerged from the bathroom. A teacher from Zaragoza, he was still short of thirty but had the slow speech and deliberate movements of a much older man. He was wearing a long maroon dressing gown over his pajamas, threadbare and discolored as the surrounding curtains and bedspreads. In some curious way, the man suited the room as perfectly as if he had lived there from birth.

"You'd better get changed for the game," he said in his fatherly way.

The evening's program included an ice hockey match between two Prague teams at the Nikolaika.

"Aren't you coming?" asked Martin.

"I wouldn't understand what was going on. I don't know the rules." The Spaniard retired to the desk. Martin knew that he would find him still ensconced behind it when he came back. He had delayed the buses' departure that morning by taking an age to stamp his last night's output of letters and postcards.

Voices and laughter could be heard in the passage outside. Someone knocked and called Martin's name.

Opening the door, he saw a dozen members of his party—laughing couples arm in arm. They looked as if they'd put in some time at the hotel bar.

The person who had knocked and called his name was Elsa, but a very different Elsa. Her hair had been piled on top of her head and buttressed with combs, her makeup completely reorganized. Her sandy eyebrows, which were usually invisible, had suddenly asserted themselves, and her floral dress rivaled the carpet in the corridor.

"Coming, Martin?" The others laughingly backed her up in a variety of languages. "Of course he is!"

"Aren't you going to the match?" he asked.

Elsa looked momentarily at a loss. She indicated a man on the outskirts of the group. He was one of the guides assigned them by the hotel, a waxen-faced man in a pearl-gray suit that had made many trips to the cleaners and was obviously a bequest from one of his Western "clients." He wore a cream-silk shirt with frayed cuffs and carried an old-fashioned dustcoat draped over his arm.

"Němeček's taking us to—where did you say it was?"

"The Tehran," Němeček replied gravely.

"Loads of atmosphere." Elsa recited what he must have told her. "Very exclusive—locals only, no tourists. Music, dancing, Czech jazz . . ." She smiled at Martin, fractionally unsure of herself but determined to make the most of her siren's role. "Just the place for a romantic *tête-à-tête*."

Two or three couples started drifting off down the passage. Someone else reminded him to take some money along. "Dollars or deutschmarks. Deutschmarks are best— Němeček here, he'll give you fourteen Czech korunas for one deutschmark. That's the unofficial rate. Or is it fifteen, Němeček?"

Martin sensed that Němeček was watching him. All he could detect, when he searched the man's face, was the boredom typical of a veteran tourist guide, but he didn't let that deceive him. There was something else there as well— something inconsistent and out of tune. He played the black market on the side, Martin told himself, *and they knew it*. They tolerated it in return for reports on his foreign charges.

"Please come, Martin. I've gone to so much trouble. There's a beauty salon right here in the hotel, and the girls really did a job on me."

Elsa's sense of irony was precisely what saved her from

seeming merely ridiculous. Her periodic outbursts of sarcasm were always directed at herself, as though she saw herself as an ideal target for mockery.

"All right," he said. The Tehran was one of the hotels where Zentner's staff might be staying. "I'll come."

The advance guard were already on their way down in the elevator, a cage enclosed by wrought-iron curlicues. They had to wait because it was the only one available to guests. On their left lay the main staircase, which debouched into the ground-floor lobby. At the end of the corridor was another staircase connecting their own floor, the fourth, with the staff quarters on the floor above. Martin had checked this on his first night in Prague. The backstairs' route to the fifth floor was open, but access to the lower floors was barred by an iron grille.

"Like my dress? I bought it specially for the congress."

"It's great."

She shook her head ruefully. "Why do I do it?"

"Do what?"

"Spend my hard-earned cash on clothes that don't appeal to the opposite sex?"

"But I told you, it's great."

"You have to invest in yourself—women do, I mean. We always have to lay out more than men, it just isn't fair. For a while I spent half my salary on adverts. 'Academic type, thirty-two, five foot six, blonde, ultrafeminine . . .' Well, aren't I?"

The elevator reappeared just as Martin was girding himself to say something nice. They rode down. There was an oriental look about the Nltava's big reception hall, with its tiled floor, potted palms and red and green lanterns. The lobby was as thick with humanity as a caravansary. New arrivals were standing in a gaggle beside their baggage, which bristled with Aeroflot and Intourist labels.

They walked over to the Čedok counter, where a dozen or more employees of the government travel agency sat watching the exit and main staircase, and had themselves signed out in a big thick ledger. Martin could guess at the entry without seeing it: "Martin, Room 425, left premises 21:30."

Outside at last, they looked around for the other couples. Martin caught sight of two cabs parked in front of the ever-present buses. Arms waved and voices hailed them through the open windows. Elsa grabbed his hand and towed him in her wake.

2

MARTIN WONDERED WHOSE idea the Tehran had really been, but not until later. Tonight there seemed no doubt. It was Němeček who abruptly took command, transmitted his party's requests to the band leader and ordered them drinks unasked—cuba libres to start with, Georgian champagne to follow. He handled things at first with a certain restraint. Once he had done justice to the bottle himself, however, he stopped addressing the waiters in a discreet whisper and bellowed for service like a millionaire playboy.

One potential reason for his behavior was a Belgian schoolteacher named Gabrielle, a horn-rimmed, bosomy brunette with whom he flirted heavily and danced incessantly. At the Nltava, Němeček had been wearing a plain gold wedding band. Martin noticed that it was missing from the hand that now raised his glass aloft.

"To all pretty schoolteachers everywhere! *À toi*, Gabrielle! *Tu es belle—magnifique, délicieuse, sensationnelle!*"

The Tehran Club occupied the top floor of the hotel of the same name, which was quite unlike the gilt-and-plush Nltava. The walls were lime green, the chairs and tables sheathed in white plastic. Batteries of multicolored lights rotated above the dance floor. The interior designer had doubtless striven to create an atmosphere of Western chic, but to Martin the place was as sterile as an operating theater.

They were the only foreigners there—or the only ones using the dance floor. Three air hostesses were sitting at the bar, which took up one side of the room, presumably marooned in Prague for the night. They were waiting for nothing and no one in particular, just killing time over a trio of soft drinks. Most of the other tables were occupied by middle-aged couples who consumed the contents of their glasses in dour and dogged silence, watching the noisy party from the Nltava without a vestige of amusement or disfavor.

The Czech jazz, so-called, emanated from a four-piece band in orange blazers. It was a medley of shop-worn hits, mainly in the sentimental vein. The jazz element was supposedly provided by the vocalist, a skinny blonde in a long green evening gown. She was currently tackling a Beatles number in heavily accented English. If Martin hadn't been familiar with the words and music, her annnouncement that they were all living in a yellow submarine would have defied his powers of comprehension.

"Shall we?"

Wayward wisps were already escaping from the edifice on Elsa's head. He got up and escorted her to the floor. She rested her head on his shoulder as if its weight, under all that hair, were too much for her neck to support.

"She doesn't sing badly, does she?"

"No." His thoughts were miles away.

"Aren't you enjoying yourself?" When he didn't answer, she went on, "Why can't you enjoy yourself a teensy bit? Why not pretend, at least? Tell me a few white lies. Pretend you like my dress, this place, this evening, what they've done to my face and hair. That's all I'm asking—a bit of make-believe, just while we're here."

She giggled into his neck. He could tell that the Georgian champagne had done its work.

"I think it was really *nice* of them to invite us both to this congress and put us in the same compartment. Aren't you superstitious? Do men think it's silly to be superstitious—I mean, don't they believe in the luck of the draw?" She suddenly stopped dancing, removed her head from his shoulder and lowered her arms. From one moment to the next, she seemed entirely sober. "Let's go. You're right, it's really awful here." She was looking past him, not at him.

As though on cue, the band stopped dead in the middle of a number. When they started up again—almost without a break—they launched into something they'd so far considered beneath their dignity: a sentimental waltz. It was like a chameleon changing color.

"Shall we go?"

Martin froze when he saw the three men and two women whose entrance had stopped the band in their tracks.

"We'll have to pay our share first." He led Elsa off the dance floor.

The new arrivals had reached the platform. The musicians bowed and smiled, the two saxophonists raising their instruments in salutation. The men reciprocated by clasping their hands in the air, boxer fashion. The leader of the party, a bald man with drooping jowls and eyes veiled by bushy eyebrows, gave the vocalist a hug. She left the stage and accompanied him to a reserved corner table, one arm wound round him like a thin green creeper encircling a tree stump.

Elsa must have grasped that the strangers' arrival had wrought an instant change in the atmosphere. She went quiet, and Martin could feel her follow the direction of his gaze when he glanced at the corner table.

What mattered was that Zimra hadn't seen him yet. For a moment, he even tried to persuade himself that he was wrong. She had changed; the color of her hair most of all. Couldn't he have made a mistake? The bar was dimly lit; besides, his constant preoccupation with Zimra was such that any woman who resembled her triggered a spurious thrill of recognition. No, there was no mistake.

She was bound to spot him sooner or later. He simultaneously longed for the moment and dreaded it. Her immediate reaction—that was where the danger lay. She could hardly fail to be startled.

Waiters converged on the party as soon as its members were seated. There was a repeat performance of the welcoming ceremony, this time accompanied by vigorous hand-shakes. The men's brusque voices and guttural Czech introduced a new note into the room. Martin's view was temporarily obscured by the waiters' deferential backs as they bent to take orders, giving him just enough time to reach a decision.

During his preparation, Carow had shown him pictures of Ministry of Security personnel who might be going to Prague, not necessarily to attend the conference itself, but because they would be needed behind the scenes. Although some of the pictures were only out-of-date photographs or faded press clippings, Martin was sure he recognized the party's spokesman as one of Zentner's deputies.

Except for Elsa, no one at their table had so far paid much attention to the newcomers. No one, that is, apart from Němeček, who drew in his horns at once. Not because he knew who they were, Martin surmised, but because someone of Němeček's type could be expected to have an instict for such things, he promptly lowered his voice and stopped flaunting his ten words of French. The others became infected by slow degrees. Something gradually permeated their ranks—some nameless but palpable sense of disquiet instilled by the table in the corner. German was being spoken there now, and the men's voices were loud and unabashed. The alien language hung over the room like a dark and menacing thunderhead in a previously cloudless sky.

Němeček began whispering. Martin saw that he was collecting dollars and deutschmarks to cover the bill. He had no time to lose.

He didn't look at the corner table. Nothing went on inside his head, except that he commanded his body to walk *slowly* to the bar. Walk slowly, speak slowly to the barman, slowly leave the room. She had to catch sight of him. It gave him a sense of mastery, being able to restrain his legs from moving too fast.

The girl in the cloakroom was taking on fresh supplies of cigarettes. She had toured the tables from time to time with

the red tray slung round her neck. She had a flat, round face
which belonged in a flat landscape but looked out of place
here. She smiled at Martin. Her smile was devoid of youth,
a fact for which her age—nineteen at most—provided no
adequate explanation.

"Leaving already?"

Martin asked for some cigarettes, naming a brand at random. He produced one of the ten-dollar bills he'd been
supplied with. "Keep the change."

Her smile became more practiced still. "We don't close
till one. I won't get away till quarter past. Are you staying
here? Better tell me your room number."

He tried to smile back. "The party of five that just came
in—are *they* staying here?"

"Yes." She paused in the act of taking the bill, smiling
no longer. "Which one do you mean, the brunette? You
want me to find out her room number?" She spoke quite
briskly, in the tone of an expert who knows her subject.
"She dyes her hair." She patted her own. "I don't."

Martin listened to the sounds behind him. Zimra needed
time, he thought—she couldn't follow him right away. Perhaps she wouldn't come at all. She wouldn't believe it was a
chance encounter, not here—not after almost six years. Perhaps she was trying, as he had done, to convince herself that
the likeness had been deceptive.

"I'll get her number from the barman."

"No, just a minute." Martin headed for the men's room.
There were some french windows at the end of the passage.
Looking through them at the sun-roof beyond, he could see
the lights of the city winking between stacked patio furniture
and umbrellas. He tried the doors. They opened, admitting a
flood of cold air which made it clear to him that he'd drunk
more than he realized. That thought alone was enough to sober him up.

She wouldn't come. Why should she? A six-year separation versus six months together—six months from which she

must long ago have dissociated herself. It was a preposterous scenario. Only a madman could have dreamed it up.

He closed the french windows behind him and went back to the bar. His companions were on the move. Němeček, whose voice had regained its strength, was at the repetitive stage of inebriation.

"Gabrielle! *Viens ici*, Gabrielle! Come on, *camarade*, let's dance! *Belle* Gabrielle, where are you?"

He started to sing, sing and dance by himself with his arms flung wide; sing, dance and stare at his legs as if surprised at what they were doing to him. That was when Martin saw her. Zimra had taken advantage of the general exodus and was in their midst. Němeček grabbed her, held her tight, tried to involve her in his solo performance.

"Let's dance, *camarade*, let's dance!"

Martin paused, waiting to see what would happen. She had changed. Yes, it was her hair he noticed most of all. It was far shorter than it had been—and, yes, it was dyed raven black. Six years ago—"My father was gray at forty"—her head had already been dusted with silver. He had liked it then, her combination of youthful looks and graying hair, probably for a very superficial reason. It imparted a subtle quality to his strong, simple desire for her body—a protective sense of responsibility toward her.

She had laughingly—laughingly!—detached herself from Němeček and was coming in his direction. The blue dress looked a shade too big for her. She was slimmer than ever. That was another thing he'd forgotten till now: his recurrent surprise at how small she looked, lying naked in his arms, whereas their difference in height seemed to vanish when they walked side by side.

He didn't know what the next move would be. He had prepared himself for this moment, rehearsed the possibilities again and again in his mind, but he still felt unsure of himself. All he could do was command his body to move, very slowly, toward her.

She walked past him, one or two steps, then stopped and turned with a cigarette between her fingers.

"Do you have a light?"

He had expected fear, or possibly that strange, tense smile of long ago. But there was neither fear in her face nor a mute appeal to be left in peace; neither that nor the least encouragement, the vaguest intimation that they shared a common past. She might genuinely have been addressing a stranger.

"Sorry, I don't smoke. Wait . . ." He felt in his pockets, recalling that she hadn't smoked in the old days. At the thought that he was squandering a golden opportunity, his composure returned.

"I have to speak to you." He pulled tomorrow's program from his pocket. He had turned to face her, so his body hid the movement from the group behind him. "It's essential that I see you—vital. Take this."

"Oh, Martin!"

Her face, which had been impassive till now, came to life. There was a searching, almost hostile look in her dark eyes. Just for an instant, he feared he might have spoiled everything by being so brutally direct, but there was no other way. It was pointless to spare her the truth, pretend that his presence was fortuitous, disclaim an ulterior motive.

"Tomorrow. Please! You choose the place."

The four thin bangles on her wrist clicked as she put out her hand to take the sheet of paper. They were the only jewelry she wore apart from some earrings with little round blue stones in them. Once upon a time, when her hair was longer, they wouldn't have been visible. She palmed the program without a word. Her face was as expressionless and dispassionate as before.

"No, so sorry." He patted his pockets and spread his hands to signal that he had no light for her cigarette, then turned away and rejoined the others. They all had their coats on by now. Němeček's long, dove-gray duster resembled something out of a silent movie.

The cloakroom girl handed Martin his coat. "It's Room 305." He squeezed a smile. A stern voice behind him said, "You haven't paid Němeček your share."

It was Elsa, with an affronted expression that suddenly made her look, despite her makeup, like a spinsterish schoolmarm.

He went to Němeček and asked what he owed, but the guide waved him grandly away and resumed his song and dance act, this time on the spot. There was an elevator, but while they were waiting for it Němeček pranced off down the stairs. They trooped after him.

Although he stumbled every few steps, hampered by the folds of his voluminous coat, he spurned all offers of help from his *camarades*. He seemed gratified by something known only to his fuddled self.

=========== CHAPTER XXI ===========

IT WAS TOO EARLY FOR A SIGNAL from Prague. That wouldn't come before midnight—more probably, not till the small hours—but Carow had no intention of turning in so soon. He could stay awake all night with ease, unlike Geissler, who was already asleep in the next room, to judge by the intermittent snores and snatches of gibberish that drifted through the open door. Being accustomed to the Center's ceaseless bustle, Carow found nights at the outstation preferable by far to the long and uneventful days since Martin's departure.

He had naturally acquired a copy of the congress agenda, so it was possible for him, in a sense, to follow Martin's movements throughout each day and evening. Although his knowledge of Prague was limited to the final days of the war, old cities changed little, least of all in the central areas to which Martin was restricted.

Thus, Carow sometimes had the feeling that he was at his agent's side, sharing in his deliberations, weighing his chances—eavesdropping on his innermost thoughts. The knowledge that he could never have done this with Rosell made him glad, after all, to have Martin on the spot.

His occasional misgivings were of two kinds. In the first place, he was condemned to sit there with his hands tied. True, a signal would be arriving from Prague within hours via a W12.6 transmitter in the Czech capital, the 150-foot aerials near the border, and the green telephone on the table in front of him—a direct line to the Organization's monitoring service. Five minutes, Carow reflected—maybe four, maybe six—plus the time required to decode the text. That was fine, but Martin was beyond the range of his advice, beyond his power to warn. Except in an extreme emergency, Carow was debarred from giving his agent a helping hand.

What preyed on his mind still more was that Martin knew nothing of these signals. The question of informing him had never been at issue. No agent, however efficient, was ever given the full picture; the rules of the game forbade it. Radio messages were the extended eyes and ears of the Organization—designed, like a lion tamer's whip, to direct an agent to his place or avert some imminent threat.

Martin would probably never know that he was being watched. He mustn't even learn of it later. Of course, if something big cropped up . . . Alone with his thoughts in the night, Carow hoped that the need to inform him would never arise. Knowing Martin as he did, he felt that the results would be incalculable.

Geissler had started talking in his sleep again. His incoherent snatches of speech were getting on Carow's nerves. Just as he rose to shut the door, the telephone in the showroom rang. It surprised him for a moment until he remembered placing a call to Johannesburg.

The specimens were spotlit. Carow didn't like the showroom by day. To him, there was something disagreeably artificial and unnatural about its array of stones. They reminded him of another shop he'd seen—one that sold aids to the study of anatomy like molded skulls and skeletal hands, transparent plastic hearts and lungs. At night, however, the place made a different impression, as though the darkness from which they had been wrested was all that could restore these rocks and crystals to the beauty of their pristine state.

"You're through to Johannesburg, caller. Go ahead."

"Frau Grapentin, please." He almost said the wrong name.

A pause. "She isn't in her room."

"But she checked in?" Carow had been in touch with the operatives who were monitoring his hospital number. No calls had been received for him. They could have operated on me already, he thought—there might have been complications, for all she knew or cared. The thought gave him a twinge of pain.

"Mrs. Grapentin and Mr. Fehling have both arrived." Another pause. "I've just been told they're out. Did you get that? Would you care to leave a message?"

He hung up without replying. Mrs. Grapentin and Mr. Fehling . . . Fehling was a young professional at the golf club, and Carow hadn't liked the desk clerk's tone. He felt a fool. The Organization was well represented in Johannesburg. His immediate reaction was to put a tail on them. The idea sprang more from habit than from genuine jealousy; of course he wouldn't do any such thing. Yielding to the sense of power conferred by his status in the hierarchy was a constant temptation—a fact that irritated him. You let too many things get you down, he told himself. It was like the sudden flash of a warning beacon.

He could hear Geissler stirring in the back room. He was

out of bed and waiting in his striped pajamas, paunch protruding, hair tousled, face flushed with sleep.

"Any news from Prague?"

Carow shook his head. "Not yet, it's too early."

"Martin's taking his time."

"Go back to bed."

"I'm awake now."

"You talk in your sleep."

Geissler looked dumbfounded. "That's what my wife always says."

"She's right."

"I never believed her."

What are we doing here? Carow thought. Two grown men, married, with grown-up children, spending our nights in the back room of a bogus shop, playing a peculiar game with pieces of our own devising . . .

"He's putting off making contact."

"It was only to be expected." Carow would rather have been alone. He hadn't told Geissler about his signal to Prague that morning, instructing Martin's baby-sitter to speed things up.

"Shall I make us some coffee?"

"There's enough left in the flask."

"I think I'll get dressed."

When Geissler reappeared he poured two mugs of coffee, adding milk to Carow's and a generous slug of brandy to his own. Carow watched him drink with one hand and, to guard against future contingencies, hook the bottle nearer with the other. It reminded him of the morning on the golf course and Geissler's pleas for approval and encouragement. He forgot his own misgivings.

"What's the matter with you?"

"Nothing, except . . . I sometimes think of Cichosz."

"Who's Cichosz?"

"I can still see him lying there."

Carow, who had genuinely forgotten the name, made an

all-embracing gesture. "If outstation work is getting you down, tell me. We'll find you a job at the Center."

"Lord, no—don't get me wrong." Geissler displayed real alarm for the first time. "My nerves are okay. That business on the border—honestly, you've got the wrong end of the stick. It's the other way round. I mean, that morning . . . It was just like old times." He gave an apologetic laugh, but its meaning was ambiguous. Was he asking forgiveness for saying what he had, or for refilling his mug from the bottle?

"When all these exchanges began—their agents for ours . . . When everything turned soft . . . The thaw, *détente*, no clear-cut picture of the enemy . . ." He might have been talking to himself now, rambling in his sleep. "It was easier in the old days. You knew who your enemy was."

The green phone rang. Geissler reacted promptly. He pushed his mug aside, pulled a pad and pencil toward him, and prepared to write. It was Carow who hesitated, reflecting how much he would have preferred to be alone at this moment, take down the text himself—digest the news for a while before it became part of the Center's operational file. He saw Geissler note the time of receipt at the head of the pad.

Carow picked up the receiver and gave his code. He repeated the groups as they came over the line, watching Geissler copy them down in big, easily legible characters. Then he took the cipher key and set to work. In clear, the message read: "Contact established. Further developments unknown."

Neither of them spoke for a moment, like children whose birthday treat has fallen short of expectations.

"Talk about handling her with kid gloves!" Geissler tore the sheet off the pad. He restrained a fleeting impulse to ask who was babysitting Martin in Prague. In view of Carow's silence on the subject, he wasn't sure what response he would get. All he said was, "Shall I pass it on?"

Carow nodded. He stood behind Geissler and looked over his shoulder while he teletyped the reenciphered signal to headquarters. Not being classified as urgent, it would await C's attention till morning.

C would be bound to call him and press for more information, but that was the least of his worries. He felt disappointed, deflated and weary. Largely, of course, because he knew it would be at least twenty-four hours before he could expect another signal.

CHAPTER XXII

1

THE PRAGUE SKY WAS STILL GRAY AND GLOOMY as midday approached. It had turned colder overnight. After a long and tedious morning symposium, the next item on the program was listed as "Purchase of Souvenirs." Národi, the quarter predestined for this communal activity, was closed to buses, so they had to cover the final stage on foot. Martin, who had left his coat behind, felt chilled to the bone. He hadn't realized till now how used he was to Ibiza's Mediterranean climate.

It wasn't Němeček who led the party. Němeček hadn't turned up for breakfast, and his place had been taken by a steel-haired matron of fifty in a thin gray costume. A stand-in or a permanent replacement? She looked so forbidding that no one summoned up the courage to ask her.

She marched ahead of the group in quick time, explained things only when expressly asked to, kept stopping and looking over her shoulder to allow her charges to file past like sheep, and counted heads again and again.

There was, in fact, nothing of sufficient interest to warrant explanation. The stores they passed were state-owned, state-run concerns. Although the windows were filled to overflowing—some with costume jewelry, others with *objets d'art* or gold watches and lighters, others with the inevitable caviare, Russian vodka and Cuban cigars—their contents looked curiously like dummy goods. Every window displayed a multilingual notice stating that foreign currency only would be accepted.

The visitors' goal was the Dùm Evropa, a large-scale pawnshop-cum-salesroom where citizens of Prague—old folk from impoverished middle-class families, Martin guessed—could convert the last of their treasured possessions into cash. This, too, was state-owned. A glance through the day's program suggested that here would be the most likely place, if any, for Zimra to make contact.

"They say you can buy things incredibly cheaply there—real bargains! Honestly, they think of everything, don't they?"

Elsa was walking beside him, visibly at pains to sound bright and cheerful. Last night had been something of an ordeal. Back at the Nltava, she had insisted on having a nightcap in the bar. Somehow, the idea had taken root in her mind that this was her last and only chance to capture Martin. The climax came outside her bedroom door, where she suggested, more or less openly, that her roommate wouldn't mind making herself scarce for an hour or two. She appeared at the breakfast table smiling—claiming total loss of memory. "What on earth happened last night? I'm sure I behaved disgracefully. I shouldn't drink, and that's a fact." But it all sounded forced, and sometimes, when she looked at him as she was looking now, her face took on the offended, spinsterish expression he'd noticed the night before.

The Dùm Evropa was a former mansion which hinted, like the Nltava, at the splendors of a bygone age. Their grim-faced guide waited, counting under her breath, until the last of the party had entered the forecourt, which conjured up images of horse-drawn carriages, flickering lanterns and couples in evening dress. The sconced lanterns were still there, denuded of glass, on either side of the door through which they now trooped into the first of the building's many spacious rooms.

"Funny, isn't it, them showing us all these bourgeois things and places. Anyone'd think that's what they were proudest of."

Elsa had expressed his feelings perfectly. She spoke in the hushed tones of someone visiting a museum. They weren't the only group of teachers or tourists. Bargain-hunters crowded and jostled past the showcases that divided the lofty rooms into aisles. To Martin, most of them looked less like prospective purchasers than the owners of the mementos themselves, keeping watch over their treasures until some foreigner bore them off. An auction was in progress in the room next door.

"Looking for anything in particular?" Elsa paused in front of a showcase filled with an arbitrary collection of useless bric-a-brac: empty scent bottles with silver tops, fragile old fans, embroidered purses, cigarette cases, ornamental combs.

She asked his opinion on something, he replied, and they walked on. Martin's sole concern was to choose the right moment to slip away from Elsa and the rest of the party. It shouldn't be too difficult in such a crowd.

Did Zimra know the Dùm Evropa, he wondered. Even if she did, would she come? He hadn't allowed himself to doubt it—hadn't armed himself against the possibility of hearing no more from her. Instead, all his thoughts since last night had been centered on the moment when he would see her again, face to face, and all his questions culminated in a single question: What entitled him to hope that she would consent to give him what he asked? He felt deprived of control over his own decisions, enmeshed in the cogs of a machine—an ineluctable, irresistible chain of developments.

He paused in front of a shallow display case. Elsa had

wandered on with the rest of the party. Beneath the glass lay a pair of barrettes shaped like two little posies of primroses. The ivory was yellow with age. The price, forty U.S. dollars the pair, seemed horrendous.

"You like them?" His interest had been noted by one of the gray-smocked sales clerks, a man with a broken nose. "Shall I bill them to you?"

Martin hadn't intended to buy the little clasps, although they would have suited Zimra's new hairstyle. He was still wavering when he caught sight of her at the other end of the room.

"The price seems awfully high."

The sales clerk, who had started to write out a bill, stopped short and gave Martin a venomous glare which made his nose look even less attractive.

"You aren't obliged to buy anything unless you wish."

"All right, I'll take them."

Forty of the Organization's dollars would buy him some freedom of movement. They would also buy him some time—time above all. Dozens of customers were queuing in front of the cash desks where payment had to be made and rubber-stamped receipts obtained before purchases could be collected.

Zimra had seen him. She walked toward him while the sales clerk was still explaining, at interminable length, the procedure to be followed.

2

LAST NIGHT, WHEN alarm would have been a natural reaction, Zimra had displayed extreme composure. She now looked far more tense and apprehensive. The shadows beneath her dark eyes hadn't been there before; they made them look even bigger. Once again, though, their expression gave Martin no clue to his chances. All he could read in them was amazement at the reality of his physical presence.

"How long have we got?"

He'd rehearsed the sentence like the opening move in a complicated game. She didn't reply at once, just walked beside him in silence as he headed for one of the farthest cash desks. When she spoke, he realized that her present train of thought had nothing to do with his game—that their conceptions of time were very different.

"Have you bought something?"

He nodded. It seemed absurd to go into details.

"I'd never have thought people would actually buy this stuff." She lingered in front of a showcase. "It's gruesome. They shouldn't exist, places like these. What sort of mind would concoct such an idea?"

The pieces in his game had suddenly adopted unforeseen positions. As though starting out from scratch, he said, "We didn't meet by accident. The fact is, I'm working for them again."

She stared at him. "Can't you give me a little time?"

"We don't have any, not now." He regretted the words before they were out of his mouth. "We could have, later."

"We already did, and it wasn't any use."

"It's about the conference. You know what I mean?"

"Not even a minute or two?"

He hesitated. They were standing at the end of the queue, yards from the cash desk. "You've done something to your hair."

"A friend talked me into it. She said I'd feel a new woman. It was silly—a waste of time and money."

"I liked it better gray."

She smiled for the first time. "But you weren't there anymore, and you were the only one who ever liked it that way."

"I planned to get you out afterward, but you didn't encourage me."

"I know I didn't. Sometimes we don't know what we want. To tell the truth, I was waiting for you to make a move."

She was setting up the board afresh—rearranging the pieces to her own advantage.

"I won't leave you behind this time."

She shook her head. "Don't talk like that—don't start all over again. Past and future . . . They make me go cold inside, those words. They're like frost and snow on a spring flower."

He recalled that she used to write poetry for her own amusement. Although she had never shown him any, she once confided, "Everyone thinks I'm immensely competent, utterly dependable and extremely ambitious. But my ideal—my picture of the life I'd like to lead—is to write a poem every day and love someone."

They had reached the cash desk. He paid and was handed a rubber-stamped counterfoil. He'd been watching the people round them all the time, on the lookout for any face that swam into view too often. Asking her to wait for him, he went off to collect the barrettes. He maintained his watch on the way, but no one aroused his suspicions. When he came back, he took her arm and joined the end of another queue.

He had always found her beautiful, not that her face was so in every detail. It lacked a certain harmony and regularity of feature. Her eyes didn't match and were just too far apart, her nose was too big—too heavy for her slender face—and her mouth too small, yet the general impression was one of beauty.

Why should such thoughts occur to him now, when he had no time for them? He had difficulty in picking up the thread of the dialogue he'd rehearsed the night before, and it was she who spoke first.

"Why did they send you? They don't often send someone back, not after what happened to you."

"It was us—the fact that we knew each other."

"You told them?"

"No, but they found out all the same."

"And the conference? How did they find out about that?"

She was all attention now, her interest centered on the matter in hand.

"From a local agent."

"What do they want?"

"Everything."

"Meaning?"

"What the conference is about, what decisions are taken. There must be an important reason for a get-together at that level." He paused. "How many days is it scheduled to last?"

"One can never tell beforehand. What am I supposed to do?"

Once again, this was nothing remotely like the dialogue he'd envisaged, but he had no time to worry about it. "How will the record be kept, shorthand or tapes?"

"Both, but the tapes are only used for checking discrepancies in the transcripts."

"How many copies?"

"Numbered copies, one for each delegation. They're typed out every night."

"And the tapes are filed?"

"Yes."

"Filed and never consulted again, once the transcripts have been made? Getting hold of the tapes would be safest. Could they be copied?"

The smile on her face might have been painted there. "Whose idea was this? What made them think I'd cooperate? Didn't you tell them it was hopeless—didn't you say I'd chosen my side of the fence forever?"

"Yes, more or less."

"So what have you got up your sleeve, a lever of some kind? Did they tell you they'd been in touch with me?"

"Just a minute. When was this?"

"Well," she persisted, "is that what they plan to blackmail me with, undisclosed contacts with the West?"

His initial reaction was rage and shock at how little they'd trusted him. Then his surprise faded. Viewed objectively, the fact that he'd been kept in the dark could almost be seen—on the contrary—as a mark of confidence. Knowing him as he did, Carow must have warned C off, so the idea of informing him had been ruled out. Carow had faith in him—trusted him to attain his objective without resorting to dirty tricks.

"They never said a word, so there couldn't have been any intention of using it against you."

"So why, Martin? Why should I play?" She tried, without success, to inject some sarcasm into her voice. "What are they offering me?"

"A safe way out. With me."

She seemed to turn this over in her mind. Then she said, "Can't you give me a better reason?"

He had his answer ready. It was one of the questions he knew she'd ask, and he hadn't found a better reply than the one he gave her now. "Do it for your own sake, the way I am."

She scanned her surroundings as if the real answer lay somewhere in the room. "Is that enough? I grew up differently, with different ideals. They may not fit the facts, but they're the only ones I have."

"Do you know my private name for you? 'Little soldier,' that's how I sometimes thought of you when we talked about these things in the old days. All right, little soldier, tell me where we stand. How much have your ideals done for either of us?"

"I see, so your bosses really don't have anything to offer." Again she sought refuge in the sarcasm that suited her so ill. "How about you—what do *you* have to offer? Could you spend a night with me? That would be worth considering, at least."

He felt her arm tremble in his. Her fear transmitted itself to him like an electrical discharge, so abruptly that he swung round, convinced that they had been under observation the whole time. He half expected to see them, two or three anonymous figures, bearing down with calm and unhurried tread. No fuss, no commotion, just the silent nod that would signal them to follow. It was almost a rerun of the sequence on the landing outside Dlubek's door. He saw it quite as vividly, like a slow-motion clip from a film with no sound track.

But no one was taking any notice of them. The big, echoing room was just as it had been—oppressively full of inanimate objects in glass cases and figures waiting patiently in line with slips of paper in their hands. The cash registers clanked and jingled as before. They were old enough to have been sold as antiques themselves.

"Zimra—"

"I've dropped the name. I'm Anna now, like my mother."

"What does your father say to that?"

"He's dead, didn't they tell you?"

Another mystery. If C and Carow knew this all-important fact, which was probable, why hadn't they told him? It not only accounted for her presence here—it changed the whole picture. Whenever Zimra spoke of "my country," Martin had always felt she really meant her father. Why hadn't they let him know?

"When did it happen?"

"The year after you left. So they didn't tell you? He killed himself." Again she looked round as though searching the room for explanations. "God, how I detest this place!" Her eyes met his. "You say memories are what count. The truth is, they count for nothing. Death puts an end to them—I've found that out for myself. I need my father, and he isn't here anymore, that's a good enough reason. Maybe you're right—maybe I shouldn't expect a better one. Very well, I'll try."

Martin felt no thrill of triumph; just a pang of mistrust. A suspicion took root inside him: Was the whole thing a well-laid trap on Zentner's part? Whether knowingly or not, was Zimra acting as bait for the Apparat, as she had at Bernau?

Whatever the truth, his only recourse was to trust her. Besides, a vague promise was all she'd given him so far.

"Can you get at the tapes?"

"Not as easily as the transcripts."

"Tapes would be better." He had no need to tell her why. All secret services were chary of being fed with disinformation, and tapes were easier to check for authenticity. "Concentrate on the policy decisions. Don't take risks for the sake of anything minor."

"What if—"

"No, let me finish. Unless you're absolutely sure, don't touch a thing. Memorize as much of the transcripts as you can. We may be able to reconstruct them later." That wasn't part of his assignment, but he said it just the same.

"If I do get hold of a tape, how do I hand it over?"

He gave her a copy of the congress program. She put it away without looking at it.

"You'd better choose the place again." He paused. "Are you sure you want to do this?"

She smiled her painted-on smile. "For you, yes."

"And for yourself."

She shook her head. "It'll kill something inside me, even if I'm not found out. Treachery is a lethal thing. Perhaps that's my real reason. I don't have my father's strength of character, or I'd follow his example. I wish we had time to talk about it."

He had to steer her away from such ideas. Her weakness might be working in his favor at present, but it wouldn't help when the crucial moment came. Purloining a tape and handing it over would spell danger and fear, and weakness wasn't the answer to those. She would need courage; or, better still, some justification for acting as she did.

"You may be doing the world a favor. Try to look at it that way." Put into words, the argument sounded shallow—unworthy of her. It was useless to pretend to her. In that case, what? A dash of hope? All he said, in the end, was,

"I'll need some passport shots of you. Coin-booth pictures will do. Enclose them with the tapes."

"You mean you still believe in promises, after all your years in the trade? Oh, Martin!"

"When the conference ends, find some excuse for staying on."

She hesitated. "I could invite one of the other secretaries to stay on with me—that would look better. We could arrange to take the midday train back to Berlin on Sunday."

"We'll both be out by then."

"An agent with illusions . . . If we had the time, I think I'd fall in love with you again."

"We'll have the time."

"We already did." All at once, she had left his side—vanished into the crowd before he could stop her.

But he hadn't wanted to stop her in reality. It was better this way. All had gone well, though not as he had planned. It was a different game with a different opening and different moves, but it had ended with the pieces where he wanted them. Who had put him in such a commanding position? For a moment, his suspicions revived. It all seemed far too easy.

He left his place in the queue and went to look for the others. Some of them he found in the room where the auction was being held. They were sitting at the back, uninterested in the proceedings on the platform. Footsore and weary after traipsing round the salesrooms for so long, they were merely taking their ease. One old schoolteacher had removed her shoes and was massaging a pair of swollen ankles.

He joined the little group and remained with it until their guide ran them to earth.

"Come along now!" she said briskly, arms akimbo. "We must get back to the hotel. Everyone is waiting at the main entrance."

The old schoolmarm had difficulty in getting her shoes on again. Martin kept her company until she did. Most of the party had already assembled, but the guide took another half-hour to round up her missing charges. Nearly all of them had bought something. They displayed their packages like evidence of good behavior.

When Elsa sat down beside him in the bus, likewise carrying a parcel tied with string, Martin was glad that he, too, had something to show for their excursion.

CHAPTER XXIII

1

THEIR SEATS WERE SEVEN ROWS BACK and well to one side. The audience seemed comatose. There had been only one round of applause—some half-hearted clapping from the rear of the hall after one of Turandot's arias—and then at a moment so wholly inappropriate that even the cast had been nonplussed. Since then, everyone had sat there twice as stiff and silent.

The congress delegates were being treated to a special performance at the Palace of Culture. Mimeographed synopses of the libretto had been distributed in various languages, but no one had troubled to read them; either that, or no one could raise any interest in the fate of the capricious Chinese princess. Martin had a sudden vision of the Ministry of Culture official responsible for selecting the opera. It might even be the sweating figure in the box on their right, a man with the lugubrious air of one whose hours are numbered.

Elsa was observing developments on stage through a pair of mother-of-pearl opera glasses, her trophy from the state pawnshop. Her hairdo was in process of dissolution, partly because she, at least, was enjoying the show—swaying to the music with an abandon that suggested it was all she could do not to join the cast in song. Elsa was in the best of spirits—back, as it were, in that girlish state of readiness to be bowled over by anything and everything her hosts served up.

She lowered her glasses and offered them to Martin. When he shook his head, she leaned over and hissed in his ear. "They're philistines, the lot of them!" A discreet cough from behind them failed to quell her scathing verdict on their fellow sufferers. "Birdbrains, that's what they are!"

The expression sounded so bizarre, coming from her, that he almost laughed out loud. He wondered where she'd picked it up; from her pupils? He still knew little more about her than that she'd been dismissed or temporarily suspended from her teaching post for belonging to the German Communist Party—something like that.

The second act seemed to drag on forever. Martin found it increasingly hard to concentrate on the stage. His thoughts strayed back to Zimra again and again. Where was she? What was she doing? Had she been in earnest? If so, would she contrive to get hold of the tapes? How would she hand them over? When? He could answer none of these questions.

He had often recalled their conversation, word for word. In retrospect, he felt he'd been absurdly optimistic. All he could do was set himself a time limit and try to refrain from idle conjecture until it expired.

The curtain came down. For a moment, the audience sank still deeper into torpid silence. Elsa was one of the first to clap and one of the last, standing in the side aisle, to keep the applause going.

"Come on," Martin said eventually. "There's bound to be a cold buffet."

The foyer was a huge, draughty hall. The tall windows

overlooked a brightly lit ice rink so crowded with youngsters that the ice itself was invisible.

Voices cleft the air on all sides, loud with relief. The buffet was taken by storm and occupied. Doormen in shabby violet uniforms stood guard beside "No Smoking" signs to which they pointed sternly as soon as anyone lit up. Martin's eye was caught by one in particular, a nondescript man who prowled in his vicinity as though he expected to catch him breaking the rules at any moment.

Martin felt himself turn cold, heard the sounds around him dwindle to a murmur. Was the long wait playing tricks with his imagination? The ageless face was blank. No sign, no movement, just the impassive look of a man employed to keep order, and yet . . . Some sense extraneous to the normal senses—something which, in Martin, resembled a chemical reaction between two body fluids—prompted him to give the man a nod. He strolled over.

"You can only smoke outside."

"Where outside?" Martin's throat felt dry and constricted.

"In the cloakrooms."

"I've forgotten my cigarettes."

"In your coat, perhaps?" The man turned away. His back, in the shabby, baggy uniform jacket, displayed more fear than his face had done.

Martin looked round for Elsa. She returned from the buffet with a laden plate in her hand.

"For you."

He shook his head. "I think I need a breath of air."

"I know what that means," she said reprovingly. "Mind you don't miss the last act."

You're imagining things, Martin told himself as he produced his token and handed it to the cloakroom attendant. "May I have my coat, please?" She laid aside her knitting and went to fetch it, then waited indifferently, chatting to a colleague. He patted the pockets. The feel of the package took his breath away. *It was there; she'd done it.* He with-

drew his hand as if the temptation to take it out might prove
too much for him. He groped in his trouser pocket for a couple of coins. The noise they made before they finally came
to rest on the counter sounded deafening, but the woman
took no notice. He smiled without knowing it. All he felt
was the tension that froze his blood like a chemical agent.

From behind him came the signal for the third act. It as-
saulted his ears like a Klaxon. He started to think more
clearly again. He would have to make a snap decision.
Could he afford to return the coat and leave its contents un-
guarded for another hour? Take the package back to the
hotel? Keep it in his room all night? No, he must get rid of it
as soon as possible.

He pulled the coat toward him and draped it over his arm.
Just as the woman put out her hand to take the coins, a
thought struck him. He retrieved the coins and gave her a
note instead. It was far too much; if the worst happened she
would remember him, but he needed the coins. For an instant, satisfaction was outweighed by his disquiet at this
near lapse of judgment.

2

HE COUNTED HOW many paces he took to cross the square
and reach the illuminated phone booth. A hundred plus four.
One-zero-four. The sum of one-zero-four was five, and five
wasn't a bad number. Martin's favorite numbers were two,
five and eight, in that order. He couldn't have said precisely
why; he just had a feeling that they brought him luck. His
room number at the Nltava was four-two-five, which added
up to eleven, which in turn made two.

He took a final backward glance across the deserted
square. Four dark-clad youngsters were slowly circling a
fountain on mopeds, their feet scuffing the ground. Martin
had noticed them while conducting a routine search for potential shadows.

It was colder in the phone booth than outside. He inserted

the coins, dialed the number, let it ring twice, and hung up
The coins tumbled out. He reinserted them and let the number ring four times before depressing the cradle with his left
hand and repeating the whole performance. This time, however, he waited, counting the rings before the other party
lifted the receiver and replaced it: six, as arranged. Then he
hung up, feeling relieved for the first time.

He left the booth and put his hands in his coat pockets, ex-
ploring the shape of the package and the way it was tied.
He'd still had no chance to look at it, nor did he know whose
number he had dialed. He would far rather have followed
normal procedure and consigned his haul to a dead-letter
box. Agents and their contacts were kept in ignorance of
each other's identity, but Carow—"C wants it soonest"—
had sanctioned this exception to the rule on grounds of urgency.

Martin didn't know how they'd get the tape or tapes out.
Probably by diplomatic bag, which pointed to some Western
embassy official, but Martin wasn't interested in that either.
The ways and means were up to Carow, and Carow knew
his business. "Give him fifteen or twenty minutes," was all
he'd said.

He looked at his watch. Nine-thirty. Being close enough
already to his rendezvous, he decided to make for one of the
livelier streets in the old quarter, buy himself a drink somewhere, and examine the package. The four youths on
mopeds stopped circling the fountain, he noticed, and put-
tered off.

Except when it became necessary to consult a doctor or
call at some government office, childhood visits to Prague
with his mother had nearly all been Christmas shopping ex-
peditions. He could remember a lot of lights, a lot of people,
his mother's constant fear of losing him in the crowd, and a
steady accumulation of parcels.

He loved these trips to the city because his mother denied
him nothing. If he stood in front of a stall where a man was
winding candy floss on sticks, he had only to point and he

got one. The only opposition she raised, if one could call it that, was that every treat was accompanied by a warning against "mentioning it at home." Prague was her secret. She never dared to spoil him back home, with their host of poor relations.

Later, in the train, he invariably felt sick after all the sweet things he'd eaten—sick, tired out and happy. His recollection of these train journeys was especially vivid. He would sleep with his head on his mother's lap and wake, blinking drowsily, whenever the train pulled into one of the numerous stations *en route*. Crowded at first, the compartment gradually emptied until, as they neared the frontier, he and his mother were alone with their stack of parcels.

Tonight there were no lively streets. The city seemed deserted—a ghost town abandoned by its inhabitants. Just as sweet things had tempted him in the old days, so he now felt eager for a drink. The craving surprised him. He had started to drink in the evenings as a means to an end, nothing more. The unwanted slugs of hard liquor had almost made him sick at first, but now he was used to them. They made him feel better, calmer, less uneasy, more confident. He had never needed them before.

Seeing the lights of a small tavern, he crossed the street and went in. The dark, cramped interior was crowded with men and women in working clothes. They stared at him as he made his way to the counter. He didn't know what it was about him—his overcoat collar was turned up, so they couldn't see his dark suit—but they all seemed to know at once that he was a Westerner, as surely as if the word were branded on his forehead. He ordered a schnapps and took a quick swallow as soon as the glass was put in front of him. He paid, drank up, and went outside. The four moped riders had reappeared.

He still had no precise idea of what the package contained. He glanced at his watch again—not the watch he'd bought in Munich, but a Spanish one. His own reposed with the rest of his things in a cardboard box at the back of a bogus shop. It belonged to a sphere of existence that now seemed infinitely remote.

His rendezvous time was drawing near. He turned into the Jáchymova, Prague's Jewish quarter, passing darkened kosher shops that looked as if they never opened, even by day. He met no one. Once he saw a gleam of light through some shutters and heard men's voices singing.

Finding the right synagogue proved unexpectedly difficult. He had memorized the street plan and been shown photos of the building by Carow, but the synagogue he was looking for, the Pinkas, seemed not to exist until he realized that he'd passed it twice already. Nothing in Carow's photographs and layouts had indicated that it was undergoing restoration and was almost obscured by scaffolding. Carbide lamps hung, hissing, over a hole in the ground. There was no sign yet of his contact.

He took the package out of his pocket. It was wrapped in plain brown paper and tied with string. To judge by its bulk, it contained two cassettes, but Martin's interest was confined to the folded envelope tucked beneath the string. He carefully withdrew it and looked inside. The passport photos were there—an uncut block of four. He couldn't see much, just the eyes, which were slightly narrowed in response to the flash. It made her look younger.

So she did want to leave! He should have felt exultant, but he couldn't help remembering what she had said about past and future, frost and snow. Before, the words had sounded high-flown, but here, in these surroundings, they made him shiver.

He restored the package to its original state and pocketed it again. He was heading for the open space in front of the synagogue when he noticed the four youths. One of them was loitering in the background beside the four parked mopeds. The other three were approaching in line abreast. Martin knew at once that it had been a mistake not to lose them.

The trio came closer, moving very slowly, until their

leader halted barely a yard away, grinning, arms hanging loose at his sides.

"Got the time on you?"

He was so relieved that they were only after his watch that he spotted their knives an instant too late, alerted by the click of the blades springing open. Two of them seized his arms and twisted them behind his back. He didn't struggle—in fact, he welcomed the pain in his wrist when they wrenched the metal bracelet off.

He heard a whistle and felt them release him. Pencils of light swept the empty square, which he now saw was full of newly planted saplings. They were headlight beams, but that he didn't realize till the car itself appeared.

The four youths vaulted onto their mopeds and roared off. Martin listened to the dwindling blare of their exhausts. Then silence fell. The car had pulled up and dipped its lights. The windows were closed. Martin felt an urge to laugh but couldn't. Having secured his watch so easily, the youngsters might have searched him and found the package. Later, they would have opened it and tossed the contents down a drain in their disappointment.

The windows of the car remained closed as he approached it. It was an American model with a customs license plate. The driver's window purred open, but only halfway. All he could see of the man was that he was surprisingly young and had sleek black hair. He wore a smart blue shirt with a button-down collar.

"Were you having trouble?"

Martin didn't reply. The man at the wheel remembered his lines.

"Do you happen to know when the old Jewish cemetery opens?"

"Nine to five, except Saturdays."

There was a thin gold band with an inset diamond on the hand that took the package. The window closed with a faint mechanical whine. Martin didn't wait for the car to drive off. He left the square and the ghetto, walking slowly at first, then quicker.

To his surprise, a street clock told him that he still had time for another schnapps. He drank it in the same bar, attracting the same silent scrutiny, and reached the Palace of Culture just as the first members of the audience were hurrying to the cloakrooms to avoid the rush.

He collected Elsa's coat but had to wait for several minutes. She was one of the last to emerge, having presumably led the applause again. Elsa was in fine fettle, cheeks flushed and hair in disarray. She said nothing, just wagged her head when she detected liquor on his breath. In some strange way, he didn't feel it was a genuine reproof. It was more like his mother's confidential warning—a secret Elsa chose to share with him alone.

CHAPTER XXIV

IT HAD BEEN TYPED ON YELLOW PAPER. Three sheaves of it lay stacked on C's desk, and each corresponded to one side of a ninety-minute tape. A fourth would follow as soon as Pauly had transcribed it. The head dragon was audiotyping the sheets herself in an office commandeered for the purpose.

Yellow was *his* paper, reserved within the Organization for his use alone. Likewise red ink. He was noted for the liberal way he annotated every document that passed across his desk. Extra-wide margins were left to accommodate these scarlet effusions. So far, however, the red pen remained untouched. C hadn't so much as added his initials. Just occasionally, Puck saw him remove a sheet from one of the transcripts, read it slowly through, and neatly replace it with a contented nod.

He looked, thought Puck, as he deposited a glass of chilled fruit juice at C's elbow, like an old man browsing through snapshots from the past.

"All set for our council of war?" C glanced up with a smile. They were both aware that he usually shunned such turns of phrase. He pointed to the transcripts. "I can't help thinking of that last powwow with Zentner. The Yellow House, remember?"

There was nothing for Puck to say. Even a nod would have been too much—spoiled the magic of the moment. That was Puck's lot in life, to hold C's album of memories for him and open it at certain places. All at once, quite another thought crystallized in Puck's mind. What if the operation didn't go as C envisaged? What if he had to retire —earlier, perhaps, than he intended? *Then* C would need him!

The idea seemed remote, especially now. Puck recalled his sense of pride and triumph while driving to the airport to meet the courier's plane that morning. C had entrusted him with the pickup. He could still feel the pleasurable pressure of the handcuff that secured the slim attaché case to his wrist—the self-importance it engendered to sit alone in the back of C's limousine. Yet the triumph he felt at this moment was greater and more satisfying by far. Oh, yes, *then* C would need him with a vengeance!

"You remember the Yellow House?"

Again Puck made no reply, this time for fear that his voice might betray some inkling of his thoughts. It really had been a yellow house—chrome yellow stucco—and was one of three such buildings placed at the Organization's disposal by the Americans after the war. That was where C's final confrontation with Zentner had taken place. Puck felt abruptly certain that the sheets he had singled out bore transcripts of Zentner's actual words.

"We've come a long way since then, Puck. Sometimes we've been on top, sometimes he has." C indicated the sheaves of yellow paper. "But this stuff will finish him if we use it right."

He doesn't even trouble to conceal his hatred any longer, thought Puck. It was a fact that had been expunged from the Organization's annals: C and Zentner were ex-colleagues as well as archenemies. More than that, it had long been debatable which of them carried more weight in the Service.

Arguments at the Yellow House had invariably revolved around the same point. Zentner advocated an "independent" Service tailored to "the new Germany of the future"; more realistically, C put his shirt on the Americans. Their power struggle could only end in victory for one or the other, and C had prevailed. He enjoyed the backing of Don Langtree, and Langtree then held the purse strings. The American eagle had, in Zentner's words, taken the Organization under its "24-carat wing." Zentner chose the other side and defected to the "Reds."

Puck sometimes suspected that the fanatical zeal with which C pursued this single enemy might really be the outward manifestation of a deep-seated personal disappointment—that it sprang from a sense of betrayal at the hands of the one man he had ever thought his equal. Puck recalled rumors that C had later tried to lure Zentner back to the West—idle rumors, no doubt, because Zentner's star had already risen in the East.

"I hope those gentlemen in Bonn will appreciate what we're giving them, for once."

Puck returned to the present with a jerk. "We're taking this stuff to Bonn? Today, you mean?"

"Yes, I think so."

"Does your date with Langtree still stand? He keeps calling, says he's got to speak to you before he flies home."

C nodded absently. "You know, Puck, most people have the wrong idea about espionage. They say it paves the way for war; I say it *replaces* it. The art of espionage consists in destroying your enemy on his own ground—bloodlessly. The Reds appreciate that. 'Sow discord and dissension among the citizens of a hostile land, subvert all that is good in the land of your enemy . . .' Know who said that?" C frowned indignantly as Pauly interrupted him by coming in with a transcript of the last forty-five minutes' worth of tape. She put the yellow sheaf beside the three already on his desk.

"They're ready for you."

"Waiting outside, you mean?"

"Yes." Pauly indicated the transcripts. "How many copies do you need, five?"

C shook his head. "Four will do."

"None for Carow?"

"He'll get his later. I don't want any of this material taken off the premises."

"Does he know about it yet?"

C gave another fleeting frown. Then he said, "Better get him for me. You can send in Ziegler and Blumenschein when I'm through."

Watching C combine the four sheaves into one, Puck marveled once more at the satisfaction, if not glee, on his usually impassive face. He also marveled at his own reaction to it. One day they'll take your toy away, said his inner voice; they'll let you play with it for a little while longer, but only a while, and then what? He went off quickly to make some coffee for the meeting, glad of the excuse to leave C alone.

"Heiner? I've got some news for you." It was C's normal voice again, dry and monotonous, running the words together as though trying to depreciate what he had to say. "Good news." He had switched on the speaker so that Puck could listen in, but Carow said nothing. "Don't you want to know what it is?"

"Of course."

"We've done it! Verbatim transcripts of the Prague conference—three whole hours of them."

"You mean *he's* done it."

"A good officer always gives his men the credit, eh? Yes, he's done it. I wasn't so wide of the mark. Amalgamation . . . Anyway, they've met. It's come, Heiner, the day we've been waiting for."

"Our suppositions were correct?"

"A hundred percent. There are dozens of centers of unrest in nearly all the relevant countries. They can hardly control them—that's why they're discussing countermeasures. They hope it'll be possible to quell the trouble without Russian intervention." C paused. "We're already evaluating the details. At least they aren't conjectures anymore. We've got the facts now."

"When did this come in?"

"You've really shown what a good agent with a high-grade source can . . . When? It only reached us this morning."

"Verbatim transcripts . . . Tapes, in other words?"

"Six hours ago, actually."

"They came by the prearranged route?"

"You're asking a lot of questions. Yes, by the overt route."

"So the goods were delivered yesterday?"

"Last night. Nine-fifty, to be precise."

"What about the passport photos, did she enclose them? When is her passport being sent?"

"Today, as arranged, by the same route. If our political masters have a spark of intelligence—"

"You've had these tapes authenticated by the bird fanciers?" Carow meant the voice-print analysts.

"He's your agent, Heiner. Why so skeptical? Yes, we've given them snippets of every voice that occurs. They've examined them from every possible aspect—regional accents, sentence structure, pet phrases. You know the bird fanciers—they say voices are unique, like fingerprints. The tapes are genuine all right." C picked up one of the yellow sheets.

"I've read most of Zentner's dialogue through myself, and there's no mistaking his style."

"Are you meeting? You want me to come?"

"How, Heiner, from a hospital bed? I'd sooner you kept your cover intact. We'll hold our little council of war without you. Then I'll fly the stuff to Bonn. This time they'll have to come down off the fence."

"Before you make any decisions"—the loudspeaker transmitted Carow's uneasiness as clearly as if he were in the room—"don't forget our agent's still on site."

C ignored the implication. "Will he keep his head down? He won't get cocky just because he's pulled it off?"

This time Carow's reply was unhesitating. "No, he'll tend to be lethargic—mentally, I mean. Low rather than high."

"An agent's brand of postcoital depression, eh?"

Coming from the old-maidish C, this was such a wildly outrageous remark that it almost gave Puck gooseflesh. He wondered how Carow would react, but his voice came through a moment later, calm and businesslike.

"For Martin, the next couple of days will be the worst of all."

"Just as long as he doesn't make waves."

"What about Borchers? Any 'waves' to be expected from *that* quarter?"

Again Puck felt a peculiar upsurge of tension. The ever-faithful Carow had given vent to something which, from him, verged on lèse majesté.

"Let us worry about that, Heiner. You look after your man. He's to lie low and do absolutely nothing. Well, I think that wraps it up. I'll call you again, either from Bonn or when I get back."

C had signified that the conversation was at an end. Before he could hang up, however, Carow's voice came through once more, urgent and insistent.

"But please call *before* you make any decisions that af-

fect our agent. We must get them out first, both of them—
agent and source.''

"Ah yes, the source. It's a damned shame, really. When
I think how valuable she could be to us. A damned
shame . . .''

"It's in his contract."

"What's the matter with you? Can't you take a joke anymore? Don't be so tetchy."

"Will I be getting a copy?"

This time C signed off with a crisp "That's all." He
shook his head, more in amusement than annoyance. "Carow always feels duty bound to stick up for his agents. He
thinks I don't care two hoots about them, of course."

There was no sarcasm in his voice. The words sounded
simply like an afterthought—an echo of the conversation
with his deputy—but Puck felt the same prickle of apprehen-
sion as before. He wondered what it stemmed from, apart
from the subtle change in his own feelings toward C.

C's face was inscrutable. He sat there straightening the
things on his desk—ink, fountain pen, papers—with a
wholly abstracted expression.

The other two, Ziegler and Blumenschein, would come
in. They would hold their four-man "council of war," but it
would be merely a gesture on C's part—merely the operation of a preprogrammed machine. Whatever was said in
conference, the crucial decisions had long ago been die-cast
in C's head.

"All right, let's get started." His hand—an old man's
hand—reached for the switch that changed the light above
his door from red to green.

CHAPTER XXV

THE DEMONSTRATORS WERE FILING DOWN THE broad Vitěz-ného Února, with its state-owned stores and high-rise office blocks. Far ahead, looming above the crowd, Martin made out the bulky silhouette of a large church or cathedral. They could scarcely be heading for that, but no one seemed to know what else their destination could be. The banners afforded no clue. The slogans they bore were generalized and multipurpose enough to suggest that they had been used on previous occasions.

The marchers' progress was anything but orderly and uninterrupted. Sudden stoppages compressed them into dense knots of humanity which dissolved, just as suddenly, into strings of scattered figures sprinting to catch up. Sometimes their advance was barred by military vehicles or redirected by policemen.

There was nothing festive about the demonstration. Martin found it completely devoid of zest and enthusiasm. Despite the numerous red-and-white banners dutifully held on high, and despite the intermittent chanting of slogans, the whole affair reminded him of a small-town carnival procession without the usual gaiety. It couldn't have been the weather's fault. The autumn day was gloriously sunny.

Martin would have confirmed Carow's diagnosis of his condition: he was feeling tired and depressed. They had been tramping the streets for nearly two hours, and this was the time of day when he customarily paid his first visit to a bar. But it wasn't fatigue alone that sapped his spirits. Other things were preying on his mind. What of the tapes and passport photos? What of Zimra herself?

The demonstration hadn't figured in their program, perhaps because it was meant to seem spontaneous. The idea had been broached by the last speaker to address the afternoon session: why not show gratitude by supporting their Czech hosts' campaign for peace and non-intervention? Motion proposed, seconded, and carried unanimously. Spontaneous it may have been, but television cameras had already been set up in the square outside the Academy, and the banners had appeared from nowhere . . .

"We're really having to earn our keep today!" Elsa, who had latched onto him again, did not intend this in any critical sense. She appeared to be enjoying herself as usual. "Do you think they'll show us on TV tonight? How exciting!" She smiled and waved at a camera mounted on the edge of a public fountain. The crowd had started chanting again, and she joined in with a will: "Friendship yes—intervention no!"

Němeček was there too, marching in the row ahead of them with his dustcoat over his arm, sweating profusely. He had reappeared as he had vanished—without a word of explanation—and taken charge of them once more. His pallid face and red-rimmed eyes suggested that he hadn't slept much in the interim.

The column shuffled to a halt. Martin saw that they were back in the square they'd started out from. The concrete slab known as the Academy of Pedagogic Sciences, a modern cultural supermarket, was painted yellow ocher, but the light of the setting sun made it look like a dirty rectangular orange.

The chanting ceased, the banners drooped. Everyone wavered, unconvinced that the demonstration was really over. Splinter groups broke off and stood clustered together, just as they did between lectures or in the lobby of the Nltava.

Assorted clouds of conversation hovered above each group, almost like national flags. There were the noisy, harsh-sounding German and Dutch contingents; the loquacious but stand-offish French; the ebullient Italians, who'd brandished more banners than they had delegates; and the serried ranks of cheerful Scandinavians whose hip flasks of schnapps kept them well-prepared for all eventualities.

Some of the groups seemed depleted by fatigue. Martin wondered if he wouldn't have done better to take advantage of the demonstration and sneak away for a couple of hours, but what could he have achieved? It was Carow's business, not his, to see that Zimra's passport turned up in time. All he could do was wait for Sunday morning and his rendezvous at the main-line station.

The delay entailed a process of adjustment to the knowledge that he could do nothing positive and was condemned to inactivity. Had it been like that in the old days? After so many years of abstinence, perhaps he cherished false or glamorized recollections of his time as an agent. In retrospect, there seemed to have been far more action and suspense. Was his memory of those days at fault, he wondered, or was it that the *drug* itself had ceased to act on him? Had his self-prescribed cold-turkey cure been too drastic, too permanent?

The groups had fallen silent now. They stood around the square, patiently awaiting further instructions. There was no sign of the buses that were supposed to take them back to their various hotels. An administrative blunder, or was their non-appearance intended as proof positive that the demonstration had been genuinely spontaneous?

Němeček was careful to keep his party together. He had no great difficulty in doing so because they were too tired to stray far. Martin suddenly remembered that he still owed the guide some money—the drinks money he'd so loftily declined.

"Here," he said, "I'd like to pay my share of our night out."

Němeček fiddled with his shirt cuff, frayed cream-silk with a crimson stripe. "Well . . . Please don't think me grasping, but Prague isn't cheap."

Martin handed him a fifty-mark note. He wondered what Němeček did with all the cash he must earn on the side. He had a room at the Nltava; free meals too, presumably.

"You must have a fortune salted away."

The man smiled his waxen smile. "Don't you believe it. The money just goes . . . ."

There was something of the gambler about him. Not what Martin would have called a "hard" gambler in the big casino class, but the kind that haunted race tracks and betting shops. On closer inspection, his face betrayed none of the attributes of the genuine gambler, none of the drive and recklessness, the implicit faith in his ability to defy the laws of chance. All that was imprinted on the aging guide's features was the sad realization that happiness didn't grow on trees, coupled with the resentment of a man resigned to paying for it.

"Women?" hazarded Martin.

"Only one."

They had drifted away from the rest and were standing a little to one side.

"You'll laugh at me if I tell you, it's such a hackneyed story—so ridiculous. An old man clinging to a young woman, keeping her sweet with money. Money for an apartment, a car, furs in winter and bikinis in summer—any idea what a 'Western' bikini costs in this place?—and all the time he knows it'll only last while the money holds out."

Could he really make so much on the side, just from minor currency deals? Martin found it hard to believe.

"I apologize," Němeček went on. "I shouldn't have started on the subject, but there's no one I can talk to these days, not about Movina. 'Zlatá' Movina, my friends call her—Golden Movina. They think I'm a fool—they say I should drop her."

"Maybe you should."

"I'd better see about our bus." Němeček enjoined the others to stick together and stay exactly where they were. He pulled on his long dustcoat as he scurried off.

Elsa sidled up. She stared at Němeček's departing figure. "What did he want?" When Martin didn't answer, she perched on the plinth of a concrete statue. He sat down beside her. Now that the sun had set, the air struck chill. She edged closer, hugging her knees.

"Did he get into trouble?"

"I reckon so."

"Changing money the way he does—it isn't really allowed, is it?"

Martin was still speculating on the main source of Němeček's income. "Maybe he spies on us."

"You can't be serious! What on earth could he find to report?"

"Little remarks he overhears, little things he finds out—nothing earthshaking. From our hosts' point of view, gathering information about us may be the purpose of this whole congress, who knows?"

"You surprise me sometimes, Martin."

"Think of the way they keep the hotel bar open after hours—think of those late-night fraternization sessions when everyone lets their hair down."

"But what would they get out of it?"

"One day, not next week but some time in the future, a man may come knocking at your door, Elsa—a friendly, engaging sort of man. You may not remember him, but he'll remind you of a good night out you had in Prague. *His* memory is excellent—he remembers every word you uttered. Maybe he'll ask you to do him a little favor, just for old time's sake—I don't know what, maybe get him a copy of some syllabus or other. Something innocuous at first, anyway."

"You mean they're prospecting for spies?"

"That's the way it's done."

She gave a sudden laugh. "They'd never pick on me, that's for sure."

Her laughter sounded genuine, her surprise unfeigned. She simply found it amusing that he should have associated her with such a possibility.

"Where do you live, Elsa?"

"You know where Cologne is? A small town nearby."

"Tell me about it."

"There's nothing important there, just coal mines. Lignite—the soft brown stuff." She sighed. "Nothing but coal mines. Where I come from, they say the Bible starts a different way: 'In the beginning was lignite . . .' "

"What about your family?"

"We've been there for generations. All teachers."

Martin could sustain a conversation without mental involvement. The spoken words were only camouflage for what really preoccupied him. The tape had presumably left the country. He wouldn't know their value until he saw Carow again—or unless he was asked for more, but that he thought unlikely. The mission was over, to all intents and purposes, and there lay the source of his nervous irritation.

What a discrepancy between his original brief and the way it had actually gone! His preliminary contact with Zimra: pure coincidence. Their meeting at the Dùm Evropa: a complete reversal of the way he'd planned it. The tapes in his overcoat pocket—yet another variation which he himself had not devised. The one thing that had threatened the mission was an almost laughable incident: four young thugs with designs on his wristwatch. It had all been too easy, he reflected, but simultaneously called himself to order. He knew from experience that things could go off smoothly when one least expected it. Why see dangers where there were none?

"I tried to get away, one time. Away from the coal mines, away from the classroom. It was the only chance in sight. When you're a woman, what other chance is there?"

Just for a moment, Martin was distracted by the surprising fact that Elsa had been married—at least, he thought that was what she'd said.

Why did it linger, his sense of foreboding—above all, of guilt for having been the cause of Zimra's involvement? What if she'd already been arrested? There was no cold abstraction about the thought. Martin knew only too well what it meant: dazzling lights, insistent voices, questions that sped from the glare and transfixed you like flaming arrows . . .

Guilt? Martin thought he knew his vulnerable points—a hint of arrogance, the fascination danger held for him—and had done his best to shield them when preparing for the assignment. A sense of guilt? That was the last thing he'd allowed for, yet he had to concede its presence; his thoughts were merely symptoms of guilt. But just as the demonstration had been intended to convey faith and strength, then petered out and come to nothing, so this idea, too, lacked strength and conviction.

"In the end I sold the ring he'd given me—for less than it was worth, naturally. Still, it did fetch the price of an air fare home, and the school gave me my job back."

He had missed another slice of Elsa's life story. Her expression, as she looked at him, epitomized all the weary disenchantment of a woman condemned to live in a world where the laws of love were tabled and enacted by men—a woman, moreover, who'd given up trying to amend them.

Martin was weak-minded enough to put his arm round her. She shivered. It might have been the cold. It might equally have been that she knew how little the gesture meant but was thankful for small mercies.

The delegates stood forlornly in the broad asphalt square, filling it no longer. It was quite dark by now. The street lamps came on, flaring up in turn like matches in a box. Applause broke out as the buses' headlights rounded the Palace of Culture.

Martin and Elsa rose. The applause gained strength when the first bus entered the square. The driver tooted back. He hammered the button with the heel of his palm, beaming all over his face. And then, abruptly and without warning, a figure materialized behind him and laid a hand on his shoulder.

Martin, who was watching, heard the horn fade out on a discordant wail, saw the smile die on the driver's face, saw him turn to stone in his seat, saw him shrivel and retract his head—all from one moment to the next, because he'd felt a hand on his shoulder. And Martin, who had seen the whole thing, felt just as instantly liberated from all that afflicts an agent after the event: fatigue, pangs of conscience and the temptation to indulge in sinister fancies.

CHAPTER XXVI

1

THE THREE CARS, NOT THE USUAL BONN Mercedes limousines but a trio of dark-blue BMWs, left the parking lot as soon as they received the signal and drove slowly up to the floodlit Chancellery. Only Puck got out when they halted beneath the projecting canopy.

Looking through the lofty glass doors, he saw C coming down the steps. He was escorted by a liveried attendant and was carrying his own black briefcase. The two sentries flanking the entrance prepared to salute. Their white gloves momentarily distracted Puck's attention; they looked too big for the hands inside, as though the rifles would slip through them when their owners saluted.

C was outside now. He seemed uncertain whether to acknowledge the sentries' salute. Then he surprised Puck by doing something he hadn't done for a long time: he reached into his breast pocket and produced a pair of dark glasses. They were big and old-fashioned, with circular lenses that looked jet-black and concealed far more than his eyes. Puck hadn't realized that this stage prop still existed.

"What is it? What's holding us up?"

Puck opened the door of the second car. C handed him his briefcase and got in. Puck got in beside him. The lead car drove off at once, silently leaving the lights of the Chancellery behind. As they purred through the densely wooded grounds, Puck wondered if C could see anything at all through his glasses.

Once out of the gate, the convoy threaded its way into the stream of traffic crawling along the broad avenue. It was still very heavy.

"Can't we go any faster?"

Puck said nothing. C knew full well that their speed was governed by traffic flow and traffic lights, and that the three vehicles had to stay in convoy for security reasons.

C leaned forward and peered out of the window. "Where are we going?"

"Don Langtree, don't you remember? He's expecting you."

"Tell the driver to turn the heating on."

"It's on already."

C settled back again. Puck waited for him to say something, but he didn't. He could usually be relied on to make a few sarcastic remarks when he emerged from the Chancellery. They seemed to clear the air, and he was always in the best of spirits by the time he boarded the helicopter. Tonight was different. When he still said nothing, Puck's thoughts returned to the dark glasses which C persisted in wearing, even inside the car.

He strove to recall when C had worn them last. Ten years ago? No, much longer. They dated from the post-war years when reaching into his breast pocket had become a reflex action. He donned them as soon as he left his desk and ventured into the outside world, ever fearful that someone might get close enough to photograph him. The whole notion had been absurd, even then, because the big black lenses were more of a trademark than a disguise, like Garbo's hat. "C's Garbo goggles"—that, in fact, was what they'd been christened inside the Organization. Surely he wasn't going to start all that again, not at the end of his career?

The end . . . Yes, that probably accounted for his change of mood—it was almost like a physical emanation. Puck's thoughts strayed still farther. The house they lived in—would C have to leave it when he retired? Puck felt at home there, especially now that C's wife was dead and they had it to themselves. He must urge C to pull some strings while he still had the power to. C was a child in these matters, but he'd see to it. He must broach the subject. Not now, of course, but later—at home.

They had reached Bad Godesberg. C never used Cologne's Wahn Airport. His helicopter waited for him on a private airstrip belonging to a machine-tool manufacturer. C had a lot of industrialist friends who were happy to oblige him in all kinds of ways. He'd soon see what his so-called friends were worth when he hauled down the flag, thought Puck, but still . . . If only C could retain his personal archive—if only his reputation and the legends that surrounded him could be kept alive after his retirement—nobody would know how much power he still wielded. He badly needed advice, and Puck was determined to provide it.

The cars pulled up in a narrow street bordered by private houses with art-nouveau windows and gratuitous turrets and oriels. In another city they would have been a drug on the market, but here, where so many people earned their bread in the West German capital, they sold at a premium. One of them had been whitewashed and converted into a restaurant. The White Peacock was "in" because it was run by the wife of a former cabinet minister.

The drivers left their cars and stationed themselves round

the entrance. C was still wearing his dark glasses. It disturbed Puck not to be able to see his eyes.

"Your glasses."

"What about them?"

"Nothing."

The thin lips twitched, perhaps in a smile—Puck wasn't sure.

"You mean they'll know who I am anyway?" C removed the glasses. Involuntarily, he screwed up his eyes in the glare from the light above the door.

The grimace had not been a smile. C's face was as humorless and impassive as ever. For a moment, as the cold blue eyes met his, Puck suspected that C had read his thoughts.

2

DONALD LANGTREE WAS a tall, thickset man who made C look frail by comparison. His name, allied with his bulk and prodigious capacity for hard liquor, had inspired the Russians to nickname him "Drink-Tree." That was in Moscow, where Langtree had spent some years as U. S. Ambassador. As soon as the concept of *détente* appeared on the horizon, he was recalled.

Langtree, who was waiting for C at a corner table, had already demolished several of his beloved highballs. He drank them long, with plenty of water. C had always hated scotch—the very smell made him queasy—and he didn't chance his ways tonight. He drank iced water while Langtree stuck to whiskey, even during the meal.

Neither of them ate much, and most of what they ordered went back untouched. The one thing Langtree would really have fancied—a big, well-marbled steak—was beneath the dignity of the house.

They began by touching on the sort of subjects that might have been discussed by any two friends who hadn't met for a while. Langtree started off in English but soon switched to German. C was a poor linguist, though he could still hold his own in Russian and read it tolerably well. The present that had given him most pleasure on his sixty-fifth birthday—Puck's personal choice—was a Russian language course.

"You're looking really fit—not a day older, I mean. Thanks for sparing the time. I know you never stay in Bonn a minute longer than you have to."

"What brings you here?"

"This and that." Langtree frowned at the bottom of his glass. "I don't know why they always land me with the dirty jobs."

"I suppose your government wants some money out of us, and you've been sent to put the screws on. You always were an expert at that."

"But it's no fun anymore—I'm getting too old." Langtree inserted a lengthy pause, rotating the tumbler between his palms. "My bank fired me on my sixtieth birthday, did you know?"

"I thought you owned it."

"Sure, but youth wants its turn at the helm. That's the States for you."

"And the banking business," said C. "It must be one of the toughest trades ever—lots of stress."

"Times are changing. You can make a fast buck out of projects that would have ruined you in the old days. Wholesale change, that's the modern credo." He looked up. "Ever think of retiring yourself?"

Both of them knew that the preliminaries were over; they were nearing the battle zone. C said, "I think about it all the time, if you want to know. It's just that the right moment never seems to come along. Any special reason for bringing it up?"

"Only that some of your friends and mine are getting itchy. There's a rumor you're contemplating retirement very soon, and they'd like to know when. Preferably from you, not East Berlin."

"Come on, Don, don't beat about the bush."

Langtree tilted his glass and drained it. For some strange reason, the more he drank the redder his hair looked. "Why in damnation do they always have to pick on me!"

"What is it, Don?"

"They want you to go. Now."

"They?" C took the glasses from his breast pocket. He laid them on the table, midway between them on the white cloth, much as if they were discussing the merits of a valuable antique: two experts preparing to negotiate a price.

"You've been in harness longer than any secret service chief I know. You've already extended your term of service twice beyond retirement age."

"They?" C insisted.

"You know how it is. Nobody wants his name mentioned, but it's straight from the top, and I mean Washington as well as Bonn. Don't pretend you're surprised. Times change and so does official policy, but you go on playing your war games—your Cold War games. You're living in the wrong age."

"The Russians haven't changed their policy."

"That's not the question. You know what happened to me—one little frown from the Kremlin and it was good-bye Moscow. Naturally, they couldn't treat you like that. You carry more clout."

"Why did they choose you?"

"Because we're old friends, and they want this business settled amicably. Because they're prepared to negotiate, I guess. Retire voluntarily while they're still scared of you, that's my advice, and my advice has never been bad."

"Listen, Don. If the Reds were heading for a crisis as grave as Berlin in sixty-one or Prague in sixty-eight, and your friends were informed in advance—I mean *accurately* informed in every detail—what would that be worth to them?"

Puck could hear nothing of the conversation from his table. Not only did he have a job to do—keeping watch on all that happened in C's vicinity—but he was enjoying his meal. It would be he, not C, who settled the bill afterward. That was another little chore he enjoyed, and he was always generous with tips—a pleasure only slightly vitiated by the knowledge that his generosity would later be rebuked by Accounts. C, he noticed, had been leaning across the table for quite some time now, talking with earnest insistence. He tried to analyze the look on Langtree's face. Was it really admiration?

C had concluded his report. Although it was almost a repeat of his presentation to the Chancellor, he felt he'd put it over far more effectively, if only because Langtree had heard him out with greater attention.

"So there it is, Don. You really think it's the moment to retire?"

"I assume these are facts you've been giving me?"

"I wouldn't have told you if they weren't. We have the transcripts of that conference—verbatim transcripts. We have a source as close to the top as you could wish for."

"Who else knows of this so far?"

C shifted the glasses an inch or two. "I'm offering it to your friends—exclusively. The full facts. Transcripts and originals. And perhaps . . ." C did not complete the sentence, as though leaving a door ajar.

Silence fell. Both were cool, dispassionate men who eschewed emotion at moments of crisis, and both realized that they were picking their way through a minefield.

"You're really sticking your neck out," Langtree said eventually. "This is dangerous territory. I'm not sure my friends would follow your lead."

"You could talk to them."

"Didn't the Chancellor buy it?"

C looked half-inclined to put his glasses on. "On the contrary, but he tied my hands. No further action on our part. That means he can wash his own hands of our operation any time he likes." He paused. "No mention of retirement, incidentally."

"What did you have in mind?"

"The situation in the Bloc is grave. Discontent, unrest, strikes. Our idea was to—well, fan the flames, if you like."

"Agents provocateurs?"

"If it came to an explosion, Don, and the West were prepared to—"

"That's politics, not espionage. You Germans make hopeless spies. Your whole proposal's out of the question."

"We'd only be beating them at their own game."

"When everyone's sold on *détente* and coexistence?"

"But Don, I *know* the Russians. Their ideology precludes coexistence. They never lose sight of their ultimate goal—never neglect a chance to take the offensive. What's happening here in Europe is only a rehearsal for their final confrontation with the States."

"You're exaggerating."

" 'Embrace and undermine'—that's what Lenin taught them."

Langtree chuckled. "Why not retire and write a book about it?"

C's hands were toying with the glasses. "So it's no deal?" His voice was dry and expressionless.

"Too hot to handle."

"What about the source I mentioned? A high-grade source, Don—a *dream* of a source for any service. I'm offering it to your friends for exploitation."

"I can pass the word, but that's all. You've done a lot for us. You presented us with the Organization on a plate when we really needed it. A few people still remember that, like me, but they're a dying breed. Why don't we come to terms right now?"

"On what?"

"Your house, for a start. I seem to think it belongs to us, correct?"

"It's bigger than I need."

"Still, you've got to admit it wouldn't make a bad retirement home. Secondly, my friends would pay you an additional pension. Even if you don't need the money for yourself, you'll probably want to keep Puck on, and you'll have to pay a secretary. I imagine you'll want to remain active, like me. Your advice would still be in demand. You could write your memoirs and give lectures.''

C looked wry. ''You've certainly done your homework.''

''Then there's your personal archive. It's debatable who it belongs to, but in this case you could keep it. They'd give you an office at the Center for a transitional period—a year, let's say—so you could come and go as you pleased. Oh yes, and there's one more thing: you could pick your own successor.''

''Meaning what?''

''Meaning I've a suspicion Bonn's toying with the idea of appointing an outsider.''

''A non-professional?''

''An administrator—a politician.''

''They'd destroy the Service.''

''Maybe they take a different view—maybe they don't want any one individual to have so much power from here on in. Well, now you know. That's the deal.''

''Why offer me any kind of deal? If my contract isn't renewed, I'll be out on my neck in seven months' time.''

''Now you're being disingenuous. They want everything to go off smoothly. This changeover affects the whole range of friendly services. No one wants any grit in the Organization's works.'' Langtree sat back. ''Puck's making signs.''

''We have to leave at eleven.''

''What shall I tell my friends?''

''I need time. It's too important a decision to rush, not purely from my own point of view. If I were the sole consideration . . .''

There were aspects of C's character which Langtree had never understood—or had he merely shut his eyes to them because he disliked what he saw? There was a hatred in C successfully disguised as love, a host of prejudices masquerading as ideals. C's legend consisted in the very fact of his having persuaded everyone that here was a man whose energies were wholly devoted to the service of a cause, a crusade against lurking evil. Not for the first time, Langtree sensed that this burning hatred was of a different order, and that anyone who troubled to examine it under a microscope, like a tissue culture, would discover it to be quite another disease.

But what was the point? He and C were allies—they were on the same side. Anyway, weren't such sinister speculations an overestimate of the elderly man who had now picked up his glasses and was replacing them in his breast pocket?

"Don't keep me waiting too long for an answer."

"I'll think about it. Can we drop you somewhere?"

"I'll take a cab. I'd hate you to know where I'm spending the night. It's never bothered you, has it?"

"What?"

"The futile vanity of old age." Langtree gave another chuckle. "The illusion of sin—the idea that, as long as you can sin, you're still alive and kicking. My wife has a simpler name for it—she calls it 'Don's third wind.' She knows it's only a breeze, but she lives in constant dread of being phoned by some madame and informed that her poor old Don has breathed his last in the arms of some trollop." He seemed about to add something. Then he noticed C's stony expression and remembered what a prude he was.

"So long, then, my old monk. Include me in your prayers."

Watching C as he left the restaurant with Puck limping along in his wake, Langtree reflected that he really did look like a monk; an abbot escorted by a friar, withdrawing to his cell for the night to pray for all the sinners in the world—especially aging men with lecherous inclinations . . .

Outside, the convoy got under way again. Puck waited, but C delivered no postmortem on his conversation with the American.

The route to the airstrip took them past the Soviet Embassy. By day the gates were permanently besieged by groups of silent demonstrators under police supervision. Now, as they drove past, only two were still there, an oldish woman and a man in his late twenties. They had secured their placard to a little handcart for ease of transportation. The wording, which was visible in the light of some lanterns mounted on the cart, said simply: WHERE IS OUR HUSBAND AND FATHER, PETER SABROCK?

Here, too, C could generally be relied on to make a few apt remarks. Like Puck, he stared out of the window as the couple and the sentries swam past in the glare of the headlights, but his thoughts were elsewhere.

"It's ages since I visited an outstation. Call Carow—warn him to expect us."

"Tonight?"

"Yes, I'm in the mood."

Puck reached for the car phone to call the outstation. He had a sudden feeling that the old man beside him was far from finished yet.

CHAPTER XXVII

IT WAS JUST AFTER ELEVEN, PRAGUE TIME, when Martin left the elevator on the top floor of the Hotel Tehran. He had expected to find the same girl in the cloakroom, but her place had been taken by someone else.

Having counted on the other girl, he was momentarily assailed by a suspicion that all wasn't well. Then he dismissed it from his mind. He was "over there"—and that was the sole reason for his recurrent misgivings. Westerners forgot that their own side, too, engaged in propaganda. Most peo-

ple in Eastern Europe regarded their existence as natural and
normal. The other girl was off duty; there was no more to it
than that.

"Anything I can do for you?"

She had a sly, conceited smile and nothing to offset it.
Music was issuing from the so-called nightclub: the same
"Czech jazz," the same vocalist wrestling with an English
lyric.

"Really not?"

"Really not."

He went inside. The East Germans' corner table was unoccupied. The band was playing to an empty dance floor.
The barman sat alone behind his counter, watching a foot-
ball match on a miniature television set.

Martin ordered a cuba libre. He hadn't drunk a thing all
evening and had no wish to now. He was in a strange mood.
He couldn't explain it to himself, but he felt good, almost
high. It had to be connected with his decision to take the initiative.

"Care to join me?"

"Thanks." The barman's smile hadn't improved much.
Perhaps it was dollars and deutschmarks that played such
havoc with the local smiles.

On the silent television set, the Bohemians were battling
against tough opposition. The lobby of the Nltava, which
had a set in one corner, had been thronged with spectators,
not excluding loiterers among the hotel staff. On leaving the
hotel, he'd found the streets deserted. Every uncurtained
window disclosed a darkened room lit by a flickering violet
rectangle whose convulsions reminded Martin of a crude
magic lantern his mother had bought him in Prague.

"Anything wrong with your drink?"

Martin was feeling averse to alcohol in any form. He
nodded at the corner table. "Nobody here tonight?"

"They checked out." The barman took a closer look at
him. "Have you been here before? Wait a minute . . . with
Němeček, wasn't it?"

"Does he bring you a lot of trade?"

"Prague isn't cheap."

They were the same words Němeček had used. Martin produced one of the Organization's ten-dollar bills and laid it flat on the counter. All the barman resented was not being able to pocket it discreetly.

"How do I earn it?"

"Call Room 305. Ask the lady if she'd join me for a drink." Martin gave him her name—Anna, not Zimra. "Say I'm an old friend."

The barman took the bill and retired to the end of the counter. When he came back, he said, "There's nothing to beat the good old-fashioned approach. She'll be right up." He leaned over, though no one could have heard him, and whispered, "Like some champagne? The real thing, not Georgian!"

"Why not?" said Martin. It was his strange new mood talking. He'd spent hardly any of the Organization's cash so far. The whole assignment had cost next to nothing— incidental expenses only.

He left the bar and went to choose a table. He suddenly thought of the real Martin, the schoolteacher. Had they paid him? Not much, if anything, or maybe they'd unearthed something about him—enough to throw a scare into him. There was some kind of skeleton in everyone's cupboard, and they never balked at rattling the bones. He looked round the room and thought: Freedom and coercion—they talk of them as though they're fixed coordinates.

When Zimra walked in, he rose and went to meet her. The four-piece band bowed low as they had three nights ago, but their salutation didn't include Martin and they kept on playing. Martin liked the Tehran Club less than ever; the pseudo-chic décor, the imitative music, the little more authentic-looking members of Prague's Communist upper crust, sitting brooding over their drinks.

She was wearing the same dress. He'd never seen her use makeup in the old days, but tonight she'd given herself the full treatment: lipstick, rouge—even mascara. Whatever the intended effect, the combination of heavy makeup and jet-black hair made her look like a youthful Indian squaw on the warpath.

"What are you smiling at?" she asked as she sat down.

"Your makeup."

"I see. I felt I needed it." She glanced round. "Isn't it a little risky, meeting here?"

"No more so than anywhere else." A waiter came and filled their glasses. "Let's not look too serious, that's all. Is the conference over? Smile occasionally."

"I'll try. What about the tapes? You passed them on?"

"Yes, no problems. Is it over?"

"Everyone left for home after a short session this morning." She hesitated. "There's something I have to tell you."

"You had trouble staying on?"

"That too."

"You told them you wanted a weekend's sightseeing?"

She shook her head. "That wouldn't have been a good enough reason. The doctor wouldn't let me travel."

"What—"

"I had it when we met at the Dùm Evropa, that's how I managed to get away. A grumbling appendix. It flared up again this morning—the pain was quite bad. No, don't worry, I'll have to have it out sometime. I'm a bit wobbly at the moment, but that's all. The doctor says, if it's no worse tomorrow, I can leave here on Sunday."

He took her hand and held it a while. "Are you fit enough to dance?" She nodded. He rose and led her to the floor. They were the only couple. "So you made your decision?"

"Please, Martin, don't expect too much. It wasn't a real decision . . . or maybe the decision was made when I took the tapes, I don't know. I just feel tired—wrung out. *They know*, Martin! They know the Organization has an agent here."

He smiled. It was fear he felt, not alarm. Fear was a normal sensation; it went with the assignment. It meant no more than the pain of an inflamed appendix, the symptom of an incipient disease. Alarm was something else. Alarm was fear without prior warning of any kind.

"Impossible, I'd have noticed." Martin surveyed the room over her shoulder. "We wouldn't be here now, unobserved."

"I'm not saying they know about you, only that they've known all the time your people planned to send an agent here. It came up this morning, just before the meeting ended."

"No name, of course?"

"Just the agent's code number: A7Z115. Can that be right? What's the matter?"

This time alarm gripped him. He suddenly couldn't dance anymore. "Let's go back to the table." *His* old agent's number! The number itself wouldn't help them—he clung to that hope—but how could anyone have unearthed it from the files?

"Does it mean anything to you?"

"It means they've got someone inside the Organization."

She nodded, and for a moment Martin thought he detected a hint of pride in her expression. "I don't know his name, but he's planted at the Center. He sent a report last week, before the conference opened."

It was serious this time. Martin wondered if Carow knew. Had they known when they inserted him? They wouldn't have told him, naturally, but if they did know—if the mole was under surveillance—how had he laid hands on such information?

"There's something else, Martin. I don't know what to make of it."

"Just give me the facts." He wasn't really eager to hear them. He had the absurd notion that, if only he could dissuade her from telling him any more, the danger would go away of itself.

"There was a border incident two weeks ago. An agent,

one of yours, was killed. That's all I know, except that it seems he'd found out about the conference.'' She paused. ''But it took place all the same. Can you understand that?''

An idea had struck him, a crazy idea far removed from reality. He would have laughed at it if his throat hadn't been tight with fear.

''Those tapes I passed on, Zimra—were they genuine?'' The look she gave him was answer enough, but he pursued the idea. ''If they weren't fakes, could they have been doctored?''

''How? They were recorded at the conference itself. They match the transcripts. I was there the whole time.''

''What if they *wanted* them to fall into our hands, even if they were authentic?''

Neither of them spoke for a moment. It was a suspenseful, fearful silence. They stared at each other like children who had strayed into a maze designed and built by giants.

''It crossed my mind,'' she said, ''but it doesn't make sense.'' She had suddenly paled beneath her makeup. She shook her head. ''I wouldn't be here now if Zentner knew I'd taken the tapes and passed them on—it isn't his style. If he did, we wouldn't have a hope.''

She was right—their chances of getting out of Prague would be zero. And yet . . . Martin couldn't think in terms of East and West, only of individuals and personalities. Knowing Zentner and C, he involuntarily pictured them probing each other's defenses and striving to infiltrate them. Quite suddenly, his crazy idea acquired a vague substratum of meaning.

''Do we really stand a chance, Martin?''

There was no point in alarming her unnecessarily. ''I think so.'' He felt in his pocket to reassure himself that the key was still there; a plain hotel key—not pretentious like the Nltava's—with a circular brass tag bearing the room number.

''Did you stay behind on your own?''

"That would have been suspicious. One of my juniors stayed on too."

"I'm going to give you a key. A little boardinghouse behind the central station, Tetinská 56, Room 17. I've taken it for two days." She said nothing, asked nothing, but he saw she was listening intently. "We have a full day's program tomorrow. Steamer trip to Štěchovice in the morning, official farewell party in the evening. Our special train to Vienna leaves at eight-ten on Sunday morning. I'd like you to move into the boardinghouse tomorrow night."

"What time?"

"Not too early. I'd sooner you were here in case someone asks for you. Midnight, let's say." He could smell the boardinghouse now. "It's a bit of a dump, but conveniently situated."

The idea had come to him after the demonstration, when he decided to stop hibernating. Carow's plan for Zimra prescribed that he should hand her over, at seven-thirty on Sunday morning, to the man who had her new passport and would take her to the airport to catch a plane to Vienna. Although he had no reason to mistrust Carow's plan, he now saw everything in a different light.

"We've got two ways of getting out. We don't have to decide right away, but I'd like us to be prepared for either."

"What do you want me to do?"

"Buy a couple of cheap shoulder bags—or better still a small rucksack, if you can find one. Not too bulky, not too heavy, not too conspicuous—the sort of thing a person would take hiking. Put in a flask of coffee and something to eat. The less we carry the better."

"Stout shoes?"

He nodded, feeling reassured. "Buy the stuff sometime tomorrow and drop it off at the boardinghouse, but don't stay there. Need any money?"

"I may as well spend my own. It wouldn't be worth much over there." It was her first note of uncertainty.

"Believe me, Zimra, you're doing the right thing."

"What else?"

He made inquiries. The last train to the station near the frontier left just before 1 A.M. That would mean spending most of the night in the open. The first train in the morning left at 5:35, which gave them too little time to reach Sěnk's pickup point before daybreak.

"Know anyone in Prague who owns a car? Someone who'd rent it out for a night?"

"Only Vlatko's brother."

"Vlatko?"

"He put the tapes in your coat."

"Ask him to borrow it and drive us. Just him, no one else. He'd have to stand by from midnight on."

They looked at each other in sudden doubt, as if nothing they were discussing had any bearing on reality. Only thirty-three hours to go, he reflected, but there was little hope associated with the thought. Even farther in the future lay the island and his house. What could they mean to her if he spoke of them? What did they mean to himself? They might have been whole galaxies away. This time she's coming too . . . that was the only thought with any claim to reality—the only one he could cling to.

"What about your colleague? I don't want her raising the alarm too early on Sunday morning."

"She's bound to, sooner or later. What do you mean by early?"

"Not before nine."

"I think I can arrange it."

"They'll question her. They won't believe she didn't know." That was real too, and Martin tried not to avoid her eye when he said it.

Her response was calm and unruffled, as if she'd already come to terms with the idea. "I know. And even if they finally believe her, she'll lose her job and all her friends. It's terrible to think how often one's own happiness has to be bought at someone else's expense. The end justifies the means, isn't that the principle?"

Martin didn't react. "I think we've covered everything."

"Perhaps that's why I'm sitting here now, because I've spent so much of my life upholding that principle. You simply shut your eyes in the end. My father used to say it was the worst thing a person could be accused of, never to have defied the call of expediency."

"Your father tried. He died."

"He subscribed to a different principle. Leave the world better than you find it—he believed that to the last."

"We ought to say good-bye now."

"When I'm over there—I mean, if we really make it—do you honestly think they'll leave me in peace? They're bound to question me. I know a lot. Even if it isn't important, what matters is *they* think so. Don't you see the irony of it? The principle persists. I'm running from one stronghold of expediency to another." She picked up her glass. "You haven't touched a drop. It must be awfully expensive."

"I'm not too keen on champagne."

She drained her glass. There were traces of lipstick on the rim when she put it down. "Just a minor detail. What about my bits and pieces?"

"You'll have to leave them behind." He beckoned to the waiter.

"I see. Passport and lipstick only."

He settled the bill. The band waved to them as they walked out. The barman gave Martin a conspiratorial grin that made him doubly glad to see the last of the Tehran Club.

Later, on his way back to the Nltava, Martin reviewed his latest findings as soberly as possible. They knew there was an agent on site. They even knew his code number. Could they connect him with it? How long would it take them? Unable to do anything but hope that time was on his side—thirty-two hours of it now—he put the thought from his mind.

There were two more important points to be considered. For one thing, they had a mole inside the Organization; for another, the tapes were not what they seemed. He thought he had fathomed their intention and lifted a corner of the veil: they hoped to provoke the West into provocation, then shout it from the rooftops. Exploiting xenophobia was a sure way of diverting attention from internal problems. It wouldn't be the first time.

This was conjecture, though, not fact. Ought he to report it? The existence of the mole was another matter. The mole represented a threat, not only to himself and Zimra, but to the Organization as a whole. Why should he hesitate?

Martin had only one means of passing a message, and Carow had repeatedly warned him not to use it lightly. It was the one point on which Carow had seemed nervous and uneasy. Would he discover that his suspicion was well-founded: that Carow, who had called this a solo run, was keeping him under surveillance? Earlier that evening, on his way to the boarding-house, he had spotted someone tailing him.

It went against the grain to expose his baby-sitter—if that was who he was—but his reluctance to pass the word was only procrastination. In his heart of hearts, Martin knew the answer. He was a paid agent; he had made a contract and accepted an assignment; he would do whatever that assignment demanded. His mind was already working on the text of the message.

CHAPTER XXVIII

1

FOR AN AGENT, THE LAST PART WAS THE WORST—he had told C as much on the phone. He might equally have called these days and hours the hardest for a case officer to endure. Because his Darvons had run out—but even more so because of the silent telephones, the absence of any word from Prague or Bonn—Carow went for a walk.

The local doctor—Carow had left his prescription behind in Munich—read him a long lecture on what he already knew: popping pain-killers was no long-term solution to his problem. Strolling through the deserted streets of a provincial town was no cure either.

He felt better, though only for a moment, when he presented his stopgap prescription at an all-night pharmacy and got a smile from the girl behind the window.

"For you, are they? You shouldn't take those things. There are better ways of getting a good night's sleep, wouldn't you say?"

She was pretty in a well-scrubbed, convent-school way, but her dark eyes and red lips were far from nunlike. The pain in Carow's back gave way to a sudden thrill of pleasure, a foolish quickening of the pulses, but the sensation had passed by the time he came in sight of the shop's illuminated window.

Geissler, who had evidently been waiting for him, opened the door. "You took your time. Half an hour, you said." He had his coat on, Carow noticed.

"What's up?"

"C's on his way here, and there's a signal in from Prague."

"Have you decoded it?"

"Yes, and you won't be pleased." Geissler looked at him uneasily. "Your agent's on the loose. He's rented a room in a boardinghouse near the main-line station. If I interpret the signal correctly, he's getting ready to cut himself adrift."

"I'd better take a look at it."

Geissler found it hard to tell if Carow had registered the news of C's forthcoming arrival. "I must go—I was only waiting for you to get back."

"He's coming straight here?"

"Yes, he wants me to pick him up. Our local hospital has a helicopter pad." Geissler shook his head. "It's never happened before, Heiner. He's never visited my outstation in his life.''

''Well, don't turn it into a ceremonial parade. I mean, don't come screeching up to the door in that Mercedes of yours.''

Carow let Geissler out and locked the door behind him. He had the sour taste of betrayal in his mouth. How could Martin do this to him? He had felt tempted to ask Geissler to keep quiet about the signal, but it would only have testified to a suspicion he preferred to disguise from everyone else.

He retired to the back room, removed the signal from the safe and put it on the desk, unread. Geissler's bold capitals seemed to stare at him mockingly. He took off his coat and fetched himself a glass of water, but forgot to take a Darvon; the other pain was too great. ''Why?'' he said aloud, as though Martin could actually hear and answer him. ''Why now? You know you can trust me.'' How could any agent in the field exist, move an inch, even breathe, without trusting his case officer?

He started to read the signal. It was very brief; just the fact mentioned by Geissler plus the name and address of the boardinghouse. The baby-sitter had appended no comment of his own, nor was it his job to do so. What surprised Carow most was that Martin had given the baby-sitter a chance to discover anything at all. If he were really cutting loose, wouldn't he have covered his tracks with greater care?

Carow put the signal back in the safe, determined to avoid snap judgments. It only dawned on him then that C would be there any minute. He went into the bedroom and exchanged his sweater for a shirt and tie. He considered putting on a jacket, but it was too hot. Although he didn't feel much different, he somehow felt better equipped for a meeting with C.

He went back and made some coffee, enough for both flasks. It was going to be a long session, he guessed—quite why, he didn't know; he merely sensed that a long and crucial night lay ahead. It wasn't just C's handful of oblique remarks during their latest telephone conversation, nor the truly surprising fact that he was turning up in person. The reasons lay deeper.

Carow had no desire to explore them. Fundamentally, he was a simple, straightforward soul, a man who was better with his hands than his head—a born farmer, he reflected, except that he hadn't lived like one. He'd involved himself in something too big for him, too devious and complex.

2

THEY SAT FACING each other across the table in the back room. Geissler had gone off with Puck to prepare overnight quarters at his home for C and Puck himself. They would be bringing back some sandwiches and replenishing the outstation's stock of soft drinks, which had run low. C was halfway through the last bottle of Coke. Ice clinked against his glass as he gestured at the room with it.

"Very cozy. So this is where all our money goes."

He had said much the same, though at greater length, when inspecting the outstation on arrival. All *bonhomie* and good humor, he claimed to have acted on the spur of the moment: high time he visited the troops, et cetera. Although he must have had a very special reason for turning up at one o'clock in the morning, they joined in the charade to a man. In the world they inhabited, pretense was all.

Left alone with him, Carow saw no need to playact any longer. He hadn't meant to expose his line of defense, but C had always surpassed him at the waiting game. In the end it was Carow who made the first move.

"What happened in Bonn? How did they take it?"

C sighed. He had removed his jacket and was wearing the usual old-fashioned expanders that held his shirt-sleeves up. Carow wondered if he bought his shirts too big on purpose, so as to be able to use them.

"I'm retiring."

Carow was surprised but wary. "Is that official?"

"Not official, but definite. Only the two of us know so

far. Langtree's medicine—he prescribed it. I didn't like the taste at first, but thinking it over on the way here—well, it's beginning to grow on me. In the future, one of you can cope with the Chancellor's vetoes. I'll be choosing my successor very shortly, as soon as we've wrapped this thing up. That's confidential too.''

No witnesses, thought Carow, but he could almost have sworn, from C's tone of voice, that the old man meant it. The Chancellor must have squelched his proposals. Carow wasn't really surprised. He had always held that the Organization should be restricted to its official function: the procurement of intelligence in foreign countries. Procurement and transmission to higher authority, neither more nor less.

Carow waited in vain for C to elaborate. ''I gather,'' he said, with paternal solicitude, ''that you're having problems with your agent.''

So Geissler had talked. C had pumped him, no doubt, but Carow felt disappointed nonetheless. He got up, opened the safe, and placed the signal in C's outstretched hand. ''Problems?'' he said. ''Not really.''

C waved the sheet of paper. ''Does he know there's someone on his tail?''

''No.'' Carow was uncertain whether C had read the signal at all.

''Just for safety's sake, eh? I understand. Never trust anyone all the way.''

''But I do!'' Even to Carow, the words sounded overemphatic as soon as he uttered them.

''Even though he's cutting loose?''

''That's a matter of interpretation.''

C put the signal on the table in front of him. ''Have you forwarded this to the Center yet?''

''Not yet. We knew you were on the way here.'' Carow wondered, yet again, what the old man was driving at.

C smiled. ''I know it doesn't really matter, but I like our operational records to be absolutely complete. Leave out a trivial little item like this, and it can change the whole picture—in retrospect. If your agent is genuinely planning to cut himself adrift . . .''

"But he hasn't any reason to.'' Carow was struck by a sudden thought. "He'll have to house his source somewhere when the conference breaks up. He's paving the way for her exit, that's all.'' He felt better. Though defensive in intention, his argument sounded cogent and logical.

"Suppose you're wrong. What else could he be planning—an escape route of his own?''

"Why should he? We already have secure routes for both of them. I don't see why he'd run the risk.''

"What alternatives might he have?''

"None as safe as ours. Martin isn't the type to take unnecessary chances. That was one of our reasons for selecting him.''

"When does she get her passport?''

"At the last minute. Sunday morning, on the way to the airport.''

"So the other way out—*his* route—it couldn't be a plane or train?''

"Why all these questions?''

"I wish I'd spent more time with him. Perhaps I'd understand him better—guess what's going on in his head.''

"You knew enough about him to make your idea work.'' Carow sensed that C was gradually coming to the point, though he still couldn't tell what it was.

"Yes, my idea . . . A hunch, but still, I'd like to have known more.'' C knit his brow. "Tell me, do women often allow themselves to be recruited because they're in love with a man—because they don't have any choice: either they help him, or they lose him?''

"In unimportant instances, yes, but not in the case of high-grade intelligence—not here. The Steffin woman must have acted of her own free will—at least, that's my assessment of her. She's an exceptional person. When you told me about those tapes, I had a momentary sense of unreality. I felt it was too improbable, too good to be true.''

"Meaning?"

"Simply that I can't see her in her present role. After all, she's betrayed her country."

"Precisely, and she's done so of her own free will—you said it yourself." C paused for effect. "Heiner, we've got to leave her on site. That's why I came, to discuss the best way of arranging it. We *can't* dispense with a source like her. Why not? For the best of all reasons, and you yourself confirmed it just now: she acted of her own accord!"

When had it begun? Carow wondered. How many years was it since he'd taken the first wrong step—retreated when he should have stood his ground? There must have been a first time, a first abandonment of ideals he'd thought must exist, even in their trade. He felt incapable of rediscovering it under the slag heap of betrayal that had accumulated since then.

Even so, how did C have the gall to approach him with such a suggestion, sitting there like an accountant who'd found a mistake in his figures? Carow felt less angry with C than with himself, for having made it possible.

"What you're proposing—it can't be done."

"Why not? Are you out of touch with Prague?" The question sounded wholly innocent, wholly ingenuous.

"If this became known, we'd never get another agent to work for us."

"You're overwrought, Heiner, I thought so on the phone. What am I suggesting? Nothing we haven't done before. We've always tried to keep our hands clean, but there are times when it just can't be done. Isn't it a bit late to turn squeamish?"

"My agent's cover—"

"Nothing will happen to your agent. I'm talking about Zimra Steffin."

"It's in his contract."

"Be damned to that! Contracts get broken—agents break them, we break them. This isn't a nursery school. 'Are your handy-pandies nice and clean? If they aren't, you won't get an ice cream!' What I'm proposing is mean, shabby and dirty—all right, I admit it, but circumstances change.''

''How have they changed?''

For a moment, C seemed about to launch into one of his endless tirades. Then he said, ''It's a question of relative interests, relative values—the value of the individual *vis-à-vis* the interests of our country. We need the woman where she is. *You'll* need her more than anyone if you step into my shoes.''

I shouldn't sit here and listen to him, thought Carow, but all he said was, ''No, it's impossible, out of court. Anyway, Martin would never leave her there. He knows she'd be in danger.''

''We wouldn't have to leave her there forever. Just for the present—just while the operation lasts. You can give that undertaking—write it into the new contract. We'll lift her as soon as the operation's over.''

''I thought it already was—apart from retrieving our agent and his source.''

''But that's just what Zentner wants! He *wants* the storm to blow over, wants to wriggle off the hook——thinks he can hold out longer than we can. Well, he's wrong. Mark my words, Heiner, he'll come a cropper before I do, and they fall harder over there—a hell of a lot harder! That's why I need the woman, because she's right on his doorstep. I need her just for now, can't you see?''

They'd never fought their many verbal battles to a finish. Carow had always avoided a showdown and given way. He knew it was now or never. ''I've always gone along with you,'' he said, ''but not this time.''

C looked suddenly deflated—flat-chested, as if the air he inhaled were insufficient to fill his lungs. He opened his mouth and said wearily, ''What's happened to Puck and Geissler?'' Then he relapsed into silence.

Anyone less familiar with him than Carow would have construed his silence—his whole demeanor—as what it appeared to be: the crestfallen acquiescence of a man defeated by superior logic.

══════ **CHAPTER XXIX** ══════

1

HE WAS SITTING AT THE TABLE WHERE the teacher from Zaragoza habitually wrote his letters. The lamp was mounted on a bronze figure of a woman in a flowing robe. Her bosom was bare, and some chambermaid had amused herself by keeping it regularly polished. The breasts were a pale, lustrous shade of gold which contrasted with the chocolate-brown of the rest of the figure.

The room looked even bigger from his little island of light. His roommate was asleep, half hidden by the crimson velvet drapes that overhung his ornate bed. Having lost his watch, Martin was uncertain of the hour. His usually accurate sense of time had deserted him. He couldn't even have predicted, when he rose to draw back the heavy curtains, whether the sky above Prague would be tinged with the first light of dawn.

His telephone call had brought no response. "Wait, do nothing yourself, stay cool." He could almost hear Carow's warning voice. "Let him come to you, not the other way round. Not under any circumstances."

I'll give him another half hour, thought Martin. Pushing the two Prague phone directories to the edge of the table, he unfolded the slip of paper on which he had drafted his report.

His mood had passed through various stages in the last

few hours. Sometimes the whole affair seemed pointless, and he wondered whether it mightn't be wiser to refrain from submitting a report. Sometimes it all seemed clear as daylight—a macabre game played by two old men who were bent on unseating each other. The one thing he did recognize, clearly and without self-delusion, was his present irrelevance to the operation. He could rely on Carow for continued support—that, at least, was a constant factor—but his remaining part in the overall picture was zero.

Not that he lamented the fact. He still felt good, and his spirits had maintained their upward trend. He enjoyed sitting there alone in the night and relished his inner suspense. Suspense . . . maybe that was the drug he'd been seeking, not action itself.

Surveying the room, he had a sudden recollection of his father coming home one day with an old cabin trunk—a big black sarcophagus plastered with labels from all over the world. It would have suited the Nltava perfectly; that, perhaps, was why he'd been reminded of it.

At home the trunk had been a complete white elephant. It took up precious space and served no practical purpose. As far as Martin could recall, his father had never explained why a resigned and world-weary prison guard should have put his marriage in jeopardy for the sake of such an acquisition. From the day the trunk appeared, it became a permanent bone of contention between him and his wife—a regular *casus belli*.

Later, Martin realized that his father's cabin trunk was a dream that had never come true; a dream of departure and new beginnings, solitude and seclusion. He was happy, sitting on his chair in the cellblock corridor. Self-containment had become his life's ideal. To Martin's mother, the big black monster was the devil incarnate, an evil spirit that had led her husband astray, alienated him from her, driven a wedge between them where none had existed—or been seen to exist—before. Martin's mother was his father's diametrical opposite. She needed friends and the company of

Hans Herlin

others. To her, sharing was everything. "My parents were divorced," Martin could hear her saying, "that's why I always like putting things together—making *pairs* of them. A pair of vases, a pair of lamps, a pair of trees outside the house . . ."

Martin had never perceived this as clearly before. Now that he did, he realized something else: they were both there inside him, his father and mother—both parental opposites. So far, he had never managed to decide which of the two ideals he favored. Would Zimra understand his indecision? Would he be able to explain it?

The thought of her brought him back to the present. He folded the message and put it in his pocket, then rose and went over to one of the windows. He groped for the cords that operated the curtains. They swung back ponderously, like carcasses on a butcher's rail. It was still dark outside. The mist that swathed the river was so dense he couldn't see the bridge. He decided not to wait any longer.

The man from Zaragoza woke up. By the time Martin turned, he had switched on the light and was sitting bolt upright. He groped for the dressing gown at the foot of his bed. He seeemed quite unconscious of Martin's presence as he got up and glided, like a somnambulist, to the bathroom. It was only when he returned that he paused in fromt of Martin's undisturbed bed.

"You still up? What time is it?" He took a pair of glasses from the bedside table and peered at his alarm clock. "Two . . . You ought to get some sleep. It's going to be a long day."

A long day and a long night, thought Martin. It made him feel good again, just thinking about it.

"What's keeping you awake?" The other man was back in bed.

A Prague phone number, a secret message, a baby-sitter who's keeping me under surveillance . . . Martin felt an urge to tell the stranger everything. He pictured his surprise—his utter amazement. He could afford to flirt with the idea because he knew he would never succumb to it.

"Nothing. Go back to sleep."

The Spaniard removed his glasses, turned out the light, and drifted off at once. He made peculiar noises in his sleep. It wasn't laughter, exactly, Martin decided as he tiptoed past the bed on his way to the door, but it did convey some form of profound amusement.

2

THE FIFTH FLOOR of the Nltava retained no traces of old-world splendor. Feebly lit by two naked bulbs suspended from the ceiling, the narrow corridor was rendered narrower still by rows of gray steel lockers. Presumably, these held clothes for which no room existed in the staff quarters flanking the passage. Naked central-heating pipes made the air on the top floor hot and stuffy. All that relieved the silence was the water gurgling through them.

Martin had no idea where Němeček's room was. He would probably have tried to secure one at the end of the passage, not sandwiched between two others, to lessen the danger that his nocturnal radio transmissions might be overheard. Martin moved at a snail's pace, partly because of the heat and partly because he was scanning the doors. None of them bore a name.

Somebody coughed in his sleep—a first indication that the rooms were actually occupied. Light seeped faintly from under one door, but it was halfway down the passage. Martin tiptoed on, feeling the sweat break out beneath his arms. At the end of the passage, just short of a dormer window, he turned and looked back. The locker on his right had no padlock. He opened it and, seeing nothing, felt inside. His fingers closed on something flimsy. A dustcoat, many times washed?

The door beside the locker opened. He removed his hand from the coat and saw Němeček's figure silhouetted against the light. A low voice, as hesitant as his own would have been, said, "Is that you, Martin?"

"I've a message."

Němeček stared at him like a deaf-mute whose eyes are his sole source of information. "Not here, please. Come inside."

The room was as cramped as Martin had imagined. It looked like the stock room of a secondhand bookshop—there were books and stacks of old magazines and periodicals all over the place. Martin took a little longer to register the rest: a narrow bed hemmed in by bookshelves, a table set in the window alcove, a small television set whose aerial was threaded through the window frame. He looked round for Němeček's transceiver, probably a W12.6, but could see no sign of it.

"So you spotted me? When? This evening, when I tailed you to the boardinghouse?" Over his pajamas, the guide was wearing a silk scarf and a dressing gown with some kind of crest embroidered on the breast pocket. He looked far frailer and older out of his everyday clothes.

"Yes." Martin refrained from adding that he hadn't found it hard. That would have been superfluous. Besides, it was against the rules for him to be talking to Němeček at all. "So you've been breathing down my neck from the start? My baby-sitter?"

"That's right, your baby-sitter." Němeček repeated the expression as though hearing it for the first time—as though it had taken his fancy. He essayed a smile, but it was still the smile of a deaf-mute. "You don't feel deceived?"

"No, not really—not anymore, at least. Exactly what were you meant to do?" Again, Martin knew he shouldn't have asked the question.

"Just watch you, like you said. Keep my eyes open and mind the baby."

"And report back?"

"That too, of course."

"Our night out at the Tehran—was it your idea?" They

were still standing. The only chair was piled high with books.

"I take all my parties to the Tehran."

"Did you know my source would be there?"

"They were getting impatient—they wanted me to help things along. I was lucky, that's all." Němeček retied his scarf. "I've never really done much, you know. Nothing like the things you do. Baby-sitting, yes, and signals—I wouldn't have the nerve for anything else, not these days." Now he was fiddling with his dressing-gown cord. "You can't stop, though, can you? You keep on going till you die in harness, like an old nag. There's the money, too, of course . . ." Even his deaf-mute's smile had faded. "You said you had a message?"

"Why didn't I get any response to my call?"

The guide bowed his head. Strands of gray hair fell over his face. "She gave me my marching orders. I had to quit the apartment."

"So the number wasn't manned anymore?"

"I should have reported it, I know, but it was only for emergencies. Besides, I naturally hoped she'd have me back. It's been two days . . ." He seemed to recollect himself. "How did you know it was my number?"

"I remembered the name. Movina."

"You spoke to her?"

Martin felt it unnecessary to answer the question. "Are you still giving her money?"

"Yes. Look, I'm sorry. I'll report it at once—I mean, tell them the number's out of commission."

"Don't bother on my account. As far as I'm concerned, the assignment's completed. This wraps it up." Martin handed him the sheet of paper. "I'm afraid it's rather long." He suddenly felt sorry for the little man. "Destroy it when you've finished."

"I'm not a fool." Němeček bridled faintly. "Not from that point of view."

"Till tomorrow, then." Martin turned on his way to the

door. "Is there a backup? Someone who'd take over if you dropped out?" The last two words were preceded by an infinitesimal pause.

"A second baby-sitter?" Němeček fought another minor battle with his injured self-esteem. "No," he said at last, "not that I know of. That's the honest truth."

"The boardinghouse—did you tell them I'd taken a room?"

"I had to."

Martin wondered how Carow would take the news. He heard Němeček say, "I reported the fact and left it at that. Mind you, it made me think twice." The sly twinkle in his pale blue eyes corrected any impression that he was just a harmless old fool. "It won't do you any good, you know." When Martin still said nothing, he went on, "It's pointless, fighting the machine. You can't stop the wheels turning. You may think you can, sometimes, but you always get beaten in the end."

Whenever he thought of the old guide later on, the same two pictures sprang to Martin's mind: Němeček cavorting down the stairs with his long coat flapping after their visit to the Tehran Club, happy to have engineered a meeting with Zimra; and Němeček in his stuffy little room on the top floor of the Nltava, playing Cassandra.

Yes, you're right, he should have said. No one ever crosses them with impunity, but sometimes you don't have any choice. You know the rules of the game. You know there's no point in pitting your strength against the machine—defying expediency, in Zimra's phrase. Everything portends failure—every lesson of experience and law of probability—but one or two people will always feel tempted to buck the odds.

CHAPTER XXX

IT LOOKED LIKE THE AFTERMATH OF A PICNIC. The table was littered with empty bottles, paper cups, plastic cutlery and paper plates, one of them an inch deep in butts and ash. The relaxed atmosphere, too, was that of a picnic shared by four men who'd sat down to eat and drink after a long day's trek.

Geissler, with his shirt-sleeves rolled up and his flushed face radiating alcoholic pleasure at this unforseen chance to play host to C, was just saying, "Remember that time at Naumburg in April forty-five, when we were holed up in those cellars with the archive? Remember all that red wine—barrels of it? It flowed like water for three whole days . . ."

It was C who had called the tune. If Carow hadn't still been so wary, he might actually have believed that the prevailing theme—four old-timers from the year dot—was spontaneous. It didn't escape him, however, that C always steered conversation back to "the good old days" whenever it showed signs of taking a different tack.

Apart from C, Geissler had done most of the talking. Like a man too long consigned to the shadows, he was basking in C's reflected glory. Puck took a back seat as usual, saying little and keeping C supplied with iced fruit juice, but it was he who made the first move.

"It's been a long day," he said, starting to clear away.

C surveyed the others with a beaming smile. "Splendid idea, this visit—I've thoroughly enjoyed it. I know I'm ac-

240 *Hans Herlin*

cused of hugging my desk, overdoing the paperwork, taking too little interest in what goes on in the field. Well, it's never too late to learn.'' He focused the smile on Carow. ''We're one big team, after all.''

Carow was reminded of a wily old politico making friends all round in the run-up to a major election. C had made no further reference to his veto, simply accepted it, and it wasn't his way to leave things in the air. To Carow's surprise, however, he went on, ''Puck's right, we've all had a long day. I could use some sleep. Will you drive us, Geissler?''

That was that, thought Carow. C had backed down and granted him absolution. Here in the field the decision was his, Carow's. He was free to wind up the operation as arranged. Ordinarily, being as tired as the rest, he would have said no more, but too many of his battles with C had ended in defeat when victory seemed assured. He felt he ought to clear the air in front of witnesses.

''So it's settled,'' he said. ''We wind up the operation as per contract.'' Recalling C's remark about the latest signal from Prague, he added, ''Just for the record.''

C's smile vanished. Carow had been prepared for some last-minute resistance, which was why he had kept the fires of his antipathy burning bright. The look on C's face—the look of a jilted woman—told him how right he'd been. C *still* hadn't given up. That was clear from the way he addressed himself to the other two.

''We're a team, as I say. Our aims are the same, right? We all have a duty to put personal considerations last. That's why I think we ought to review the whole—''

The green telephone, its buzzer muted for the night, began to coo like a ringdove. Carow glanced at his watch and noted the time: 2:38 A.M.

''That's Prague,'' said Geissler, stifling this superfluous remark with his hand. C, whose punch line had been nipped in the bud, seemed temporarily thrown off course. ''Were you expecting anything?'' he asked in a hesitant voice.

Carow shook his head. He picked up the receiver. Geissler joined him at the desk and nodded to show that he was ready. Carow started to dictate the enciphered signal. In his surprise at its length, he forgot about C. He had a presentiment of disaster.

He was so preoccupied with Martin and Zimra that the mechanics of decoding the baby-sitter's signal came as a relief. He threw himself into the task, concentrating on the individual words to such an extent that their context escaped him. It was Geissler who supplied his first inkling of what the message signified—of the blow their operation had sustained. Geissler swallowed hard and said, "Damnation, the whole thing was a plant! They've been stringing us along from the start."

Carow ran through the text a second time. When he rose from the desk, C was still standing in the same place with the same expression on his face. He held the signal out, but the old man didn't take it—didn't even seem to see it. It was Puck who took the sheet from Carow's hand. He read it over, first to himself with silently moving lips, then aloud for C's benefit. Nothing in his unemotional voice conveyed either shock or dismay.

C took the sheet at last. He read the signal without a flicker of expression, then shook his head. "What's your agent up to—trying to earn himself a medal or something?"

The others looked at each other, doubtfully and incredulously, before swiftly looking away. None of them wanted to admit that the same thought had struck them all at the selfsame moment: Their old lord and master was shying away from the truth—refusing to accept that his operation had foundered.

To Carow's surprise, it was Puck who first spoke up for Martin. In a dry, matter-of-fact voice, he said, "He's on the spot—he should know."

C snapped awake. "I gave orders. That man was supposed to keep absolutely mum." He struggled for words but could only repeat himself. "Absolutely mum! Well, isn't that what I said? What more does he want? We've got the tapes? There's no doubt about the tapes—they're genuine, everyone says so. Good grief, I *know* Zentner—I've known him for thirty years. Are you trying to tell me some lousy agent can read his mind better than I can? It's rubbish, I tell you—pure and unadulterated rubbish!''

Carow cleared his throat. ''But don't you see what it means? We'd come a cropper if we acted now.''

Once again, it was Puck who came to his support. ''That was the danger from the start, wasn't it?''

''Meaning what?''

''You and Zentner—the fact that you know each other so well.''

''But those tapes—''

''Nobody doubts they're genuine,'' Puck broke in. ''The agent doesn't either, but you can't dismiss the possibility that Zentner guessed what you had in mind. Look at it from his angle. He was in a tight spot, so what did he do? What *could* he do? He invited you into his parlor—come on in, he said, send in your runners. Knowing you, he guessed how tempted you'd be. I warned you what to expect when Blumenschein started raving about time bombs and detonators. Try it, I said, and he'll spring the trap. This is Zentner's best hope. It'll take the heat off him. He'll parade your agents before the international press. They needn't all be yours, even—he'll dig up enough to warrant an outcry. 'Look,' he'll say, 'there's the West for you, always trying to stir up trouble in peace-loving countries.' And his own people will swallow it whole—the ordinary folk, I mean. They'll grit their teeth and close ranks. As for the rest, he'll handle them with ease.''

Carow stared at Puck with growing admiration. Had he really said all these things at the meeting? As far as he could recall, Puck had followed his usual practice and refrained from commenting. If he hadn't known how close the two men were, he might almost have felt that Puck was reveling in C's discomfiture.

C shook his head. "The bastard! And I nearly had him."

"It's just his style, admit it."

Puck's final argument seemed to set the seal on C's collapse. Carow felt his old loyalty to C revive. "Why don't we wait till Martin and the Steffin woman are out? They may have some more information for us."

Nobody spoke for a while. Then Geissler harked back to his original remark. "They must have planned it like that from the outset. That agent, Cichosz, the one who got shot on the border after bringing us word of the conference—they probably fed him the information and gave him a clear run because they wanted it to reach us."

C, with the signal still in his hand, looked round as though striving to remember where he was. Carow felt sure he was missing his office, his desk—wondering, perhaps, if all would have turned out differently had he never left Munich. At last he turned to Puck.

"Let's go home."

"Right away, you mean?"

"Of course."

"I'd have to dig the pilot out of bed."

"Then do so, for God's sake." He handed the message form to Carow. "File it, Heiner. I see no prospect of further action." He was turning away when Carow stopped him.

"If Borchers has been under surveillance, how did he manage to pass this information?"

"What information?" It was the weary voice of an old man who wanted to be left in peace.

Carow refrained from rubbing it in. "You'd better have him picked up at once."

"Yes, tomorrow. Today, I mean."

They could hear Puck phoning from the showroom. C looked suddenly relieved, as if the very thought of being home within the hour had given him a shot in the arm. "When they're out, Heiner, make sure they don't talk. I don't like any agent knowing so much about an operation. It makes me uneasy."

"Martin isn't the talkative type."

"If you say so—you know him better than I do." C hesitated. "The room in the boardinghouse—that changes the picture slightly, doesn't it? You know the man. What do you think he'll do? Will he use our route? Be honest."

Carow chose his words with care. "He's in an awkward position. We didn't tell him anything about the baby-sitters."

"You mean there's more than one?" C looked surprised.

Carow ignored this on the grounds that it was unimportant——his business. "He'll understand. Martin knows the form. What's more awkward is the Borchers affair—the fact that we concealed the existence of a potential leak."

"We had it plugged."

"But he'll feel we didn't fully trust him—or were careless, which is just as bad. Worst of all, he won't know where his greatest danger lies or how much Zentner really knows. Not even we can tell him that, so he may feel tempted to use a route of his own—if he's got one ready.'" Carow brooded for a moment. "But then, of course, he'd never know for sure . . ."

"Know what?"

"Whether he was right *not* to trust us."

"Just a minute. You mean he might risk his neck to find out?"

"The risk wouldn't deter him." Carow took another few seconds to marshal his idea. "I think he'll delay his decision till the last possible minute. Any little factor could make up his mind. He may not even make the decision himself. He may leave it to chance—one card for their route, one card for mine, higher card wins. Plenty of agents are like that. That's why I can't answer your question."

"His route—what could it be?"

"I already told you—I don't know." Carow didn't feel he was lying to C because the report was still in the outstation safe, not on file. The man who'd shadowed Martin in the train to Vienna had noted an outwardly innocent contact. A

routine identity check conducted the same night, during the
return trip, had made the contact seem less innocent:
Miroslav Sěnk of ATAP Airlines, a man who used to fly refugees out of Czechoslovakia. A coincidence?

"Would he need outside help?"

C's question was altogether natural and logical, Carow
told himself, not a mind reader's *tour de force* . "Yes," he
said, "probably."

"He shook off surveillance that first night in Munich.
Any pointers there?"

Carow's report on his preliminary meeting with Martin
had contained a mere two lines on the subject, so C's powers
of recall were still in working order. "He'd just arrived. He
wanted to show us he hadn't lost his touch. Besides, he
hardly knew a thing about the operation."

"What about here?"

"We were together all the time." Carow was puzzled by
C's persistence. What was he getting at—what was going on
in his head? Carow wondered whether to warn Geissler not
to mention the Sěnk report if C questioned him, but what
could C do at this stage? The operation was dead. All that
remained was to collate the files and give them a decent bur-
ial in Records.

"So there's nothing; no indication at all?"

Puck returned, absolving Carow from the need to reply.
The pilot had been alerted, so they could leave. C's interest
in Martin seemed to have waned. Geissler fetched his coat,
ready to drive him and Puck to their helicopter.

After they had gone, Carow sat down at the desk and
drafted some alternative signals for transmission to Prague.
His final choice of words read as follows: "Report extremely valuable. Routes still secure. Mole identified."

He knew the signal was superfluous—symptomatic more
of weakness than strength. The last thing Martin needed
now was cheap encouragement. Perhaps because he needed
some himself, Carow overcame his hesitation and sent the
signal off.

CHAPTER XXXI

"MARTIN, MARTIN!"

He woke, and the dream receded at once. It clung to his subconscious as though too secret to be entrusted to his waking self. All he could remember was that it had some connection with water: a broad expanse of flooded fields with only the tips of some fence posts showing.

"We're back, we'll be landing any minute. I bet you didn't see a thing!"

He felt cold although, on opening his eyes, he saw that Elsa's head was framed by a solar halo. Her curly fair hair looked translucent, her prominent ear-lobes pink—irradiated by sunlight.

"I combed the whole ship for you. You simply vanished."

Martin sat up stiffly. He now saw where he'd gone to sleep: on one of the white wooden benches on the paddle steamer's afterdeck. All at once, his ears registered the appropriate sounds—the throb of the engines and the roar of water gushing through the massive paddle boxes.

"What a shame you missed it all! You could have slept tomorrow, on the train." Elsa's face was aflame from the sun.

Tomorrow, he thought, really awake at last. He said, "You'll be peeling by tonight."

"You should see me in summer. Red as a lobster."

Was this weather good or bad from Sěnk's point of view? Navigation would be easier in fine weather, but perhaps he preferred rain and a low cloud base. From his own and Zimra's point of view they were good, these dry, sunny, Indian summer days. It wouldn't be so cold before dawn.

"Do you like your women nice and brown? Most men do, don't they? I envy any woman who tans easily." She laughed. "But then, I envy any nice-looking woman."

"What's nice looking?"

She answered without a moment's hesitation. "Tall, dark-haired, blue-eyed, tanned. All the things I'm not."

"You've got blue eyes."

"My passport says gray."

"Passports always get things wrong."

"Maybe, but it's the combination that counts. Shall we watch them tie up?"

The other congress delegates had already thronged the rail on the starboard side. There was a good view of the city, and camera shutters were clicking away. A gray police launch glided past. A middle-aged couple in an orange kayak were paddling hard to escape the steamer's wash. A bridge loomed up ahead, and beyond it lay the quay flanking the broad Boulevard Engles.

"Don't let go of me!" Elsa mounted one of the chairs to enable her to see over the others' heads. Martin gripped her outstretched hand.

Elsa would be the first to notice that he wasn't on board the train. What would she do? Although it wouldn't matter by then, Martin couldn't help picturing the scene at the station, the unscheduled delay, the locked doors, the uniformed men with dogs on either side of the train, the policemen in the train itself, asking questions. The others would draw their own conclusions from these inquiries. Martin saw their faces, heard their remarks. What a shabby way to repay their hosts' hospitality!

"This time tomorrow we'll all have gone our separate

ways." Martin couldn't think why he'd said it. Sentimentality was the last thing he could afford at this stage.

Elsa looked down at him. "Have you bought your presents?"

They'd been for another shopping expedition before the boat trip. Someone had suggested that their hosts—guides, interpreters, Čedok staff—might appreciate some farewell gifts. These were to be presented at the Nltava's grand soirée that evening.

"No, have you?"

"Only Němeček's."

"What did you get him?"

"A pair of cuff links."

On the way to the shops, Němeček had given Martin a message from Carow. Its contents had left him more perturbed than reassured.

The steamer slowed, almost to a standstill, and lowered its spindly smokestack. Elsa climbed down off her chair as they plunged into the gloom beneath the bridge. Traffic could be heard overhead.

"I've never seen *you* wearing cufflinks," she said.

"I lost so many I gave up."

"Are you going straight home from Vienna? Back to all your Spanish señoritas?"

"Not right away, no."

"Taking some more time off?"

"A week, maybe." Ever thorough, Carow would be bound to spend a week with them in a safe house. Martin's thoughts returned to the message. *Report extremely valuable* . . . As he understood it, that meant his report had killed C's operation stone dead.

"How about you? Going back to your classroom among the coal mines?"

"I'm suspended at the moment."

"Why?" He only had a dim recollection.

"For leading my pupils astray—filling their heads with dangerous ideas. Actually, all I'd like them to do is spare an occasional thought for something other than mopeds and pop records and discos and how to raise the price of a joint.''

The steamer was nearing the shore. Men were standing on the quay with coils of rope at the ready.

"What sort of dangerous ideas?"

"Brecht, for instance. 'Make sure, when you leave this world, not only that you were good, but that you leave a good world behind you.' That was my last German literature class—a debate on his appeal to mankind."

Involuntarily, he thought of Zimra. Was she afraid of to-night and tomorrow? More probably, she was concentrating on what she had to do today.

"Maybe they're right. Maybe you ought to stop teaching kids things like that."

"Why? Don't you believe in the possibility of a better world?"

"I never look beyond tomorrow."

"That isn't enough."

It was, he thought. It would be more than enough if he saw Sĕnk's Bell JetRanger in the sky tomorrow morning. He would hear it first—or rather, he'd hear the wild duck take wing, startled by the huge and outlandish bird above them. Sĕnk would fly low, especially on this side of the border. There was a copse beside the clearing they'd agreed on. That was where he would first catch sight of the helicopter, skimming the poplars, making them bend beneath the down-draft of its rotor blades . . .

"You wouldn't be here if you really thought it was enough, you'd have stayed behind with all your sun-tanned señoritas and never come at all."

She was right, of course, in some strange way, even though his original motives now seemed blurred and re-mote. He had come to prove something to himself, but what?

The steamer's big paddle wheels abruptly reversed, then stopped. The vessel lurched as it brushed the quayside. Elsa lost her balance. He caught her as she fell and held her.

She released herself from his arms. All of a sudden, she
had two faces. One was severe, acerbic and close to tears;
the other seemed hugely amused—almost convulsed with hi-
larity. It was the other that triumphed in the end. "I hope
you're going to dance with me tonight, lots of times."

He remembered their evening at the Tehran. When the
East Germans entered the bar, Elsa had suddenly stopped
dancing and raised her head from his shoulder. She had
worn the first face then.

"You know," he said, "there have been times when I
thought you were playing a part."

"What sort of part?"

"The naïve fellow-traveler—the slightly scatty, rather
overexcitable schoolmarm who makes a lot of wild remarks
about free love in the East and microphones hidden in hotel
bedrooms."

"And what is she really?"

"A sort of—well, spy."

"Oh, Martin, Martin!" She put her head on his shoulder,
but only long enough to hide her face for a moment. "You
really meant that?"

"Then there was another time—"

"A spy? A Mata Hari who breaks men's hearts and so on?
That's the nicest thing a man ever said to me. I love you for
it, really I do. You're a sweetheart."

"You think spies are nice?"

She stared at him in surprise. Then she said, "There must
be a few nice ones among them, wouldn't you say?"

The passengers ahead of them had started to go ashore.
The passengers behind them began to shove and jostle. They
found themselves in the midst of the exodus, shuffling along
a step at a time.

Measuring posts were bolted to the quayside. Martin noticed how low the river was. The water-meadows in the
Vltava lowlands—that was what he must have been dreaming about! They wouldn't be flooded as they so often were
after a long spell of rain.

The frequency with which this thought recurred—did it mean that his mind was made up, irrevocably?

CHAPTER XXXII

THERE WAS NOTHING ON THE CONFERENCE table but a black Uher tape recorder. The voice on the tape filled the room. Though almost unaccented and devoid of special characteristics, it conveyed an impression of the speaker: a giant of a man, slightly asthmatic from overweight and too much tobacco smoke.

C had begun by listening from his desk. When one side of the tape ran out, he reversed the cassette and moved nearer. The two men might have been in conclave, thought Puck, one visible but silent, the other disembodied but articulate.

Ever since arriving at the office—far later than usual—C had done nothing but play the tape over and over again; a composite of Zentner's dialogue, specially edited for his own use. He saw no one, signed no letters, told Pauly to cancel all his appointments. Twice the head dragon called Puck out and enlisted his support, but C merely waved them both away. The light above his door remained red.

"Want something to eat? It's nearly three. You didn't have any lunch."

C continued to gaze at the rotating spools. Puck was tired of the voice, tired of watching C do battle with the thoughts that were searing him inside.

"Forget it. What more do you want? Don't make the mistake so many people make—the ones who don't know when to stop. You've been king of the castle long enough."

C looked up for the first time. "And I'm losing it for want of a nail." He tried, without much success, to smile. "To paraphrase the old saying, 'For want of a nail the shoe was lost; for want of a shoe the horse was lost; for want of a horse the king was lost; for want of a king the battle was lost . . .' "

Puck stared at him, no more reassured than before. At least the tape had stopped. The room regained its traditional hush, its familiar sounds. The drinks dispenser and ice machine emitted a discreet hum. Somewhere in the grounds, bulldozers were carving out the foundations of a new annex.

"It would never occur to an outsider that we'd lost the battle."

"But *you* think we have."

"I don't think it's a question of winning or losing. Properly speaking, it's a draw. To outsiders, it could even look like a victory."

C gestured at the empty chairs round the circular table. "The mistake began right here, at that preliminary session. Ziegler was right: we had all we needed. I shouldn't have listened to Carow. Agents, agents, agents . . . Martin was superfluous! We had it all here on the table—on file." He paused for thought. "Do you think they've turned him?"

"Who?"

"Martin. Look at it in the light of our latest information. They know he's coming, so they pick him up and turn him with the aid of that woman. They give him the tapes as evidence that he's still on our side. Then they get him to send that last signal. They know it'll take the wind out of our sails."

My God, thought Puck, will I be glad when it's over! Ploy and counterploy, bluff and double bluff, a maze of mistrust so convoluted that even its designers lost their way . . .

"Your best plan," he said, "is to forget there ever was an Operation Bear-Hug."

One of the phones started purring. C made a dismissive gesture. Puck walked over to the desk and took the call.

"It's Pauly, she's got Geissler on the line. He says . . ." To his surprise, C rose at once.

"Yes, that's for me." He took the receiver out of Puck's hand. "Geissler? Good—excellent. One moment." He cupped his hand over the mouthpiece and looked at Puck. "Did you say something about lunch?" Sitting down behind his desk, he pulled a pad toward him and picked up one of his needle-sharp pencils.

Puck heard no more of the conversation while he prepared C's lunch in the miniature kitchen: Welsh rarebit and coffee with vanilla ice cream to follow. C was still on the phone when he returned with the tray. "Yes," he heard him say, "you've been a great help. And Geissler, don't feel bad about Carow. There's only one brand of loyalty, and that's to the Organization . . . No, we'll handle that from this end. Good-bye."

Puck spread a white napkin on the desk and laid it for lunch. C began to eat at once with gusto, periodically consulting the pad beside his plate. It was covered with notes in his spidery handwriting. At length he said, "That ice cream was really delicious."

"Would you like some more?"

"Please, if there is some. Then go down to Records for me. Check through our list of free-lance flyers." He consulted his notes again. "Šěnk's the name—Miroslav Šěnk. He runs an outfit of his own called ATAP Airlines. I'll write it down for you. We may have something on him."

Puck brought a second helping of ice cream. "Pauly's got a couple of urgent requests for you. Bonn wants clarification on one particular point in your memo, and Ziegler—"

"No, not now. Get me Kurella right away. I may want Borchers, too, later on."

"Borchers?"

"I don't know yet. Maybe it's better if it doesn't come

from me." A thought struck him. "Has Kurella found out how he got at that information?"

"Not for sure, but the answer's probably quite simple. The poison register showed that Carow hadn't returned Martin's source book. Borchers must have seen it and drawn his own conclusions."

"Carow . . . I'd always had him down to succeed me, but he's made a hash of this business." C's thoughts had strayed for a moment. "But there's no real evidence— against Borchers, I mean?"

"Peppermint remembers some talk about an agent, but it seems to have been the man we lost on the border, and that falls well within his province."

"Where is Borchers now? I hope they're keeping tabs on him."

"In his office, Have you decided when to pull him in?"

"Without any solid evidence? You know what that would mean, Puck. There'd have to be a lengthy judicial hearing— we'd be knee-deep in snoopers from the Constitutional Protection Bureau, and that I wouldn't fancy. I think I've got the answer, though. Borchers will smell a rat, but the temptation may prove too much for him." C scribbled something on a fresh sheet of paper and held it out. "See what we have on this Sĕnk character, would you?" He started to spoon up his second helping of ice cream.

Puck lingered in front of the desk. "Is this anything to do with . . ."

C looked up. "Bear-Hug?" he said, through a mouthful of ice cream. "How could it be? The operation's dead, the battle's lost—you said so yourself. Really good ice cream, this. Absolutely first class."

His mood was transformed. Although the previous night's lack of sleep still showed in his face, with its watery eyes and pendant folds of flaccid skin, his features were undergoing a mysterious process of regeneration. The smile had a different quality. Its gleeful expectancy reminded

Puck of a child whose broken toy is about to be exchanged
for a new one.

CHAPTER XXXIII

IT WAS 6:30 P.M. IN PRAGUE WHEN THE grand farewell
soirée opened with a drinks party at the Nltava. Attendance
at cocktails was limited to delegates staying at the Nltava itself. Those billeted in other hotels would be ferried there for
the main proceedings by bus, or, if they were close enough,
make their way along the embankment on foot. It was a mild
evening.

"The Minister of Culture's coming," Elsa reported
knowledgeably. "What with all the speeches and toasts, we
won't be through with dinner till eleven. That's what Němě-
ček says, anyway."

"Where is he?" Martin scanned the lobby. Well over a
hundred guests were standing there cheek by jowl. It was all
the waiters could do to keep their glasses filled.

"He must be somewhere around." Elsa was wearing her
floral dress, this time supplemented by an artificial flower in
her cleavage. She had paid another visit to the hotel beauty
parlor with much the same disastrous results as before.

"Did you give him his cuff links?"

"They aren't to open their presents till after dinner."

"Why not?"

"That's what was decided. So everyone can enjoy them, I
suppose."

"Maybe they'll sell the presents and split the proceeds. In
a socialist state, everyone should get the same."

She looked at him askance. "What's the matter with you? That wasn't a very nice thing to say. Mind you, it wasn't as bad as your *faux pas* at our last discussion group. That was the limit!"

Their last discussion group had been a hurriedly convened affair with only one item on the agenda: Who was to thank their Czech hosts on behalf of all the congress delegates? Arguments raged interminably over what the speech should contain and who should deliver it. They had almost agreed on an East German candidate when the West Germans lodged a veto. And so it went on until Martin turned to Elsa and said, in the midst of a rare and unexpected lull, "Liberty, equality, fraternity—why don't we all trot out one sentence each?"

He deposited his glass on a waiter's tray. "I'm going to see if I can find Němeček."

"Don't worry, he'll turn up. Why so fidgety? Maybe you ought to try something stronger than tomato juice. Soft drinks don't seem to agree with you."

Martin elbowed his way to the outskirts of the lobby. He knew that the evening would drag on forever, fraying his nerves. He was bound to think of Zimra, wonder when she was leaving her hotel, imagine her arriving at the boarding-house, speculate—of course—on what would happen in the morning. They were useless, debilitating thoughts, so he decided to switch off and concentrate on one thing only: keeping Němeček in sight.

He had another reason, too. If danger were looming, it would strike at the weakest point first. They would arrest the old guide, cart him off and grill him until he told them all he knew.

"Look at that! They've really done us proud tonight!"

Elsa had joined him and was peering through the big glass doors of the dining room. It was the size of a theater, all stucco and gilt. Strings of flags hung from the walls and chandeliers. There were flags everywhere, and Martin saw that the snowwhite tablecloths were also adorned with flowers in the various national colors. The spacious stage on the right was concealed by a red curtain bearing the motto of the evening: "Many Voices, One Belief!"

"The orchestra will be playing there"—Elsa pointed to the stage—"after the meal, and the bar will have a band of its own. The police have granted the hotel a special license for the night. Some people won't be going to bed at all— they'll go straight on from the party to the station. Know what Němeček told me? After the last congress, the train was held up for two hours because they lost a group of trade unionists!"

Martin strove to picture Elsa's homecoming. Did she have any friends—small-town friends she could impress with accounts of her trip—or would her memories belong to her alone, to be periodically dusted off and played like an old phonograph record? He couldn't visualize her life beyond tonight; but then, he had no clear idea of his own immediate future.

"Did you find a present for Němeček?"

"What's that? Oh, er—yes." He was still scanning the animated throng for Němeček's wan face. In default of a better idea, he'd decided to give the guide his surplus cash. He'd counted out as much as he needed himself—a small reserve for rail fares or for Vlatko and the car—and stowed it away in the clothes he'd be wearing, together with his passport, his deck of cards, and the ivory hair clasps. The rest of the money was in an envelope in his pocket.

"Aren't you going to tell me what it is?"

He caught sight of Němeček bearing down on them, waxen-faced as ever. He had a white carnation in the lapel of his pearl-gray suit and Gabrielle, the Belgian schoolteacher, on his arm. Martin breathed a sigh of relief.

Němeček forged a path through the crowd. Noticing that Martin had no glass, he beckoned one of the waiters. "Champagne for my friends!" he said grandly, and went on to propose a toast: "To the free exchange of free love!"

A moment's embarrassed silence followed. The people

round them edged away. Then someone—Elsa?—began to laugh and the rest joined in because it dawned on them that Němeček had been hitting the bottle.

"He's a wild, wild man!" Gabrielle giggled. She looked quite naked without her horn-rims. *"Un vrai mâle!* Just imagine, he proposed to me—he swears he wants to marry me, *sans blague!* You know what he said—I mean, the way he put it? He said, *'Chérie,* let us speak with one voice and believe in one love!' He's drunk, of course."

She proceeded to broadcast Němeček's proposal to everyone in sight. Martin eventually managed to get him on one side and held out the envelope. The guide misunderstood for a moment, because he recoiled, staring at the envelope as if it were a bomb. It occurred to Martin that Němeček must have thought he was passing a message in public. He stuffed the envelope into his baggy jacket pocket. "A present for you—a good-bye present."

"From you personally?"

"Yes." He watched Němeček transfer the money to his breast pocket.

It was Organization money, Martin reflected. He would be asked for a detailed list of expenses. The people in Accounts were persnickety in the extreme. "Farewell gift for a baby-sitter?" They'd never swallow *that*—they'd expect him to justify every last item. "Or we'll have to deduct it from your remuneration." Remuneration . . . They always insisted on calling it that.

He had a vivid mental picture of his forthcoming clash with Accounts. It seemed entirely real and immediate—far more so than any other idea connected with his return. The notion tickled him, but he wasn't aware of having laughed until he saw surprise on Němeček's face.

"Having a good time?" asked Němeček.

There was no need to answer. The dining-room doors were flung wide and the chandeliers blazed into life. The gala evening had begun.

CHAPTER XXXIV

1

BORCHERS WAS STILL AT HIS DESK IN THE Center when eight o'clock came. As long as he remained there, he felt safe. Danger lurked outside, perphaps within yards of where he sat. They might arrest him in the grounds or let him go home first, for his mother's sake. He was prepared for either contingency. All he hated was the fact that they'd left the time and place to him. It was like compelling a man to dig his own grave.

He took the framed photograph of his mother from the desk, opened the retaining clips, and removed the back. Then he took the message he'd drafted, a slip of paper the size of a calling card, and inserted it between the photograph and the cardboard backing. Kurella would expect him to leave his message in a dead-letter box, and he, Borchers, would foster that expectation. It wouldn't occur to them, or so he hoped, that he'd plant the message in his own home. Using his mother without her knowledge was an ironical twist that appealed to him.

Yet the whole thing seemed somehow pointless. Either they'd fed him the information to lure him out of his burrow, in which case they'd arrest him come what may, or . . . Or what?

This was the question that haunted him and made it so hard to decide. Was the information spurious—a marked card? The case had been discussed at a specially convened meeting. Because of a sudden emergency, an Organization agent—code number A7Z115—was to be airlifted back across the Czech border. The pickup would be made by helicopter at dawn tomorrow . . . Just at that moment, Kurella had turned up and the meeting was adjourned.

Had the disclosure been a subterfuge or a genuine blunder—an oversight? Although Borchers found the latter hard to believe, he found it even less conceivable that they would risk an agent's life on his account. The information must therefore be authentic. Ergo, he must pass it on.

Borchers had expected total silence from his "friends" after telling them, in his last message, that contact would be severed forthwith. Instead, they had transmitted an urgent request for all available details on A7Z115. This was an impossible request, and they knew it. Borchers took it as a sign that they, too, had written him off. He had no friends left outside. He was too old a hand not to realize that an agent whose cover is blown becomes a non-person. No one wants to know him anymore.

This thought brought him back to the problem in hand. He picked up the telephone. Although he was prepared for a long wait, his mother answered at once.

"I'll be late for supper."

"What do you mean, *will* be late? You're late already. How do you think I've been coping here, all on my own? You might at least have called me earlier!"

He almost bit her head off, he was so tired, so inwardly bereft of hope. Then he thought of the man who was listening in or recording their conversation on tape, or both.

"Why not call Nurse Karin and ask her to come over?"

"Call her? How am I expected to get to the phone?" As soon as she realized what she'd said, she went on, "Very well, I'll do that."

"Fine. Take care of yourself."

"What's the matter, is something wrong? Trouble at the office?"

"I'll try not to be too late."

Borchers got up from his desk. The die was cast. They now knew he'd try to forward the information. He put his coat on. There was ample room in one pocket for the photograph frame. In the other he could feel the dummy package containing blank sheets of paper.

He turned at the door and glanced back. His office looked as neat and tidy as usual. He might or might not return tomorrow morning—it all depended. Remembering that tomorrow was Sunday, he amended this to Monday. It didn't really matter anymore. Not even his mother mattered now. That chapter of his life was closed too. She would have to sharpen her claws on someone else.

He must finish the job. The only problem was that until now he'd always had faith and pride in his "work," dirty though he sometimes acknowledged it to be. That was how he'd lived, like a fish born in a polluted river. Creatures accustomed to pollution could live and breathe in it because they knew no other environment, but *his* river, he felt, was beginning to dry up.

2

BORCHERS WASN'T CERTAIN that he'd shaken them off when the cab dropped him near the palace. He'd given himself plenty of time—over two hours—before passing the word to his "friends" from a public call box.

He walked quickly into the park without bothering to see if anyone was on his tail. The grounds were unlit, but it was a fine night. The statues flanking the main avenue looked more lifelike than they did by day. Already stacked beside their plinths lay the wooden shuttering that would protect them from the winter frosts. The official season ended tomorrow, the last day of September.

Borchers crossed over to the left-hand side, counting statues, until he came to an armless figure whose face had been

ravaged by the elements. Then he stooped and thrust the
little package into the recess behind its feet.

He waited for his shadows to make themselves known,
but nothing happened. Almost indifferently now, he re-
traced his steps. The big sweep of gravel in front of the palace was deserted. Farther away, on the other side of the
canal, stood a brightly lit restaurant.

A man came strolling along the path toward him. He had
his coat collar up and was towing a dog on a lead. He gave
Borchers a friendly nod and a smile as they passed each
other. Nothing in his manner or appearance seemed suspicious. This was one of Munich's better—more expensive—
residential areas, and the folk who lived and exercised their
dogs here at night felt financially entitled to walk the streets
in safety.

They were waiting for him when he got home. He had left
his car in the street that morning. Now it was sandwiched,
fore and aft, between two identical Opels. Although he
couldn't see their faces through the tinted glass, he knew
they were inside.

What would they do? They were probably wishing he'd
come by car. Arresting him in the underground garage
would have been decently inconspicuous, but here in the
street? This, too, was a respectable area; not quite as exclusive as Nymphenburg, but eminently respectable. The folk
who lived here were likewise entitled to be spared all knowledge of wiretapping and intercepted mail, let alone the sight
of a respectable neighbor—a man so touchingly devoted to
his invalid mother—being arrested in public.

Borchers sympathized with his prospective captors' di-
lemma. He knew how much the Organization paid such operatives, and it fell far short of what was required to live in
this part of town. Anxious not to make things harder for
them than necessary, he walked across to the leading car.

There were two men inside, neither of whom he recognized. Although they had obviously identified him, one of

them said, "Herr Borchers? I'm afraid we must ask you to come with us." He sounded genuinely apologetic.

"By all means. Ready when you are."

They exchanged hesitant glances. The elder of the two, whose eyes were unnaturally magnified by the glasses he wore, indicated the apartments. "You can pack a few things if you like. One of us will have to come with you, of course."

Borchers looked across the street. The breakfast-room curtains were open. He caught a glimpse of the nurse. She took something from the table—he was too far away to see what—and bore it off to the living room. A book to read aloud to his mother?

"That won't be necessary." Borchers produced a key ring from his pocket. "There's a bag with everything I need in my car. If you'll get it for me, we can go."

The older man spoke again. "You don't want to say good-bye to your mother?"

They would naturally have been briefed on his background. That was the basis of his plan, though he was far from certain that they'd fall for it.

"It's better for her this way, believe me. I've only one favor to ask." He took the framed photograph from his overcoat pocket. "I've had this on my desk for years. Would you give it to her and ask her to keep it for me—I mean, till I'm . . ." He left the sentence unfinished, not daring to look them in the face.

To his surprise, he heard the older man say, "Here, you give it to her." His companion, a much younger man with outsize sideburns, took the photograph. He was halfway across the street when the older man called after him, "And be nice about it!"

"Thanks a lot." Borchers thought of the report the older man would have to submit—if he wasn't wired for sound. "The whole thing's bad enough as it is," he added, mindful that filial devotion might be the one mitigating factor at his forthcoming trial. "She really depends on me, you know."

There was no real emotion behind the words. His only genuine emotion—a painful one—sprang from the knowledge of his ultimate solitude and friendlessness. When they finally drove him away, any feeling of solidarity he had left were reserved for the man who wore the other half of the handcuffs.

═══════ **CHAPTER XXXV** ═══════

THE NEW DAY WAS AN HOUR OLD WHEN Martin entered the Pension Racek. The only light in the long, narrow hallway came from an aquarium let into the wall beside the breakfast room. No fish were swimming or oxygen bubbles rising in the greenish water. All that could be seen in its murky depths were some pebbles and a few skeins of waterweed.

The man who had rented him the room was slumped in a chair in front of the key rack, breathing stertorously with his mouth ajar. He was wearing a black leather cap. Although he was fast asleep, it lent him a strangely industrious appearance.

A narrow flight of stairs, steep and uncarpeted, led up and away past the sleeping man's cubbyhole. He woke with a start as soon as Martin set foot on the first step, almost dislodging his headgear. "Who's that?" he grunted, readjusting the cap with one hand and switching on the desk lamp with the other.

"Number seventeen," said Martin.

Racek, if Racek it was, swiveled the lamp so that it shone full on Martin's face. He left it there for a while before he spoke.

"You certainly believe in keeping your girlfriends waiting."

"Sorry I woke you. I couldn't have been much quieter." Martin pointed back along the passage. "What happened to the fish?"

"Search me." The man removed the light from Martin's face. "They say you've got to have the right touch. I restocked that thing three times this year, and they all died off—God knows why. Maybe it's the smell in here . . . Oh well, don't let me keep you." He switched off the light and settled back in his chair.

The smell was heavy and cloying, not unlike a smoke pastille but clingier and more animal. Martin found it almost as strong when he reached the second floor. Room 17 was on his left. He had looked around for emergency exits the day before, but without success. The only way out led past the man downstairs, who seemed to spend twenty-four hours a day in his chair.

He knocked. No one answered, so he said his name. He expected to see fear in her face when she opened the door, but the long wait had drained it of expression. The fear was in her voice when she spoke.

"It's been awful, waiting all this time."

Martin took her in his arms. He could feel how cold she was, and how soft. "How long have you been here?"

"Ages." She gave a little shrug. "Two hours, that's all."

He kept his arms round her. "I don't blame you—I mean, who wouldn't feel scared on their own in a place like this?" The more normally he behaved, he thought, the better. In essence, it was all he could do to help her.

"Anyway, I'm glad you're here at last."

He ran his eyes over the room; the twin beds, the dark, bare floor, the gray, bare walls. The ancient curtains—real lace curtains, strangely enough—were torn and flecked with mildew, and several rings were missing. There was no running water, just a brown washstand with a jug and a basin on it. She had laid out her purchases on one of the beds—neatly, with the precision of a soldier displaying his kit for inspection.

"Did everything go all right?" He examined the shoulder bag and the small rucksack.

"There's coffee in the flask," she said behind him, "and some sandwiches, if you're hungry."

"Hungry? That banquet lasted nearly four hours."

"Maybe in the morning . . ."

"Yes, some coffee will do us good then. What about the car?"

"Vlatko will drive us if we want him to. He's waiting for a call."

He repacked the bag and rucksack and put them down beside the door. It occurred to him that he had never mentioned her second possible route out of the country. She interpreted his silence correctly, because she said, "Is anything wrong?"

In a sober, noncommittal tone, he told her about Carow's prearranged escape routes. Again she read his mind.

"You don't trust your own people?"

"I wouldn't go as far as that." He hesitated, groping for some way of conveying what he felt but hadn't yet defined, even to himself. "I do have the reservations, though. There's the question of the mole, the number of people in the know, the various channels of communication, the man who's supposed to take charge of you, the drive to the airport, checking in . . . Above all, there's the fact that we'd have to split up. What do you think? How do you feel about it?"

She shook her head. "I'm no great help. I feel . . ." Now it was her turn to grope for words. "Dead inside—squeezed dry of any certainty I ever had. I feel I'm deserting my country, and the thought still appalls me. I feel I'm betraying my past, and I'm not sure what sort of future I'm exchanging it for." She smiled sadly. "Get me out first, Martin. Maybe then I'll be able to tell you what I really feel."

His fingers twitched. It was all he could do not to take the deck from his pocket and turn up two cards. If he'd been alone, he would probably have done so.

"If we take the car, we'll have to leave Prague by five——that's in four hours' time. Otherwise, we'll have to wait another three hours after that. Seven more hours in this place . . ."

"The waiting wouldn't worry me." Her smile broadened and changed. "This is the first time we've been alone together, in a room by ourselves."

"Some room!"

"It's still a room. Have you noticed the smell?"

"Yes."

"What is it?"

"Horsemeat—cooked horsemeat. There's a horsemeat butcher next door. The man downstairs thinks it kills his fish."

"I don't mind it. The room, I mean, and the smell." She put her arms round him.

"One moment." He turned away and switched off the light, then walked to the window. The street below was as narrow and confined as the building itself. It was too dark to see anything clearly, but he stared down for a long time. At last he said, "I think we should leave here."

"Now, right away? But—"

"We'll find another boardinghouse." He switched on the light again.

"If it's the smell, I honestly don't mind." Then she understood. "But nodbody knows we're here."

"Nĕmeček does."

"He's one of your people."

Martin took the deck from his pocket and shuffled it. Zimra said nothing as he turned up two cards, just watched in silence. It was impossible to tell whether the sight perturbed her or not.

"Let's go," he said. He handed her the rucksack and slung the bag over his shoulder.

It wasn't till later, in another room so like the first they might never have left it, that he wondered what had really prompted him to change quarters. A simple precaution? A sixth sense more akin to animal instinct than human deliberation? He couldn't account for it. It was enough that he felt better when the door of the second room closed behind them. He realized, too, that one decision had entailed another.

"I'll call Vlatko, all right?"

"Of course."

Their new room was on the first floor. While making the call from a pay phone on the corridor wall, he thought of another reason for choosing *his* route: it would take him back to the land of his childhood.

He'd been fourteen when his father died. There was no memory; just debts and the house. The house had been publicly auctioned, and he had a vivid recollection of the open-air sale, the handful of prospective buyers, the auctioneer, his mother and himself. He also recalled his sense of anguish. That one nostalgic journey with his mother—that didn't count. What counted were the fourteen years he'd spent there.

In some strange way, it seemed to him now that his entire subsequent existence had added nothing to those years—that all he knew of life had been learned on the frontier. Revisiting the scene of those formative experiences would be a voyage of rediscovery. Perhaps he also felt, having spent fourteen happy years there, that the area itself boded well for the morning ahead of them.

I must tell her, he thought—I must explain and set her mind at rest. But all he said, when he rejoined her in the room whose resemblance to its predecessor surprised him yet again, was, "He'll be here at five sharp. That gives us three hours' sleep."

She stared at him in amazement. "You honestly think I'll be able to sleep?"

"Why not? Of course you will. We've a long day ahead of us—and a long walk."

But when they were on the bed together, he with his arms round her and both fully dressed, he felt her tremble.

"Don't worry," he said, "everything's going to be all right." He cradled her head against his chest.

He said it although he realized that her fear would be slow to subside. For that she needed more than words, more than an embrace. He remembered how many years he had taken to cure himself of the disease, and even now his body had never really rejected it. It lurked there still, like a dormant bacillus for which no cure had yet been discovered. Her body, too, would continue to harbor it.

In a year's time—no, years from now—she would still wake up in the middle of the night, trembling, and see this room and imagine that their ordeal was yet to come. The room would always exist, every object in it imprinted on her mind by fear. "We'll be out of here soon," he wanted to say, but he was too tired. Neither awake nor asleep, he drowsily, alertly, kept watch over the woman in his arms.

But he was happy nonetheless. He felt the weight of her head on his chest, the unexpectedly firm pressure of her body against his. Even clothed, their bodies generated an intimacy of a kind no woman had shared with him in years. It made him feel secure, being united with her in this semisleeping state, as if that fact alone were a guarantee that their escape would succeed.

CHAPTER XXXVI

CAROW HAD NEVER BEEN SERIOUSLY WORRIED BY Geissler's drinking—in fact, Geissler with a bottle of brandy in front of him became, so to speak, a better man. Inhibited when sober, he tended to conceal his inhibitions beneath a brisk, brusque veneer. When he drank, on the other hand, he blossomed forth into an amiably eloquent raconteur with a fund of good stories. Tonight was different, however, and when Geissler polished off one bottle and rose to fetch another, Carow caught him by the arm.

"Give it a rest! Go back to bed, go for a walk—do anything, but stop soaking."

Geissler shrugged off his restraining hand and walked to the only window, where he stood staring out across the yard. He had slept till midnight, tossing and turning, and then devoted himself to the bottle. He didn't speak for over an hour, just sat there in the self-contained seclusion of his brandy trip. He would fiddle with a backgammon piece from time to time, but all Carow's invitations to play were rejected with a shake of the head.

Carow himself would have welcomed a game. The concentration it demanded might have taken his mind off things more effectively than the book he was trying to read.

"Let's play. Drinking doesn't agree with you tonight."

Carow was reminded of his farewell party at headquarters—of the Organization's approach to drinking in general. Many a Center executive's desk resembled a well-stocked bar. Excuses were never lacking: birthdays, the approach of the weekend, the success of one operation, the failure of another. The real reason, Carow had always felt, was something quite different. Communal drinking had become a rite designed to transubstantiate hard liquor—as opposed to bread and wine—into friendship and mutual trust.

He set out the pieces on the board. "What's eating you?" He had already asked the same question in several different forms without getting an answer. This time Geissler rounded on him. His shirt gaped open to reveal a protruding paunch. He stuffed it back into his waistband with a series of fierce, convulsive movements.

"You know it all as usual, don't you? Good old Mama Carow, breast-feeding her beloved agents! You and your heart of gold, I *don't* think! You're so damned smart it hurts!'' The words erupted with such violence that Geissler's face became distorted as he spat them out. ''Nothing's eating me, except that thirty years in this lousy trade are enough for any man. Leave me alone!''

He stooped unsteadily to take another bottle from the drinks cupboard, then clutched it to his chest with both hands and tottered into the bedroom. A minute later, Carow heard the clink of bottleneck on tumbler as Geissler tried to pour himself another slug.

When had he started boozing? Carow searched his memory, as if the time might furnish some clue to Geissler's state of mind. Earlier in the evening—that was when. The first symptoms had followed closely on a brief call from Kurella—Geissler had taken it himself—to the effect that Borchers had been arrested. Carow's hand, which was idly propelling a backgammon piece to and fro, came to a sudden halt. His whole body seemed afflicted with the same paralysis. So did his brain, except for the single thought that kept racing through it: *They're up to something!* It was continuous and unstoppable, like an illuminated ticker tape unreeling inside his head. *They're up to something, they're . . .*

Geissler was lying on the bed fully dressed. He didn't demur when Carow removed the glass from his hands and sat down beside him. He smiled, but it was such a sick smile that Carow himself felt nauseated.

''What's happened?''

Geissler raised one hand. It flopped back on to his stomach. ''Stop mothering me.''

''They're up to something, aren't they?''

Geissler heaved himself into a sitting position, shaking with laughter. Carow gripped him by the shoulders until the laughter ceased and Geissler sank back.

''I don't know what's behind it,'' he said at last. ''C brought it up last night, when I was driving him to the chopper. He really went to work on me. How does he do it, Heiner? Tell me how he gets you to do these things? *We're* friends, aren't we, old pals from way back? Goddammit, give me a slug of that brandy!'' He rolled over and reached for the bottle, but underestimated the range.

Carow stood up and moved the bottle out of reach. ''How does he do what?''

''Why can't you leave a man in peace? What time is it?''

''Three o'clock.''

''Three o'clock? You're crazy, asking me questions like that at three o'clock.'' Geissler swung his legs to the floor and propped himself on his hands. ''He asked you the same things, don't you remember? I mean, about Martin's plans. You *must* remember—he's your goddamned agent.'' Geissler's face registered relief and hope, but only for an instant. They might have been painted there, and the paint faded fast. ''C wormed it out of me—that report on the Czech flyer.''

''You mean about Martin meeting him on the train?''

''Last night, when C was asking questions, you kept quiet about it. He went on and on, but you didn't say a word. I knew you must have your reasons, but C got it out of me—I don't know how.'' Geissler tried to stand up but failed. ''Jesus, I need a shower.''

Carow experienced a momentary sense of relief. It was three o'clock in the morning. He was overtired and overwrought. For the past six days and nights, he'd been living in spirit with an agent whom he'd promised to retrieve from the Bloc unscathed. His imagination was running riot—making him see things that didn't exist. It would all be over in a few hours' time.

''Is that all?'' he asked, hoping against hope.

Geissler stared at him, and again he was convulsed with laughter. The frightful sound ceased as abruptly as it had begun. ''So you don't care? I drink myself silly, and you say, 'Is that all?' You're just like him! I rat on a friend, and C manages to make me feel it's all quite innocent—until he starts on his loyalty jag and says there's 'no need' for you to be informed.''

''So you gave him the gist of the report?''

"Yes, and pretty damned lousy it made me feel."

"But you know that's how he is—how we both are. We all do it—we all keep secrets from each other. It's a time-honored principle. The system wouldn't work without it."

Geissler shook his head. "Why can't I trust you? Why can't you trust me? Yes, that's all! Your rotten principle turns my stomach."

"Why did C think it mattered so much? Did he give you a reason?"

"Since when did C have to explain himself to anyone? Actually, I know the reason. They used it as a marked card for Borchers and slipped it into his hand. They wanted some proof before they pulled him in. That was C's idea."

The ticker tape in Carow's head began to unwind again. "Did he tell you in so many words?"

"You know he never would. Kurella let it slip when he phoned."

"Did Borchers have the goods on him when they picked him up?"

"Presumably—how should I know? You don't think . . ."

Somewhere, a telephone started chirping.

Geissler struggled to his feet and stood there swaying. "Listen, Heiner, I didn't have a clue about *that* . . . Isn't that the phone?"

"I'm going." Carow debated whether to take the bottle with him, then left it. Brandy was a lot less self-destructive than Geissler's remorse. Personally, he needed a Darvon. He was on his way to fetch a glass of water when he realized that the insistent chirp was coming from the direct line to the monitoring service.

"Carow."

"We have a signal for you."

Eagerly as he had waited on previous nights, he was expecting no more signals at this hour. "Who from?"

"PAU/37. Are you ready?"

"One moment." So it wasn't Němeček! Carow swallowed two Darvons. Unable to find the pad and pencil right away, he was about to call Geissler when he heard water gushing from the shower in the bathroom. He found a piece of paper and something to write with, glanced at his watch and noted the time: 3:16 A.M.

"Carry on."

He was still sitting at the desk with the short decoded message in front of him when Geissler came in, naked under his bathrobe. Geissler's feet were dripping wet, and he was drying his hair on a towel. He seemed to have sobered up a little, but his face was a disaster area. Carow doubted whether his own looked any better. He picked up the sheet of paper and held it out.

Geissler shook his head. It might have been an indication that he didn't want to know or hear any more—either that, or he was shaking the water out of his ears.

"Němeček?" He had finally taken the message and was peering at it. "It's the booze. I can't see straight."

Carow waited until his silence prompted Geissler to look up. "They've got him."

"Němeček?"

"An hour ago."

Geissler subsided into a chair. His bathrobe sagged open. Noticing it, he blushed and covered his nakedness. "He'll lead them to Martin."

"He can only tell them what he knows." Perhaps he was going blind too, Carow thought. It might have been the Darvons taking effect, but he couldn't see Martin endangered by Němeček's arrest.

"But he knows about the boardinghouse."

"I can't believe Martin didn't spot him. Němeček's job was to keep an eye on him in the hotel, during the official program. He wasn't up to anything else, and if Martin caught on . . ."

"You mean he'd allow for Němeček's arrest?"

"A runner inside the Bloc has to allow for everything." Thinking of Martin reinforced the soothing effect of the drug. At this moment, Carow felt positively proud of him,

just like—Geissler was right—just like a proud parent. Or
was he only deluding himself? Was it because he remembered his self-imposed ultimatum, and because time was
running out?

Neither of them spoke for a while. Then Geissler said,
''So you had a second baby-sitter on site?''

''For safety's sake, yes. A nice, innocuous sort of person.
A schoolmarm.''

''Was that her cover?''

''No, she really is one—was one, I mean. Only a proba-
tioner, but very promising.'' Carow looked up. ''I naturally
didn't mention her to you. On principle.''

''There's teamwork for you,'' said Geissler, but he didn't
sound resentful anymore, just resigned. ''Now do you see
what I mean? The whole thing's schizophrenic.'' He walked
over to the teleprinter and clipped the signal to the board,
ready for transmission. ''What now?''

''How long will Němeček stand up to interrogation? You
know the man.''

''Not long enough. Not till tomorrow, and we don't know
what *they* know.''

''You realize,'' said Carow, ''that the other route is Martin's only hope if Němeček talks?''

''That was all Kurella told me, I swear. They fed Borchers the information so as to catch him red-handed. They
know what they're doing, for God's sake.''

''When would Sěnk have to take off?''

''I forgot to tell you. C instructed me to find out where his
Bell JetRanger is based and whether there's a flight scheduled for today.''

''Well?''

''Sěnk has given advance notice of a flight from Munich
to Zermatt, but he naturally wouldn't have stated his true
destination. Take-off's scheduled for seven A.M.''

''How long would he need?''

''To make the border? We don't know the rendezvous.''
Carow rose and went over to the built-in wardrobe. He

took out his jacket and overcoat. "A JetRanger—does it have the range for a two-way trip?"

"Like I said, that depends on the rendezvous, also on whether there are any holdups and how soon he locates them. He'd have enough juice for normal purposes." Geissler paused. "You think they'll both try to come out that way?"

"Martin won't leave her behind."

"Šěnk will do his damnedest to reach German territory, that's for sure. Landing in Austria would create complications."

"Can you round up some men? Station them at likely points along the border. If they really do fly out, I don't want some local police sergeant trying to earn himself a commendation. This operation's mine till it's over."

"What are you going to do?"

Carow had pulled on his overcoat. He checked the pockets for his car key and gun. "I've got to find out what really went on with Borchers. Are you all right now?"

"Not too bad."

"Call me if anything develops at this end. If you can't raise me in my car or at the Center, try my home. Well . . ."

They stood looking at each other for a moment or two, both at a loss for words, both aware that there was no more to be said, and that anything that did spring to mind would be no help to either of them. Geissler accompanied Carow to the door. There, at the very last moment, he said, "Take care."

It wasn't until his Porsche was speeding through the darkness, with the autobahn almost to itself, that Carow thought twice about Geissler's parting remark. On the doorstep it had seemed a rather trite but not unnatural thing to say—an attempt to mitigate the awkwardness of their leave-taking. *Take care* . . . Sitting there alone behind the wheel, Carow found it ominous, like a warning to a friend *en route* for enemy territory.

CHAPTER XXXVII

1

THE ROAD WAS GETTING STEADILY WORSE; they could feel it playing havoc with the worn-out shock absorbers. They sat on the floor, clinging to anything within reach: the corrugated iron sides, the metal ribs on the floor itself, the crates that slithered to and fro whenever the vehicle rounded a bend.

From time to time, Vlatko tapped the partition behind the driver's seat to signal that all was well, and that he was continuing to follow Martin's penciled route on the map. His brother, a dog breeder, normally used the van for transporting animals between the city and his kennels in the country. For Martin, the smell that clung to the interior held a very special significance.

Hitherto they had sat in total darkness. Now a small gray rectangle took shape before their eyes. Not really a window yet—it wasn't light enough for that—but for the first time since they drove off into the night, Martin felt that even this endless journey would have to end sometime.

"Everything all right?" He put out his hand. Zimra was only a darker shadow in the gloom.

"When does it get light?"

He found her hand. It was small enough for him to enclose in his own. "My father used to call this the worst time of all at the prison where he worked, for the guards as well as the inmates. The hour of atonement, that was his phrase for it. A new day dawns, but you know it doesn't dawn for you.''

''You've never told me about him, only your mother.''

''That's because she was so lovable and uncomplicated, unlike Father. I never felt I knew him properly. He was an inscrutable character. There was something—I don't know—something of the desperado about him. He taught me a lot of things that horrified my mother.''

''A strange life, wasn't it, working in a prison?''

''I don't quite know how he felt about it. He was a policeman by training—a small-town policeman. He lost his job when the Germans marched in. Prison work was the only kind he could get that had anything remotely to do with police work.''

''And you lived near here?''

''We'll be passing the village later on. Not that there's much to see these days—it's too near the border. Frontier folk, we were. The frontier meant everything to us, good and bad. As children we got all our fun from it—and our thrills. Plenty of youngsters used to earn a living from it for their families. If a boy was smart and plucky enough and had a father who'd teach him the tricks of the trade, he could bring home as much in one night as his father earned in a month.''

''Did you do that.''

''Sometimes.''

The van's wheels lost traction on a bad patch of road. It slowed almost to a standstill. ''Not much farther now,'' he said.

''It's lonely in the dark. Tell me some more.''

''About life out here? Well, you got your first introduction to it from the old folk. With me, it was my mother's father who told me about frontier landmarks with names like Devil's Spring and Duck's Bill and Golden Tree. You listened and listened and asked innumerable questions and begged to be allowed to see everything for youself. And one day, when you'd pestered him long enough, your grandfather would take you fishing or hunting rabbits or setting beaver traps—there are plenty of beavers still, down by the river. You learned where all the places were he'd told you about and how to get there and how useless it was to rely on maps. You learned to recognize the sounds in the woods and the lowlands, the daytime ones and the nighttime ones, and how animals react to intruders.'' Martin sighed. ''It was one big playground—a children's paradise.''

''And smuggling?''

''That your father taught you. There were nights when your parents undressed you and bandaged you up in yards and yards of lace till you looked like a mummy, and you could hardly breathe with your shirt buttoned over the top. You had to know all the routes across the frontier like the back of your hand. You knew which ones to use and which to avoid at all costs, and which times were safe or dangerous.'' He sighed again. ''It became instinctive in the end.''

''You went across all by yourself?''

''Not always. Sometimes we'd be ten or fifteen strong—a whole gang of youngsters. We smuggled everything. Coffee, food, cigarettes, silk stockings—even people, occasionally. It all depended on the season of the year—that's what determined the kind of things you took across and brought back. And when you got home in the morning you'd be tired out and proud and happy as hell.''

''So this was really where you learned your trade?''

''In a way, perhaps.'' He had never looked at it like that, but maybe she was right in assuming the existence of an unbroken thread.

''What else?''

''What else did I learn?'' Martin hesitated for a moment. Then he said, ''How to catch people on the run.'' A tremor ran through her hand, but he went on. ''Prisoners used to break out of Father's jail sometimes. They thought they stood a good chance—they thought it would be easy, what with the maze of waterways and the dense woods and the frontier being so close. There was a team that specialized in recapturing them. Father belonged to it because he'd been born here. He knew every bend in the river, every path and gulley, every forester's hut, every conceivable hiding place—every tree for miles, or almost. He could read a trail, too. He could tell from a snapped twig how far ahead a runaway was. Fresh breaks aren't discolored; older ones turn brown.'' He lapsed into silence.

"Go on."

"There were dogs, too—pickups full of specially trained tracker dogs. My father let me run them on the leash. That was another tip I learned: runaways don't stand a chance against dogs on rainy days because rain keeps scents fresh and distinct. Dry weather is a boon when dogs are after you. It scrambles scents together and makes them harder to identify—dry, sunny weather like the kind we've been having these past few days."

"Did many of them make it?"

"No, not many, thanks to the dogs and men like Father. I don't know how many tried, but he told me only a handful had evaded recapture since the jail was built, and that was before the turn of the century. Nobody got clear while he was there. I remember he used to admire any convict who remained at large longer than twenty-four hours."

The rectangular gray shape was slowly turning into a window filmed with dust from the road.

"My memories are quite different," she said. "Towns are another matter—I mean, townsfolk are poor in a different way."

"My mother used to say that too, more or less. That's why she always refused to move there."

"We had a wretched little apartment. Two rooms and a kitchen, no sun—not a proper apartment, just a noisy cocktail shaker of a place. I used to lie in bed at night—not 'my' bed, because I shared it with a brother and sister—and it shook and rattled every time a train passed the window."

"Was that in Poznań?"

"Poznań first, then Berlin, but one thing never changed: the smell of fresh paint. My mother's brother worked at a paint factory. Being in charge of the warehouse, he used to filch cans of the stuff. My mother was always busy painting something or other in a vain attempt to make our place look brighter and cozier: window frames, doors, kitchen cupboards, walls, even floors. She had to use any colors my uncle could get hold of, so we ended up with a weird assortment of greens and blues and reds and yellows. It was a mania of hers, redecorating. I still feel sick when I smell fresh paint." She paused. "For me, the mornings were a hopeful time. Suddenly, the whole city became my apartment—a great big apartment filled with sunlight. We couldn't go smuggling, of course . . ."

Was she smiling? Something in her voice made him wonder.

"But we did have other resources. If you were little, you went scrounging. Five minutes' walk away there was a dairy shop with a man behind the counter who couldn't say no if you smiled at him—as long as you chose a moment when his wife wasn't around. If you were bigger, you stole. Not strictly because you were hungry. Cold and hunger don't mean so much when you're young—at that age, there are worse things than going to bed with an empty belly. Once, when my father was home, he told me I'd been wrong to steal. He looked at me, very sternly, and said, 'Bread or no bread—that's what makes history.' My father talked that way to everyone. He made no allowance for the fact that I was only a child of seven or eight. I didn't understand what he meant, but I could tell he was deadly serious. My mother had been listening—she was up a ladder with a paper hat on her head, painting the ceiling. She just laughed. I've never forgotten that scene—the earnestness and conviction in my father's voice, and my mother's sarcastic laugh . . ."

She broke off. The van had come to a sudden halt. They sat there with bated breath until Vlatko tapped the partition three times.

2

IT WAS STILL so dark when they got out that the rear window might have been a hallucination.

Vlatko, who was holding the map, said, "I hope we're in the right place."

For a moment, Martin wasn't sure. They were at the mouth of a road, but it should have been wider. Then he saw that it really was the old road reduced to a semblance of a path by encroaching vegetation. Bending down, he saw that even the asphalt surface had been ruptured by weeds.

"This is it, all right."

Vlatko gestured with the map. "There's supposed to be a village here."

The sky was devoid of moon and stars. Similarly unrelieved by any pinpoints of light, the level expanse of countryside before them stretched away like a second sea of celestial gloom. In the distance, a little to the north, the skyline seemed to condense and grow darker still. That, thought Martin, was where the forests of the Rejt began. A gentle breeze was blowing from the west, laden with the scent of stagnant water.

"Everything's fine. What time is it?"

"Five past six. We ran a little late. I didn't know the roads would be so bad."

"We still have an hour before it gets light. That'll be plenty."

It was colder than Martin had expected. Zimra was marking time and hugging herself to keep warm and drive the stiffness from her limbs. Martin fetched the little rucksack from the van and helped her on with it. The bag he shouldered himself.

"You'd better start back now, Vlatko."

Vlatko didn't notice the money in Martin's hand because he was looking at Zimra. "So you're really going?"

"Yes," she said, "I'm going."

"I could wait an hour or two."

Martin moved away. He felt it was something that concerned the two of them alone. They hadn't had a chance to speak before, in all the feverish haste of their departure from the city.

"You think your father would have approved?" he heard Vlatko say.

"Please, Vlatko! Please go. Take the money—for expenses. And thank you for everything."

"Well, would he?"

"Please!"

He shook hands with her, then turned to Martin. His face was as ageless and expressionless as it had been in the foyer of the Palace of Culture. He proffered the map, but Martin said, "I won't be needing a map from here on. Dump it somewhere on the way back—not too near here, though."

They stepped aside while Vlatko turned the van. He had wound the window up, so they saw nothing of him as he drove past. The next bend was only a few yards off. Zimra didn't speak until the rear lights had vanished and the sound of the engine died away.

"There was only one answer," she said, "and I couldn't bring myself to say it."

"Come on, it's time we went."

They headed west in silence. The road provided them with just enough room to walk abreast. The remainder was overgrown with weeds and waist-high grass.

"Were you very attached to him?" Martin had no need to specify.

"It wasn't as simple as that. In the beginning, I think I was plain miserable. I resented his calling me Zimra and giving my mother a hard time. As a child, I was just a pocket edition of her unhappiness. Father was a professional hero. Half his life he spent fighting fascism. The other half he spent behind bars, ruining his health. He reduced us to penury for the sake of the things he held sacred—he dreamed of an egalitarian utopia while my mother worried about coal for the winter."

Zimra paused to adjust the straps of the rucksack. It was a moment or two before she spoke again.

"Later on, of course, I grew to love him for the very same reason—for his rocklike faith. I discovered other things about him—less admirable things. He was a tyrant, he drank, he had affairs with other women; but none of that mattered. I loved him because of the one thing he clung to all his life, and that was his belief in a better world."

"Why did he kill himself?"

"He fell into disfavor. I don't mean the first time, in Stalin's day—this was later on. 'The dictatorship of official-dom . . .' That little phrase, plus a few other indiscretions, cost him his Party posts. He went to jail for another two years. Then they released him. I remember Mother calling me the day before he came out. She was terribly agitated, asked if I'd go and fetch him, said she couldn't face it.

"It was awful. I'm built like her, but Father had always been a bull of a man. He was a blacksmith's son, and he'd served his apprenticeship in the trade. Blacksmith, not Party iffical—that's what it said in all his various passports. He insisted on it.

"Well, now he was a physical wreck. Nephritis, edema, rheumatism, chronic insomnia—we had to put him straight to bed. After a week—on a Sunday, it was—he called us all in. Mother, me, the few friends he had left. He said he had something to tell us.

"He harangued us for an hour or more, even though Mother kept begging him to save his strength. He spoke of his faith in the future and urged us never to forget that it was just beyond the horizon, this better world of his. All we had to do was scale the final slope. It sounded crazy, of course, but not to him. Then he sent us out of the room and shot himself. He was so weak he had to hold the gun with both hands.

"Mother died six months later. She had herself cre-mated—she'd left special instructions, though it was some-thing she'd often argued about with Father, being a

Catholic. Their urns shared the same niche till three years ago, when he was rehabilitated. Then his ashes were transferred to the central cemetary—the Socialist Memorial Park—and walled up behind an ornate plaque. That would have infuriated him, though he'd naturally have been proud of near neighbors like Rosa Luxemburg and Karl Liebknecht.

"It's strange, but Father means even more to me now that he's gone. Living as he did, clinging to his idealized picture of the world—anyone like that is bound to come to grief or end up a very lonely man, but it doesn't mean he was wrong in principle. I know I'm letting him down—I can feel it. I wouldn't go back now even if I could, but Vlatko was right. He wouldn't have approved."

They trudged on in silence, Martin setting the pace. A thin, pallid finger of light had touched the skyline behind them, but they didn't notice it because they were heading west without a backward glance. After half an hour the smell of water became stronger. Once they saw the dull glint of it through a half-felled patch of forest. Another time the road forked and Martin bore left without a moment's hesitation, only quickening his pace. All of a sudden they came to a fenced field with cud-chewing cattle belly-down in the grass. There were a number of open-sided barns and water wagons to be seen, but no houses. Martin paused and looked round, then walked on. A few more steps brought them to a substantial mound of bricks overgrown with grass and thistles.

"Is this it?"

"Yes," he said, recalling that his mother had asked the same question. The mound of rubble still preserved the outlines of a house. Standing there in the first light of dawn, he could picture everything as it used to be. There was the front door, and beside it the bench on which his grandfather had given him his first lessons in frontier lore.

"When did they do that—knock everything down, I mean?"

He didn't answer, so vivid was the feeling that his senses had deceived him. The house was merely playing a macabre game of peekaboo—playing dead. A little time, a little patience, and it would rise again, resurrecting itself brick by brick like a slow-motion film in reverse.

"Martin, look!"

He turned and stared at her for a moment, half-bemused by her sudden recall to the present. She was pointing to something in the distance. Walking in an overcoat had made her perspire, but now she was shivering in the chill morning air.

"What are those? Watchtowers?"

Her face was almost expressionless again because fear and suspense had emptied it of emotion. She looked particularly beautiful, he thought. "You're looking lovelier than ever." The trite, stereotyped words were on the tip of his tongue, although he knew, if he followed the direction of her outstretched arm, that he would see the watchtowers too.

It was an effort to tear his eyes away from her. The light had changed. The wooden towers were strung out across the dead landscape at wide intervals. Martin found nothing sinister about their gawky silhouettes. They reminded him of the raised blinds built by local hunters, who had used them for shooting hare. At the height of summer, before the hunting season opened, he had often dozed off in a blind like that, snug and secure beneath its roof of logs and bark.

"Everything's fine." My signature tune, he thought. "I knew they were there."

"But where are we going?"

He took her hand. "It won't be really light for another half hour, and by then we'll be safe under cover. Come on, we can rest once we get there."

CHAPTER XXXVIII

IT WAS ALMOST DAYBREAK WHEN Carow's Porsche turned into the cul-de-sac. He saw no sign of life. This was a quiet road, even on weekdays. Its residents could afford to miss the morning rush hour, and the first cars to be seen there were family runabouts driven by mothers taking their children to school. Today was Sunday, though. He'd been away for precisely eleven days.

A Volkswagen convertible was parked in front of the double garage. It was black, like his Porsche, with a fawn fabric roof. Carow knew no one who drove such a model. He parked beside it and let himself into the garden by a side gate.

The lake at the foot of the gently sloping lawn was steel-gray. White with hoarfrost in places, the grass shimmered with moisture. A few birds were already singing. As he inserted his key in the door, he felt like a stranger who should really have rung the bell.

Some luggage was standing in the hall—two Samsonite suitcases and his wife's black-and-white-checked golf bag. The handles were still adorned with airline tags. He hadn't heard from Isabelle since his call to Johannesburg. Had she told him when she expected to get back? He couldn't remember. Everything beyond the confines of the outstation had lost its importance. Presumably, she had arrived late last night.

He hesitated, wondering whether or not to take his coat off—wondering why he was there at all. When he'd pulled into a deserted layby, fifty or sixty miles along the autobahn, most of his pent-up anger had been dissipated by half an hour behind the wheel of a fast car. What was the point of descending on C at crack of dawn? What did he really have to go on? The fact that he hadn't turned back stemmed more from an indeterminate emotion than from any clear idea of what he proposed to do or say. But when he reached C's house—so ostentatiously guarded, so glaringly floodlit—the prospect became too much for him. Reporting to the man on the gate, getting C out of bed, stating his business on the house phone . . . He had decided to drive on here instead.

The pointer's heavy breathing could be heard through the drawing-room door. He was asleep on his pigskin bed when Carow walked in, with a piece of rag between his forepaws. Holding onto something in his sleep was a habit acquired in old age, as his health began to fail.

It was darker inside the house than out. The drawing room, whose self-conscious elegance had always made Carow squirm, looked dowdy in the gray light.

The pointer woke up and raised his head. Carow walked over to the fireplace. The dog's open sores gave off a foul stench. Carow had to steel himself to bend down and put his hand on the grizzled head. "Okay," he said, "let's take a walk, the two of us."

He opened one of the french windows to spare the pointer a trek across the slippery tiles in the hall. The dog struggled up and stood there, tremulous with exertion, then quieted. Carow was following him out onto the terrace when he heard footsteps descending the stairs.

"Is that you, Heiner?"

Isabelle was wearing a terry-cloth wrapper. She must have heard him parking his car outside the garage because she was sedulously combed and made up. Amazing how fresh she looked, Carow thought. Not many women of forty-nine would have looked so consummately rested after a tiring twelve-hour flight and half a night's sleep.

"Did you come from the hospital?"

It seemed ridiculous to keep up the pretense, but force of habit prevailed. "Yes," he said. "When did you get back?"

She brushed past him and closed the french window. The pointer remained outside, forlorn and bewildered.

"Couldn't you have called first?"

Called where? he thought, but he said, "Sorry I woke you." He looked at the dog through the glass and regretted having to keep him waiting. "I've had a long drive, I need some coffee." He hoped she would go back upstairs, but she followed him into the kitchen and sat there in silence while he boiled a kettle.

"Like some tea?"

"No thanks, it's too early for me."

He carried his coffee to the table. Isabelle's red wrapper hung open, and she was naked beneath it. Her bare legs were tanned and shapely in a way that testified to regular exercise on a golf course. In the instant before she crossed them, he caught a glimpse of her pubic hair. His sole reaction was to think of Geissler clutching at his bathrobe that morning.

"Do they allow you to take your coffee as strong as that?"

Looking at her practiced smile, more camouflage than anything else, he was suddenly tired of deception and evasion, revolted by charades and masquerades in general.

"That black convertible—who does it belong to?"

"All right, let's stop pretending." She might have read his thoughts. "It's time we faced facts. We ought to have done so years ago."

"I asked you a question."

She stiffened. "Kindly don't take that tone with me."

"Fehling?" Carow drank his coffee. He searched for something meaningful to say but found it hard enough to grasp what lay at the root of the situation: a married couple whose life together had become a bad habit—one that entailed hurting each other. On another occasion he might have tried to change the subject and paper over the cracks. As it was, he rose and said, "Excuse me, I have to make an urgent call."

He went into the study, and again she followed him. He dialed the outstation. Geissler answered at once. "Any news?" There wasn't. "The chopper took off at six fifty-five." He already knew, having called the airport *en route*. "Okay, stay by the phone. I'll be at the Center by eight." Isabelle's presence inhibited him from asking how Geissler was feeling. Besides, his voice sounded normal and alert. He hung up.

"Are you through?" she said. "Now can we talk like two mature, sensible people?"

Carow looked at her. "Is he on the premises?"

"There are going to be some changes, I'd like to get that straight. And don't make me say things I'd honestly regret."

"Things like 'This is my house'?" He could have bitten his tongue. There was no point in hurting each other anymore. "I'm sorry. Let's not say anything we'd sooner not—either of us, right?" He glanced at the shivering dog on the terrace. "I'll take him for a walk. I don't suppose anyone else has in the past few days."

Carow went into the drawing room. At the door to the terrace he turned. "How did you make out in Johannesburg?"

"Runner-up. Not bad against that class of competition. I might even have won, with a bit of luck."

He went outside. "Come on," he said, putting out his hand to the pointer without touching him. He walked slowly to enable the animal to keep up. It was broad daylight now. The hoarfrost had gone from the grass and the lake was green. It was going to be a warm, sunny day. Good flying weather.

They had reached the lakeside and were standing under a

big beech tree. He took the gun from his pocket and flipped the safety catch. It was Sunday, he remembered again. He wondered what to do with the dog afterward. With a human being he would have known, but whom could he call on a Sunday to dispose of a pointer's carcass?

============ **CHAPTER XXXIX** ============

THE WATER LAY TO THEIR RIGHT. It stretched away for as far as they could see; not a river, not a lake, but a motionless gray mass congealed around wooded islands. The water level was very low, as they could tell from the paler corrugations of soil on the shore. They could also see how much power the water developed after rain. Overturned trees lay everywhere, roots still clinging to the earth, trunks and limbs half submerged and coated with mud. At dawn their surroundings had resembled a primeval landscape untrodden by man. Even now, in the full light of the sun, the place looked bleak and desolate.

They stared at each other, straining their ears. The sound drew nearer, receded, circled, changed pitch. "Could be," he whispered. Now beyond the nearest wooded island, it acquired a strange, throaty, fluttering quality. He shook his head.

Three mallards burst from the trees in arrowhead formation and touched down with their webbed feet fully extended. They folded their wings into place and, still preserving their original formation, became a trio of motionless objects on a sheet of motionless water.

"They fooled me," she said. "For a moment I thought it was the helicopter."

Martin glanced at the watch in his palm. It was Zimra's, and the strap was too short for him to wear it on his wrist.

"Ten minutes to go. He'll try to be right on time. Not too early, not too late."

"How will he manage it?"

"Gypsy's that type. You'll like him."

"I certainly will, if he makes it."

He had found conversation difficult since they reached the spot, and most of the time had passed in silence. They were sitting beneath some hazel bushes that screened them from the air. Immediately in front of them, a grassy slope ran down to the field where Šěnk would land, a green rectangle lush with grass and broad-leafed coltsfoot. A belt of reeds separated the pickup point from the water. To the left of the field stood rows of newly planted poplars. They had already shed their leaves, and between their slender trunks and branches could be seen another field containing two tumbledown shacks.

Martin had taken quite a time to find the right place when they reached the area before daybreak. Too many things had changed over the years. Stretches of woodland had been cleared, streams had altered course, and one field resembled another.

He unscrewed the cap of the vacuum flask. Only a mouthful of coffee remained, and that was cold. Zimra shook her head, so he poured the dregs away. He glanced at the watch again. "Right," he said, "you'd better take your coat off now." She looked at him inquiringly. "You'll be able to run faster without it." He pointed out the spot again. "As soon as I give the word, make a dash for it."

"What about you?"

"I'll be right behind you. But don't look back—keep your eyes fixed on the door of that helicopter. Head straight for it and jump in quick."

Kneeling because the foliage above them left no room to

do otherwise, he helped her out of her coat and draped it loosely round her shoulders. It was still cold, so she held it together by the lapels.

He was just removing his own coat when he heard the muffled whop-whop-whop of rotor blades. The sound hadn't made a gradual approach, didn't gain in volume and intensity; it was simply there from one moment to the next, a steady succession of muffled handclaps. Whop-whop-whop . . . Every beat seemed to bludgeon Martin's eardrums.

Halfway out of his coat, he abruptly found himself unable to move, like a man in a straitjacket. A dark shape loomed overhead, pinning him to the ground. The moment when both were there and pinning him down—the noise and the shape—seemed endless, but they moved on as swiftly as they had come. A shadow darted across the field like some fleet-footed beast, whereas the military helicopter flailing the air above it looked huge and ponderous. Its receding whop-whop-whop sound almost friendly.

"What was that?" Zimra lay sprawled on her back. He pulled off his coat and helped her up. A twig had scored her forehead and left a thin, rapidly reddening scratch there. "Wasn't it ours?"

He replaced the coat round her shoulders. "No, one of theirs." He noticed that his palms were moist. "They fly routine patrols along the border." He paused. "There'll only be the one, so we're lucky it came when it did." He looked in the direction it had gone. The three mallards had disappeared. Everything seemed peaceful and deserted again.

He turned toward her. She had the look he loved so much. He pressed his lips to the scratch on her forehead. His one desire at this moment was to stay here forever. Even if the JetRanger came to pick them up, he would rather have stayed with her beneath the hazel bushes than left their refuge and run across the field. Incapable of putting what he felt into words, he drew her close. There was a suspicion of silver where her hair had grown out at the roots. It reminded him of the barrettes he'd bought. He produced the little package from his pocket.

"For me?"

He nodded. She undid the string, tore open the wrapping, and lifted the lid of the box. Again the silence was broken by the whop-whop-whop of a helicopter. Neither of them had even an instant's hope that it was Šěnk; the Czech machine had returned. She dropped the box and the clasps went flying as he swiftly hugged her to him. The heavy aircraft blotted out the sun, hovering low overhead with the rocking motion of a massive cable car. Then it banked away to the left and soared clear of the poplars like a bead running up a string.

Martin kept his eyes on it while Zimra started searching for the clasps in the grass. He saw its dark bulk sink down beyond the plantation. For a moment it seemed about to land. It hovered there, rocking a little, then gained height and resumed it former course along the frontier.

"They're lovely. Really lovely."

She had evidently found the barrettes, but Martin was still staring at the spot where the helicopter had brushed the ground. Although he hadn't been able to see anything through the poplars at this distance, the picture in his mind's eye was an alarming one: figures leaping from the chopper's open door to the ground, rifles in hand—Czech Army sharpshooters.

"Did you get them at the Dúm Evropa? I hope you didn't pay too much for them."

He looked at her. Was she really so calm, or was her serenity a pretense? She seemed to be debating whether or not to put the clasps in her hair. The she replaced them in the box and shut it. This time she looked him straight in the eye.

"Do we still have a chance? It's after nine, isn't it?"

It was five past. "He'll come," Martin said.

"How far is it to the border?"

"As the crow flies, two or three miles."

"And on foot?"

"More, because of the waterways."

"Maybe we could manage it tonight."

Martin shook his head. "He'll come," he repeated, clinging to the thought. Although he had no real hope left, he felt strangely undiscouraged. He put his arms round her. Silence enveloped them once more.

═══════ CHAPTER XL ═══════

TO CAROW ON THIS SUNDAY MORNING, the Organization's headquarters looked more mysterious and deserted than ever—bleaker, too. Rain had abruptly and unexpectedly begun to fall from a sunny sky, as though the elements were out of phase.

Carow had been coming here now for over twenty-five years. He had watched the Center expand, less by coordinated degrees than with the alternate growth and regression of a tumor. But he wasn't thinking of that as he drove to his office through the rain along narrow, deserted asphalt roads. The same old feeling of security had possessed him as soon as he passed the main gate and entered the complex. He felt safe, but not in any superficial sense. It was almost like a return to the womb.

The feeling soon faded. All he felt now were the pains in his back. He wondered, yet again, if confronting C would serve any useful purpose.

C was entrenched behind his desk when Carow entered the inner sanctum. Although the red light was on, none of

the secretaries had been there to play Cerberus. Puck was
clearing away the remains of a working breakfast.

"Had anything to eat yet?" Carow didn't reply, just
stood there with his hands in his overcoat pockets. A note of
uncertainty crept into the old man's voice. "What's wrong?
Don't just stand there, Heiner, take off your coat and sit
down." Carow's continued silence evoked a sigh. "So
Geissler talked?"

"Yes."

The objects on C's desk had been displaced to make room
for his breakfast. Slowly and carefully, he began to restore
them to their original positions: the four telephones, the
pads of yellow paper, the desk set with the red ink and old-
fashioned fountain pen, the battery of sharpened pencils.

"Any special reason for turning up at this hour? Your
man isn't out yet, is he?"

Puck had retired to the kitchenette. Carow strove to recall
when he'd first had doubts about the man who had claimed
his loyalty for so many years. "Why did you feed Borchers
that information?"

"Let's not swap roles, Heiner." C's tone was wholly
amiable; he might have been offering well-meant advice to a
favorite son. "We had no really solid evidence against
Borchers, so we tried to nab him red-handed. Unfortunately,
there was a hitch. He managed to evade surveillance."

"And you didn't inform me?"

C ignored this. "He tried to be too clever, though. He left
a blank message in his dead-letter box and hung onto the real
one. Crude, but it nearly worked. Kurella spotted the truth
as soon as the men who picked him up submitted their report. Borchers had planted his message at home. We were
late, but not too late. On the contrary, the operation was a
total success. When his contact called at the apartment, we
picked him up as well—two birds with one stone, eh? You
say you didn't know? In that case, I find your presence here
all the more—"

"You took one hell of a risk."

"It was one of those things. You can't plug every last gap."

"What if it had really gone wrong?"

"The information was pretty imprecise. No exact details of time and place." C looked up. "Besides, it wasn't the route we've arranged for Martin and his girlfriend. If he sticks to instructions, he'll have nothing to fear."

"They've arrested Němeček."

"Who's Němeček? Oh, yes, I remember . . ."

"Are you sure Kurella's men turned up in time?"

"Absolutely, I already told you."

C was still dissatisfied with the arrangement of his desk. He shifted a yellow pad two inches to the right, pulled the desk set fractionally closer. "When did the report of his arrest come in?"

"Three-sixteen."

This time, C's face registered surprise. "There's nothing on my desk about it. Why wasn't the message passed on?"

His hands continued to make fine adjustments. Watching them, Carow felt that this was where the answer lay—this was the source of the truth he'd been seeking. He was as close to it now as he would ever get: C, chafing at a signal that hadn't been forwarded, fussing over the arrangement of his desk like any petty bureaucrat.

"I promise you this, Heiner. If anything happens to Martin and the Steffin woman—not that I think it will—we won't leave them in the lurch."

Suddenly, there was nothing left for Carow to say.

"We'll get them both released as soon as possible. It may take time, of course—*they'll* try to capitalize on the situation, Zentner most of all, but we'll make them an offer they can't refuse . . . Come on, Heiner, we've always seen eye to eye in the end, the two of us." C's voice rose. "I'm not asking for your approval, but I can request your compliance."

"He was our agent!" They were talking as if the worst

had happened, thought Carow. Had C heard something from Geissler he didn't know about?

"Very laudable of you, Heiner. I mean, it does you credit, this absolute loyalty to an agent, but don't forget—"

Carow cut him short. "I told you I wouldn't go along with you, not this time. I'll send you my formal resignation." He turned on his heel and walked out. C made no attempt to stop him.

Later, sitting at his desk with a sheet already in the machine, Carow realized that resigning wouldn't be enough. If Martin and the woman failed to make it, he couldn't extricate himself by signing a piece of paper. He had survived too many of his self-imposed ultimatums.

When taking off his coat, he had removed the gun and put it on his desk in the usual way. He wondered whom to ask about the dog. He pulled the telephone toward him but waited for fear of missing a call from Geissler.

He looked at his watch. It was nine-fifteen, too early for Geissler to have heard yet.

═══════════ CHAPTER XLI ═══════════

THE SKY WAS RENT BY THE SCREAMS OF high-flying gulls. Alarmed by something, they soared above the trees in their hundreds. Martin had never seen gulls keep such strict formation. Even land-based gulls were loners and individualists.

Abruptly, the birds altered course. Their tight formation broke up and they scattered in all directions, protesting shrilly. It looked as if the sky were raining feathers.

He listened hard. Another, even more insistent sound could be heard above the birds' strident chorus: the throb of a turbine-engined helicopter—not a muffled bellow this time, but a light, high-pitched whiff-whiff-whiff. It reminded Martin of twigs springing back into place in the wake of someone running along an overgrown path.

"There he is!" He said it before he saw anything. He was suddenly filled with a hope whose existence he would have denied only moments before, so endless had the final minutes of waiting seemed.

"It's him. Get ready."

Keep coming, he thought, and the thought became a prayer: *Keep coming!* The miracle was going to happen after all. They would take to the air and soar away. A quick sprint of seventy or eighty yards, down the slope and across the field, and all would be blotted out: last night, the last seven days, the last six years. *Keep coming!*

The Bell JetRanger swept into view above the poplar plantation. Compared to the other machine it looked small and dainty—almost toylike—with a long, slender pencil of a tail. The elongated cabin was a Plexiglas teardrop, and reflected sunlight hid the occupant from view. The miraculous toy seemed to be flying by itself. All that dispelled the illusion of unreality was the swelling note of its engine and the rhythmical whiff-whiff-whiff of rotor blades.

It was over the field now and slowly descending. They both stood up, Martin holding Zimra tight by the arms. When he saw the grass and coltsfoot flattened by the helicopter's downdraft and its skids hovering only a few feet from the ground, he released her.

"Now!"

He stayed close behind her as she raced down the slope and across the field. The skids brushed the ground. *We're on our way,* he thought, *we're on our way!* The Plexiglas door opened, and for an instant he fancied he saw a swarthy face, a welcoming grin, when all he could really see was an outstretched hand.

Ten yards short of the helicopter, Zimra came to a sudden halt. He couldn't understand why she should freeze, stagger, and fall to the ground. Her dress rode up, baring her thighs in a strangely indecent way. The helicopter's engine had drowned the reports of the snipers' rifles, but he saw the wound in her leg and the blood. He flung himself to the ground beside her.

"Keep going!" he yelled. "You've got to—I'll help you!"

They were under fire, he knew that now. While diving for the ground he had seen bullets hit the main chamber of the JetRanger's turboshaft engine and strike home near the fuel tank.

On the ground they were relatively safe. Martin guessed that the shots were meant for the helicopter rather than themselves. He raised his head in time to see the outstretched hand disappear. Was Sĕnk shouting something? If so, his voice was drowned by the high-pitched whine of the engine. The cabin trembled and swayed, and Martin realized that Senk couldn't wait any longer. The most he could do for them now was draw the snipers' fire by taking off. Martin was galvanized by the thought.

He knelt and gathered Zimra into his arms, then stood up. He didn't feel the weight of her body as he covered the few yards that separated them from the helicopter, whose door was still open.

No, no, no! Her cries of protest were not so much audible as tangible—transmitted by the body struggling in his arms. But it seemed too late anyway. The trembling cabin floated above him, unattainably far from the ground, then dipped for the one brief instant it took him to hurl her bodily through the door.

Martin collapsed and lay still, pinned to the ground by exhaustion, fear and the downdraft of the accelerating rotor blades. The helicopter rose, not slowly, under the weight of its additional burden, but almost as though bounding into the air with relief.

He heard the engine overhead. It struck a false note now—a receding whaff-whaff-whaff that dwindled until he could clearly hear the rifle shots at last. He rose to his knees. Beyond the stiff and leafless trees that fringed the mirror-smooth expanse of water on his right, he caught a fleeting glimpse of something that might have been a cabin roof aglow with reflected sunlight.

He was often to recall the thoughts that possessed him now. That dying would be better than returning to prison—easier, at all events, than years of reincarceration in some dismal place of penance where life was ruled by hatred and fear. Worse still, that everything had ended so nonsensically—that Zimra, if she survived, would live in a state of freedom quite as fearful and repugnant to her as his own state of bondage.

It couldn't be the end, he decided.

He scrambled up and stood erect in the middle of the field. He was exhausted but no longer afraid—indeed, he felt a sort of curiosity as he stood there waiting for the sound of the shot and the pain that would deliver him from the other, far more agonizing pain inside him: the short, sharp pain that spelled peace and repose, pardon and absolution.

But the shot never came. For a moment there was nothing round him but the silence of the deserted field—a silence so profound that he had to delve deep into his memory to recall its like. Then the gulls started screaming again and he saw armed men coming toward him through the long grass, invisible from the waist down.

CHAPTER XLII

WHEN THE TELEPHONE STARTED RINGING, Carow noted the time on a pad before lifting the receiver. The typewriter had gone. So had the sheet of paper, but the gun still lay beside him.

"Carow."

"He made it!" It was Geissler's voice, tired and a little unsteady. "One bullet smashed his elbow and grazed a rib, another hit the chopper's main combustion chamber and another missed the tank by a whisker. He only had two minutes' worth of fuel left when he landed."

"Let's do this by the book, shall we? Give me the time first." Geissler was taken aback—Carow could sense his surprise—but he came to heel at once.

"Šĕnk reached the rendezvous at nine-twenty. He'd been delayed by a patrolling Czech Army chopper, but that sheered off. Everything seemed to be going fine. He was over the pickup point, and he could see the two of them running toward him. Another ten yards, another few seconds, and they'd both have been safely on board."

Carow noted the time, 9:20 A.M., unconscious that he'd been doodling. It was a crude, childish drawing of a helicopter. "What went wrong?"

"Czech sharpshooters. They opened fire from a poplar plantation. The woman got to within ten yards. The she was hit, probably by a ricochet. Šĕnk stopped a bullet at the same time—aimed shots. They were obviously trying for the chopper. He knew he couldn't wait any longer. He was just about to take off and draw the Czechs' fire when Martin made his move. He says he still doesn't know how Martin managed it."

Carow's pencil skidded across the pad. "What do you mean?"

"He literally hurled her into the cabin."

"You mean they're out?"

"She's got a nasty thigh wound, but it looks worse than it is. She's suffering from shock, too, but that's only natural."

He still hadn't said anything about Martin, but Carow didn't press him. "Go on."

"Like I told you, he hovered over the field for a few seconds to draw their fire, piloting the chopper one-handed. He knew there was nothing more he could do for Martin. If he and his machine were to stand the slightest chance, he had to get out of there soonest. There was the woman to consider, too, yelling at him to turn back and bleeding like a stuck pig—he thought she might die on him. He was right to go when he did, that's for sure.''

"Nobody's blaming him."

"So he hightailed it back across the Austrian border. The damaged turbine gulped twice as much juice as usual, but he made it—landed ten miles inside West German territory— right next door to a hospital, what's more. Damned cool customer, Šenk.''

"You spoke to him personally?"

"Yes, before they carted him off for surgery. He kept on assuring me he'd done his damnedest. I believed him, too.''

"And he doesn't know what happened to Martin?"

"I'm sorry, no. He saw him lying on the ground, but that's all. He doesn't even know if he was hit or not. The woman isn't up to making a statement yet, but she should be by the time you get here.''

"Thanks for calling so promptly."

"Heiner, the fact that he was lying on the ground—it doesn't mean—"

"Of course not. Thanks again."

"Will you be coming right away?"

"No, I think I'll tie up the loose ends from here. You take over at that end. Are you back at the outstation?"

"Yes, I just got here."

"Very well, wrap things up. You know what to do."

A picture took shape in Carow's mind: C at his desk. Outside the throne room, nothing existed for him. His world had shrunk to the size of a desk top measuring three feet by six. C's desk was symbolic of his power. He needed nothing more; only his telephones, his yellow paper and red ink. Seated at his desk, without ever having to leave it, C could observe unobserved, like a voyeur. He could probe the ultimate secrets of a human life. By using one of the instruments on his desk, he could alter the course of events, shatter hopes, sow fear and consternation. An old man's hands, an old man's voice . . . Not an executive, simply a model bureaucrat who could always claim to be acting as a faithful servant of the state.

Carow saw another picture take shape—quite why, he didn't know. It was a battlefield in ancient times, a wide plain littered with corpses and overlooked by a brilliant blue sky. After battles like these—so he must have learned at school or read later on—the survivors went and strewed salt on the dead. What do we do with *our* putrefaction, he thought—how do *we* kill the stench? We put everything on record and file it . . .

"I thought you'd want to question the woman yourself," he heard Geissler say.

"Give her time. C will tell you to put pressure on her. At least give her time." Carow thought of his promise to Martin about her file; another promise he hadn't kept. "Protect her for as long as you can."

"Is everything all right? Did you speak to C? What—"

"Tell me," Carow broke in, "any idea what one does with a dead dog? It's my pointer. I had to shoot him this morning, and God knows what I'm going to do with the body."

"What's the matter with you?"

"Nothing, why? So you don't know either?"

"Have you tried the animal welfare people?"

"No . . . Yes, maybe that's a good idea. Thanks. Don't let me keep you. You'd better get on with the job."

Carow replaced the receiver, rose, and walked to the window. The rain had started again—fine rain falling from a sunny, almost summery sky. The asphalt roads were steaming.

It wasn't the first time he'd contemplated suicide. The act of putting the muzzle to his temple had always seemed unduly theatrical, apart from being a futile demonstration capable of changing nothing. He still felt the same at heart, so he pinned no particular hopes on the idea as he stood at the window, watching the rain.

He wasn't found for several hours. Geissler tried to call him to report on his preliminary interrogation of Zimra Steffin. When he couldn't get through, he raised the alarm.

Carow had discharged the Belgian nine-millimeter automatic into his right temple. There was no farewell letter. His time of death was officially set at 11:15 A.M. This was deduced from his last telephone call and the report lying on his desk. He had carefully completed his notes on the operation. For the record.

EPILOGUE

1

Someone must almost certainly have kept a tally of the times they'd met, though the lawyers themselves had no recollection. For reasons beyond their control, the intervals between their negotiating sessions varied widely. Certain conventions had grown up over the years. One was that, when "business" had been concluded, they and their wives dined out together. Like their meetings, the choice of restaurant alternated between the western and eastern parts of the city.

The two attorneys dealt in an awkward commodity: people. They were responsible to their respective governments for the ransoming of prisoners and their transfer from one German republic to the other. Although their many years of acquaintanceship had never ripened into friendship proper, they treated one another with courtesy and respect. Even when they were discussing money—always the most delicate issue—they did so in the most fastidious manner.

Thus it was on this particular September afternoon, when the pair had convened yet again in the western part of their divided city. Producing a neatly typed list from his brief-case, the East Berlin attorney handed it to his West Berlin colleague with a few well-chosen words of personal depre-cation.

"I did all I could to persuade my principals that this isn't an opportune moment, but I'm afraid the old scale of charges can't be maintained."

"That," said the man from the West, "will create prob-lems. You realize, of course, that I can't sanction any price increases without referring them to Bonn."

The man from the East nodded. "I warned them that ne-gotiations might be substantially delayed."

He produced a second list. Unlike the first, which con-sisted of several closely typewritten sheets, this was a single sheet only. The six names on it were divided into two col-umns of three.

"However," the man from the East went on, "perhaps we could deal with this first. It concerns three of your"—he hesitated as though repelled by the word he was obliged to use—"agents. No cash transaction involved. We propose a straight swap for three of our . . ."

"Agents?" said the man from the West, smiling.

"Yes. We suggest using the Plauen-Hof checkpoint. Usual procedure. Of course, I can't personally vouch for the relative value of the persons concerned."

"I've always found both our principals extremely realis-tic in these matters. May I see the list?"

The names meant nothing to the man from the West. It wasn't even curiosity that prompted him to glance at the first item in the column headed "West." It seemed that someone named Martin had been sentenced, almost exactly six years ago, to fifteen years' imprisonment for espionage and aiding and abetting an East German national's escape from the Czechoslovak Socialist Republic. He forgot the name and details at once.

"No problems that I can see," he said. "I'll pass this to the proper department right away. There's bound to be the usual red tape, but I think I should have a go-ahead for you very soon." He laid the second list aside and picked up the longer one. "What price increases are you proposing per head?"

The East Berlin lawyer jotted down a figure on a slip of paper and pushed it across the table. "Shall we adjourn, or do you have a little room to maneuver?"

The West Berlin lawyer added a figure of his own to the slip and pushed it back. "A little," he said.

They proceeded to bargain in an urbane and friendly fashion, both fundamentally convinced that terms would be agreed in the end. Their dinner was at stake, after all. These occasions always passed off in a far more convivial and easygoing atmosphere when a bargain had been struck beforehand.

2

WHEN THE LIST REACHED the Center—with a request for approval or rejection—Martin's inclusion proved something of a headache. It wasn't simply that the name meant nothing to most of the people whose desks the list passed on its tour of headquarters. Diligently though the files were combed for an agent by that name, no dossier or source book came to light. Not even the central computer spat him out.

One clue, however, was furnished by the year of the agent's conviction. He dated from a period when the Organization was still ruled by the legendary C. Many changes had occurred since then. C himself had stood down—after a further one-year extension—and gone into honorable retirement. His suite of offices at the Center, the celebrated desk with its four telephones, yellow pads and red ink, the conference table and photographic blowup of the Wall—all these relics were left untouched for three years after he retired. Then the people from Accounts put their foot down and reallocated the premises for other purposes.

C's departure from the Organization had been copied by many of the old guard. Puck, who accompanied him into retirement as a matter of course, shared the place at his side with Pauly. Blumenschein outlasted him by six months, and Ziegler retired a year after that.

Some survivors of the period were still there, of course, and even had a vague recollection of the case. Without knowing the name of the agent himself, they claimed that the operation had been an outstanding success—another glorious page in the Organization's annals. Others, whose recollection of it differed entirely, held that it had been an unmitigated failure. Their version seemed the more likely because Carow, then one of C's joint deputies, had committed suicide as a result.

Of course! All at once, plenty of people recalled the whole affair perfectly: Carow had been to blame for everything. He'd picked the wrong agent and been vain enough to act as his own case officer. Carow had known the truth of the matter, but Carow was naturally past talking about it.

C himself, however, was still alive and open to consultation. What was more—now that everyone came to think of it—he had been permitted to take his complete personal archive with him. Accordingly, the list was forwarded to C with a polite request for his comments on the name Martin. The "grand old man" was still revered—still ever so slightly feared.

By the time the list came back—"Nothing in my files," read the four-word note against Martin's name in C's microscopic handwriting—a clerk in the Cashier's Department had turned up proof of the agent Martin's existence. The file had never been closed because the account remained unsettled. It contained a voucher signed by Carow stating the "remuneration" payable to the agent under the terms of his contract. Martin wouldn't get the entire sum owing to him, of course, because he had never submitted an expense account.

Many people think it was this that eventually worked in Martin's favor. They overlook the fact that the list ended its tour of the Center on the desk of Carow's successor as joint deputy to the Organization's new director, a senior civil servant from Bonn; in other words, that Karl Geissler, too, approved the exchange.

3

THE TRANSACTION WAS completed five weeks after the lawyers' preliminary meeting. It was early afternoon on a sunny, cloudless October day.

First to reach the checkpoint were the cars containing the trio of East German agents. Thanks to a misunderstanding, they had turned up too early.

The cars stood parked beside the road with their windows up, just short of the West German frontier post. It was a weekday, and border traffic was light. After an hour, word came that all was ready on the other side. Gingerly, blinking up at the sun, the first of the East Germans got out. With two escorts, he walked through the gap beside the barrier. The same process was initiated on the East German side, timed so that the men would meet midway between the toll bars.

The second pair of agents were just being exchanged when a private car appeared on the West German side of the border and pulled up some way from the barrier. The driver was a swarthy man with a stiff left arm, and beside him sat a slender, gray-haired woman.

At Geissler's suggestion, news of the forthcoming exchange had first been conveyed to Miroslav Šenk, coupled with a request that he break it to Zimra Steffin. He had felt apprehensive about doing so, but his fears were allayed when he called her at her place of work. Zimra had reacted calmly. After an almost imperceptible pause, she asked if she might accompany him to the frontier.

She'd said little during the three-hour trip. Once again, it was her composure that surprised Šěnk most of all, but now she turned and looked at him inquiringly—doubtfully. "May I go meet him?" she asked at length.

He put his hand on her arm. "You'd better be prepared. He'll have changed."

"Martin? Not really—not as much as I have."

He watched her get out and walk toward the border. Some distance from the barrier she came to a halt and stood waiting.

MARTIN HADN'T MINDED going last or waiting for the other two to cross the frontier ahead of him—in fact he'd welcomed the delay. He could see, as he set off, that his opposite number was likewise flanked by two men.

They met at the halfway point. Their escorts had stopped a few yards short of it, so they were alone when they passed each other, one heading east, the other west. For an instant, they held each other's gaze.

Martin was puzzled by the look on the stranger's face. He could discern no joy there, no eagerness or expectancy. The man seemed more bemused than anything else—unable to fathom what was going on. Martin wondered if the same thought was running through the stranger's head; if he himself looked just as lost, just as uncertain of what his homecoming signified.

Then he caught sight of Zimra. For more than a year, he hadn't known whether she'd survived or not; nor had he been sure, when her first postcard reached him, whether he'd done the right thing that day on the border.

Martin was still unsure of it now, while walking up to her. He halted a yard away. Her hair was gray again—a different gray, of course. He stood there, not venturing to speak or touch her.

A man got out of another car—a blue BMW—and strolled over to them. He hesitated for a moment, taken aback by the color of Zimra's hair. He remembered it jet-black and hadn't known that she dyed it. He held out his hand to Martin.

"Remember me?"

Martin looked at the man: slim and wiry, with a pepper-and-salt crew cut. The only thing that struck him was a fleeting resemblance to Carow.

"Not Geissler?"

"It's all those missing pounds." Geissler smiled. "Congratulations on your release. We've got a few question for you."

"Now?"

"You're a runner. You know the form."

"But not this minute, surely?"

Geissler's smile didn't waver. There was a hardness about it which Martin had never detected in Carow's face. "Nine years we've saved you," he said. "That should be worth a week of your time."

Now and only now, Martin took Zimra's hand. It was cold, and it trembled in his as she walked beside him to the blue BMW.

HANS HERLIN, an author of international reputation whose books have been published in eighteen countries, was born in Germany in 1925. He worked in journalism and in publishing until 1972 when he began writing books full-time. He now lives in Normandy, France, where he is working on his fourth novel.

LEWIS PERDUE

THE DELPHI BETRAYAL
From the depths of a small, windowless room in the bowels of
the White House, an awesome conspiracy to create economic
chaos and bring the entire world to its knees is unleashed.
☐ 42393-4 THE DELPHI BETRAYAL $3.50

QUEENS GATE RECKONING
A wounded CIA operative and a defecting Soviet ballerina hurtle
toward the hour of reckoning as they race the clock to circum-
vent twin assassinations that will explode the balance of power.
☐ 41436-6 QUEENS GATE RECKONING $3.50

THE DA VINCI LEGACY
A famous Da Vinci whiz, Curtis Davis, tries to uncover the truth
behind the missing pages of an ancient manuscript which could
tip the balance of world power toward whoever possesses it.
☐ 41762-4 THE DA VINCI LEGACY $3.50

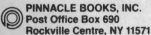

FOUR FROM
GERALD PETIEVICH

"Gerald Petievich is...
a fine writer...his dialogue
is pure entertainment."
— Elmore Leonard,
Author of *Stick*